STORIES FROM THE

Blue Moon Café

STORIES FROM THE
Blue Moon Café

THE AMERICAN SOUTH IN STORIES, ESSAYS, AND POETRY

EDITED BY SONNY BREWER

NEW AMERICAN LIBRARY

New American Library
Published by New American Library, a division of
Penguin Group (USA) Inc., 375 Hudson Street,
New York, New York 10014, U.S.A.
Penguin Books Ltd, 80 Strand, London WC2R 0RL, England
Penguin Books Australia Ltd, 250 Camberwell Road,
Camberwell, Victoria 3124, Australia
Penguin Books Canada Ltd, 10 Alcorn Avenue, Toronto, Ontario, Canada M4V 3B2
Penguin Books (N.Z.) Ltd, Cnr Rosedale and Airborne Roads,
Albany, Auckland 1310, New Zealand

Penguin Books Ltd, Registered Offices: 80 Strand, London WC2R 0RL, England

Published by New American Library, a division of Penguin Group (USA) Inc. This
is an authorized reprint of a hardcover edition published by MacAdam/Cage
Publishing. For information address MacAdam/Cage Publishing, 155 Sansome
Street, Suite 550, San Francisco, CA 94104.

First New American Library Printing, December 2003
10 9 8 7 6 5 4 3 2 1

(NAL) REGISTERED TRADEMARK—MARCA REGISTRADA

New American Library Trade Paperback ISBN: 0-451-21042-5

The Library of Congress has catalogued the hardcover edition of this title as follows:

Stories from the Blue Moon Café / edited by Sonny Brewer.
p. cm.
ISBN 1-931561-09-5 (hardcover : alk. paper)
1. Southern States—Social life and customs—Fiction.
2. Short stories, American—Southern States. I. Brewer, Sonny.

PS551.S74 2002
813'.0108975—dc21   2002009685

Printed in the United States of America
Design by Dorothy Carico Smith

TABLE OF CONTENTS

For my wife, Diana . . . truly the Goddess of the Moon,
Emily, John Luke, and Dylan . . . whose orbits hold firm my center.

Acknowledgments

Where does one begin? My great fear is that I will fail to include someone in these few lines who knows damn well that without his help, without her support, I would've fallen on my face with this project. But, with that disclaimer, I will go ahead and make the list: Diana Brewer, Melissa McAdams, Ashley Clayton, Jim Gilbert, Chris John, Suzanne Barnhill, Martin Lanaux, Skip and Nancy Jones, Betty Joe Wolff, John Sledge, Mary Lou Hyland, Frank Turner Hollon, Pop and Virginia Hollon, Kathy Lynch, Lynn and Cori Yonge, Bill and Cynthia Staggers, Charlotte Cabaniss, Mac Walcott, Mac McCawley, Hillary Martin, John Borom, and Kyle Jennings; then, MacAdam/Cage's David Poindexter and Pat Walsh, Scott Allen, Anika Streitfeld, Avril Sande, Cindy Watson, and Melanie Mitchell and Amy Long. If I left your name off, I'm sorry. Please know that if you helped me even minutely, to the granting of your good-will, I thank you.

INTRODUCTION

Sonny Brewer

Something was bound to happen.

Southerners are amenable to signs and portents, and there it was in the one month of November, two full moons hanging in the sky over Fairhope, Alabama. Wouldn't come about again for a bejillion years, or some such long time. Then there were the meteors, the sky all ajitter with them, in the middle of the month, book-ended by the moons, the last one kind of blue with a rainbow around it. Made me think of Robert Bell's fictionalized Fairhope in his novel *The Butterfly Tree* and the opening to Chapter Four, where he sets the scene inside the Blue Moon Café, whose proprietress published her "thinkings" on the covers of book matches. Bell spoke of the night moving restlessly outside the café.

If I were to claim that the event was foretold in the heavens, blue moon or no, I couldn't do it with a straight face. After all, the little stone church on the corner in downtown Fairhope has been remodeled into a theater, though not an unnatural progression, I think. (Coincidentally, we had set the stage to look like the interior of a café.) And it was a Saturday night, not a Sunday morning. There was no choir, our longhaired troubadour and his Dobro not even close. Still, I will argue that something definitely Devine (thank you, Ms. Loos) did occur on this night when the sky was moving so restlessly.

It went something like this: Our annual literary slugfest (we call it Southern Writers Reading), a gathering of writers for an event that looks something like a writing conference, held annually in Fairhope on the weekend before Thanksgiving, was winding down. It had been way too much fun. Nobody really wanted the party to end. A friend from a local college, who helps to organize similar writerly events, had leaned her head close to mine at one point, and asked in a whisper, "How the hell do you guys pull this off? You don't even print brochures. You have no printed schedule of events."

My honest answer to her: "I don't know."

Anyway, to prolong the evening, I think, as much as anything else, and to add a kind of "same station, same time next week" promise that it really wasn't all done, I interrupted a question to one of our authors from someone in the full-house audience, a cozy hundred-or-so souls. Just butted right in with, "Hey! Let's do a chapbook. All you writer guys and gals, would you throw in a story? You people in this theater would buy the book, right? If we get moving on it, we can have the chapbook ready by next Southern Writers Reading."

You hold that "chapbook" of 351 pages in your hands. The time frame from that Saturday night to this anthology was less than a year. It did this snowball thing, too. In the theater that night were Jill Conner Browne, Michael Knight, Melinda Haynes, Suzanne Hudson, Frank Turner Hollon, William Gay, Tom Franklin, Beth Ann Fennelly, Douglas Kelley, Barbara Robinette Moss, and Sidney Thompson. Missing SWR alumni included Rick Bragg, who was in Islamabad, Pakistan; Marlin Barton was at a book signing, and Tom Kelly was at a turkey hunting lecture. David Poindexter of MacAdam/Cage Publishing, also in the crowd that night, said, "You get this group of people to come through with stories, and MacAdam/Cage will publish the book." And, no one, not even those absent that evening in November, begged off. Naturally. Southern writers don't joke around about writing.

Then M/C editor Pat Walsh said, "You know there are some really talented authors who live right there in your town. Why don't you invite them in?" Okay. Around the corner and down the street we found Jim Gilbert (behind the counter at Over the Transom Bookstore), W. E. B. Griffin, Winston Groom, C. Terry Cline, Jr., Judith Richards, Jennifer Paddock, Monroe Thompson, and Richard Shackelford (M/C, bless them, allowed me these last two, ignoring the example of a successful New York agent who'd told me some months earlier, "We don't do dead writers.").

The orbit of this thing grew wider. Standing in my bookstore one afternoon, talking to bookseller Virginia Hobson Hicks in Brunswick, Georgia, where Pat Conroy did his first book signing . . . well, you guessed it. Then I ran into Silas House in Gulfport, Mississippi, one night, and we sat up talking until three in the morning and—yes, he's in here, too. Caught in the spiral were Bev Marshall down in Louisiana, and Tom Corcoran (a former Fairhoper) in Key West, and Fairhope-born Patricia Foster up in Iowa, and home county native Brad Watson at Harvard, and George Singleton in the Carolinas someplace, and out in California, Mississippi-born Steve Yarbrough.

Good Lord, what a bunch of fine writers!

I must add, too, that these writers' generosity equals their skill and craftsmanship. They have donated the fee that would have been paid to them for their submissions to the Fairhope Center for Writing Arts. That's good. One of the Center's principal purposes is to provide scholarship money for budding writers in our area. And we'll ask for judges from among the authors in this collection.

Before turning you loose for the real pleasure of these writers' genius, four sentences about my hometown: Fewer than 15,000 people live here in Fairhope, but not too long ago, three local writers were on the *New York Times* bestseller list simultaneously: W.E.B. Griffin, Jimmy Buffett, and Winston Groom. We have a good view from these bluffs, proclaimed the highest on the U.S. coast from Maine to Texas, of Mobile across Farragut's "Damn the torpedoes . . ." Mobile Bay. And Fairhope—clean and lovely, art-charged, at times eccentric—has as strong a sense of place as Greenwich Village or New Orleans or fill-in-the-blank. In Hemingway's short story "A Clean, Well-Lighted Place," the old waiter says, "Each night I am reluctant to close up because there may be someone who needs the café." . . . Fairhope, with its doors open wide, has that café feeling that more and more people seem to find they need.

With all that, under those auspicious November skies something was bound to have happened. It did. And yet, as far as the supply of Southern storytelling goes, we've stopped in the middle of the sentence. It might happen again. We'll see.

Final Spring

Marlin Barton

"He ain't worth a damn," the boy riding beside him says. "He's a fool."

Rafe Anderson looks again and sees the man himself up ahead, catches glimpses of him through the long column of riders, all of whom wear thread-worn butternut or civilian clothes, except for the officers. Rafe thinks for a moment that he is glad not to wear gray. He knows if there are sharpshooters, they'll choose gray first, spread a bloody rose across the lapel, in honor of high rank, like some undertaker's final touch.

Now a shame fills him, though, as if it rises out of the yellow dust kicked up by the horses. It coats his throat like a bitter paste; he spits in a vain attempt to expel it. He should be proud to wear gray, he thinks, just as he was in the beginning when he kept his buttons shined and was afraid that the fighting would be over before his company reached Virginia. But this isn't the beginning.

The man himself, Davis, wears a black coat, dark as iron. His back is stiff, his head straight. He rides well, as if he's on parade along some Richmond street, Rafe thinks. He has seen Davis standing before the large tent in camp in the evenings. The man is gaunt but with dark, alert eyes and a strong chin above the small goatee. He even spoke to Rafe once. "Good evening, soldier," he said. "The heat of the day seems to be leaving us." His tone had been formal, yet warm, nothing in it that said this was anything more than a field inspection of troops, no acknowledgment that they were riding south, as quickly as they could move with worn-out horses and heavy wagons.

"I tell you, he ain't worth a shit," the boy says. "He's worse than a fool."

Rafe tries again to ignore him. He'd never seen the boy until a few days before in Greensboro when a handful of new men joined the company, but the boy has stayed beside him like some half-starved dog, willing, it seems, to take any punishment Rafe might give. And the more he talks, the more Rafe wants to kick him until he whimpers.

"If Davis thinks he can set up again in Charlotte, he's crazy. Stoneman can't be too far behind us. And who knows where in the hell Wilson's Raiders are."

Rafe finally turns to look at him. The boy—who has just turned twenty, he told Rafe this early on, volunteered it for no apparent reason—quickly lowers his head and stares at the ground. He doesn't wear a hat and his hair is long and blond as cornsilk. If it weren't so dirty and matted, it would look like some young girl's pride. His face is smooth, only a small patch of short, wispy hairs at his chin, one shallow pockmark at his cheek, which somehow makes him look even younger. And his curses sound like those of someone not yet comfortable with the language of men.

The boy risks a glance now, but he keeps his head down, his shoulders hunched forward. Rafe sees the flash of blue eyes, and for a moment the boy resembles something more than a beaten dog. Rafe isn't sure what, though. It's nothing he can quite recognize, but whatever it is perhaps it's what has kept him from striking the boy.

They ride in silence for a time, for which Rafe is thankful. He tries to imagine that he is back in Alabama, in Riverfield, riding somewhere after church, maybe to court a woman. But he can't hold the image, can't even picture what woman it might be. All he can remember now is the fighting outside of Atlanta, the smoke in the distance like some portentous sign in the air that could only be denied by the strongest of wills, and then the days of riding after Sherman, annoying his rear guard. Federal rifle fire would come pouring out of a tree line as if green leaves suddenly caught flame, and riders all around him would fall in twos and threes. Then they'd form ranks and ride toward the fire, returning it, charging the line, more of them cut down. And each time they were asked, they charged again as if out of some awful habit.

Again he catches glimpses of Davis up ahead, and each time he sees the squared back and shoulders, Rafe tenses, rises in the saddle, his own back a little straighter than before. Not enough for anyone to notice probably, but enough for him to feel, and that is all that matters to him.

"They're going to hang that son of a bitch when they catch him," the boy says. "You think I'm going to lose my life for a man who's already dead? I ain't no fool."

"Whether you lose your life probably ain't up to you," Rafe says, staring straight ahead. "And from what I've seen and heard from you, your mama should have done you like the sick runt in the litter, drown you in the creek."

"My mama run off years ago."

"Sounds like she had the gift of prophecy."

The boy is sullen for a while. Rafe knows it won't last long, but for a time he listens only to the steady sound of horses' hooves hitting against dirt packed hard as brick. The dust is not as bad as before, but Rafe spits again.

"It ain't just Stoneman or Wilson that worries me," the boy says finally, somehow hopefully, as if he has come up with a topic Rafe will surely want to hear. "It's the marauders. You know they're out there, don't you? They're following us. I don't blame them, either."

"You don't know if we're carrying gold. It's just rumors."

"Rumors of riches is riches enough for some."

Rafe knows he is right, but as long as they stay as large a force as they are, an attack by marauders isn't very likely. The thought sickens him, though, soldiers turned desperate enough and sorry enough, sorry as this boy beside him, to turn on their own. For a moment his mind fills with images of buzzards and carrion.

The shadows of the column of men and horses begin to grow long and obscured against the road and the barren fields beside them, but they ride on, past the beginning of dusk. Just as he begins to think that they may ride into the night, or all night, the order to bivouac is passed along.

They camp in a large pasture, and he can see at the top of a rise the roofs of the officers' tents pointing toward a low sky. Night comes and fires begin to appear and melt small pieces of the dark.

They do not have tents themselves, and most of them don't have blankets. Many are barefooted, but at least it's no longer cold. Spring has come, and Rafe knows they have fought through their last winter. No one else will lose blackened, frostbit toes or go all night without sleep because of a trembling so deep inside they can't stop.

Rafe takes care of his horse, rubs him down, then sits on the ground and eats some of his hardtack. What he has left of it will have to last. He's grown thin on it, but not as thin as some whose faces look like penciled drawings of dead men waiting to fall.

"You want me to find a little wood and make a fire?" the boy says.

"Why? There's nothing to cook. And I don't want what passes for coffee." Rafe had hoped the boy would not sleep near him again, and he wonders why he doesn't send him away, force him to go elsewhere. Maybe he just isn't worth the trouble.

"I've got a little salted meat I can fry up. You want some?" the boy says and looks away quickly.

"No, I don't want any. But where the hell did you get it?"

"I've had it. Been saving it since Greensboro."

"Make a fire if you want, then lay down in it for all I care."

The boy walks off slowly, his head down, his arms dead at his sides. Rafe watches the hunched shoulders until they disappear into the dark and he wonders if the boy has ever known how to walk like he wanted to be a man.

He lies back on the ground and closes his eyes, but he still sees the boy's slumped outline just as it disappeared. He begins to think of retreats—out of Mississippi, across Alabama, then from Kennesaw Mountain and Atlanta. Seemed like that was all Johnston knew how to do. There was a fool if there'd ever been one, not Davis. Johnston knew how to retreat better than any general in either army. They'd gotten good at it, could slip away from the enemy and leave them guessing where they'd gone as if they were ghosts, or at least formless shadows of what they'd once been. And every time they ran—because that's what it was, running—they were hungrier and dirtier and sicker in ways that no doctor could help. There was no medicine for what they had. And the part of them that was diseased could not be cut away with a scalpel or a bone saw.

It surely hadn't been that way under Forrest. They *fought* then. And now, when he looked at Davis riding up ahead, at least he saw a straight back and squared shoulders, not some dog about to whimper and slink away.

He takes his boots off and sits completely still in the dark, hungry, then thinks of the miles he has ridden. He knows they don't have many more. Stoneman will catch up with them, or someone else. And though he is tired in a way he could never have imagined four years ago, thoughts of the end do not bring relief, only a stronger sickness in his stomach, a sickness that must feed off itself since he feels only emptiness inside.

In a little while the boy comes back and starts a fire. Rafe watches him across the tops of the small flames, sees how intent he is on cooking the pieces of salted meat, as if he wants to please. Rafe has not even asked his name. He knows that only five years separate them. The boy probably thinks it's more, he realizes, many more. But Rafe knows that it's not really years that divide them.

Some of the men nearby must have smelled the meat cooking. A few begin to gather around them with hopeful faces at the fire's edge. One carries a banjo, as if he plans to sing for his supper. Rafe knows them all. There is Calvin, who has dark hair and thin features and who lost a brother at Cold Harbor, and William, who is from down in Marengo County, Alabama, near Sweet Water, and who speaks so often of his wife that Rafe wonders if she can really be the saint that William makes her out to be. And finally there is Silas, who speaks little except through his tenor singing voice and the music he plays on five strings. Rafe has ridden with them for two years now, ever since the wound in his foot healed and he was placed in their cavalry company.

"Y'all ain't looking for something to eat are you?" Rafe says. He knows they will not ask.

"Just the pleasure of your fine company and your new friend here," William says, then laughs.

They all glance at the boy, who will not return their looks.

"We ain't exactly got enough to go around," Rafe says. Then he turns to the boy. "Give Calvin here my piece. He's looking poorly." Which is the truth. He does look weak. They all know it.

"I'm all right. I don't need it," Calvin says.

"Give Calvin my piece," Rafe says again. This time Calvin remains silent.

"You reckon Davis is running to Mexico?" William says. "That where we're escorting him?"

"He ain't running nowhere." Rafe's voice is harder than he means for it to be. "He won't leave the South. You mark my words. He'll face whatever he's got to."

"You may be right about that, but I don't really care where he goes. All I know is, I want to go home to my wife."

"I hope he doesn't go to Mexico," the boy says suddenly. "Let him suffer like we've had to." He hands Calvin a piece of meat and begins to eat his own, but he looks quickly around the fire, then back at the greasy meat in his hands.

"Children at the table should be seen and not heard," Rafe says.

"I'm not a child," he says, and his voice almost breaks. "I'm twenty, and I've seen enough fighting to know I don't want to see any more."

"Where?" Rafe says. "I'd be mighty curious to know."

"I was at Chickamauga and Lookout Mountain. Then at Kennesaw Mountain and Atlanta."

"Nowhere before that?"

The boy remains silent at first, licks his fingers nervously. "Ain't that enough?"

"Sounds like you joined up a little late," William says.

"I was too young before."

"Where you from?" Rafe says.

"North Alabama."

"You didn't do a little cave hiding up there, did you?" Rafe says. "Trying to stay away from the round-up patrols, not wanting to do your time? I've heard about some of those people up there."

"No," the boy says. "I said I was too young. When my time came they conscripted me sure enough. I'll say it. They damn sure did. But I *didn't* hide and wouldn't have. And I told you, I seen my damn share of fighting. But I ain't fighting no more. If they come for Davis, they can have him."

"We'll see about that," Rafe says. All the men stare quietly at the fire, as if not wanting to add flame to the moment. "You'll do what you're told, or you might find yourself dead anyway."

"Maybe so," the boy says. "But I'm through fighting."

The sound of soft notes arises now from Silas's banjo. At first the notes seem random, as if he's trying to find his voice, then a tune that they all recognize emerges. Silas begins to sing in his high tenor:

> The wounded men were crying
> For help from everywhere.
> While others who were dying
> Were offering God their prayer.
> "Protect my wife and children
> If it is Thy holy will."
> Such were the prayers I heard
> That night on Shiloh Hill.

Silas lets his voice trail off without finishing the song. All the men remain silent. Each of them, Rafe knows, is remembering the fields of dead they've seen, twisted bodies on burned ground, bottle flies crawling over their faces. The fires around them begin to die and the dark becomes solid again. Their own fire will not last much longer. But it doesn't matter. There is nothing left to cook, and they do not need to see. All they need now is silence.

But the boy speaks, as if he must. "How about this one?" he says. He begins to sing in a tuneless voice.

> May that cuss Jeff Davis float
> On stormy sea, in open boat.
> In burning brimstone may he be,
> While little devils dance in glee.

Rafe strikes the boy's face once, knuckles against thin cheek, and the boy sprawls backward onto the ground and lies there still, as if he will simply go to sleep now that he's flat on his back. He doesn't even reach up to touch his face where his cheek is torn.

"Get up," Rafe says. "Fight me. If you know how."

"No."

Rafe feels an anger inside that he knows is larger than this moment. It fills him in a way that food could not.

The boy raises up. "I told you I wasn't fighting anymore. I meant it."

Rafe looks at the boy outlined by the dying fire. He can't see his face clearly any longer, and his figure isn't that of anyone or anything Rafe can recognize. He merely looks down in his lap now at his clenched fists and in the darkness they look like small, fire-split stones.

He awakens at daybreak to the sound of horses and men. Then he sits up and eats some of his hardtack beside the cold ashes of last night's fire. The boy is saddling his horse, and Rafe finally gets up and begins to saddle his own.

He soon hears the voice of his lieutenant. The company has orders, the man says, to detach from the escort and ride back toward Salisbury. Davis and the column will reach Charlotte by evening, and they want to know if Stoneman or his advance have made Salisbury or beyond. "We're to ride back far enough until we hear something we can trust," he says.

They mount, and Rafe feels the soreness in his legs from yesterday's ride as he searches for the other stirrup with his foot. He stretches his legs out, and the old wound in his foot hurts. It is often painful in the morning, a daily reminder of the fighting at Seven Pines. He remembers the charge out of the flooded swamp, the unsupported run across the open field right into a Federal abatis. The grapeshot had cut them down like so much cane at harvest.

They ride toward the road and form a small column. William is beside him, and the boy finds a place directly behind. He has not spoken, though Rafe has caught the boy looking at him. Whether it is in anger or disgust or hurt, he does not know.

The lieutenant orders forward, and they begin to move.

"This ain't exactly the direction I want to be headed in," William says. "Home is south."

"It's the direction we've got to go," Rafe says.

For a while the ride is easy. The sun isn't yet high enough to raise the heat of the day, and the dew is heavy still. It keeps the dust settled.

Rafe recognizes houses and fields they passed the day before, and somehow the sight of them makes him sink inward as William continues to talk of home and his wife. He finds himself trying to block out William's stories, and he remembers the sound of Davis's voice that one evening in camp. He pictures again the straight back and squared shoulders in the black coat, and he raises himself in the saddle.

"You're a good talker, William," he says. "Reckon you could hold forth on another subject besides what all you're going to do once you get home?"

"I'm sure I could." William laughs.

"How about we see what's on the mind of the boy behind us. He's mighty quiet," Rafe says.

"Nothing's on my mind, except what we might meet ahead."

"Marauders or Yankees. Take your pick," Rafe says. "The marauders probably won't shoot when they see we don't have gold."

They ride into the heat of the late morning, and the dust begins to cloud again. They stop at noon only long enough to water the horses. Rafe is more tired than he realized, but he doesn't know why really. They haven't done any hard riding, just steady.

Later they stop at a crossroads store that he imagines has very few goods, if any, and the lieutenant and two other men go inside to ask if there's been word on Stoneman. After a few minutes, they come out and the column continues toward Salisbury. No word of any news is passed along.

By late afternoon dust and sweat cover his face and his back feels sore. What little water is left in his canteen is soured from the heat and tastes like rotten wood. Bare fields that should be filled with young tobacco plants stretch out on either side of them toward tree lines of hardwoods and pines. He wonders if the turkey hunting is good through here, and he imagines that it is. Or at least that it used to be. He knows smokehouses probably hold only what game people can kill, if Federal troops haven't cleaned that out too, or Confederate.

The column turns at a right angle away from the road and they head toward a small grove of young oaks that grow along a small river near the tree line.

"About time we took a rest," William says. "What do you think, Rafe?"

"I'll rest if it's time to rest."

"I wouldn't expect anything less from you. What about you?" William says to the boy.

"I'm ready to quit anytime."

They water their horses, drink right beside them, and fill their canteens. Then they tie the horses to saplings and let them graze on what they can reach. Rafe rubs his down good before joining the men beneath one of the oaks.

He sits with William and Silas, and Calvin takes a place beside them. The boy stands nearby, looking at them with sidelong glances, like a girl at a dance, Rafe thinks, trying to decide if she wants to dance with a boy or a man.

"Come and sit," William says. "Just don't sing us any songs. Best leave that to Silas."

The boy walks toward them slowly, takes a seat on the ground without really looking at them.

"So do you have a name?" William says.

"His mama never gave him one. Did she?" Rafe says.

He sees the boy wince, but doubts anyone else notices. If they do, they don't know why.

"James. She named me for her dead brother." He looks at Rafe a moment. "That's what I was told, anyway."

"Reckon Stoneman's at Salisbury yet?" Calvin says. "Y'all don't reckon we'll run into his advance, do you?"

"We'll hear some word before that," Rafe says and hands Calvin a piece of hardtack. "Don't you worry."

"What difference does it make?" the boy says. "If Davis would just keep on moving he might could get away from Stoneman, but Stoneman ain't the only one out there. What they got us doing here ain't nothing but a waste. We all know it."

The boy looks at Rafe again, seems to force himself, as if turning his head takes an act of physical strength. But Rafe says nothing this time. He isn't sure why.

For a moment there is an awkward quiet that not even William tries to fill. Then they hear yells, one after another that finally join together and sound strangely like those that have come from their own throats so many times that Rafe feels as if they are hearing some cry of unspoken desperation that has belonged to them all, and the woods behind them explode with a rush of movement and Rafe sees each attack he has ever been in from a vantage point he has never known. He feels caught in some confused dream of horses and fire in which they are charging at themselves, and for a moment he can make no sense of anything.

Riders come slashing and firing out of the tree line. A few wear gray, most of them butternut. Rafe stands quickly, believing what he sees but not wanting to, and pulls his cap-and-ball revolver from his belt, holds it two-handed, and begins to fire from a crouched position at men who look like himself. The horses, he thinks. They've come for the horses. He keeps firing, unaware of Silas or William or Calvin or the boy, afraid that one of the mounted riders may not be a marauder but one of their own, but he's too afraid not to shoot. A rider gallops at him, shouting, sword raised the way Rafe knows he has raised his own and slashed at heads and necks and arms with hard steel, and he hesitates, looks at the rider's face for one he might recognize, but he has to fire and he does. The man falls backward, jerks forward in the stirrups, then hits the ground just as another horse rears and comes down upon the man's chest with shod hooves.

Smoke clouds the air and the yelling grows louder now as the wounded holler and the men on the ground answer the yells of the riders until Rafe hears what seems like one chorus of voices singing a strange dirge that laments their end.

But he spins and runs toward the horses where their carbines hang in scabbards. The riders are already cutting the tied reins and running the horses off. Rafe stops, places another loaded cylinder in his pistol, and fires twice at the back of a man, then watches him fall forward, clutching the horse's neck. He doesn't fall until the animal rears.

Rafe shoots at a man who wears gray and misses, but the riders have most of the horses cut loose now. They holler and slap at them, drive them toward the road. They have taken so little time, as if such work has come natural to them. Rafe raises his pistol again, but to shoot at them now would be useless.

It is over. All of it, not just this fight, but the whole of it. He wonders how it could have come to such a day as this. He knows he doesn't have an answer, but he begins to hear the boy's voice in his head, as if it has become his own. He will not listen though, will not let the boy's words form. Instead he fires shots from his pistol at marauders who are no longer within range. A fine dust blows across the field.

He finds William standing beneath the shade of one of the oaks. Silas is beside him. They both lean down, as though over the body of some dead animal they've found while out walking.

"Calvin's dead," William says. He straightens up. "I guess we don't have to worry about him anymore."

Rafe does not speak. He walks over to them, but it isn't Calvin he looks at. It's the boy who lies beside him. His ash-blond hair is matted with blood now, his cheek and mouth broken open from what was probably the butt of a rifle. He looks as if he's trying to call out to someone too far away to hear. His arms and legs are twisted beneath him, and even though Rafe has seen the dead in all manner of odd repose, the boy's body doesn't look quite like any he can recall. What he sees broken and still before him looks somehow like his own pale shadow.

THE BLUES IS DYING IN THE PLACE IT WAS BORN

Rick Bragg

BELZONI, Miss.—The blues is, when polio freezes your fingers and shrivels your legs, you play a baby-blue Epiphone guitar on your lap in a wheelchair, chording the strings with a butter knife. CeDell Davis, crippled by that disease when he was ten, almost sixty-three years ago, lives inside the blues.

The blues is, when you find the fine, big woman of your dreams, she dies in your arms of a heart attack just before dawn. James (T-Model) Ford, who swears he would have married her, is wed to the blues.

The blues is, when the searing light from your welder's torch slowly, gradually burns much of the sight from your eyes, you sit on your porch in the cool damp of the afternoon and sing to the rhythms in your own mind, then go into town for a bottle of Wild Irish Rose. Paul Jones, who knows the narrow roads in Belzoni so well he does not need to see that much to drive, has surrendered to the blues.

"I believe in God, but the Devil, he's got power, too," said Mr. Jones, who, with Mr. Davis, Mr. Ford and a scattering of others, is among the last of the Delta bluesmen who still live in the cradle of the blues. "Most of what you sing about is suffering."

Musicians who were not born here, who have not had their spirits or their bodies broken, who have never looked at these endless cotton fields and hated them, can never truly play the blues, said Mr. Ford, who now lives in Greenville, Mississippi, and Mr. Davis, who lives across the Mississippi River in Pine Bluff, Arkansas. Outsiders might play a tune from the Delta, Mr. Jones said, but there is no feeling in it.

"It's just," he said, "something you hear."

But here in the Delta, where most of the legendary juke joints have slowly shut their doors and most of the bluesmen have died off or moved away, the blues is fading from the very place it was born, say the people who play it and others who live here.

They know their music survives, in the music collections of yuppies, in college seminars on folk culture, in festivals and franchised venues like the House of Blues, B. B. King's clubs, and others in the United States, Asia, and Europe.

But there is little live music left, the bluesmen say, at the source. They play at festivals and the few weekend clubs that have endured, but even on the jukeboxes in the surviving bars and fish houses there is little Delta country blues. Hip-hop thuds from cars. Gospel, country, and soul music, sister to the blues, dominate the radio.

"I made two thousand dollars in one night in Japan," Mr. Jones said, but here he may make three hundred, if the phone rings at all. Like Mr. Davis and Mr. Ford, he has been recorded by a label in Water Valley, Mississippi, called Fat Possum Records, which also aids the men in booking shows here and around the world. No one is getting rich, but, Mr. Jones wonders, if he had not been picked up by that small label, would he have slowly disappeared, too?

Matthew Johnson, who was one of the founders of Fat Possum ten years ago, said he never wanted to be a folklorist; he "just wanted to make records that rock."

CeDell Davis says crack cocaine and the culture it bred turned the already tough juke joints into slaughterhouses over the last fifteen years, driving people away and all but silencing the small live shows that are now mostly folklore.

But the people of the Delta will come back to the blues, he said.

"The blues is about peoples, and as long as there's peoples, there will be blues," Mr. Davis said. "The blues tells a story. Hip-hop don't tell no story. It don't tell no story about women, men, trains, buses, cars, birds, alleys, stores.

"The blues is about things."

When you sing the blues, here in one of the poorest, most unchanging corners of the country, you hand everybody who listens a piece of your pain, fear, and hopelessness, until there is such a tiny piece left, you can live with it. Sometimes, as Mr. Jones showed when he sang on a side porch one afternoon, it sounds a lot like church.

Take away my sins and give me grace.
Take away my sins and give me grace
Oh angels, Oh my Lord
Wish I was in heaven sittin' down.

It is the very authenticity of the blues that endangers it. Mae Smith grew up in Lula, Mississippi, where a man named Frank Frost pushed a broom at her school. Later, she found his name in a history of the blues.

"I thought he was the town drunk," said Ms. Smith, who helps run the Delta Blues Museum in Clarksdale, Mississippi, and holds the title of interpretation specialist. Many blues players live hard and die in obscurity, and a piece of Delta history vanishes.

The Delta, like the blues, belongs to black people, the people here say, though many do not own enough of it to root a vine. It was their sweat that cleared its vast forests and transformed a nineteenth-century jungle into the richest farmland on earth.

It lies in the deltas of the Mississippi and Yazoo rivers, an indistinct triangle of vast fields, islands of trees, and small towns extending south from Memphis for about two hundred miles, covering an area about seventy miles wide on both sides of the Mississippi.

No other place, bluesmen say, could have nurtured the blues. What other place saw such toil, such pain?

What other place could produce a man like T-Model Ford, whose ankles are scarred from two years on a Tennessee chain gang, who walks with a cane because a jack slipped and a truck crushed one leg, who sings about pistol fights, abandonment, murder, and adultery, and smiles and smiles?

BACK-DOOR MAN

In Greenville, in a small house behind the funeral home, the amplifier crackles like lightning in a box as he plugs in the guitar he calls Gold Nanny, sister to Black Nanny.

I should have left you, baby
Gone on back to Mexico
I kept messin' with you, baby
Now you got me on the killin' floor.

Some days, a bus full of Japanese tourists will roll up. They take his picture, as they would photograph any other endangered species.

He did not sell his soul, as legend says Robert Johnson did, to master the blues. The Devil, people say, would run from Mr. Ford.

He killed a man in Tennessee when he was young, stabbing him in the neck with a switchblade after the man buried a knife in his back. "They gave me ten years," he said. "Mama got a lawyer and got me out in two."

Once, when asked if he had killed anyone else, he replied, "Do I count the one I run over in my Pontiac?"

He was, in his wilder days—which have lasted pretty much all of his seventy-nine years—a bar fighter and a moonshine drinker. "I have fathered twenty-six living children," he said. "I have married five times, and I have divorced from all of them."

Then, quick as he can change chords, his voice slipped from bragging to blues.

"There was a woman I would have married, if she had lived," he said. "She was a big, fine-looking woman, but she died in my arms. Four years ago. Best woman I ever had. I loved her."

She was married to another man, so Mr. Ford—what people here would call her back-door man—was not welcome at her funeral. "I just stood on the road and watched," he said.

He thought about that a bit, then told a young man, a drummer who was napping on his couch, to "go out there behind the seat of that truck and get me that bottle of Jack."

His big hands danced across the strings. "I get to drinking," he said, "and I'm a bad man."

Sent to the doctor
Shot full of holes

Nurse cried,
"Save his soul."
I'm a back-door man
I'm a back-door man
What the mens don't know
The little girls understand.

BEYOND BLUES

If T-Model Ford is a character from one of his songs, CeDell Davis is the sadness not even the blues can describe.

When he was a little boy, a man working in a pea patch near his house in Helena, Arkansas, dropped a harmonica, and Mr. Davis found it in the weeds.

"I liked the sound," he said. He unwrapped wire from a broom handle and stretched it on a stick to make a crude guitar. He learned to play a real guitar, a big Gibson.

Then the polio twisted him. "They said I would die, and when I didn't, they said I could never care for myself."

He figured a way to steady his guitar in his lap, above his useless legs, wedged a butter knife between his thumb and fingers that were stiff and clumsy, and, over time, learned to strum with one hand and pinch the strings with the knife in a way that makes the instrument seem to cry, as if alive.

He traveled the world, in fame and pain. He played in New York to packed houses, and in St. Louis, where he was trampled by a panicked crowd during a police raid. The worse of his bad legs was shattered.

Like Mr. Jones and Mr. Ford, he made some money, squandered it, got cheated out of some, and now lives in a small house that from the outside gives no sign a legend is inside.

But some days he gets out his guitar, "Bessie, named for a pretty, light-skinned woman I used to know," and music blows through the screen doors and sweeps the sadness away.

If you like fat women
Come to Pine Bluff, Arkansas,
You know they got more fat women
Than any place you ever saw.

DUCKING AT SYLVESTER'S

To Paul Jones, the blues will always smell like tea cakes. It was what his mother baked as she sang. His daddy was a guitar man. By the time he was eight, he knew his destiny.

"The Belzoni police stopped me and my daddy one time, but they just said, 'Hey, get that boy out and let him play,' and they took me to the station and I played, and they threw quarters in the hole in my guitar."

He played the harsh clubs of the Delta, like Sylvester's, where his sister was shot by accident by a jealous woman, where a man fired a shotgun at him as he played. The closest he came to dying was about 2 AM, coming back from Oxford, Mississippi, when his 1974 Chevrolet broke down. It was seventeen degrees, and he almost froze.

Though he played all his life, it was welding that paid the bills.

He would like to pass his music on, "but I got five kids, and nary a one of them plays."

Ms. Smith of the Blues Museum in Clarksdale said the music that was once such a part of daily life here must now be kept alive by programs like the one in her museum, which is teaching blues to about forty students.

Venessia Young, a seventeen-year-old high school senior who plays wicked guitar, is one of them. Her classmates refuse to listen to blues.

But when she hears it, she hears something Paul Jones and CeDell Davis and T-Model Ford hear.

"I'm going to attend Mississippi State next year, and they want me to play in a jazz group," she said.

"But that music, I just don't feel it."

Bitsy

Jill Conner Browne

When my daughter, BoPeep, was about six or seven years old, she went to New Orleans with her Godparents, Joanie and Buster, and their granddaughter ('Peep's Godcousin?), Ali, who would have been about four. I figured Joanie and Buster had completely lost their minds to want to take not *one* but *two* (2) small children to N.O. for a weekend—but 'Peep adores them and it also gave *me* a free weekend, so I figured, "So what if they're crazy? They're extremely nice otherwise," and so, off they went.

On BoPeep's solid recommendation, they went to dinner at Mandina's on Canal Street. Mandina's is very similar to a restaurant we know and love in our hometown of Jackson, Mississippi, Crechale's—in décor, atmosphere, and food, respectively: zero, very loud, and so good you can't stand it. Mandina's has good *everything* but the gumbo is outstanding and the crab claws are my personal favorite. Actually, you could throw the crab claws on the *floor*—it is the *goo* the crab claws come swimming in that is The Best Stuff You Ever Sopped a Hunk of French Bread In—ever in the history of the world, living or dead.

Anyway, 'Peep and Ali were Acting Big and Going to the Ladies Room Without a Grown-Up and getting a major charge out of it. Remember how cool you thought you were when you could finally start going to restaurant restrooms without a parent? I wish I could feel that mature *now*—about *anything*. Anyway, Joanie and Buster had wisely selected a table that was in direct line of sight with the powder room so they could at least get a description of the kidnapper, should the need arise. This is why I trust them so completely and chose them to be Godparents to my only child—they think of details like that.

So dinner was pretty much over and 'Peep and Ali had made their sixth and final trip to the Facilities. Buster had gone dutifully to pay the tab, Joanie waited for the girls at the table. Well, they didn't come and they didn't come and so, by and by, Joanie ambles over to the Ladies Room to check on them.

The Ladies' Room at Mandina's is designed like this: the outside door opens into a tiny, tiny, tiny—*a real small*—space with a mirror on one wall. Another door then opens into the actual space that contains the potty and sink. This is also a very small area. As Joanie enters, she is aware that there is another person already crammed in there (it could not have escaped her attention, since they were practically forced to embrace in order to fit both of them in there at the same time). The Other Person is obviously waiting, somewhat *less* than patiently, to use the restroom. Joanie did not actually *look* at this person, she was totally focused on trying to extricate the girls from the potty room in what was already too late to be a timely fashion.

She knocked on the door and made the usual Mom-type comments. You know, "Hurry up, girls, someone's waiting, are you all right, do you need help," etc. The only reply she receives is *gales* of laughter of the shrieking sort that is peculiar to Small Girls. She, of course, knocks more firmly on the door this time and *demands* that they come out *right now*. They open the door a crack and in that piercing whisper that is really more of a shout—that is also peculiar to Small Girls—they inform Joanie that they *can't* come out because *there's a boy out there!*

This is the first time Joanie actually *looks* at her very close neighbor in the very tiny room. She turns slightly, eyes downcast, and her gaze takes in two very large *furry* feet—in high heels. Moving slo-o-o-wly up, she notices two fairly substantial, equally furry, legs encased in stockings, emerging from a very short, very tight skirt. Climbing still higher, she finds she is face to face (or would be were Joanie significantly taller or her companion significantly shorter; truth be told, Joanie is taller than most toddlers but a fair number of middle-schoolers can see the top of her head; however, as Buster can attest, one should never confuse her diminutive size with any corresponding lack of power) with what is very likely The World's Largest Transvestite, complete with chest hair, make-up, five-o'clock shadow, a bad wig, and a necklace that inexplicably reads, "Bitsy."

He/She had apparently knocked on the potty room door and asked if "anyone was in there" and his/her voice had clearly said "Boy!" to the little girls on the other side of that door, and they had stayed locked in there, howling with hysterical laughter at The Very Idea.

Joanie, however, is standing toe-to-toe with him/her and finds they have Nothing to Talk About. None of the usual stuff that Women Talk About in Restrooms seems appropriate somehow. She smiles weakly and turns once again to The Door. She raps sharply this time and speaks in that Mother Tone that Cannot Be Ignored. "Come out *now*," she says quietly, death threats dripping from every syllable.

At the first opening of the door, he/she pushed him/herself through, shoved the girls out, and slammed the door in a Decidedly Huffy manner.

Joanie and the girls exploded out into Mandina's in absolute convulsions of laughter to find an Utterly Bewildered Buster. They explained it all to him in the car.

Mostly they explained to him that this is the Very Reason that women Always Go to the Restroom in Groups—you just never know *what* will happen and you sure don't want to *miss anything*!

S. Trident

C. Terry Cline, Jr.

U.S. Government Surplus Sales
c/o Pentagon, Dept. of Defense
Washington, DC 20301

September 23, 1979

Dear Sirs:

Enclosed is my check in the amount of five thousand dollars. I wish to bid this sum on Surplus Lot #5234-1-A as listed in your surplus catalogue of June 30, 1979, under the heading "S. Trident." As I understand it, this is for 33? acres of land plus existing structures and equipment.

Thank you,

C. Terry Cline, Jr.
115 North Avenue
Fairhope, AL 36532

U.S. GOVERNMENT
Sales and Surplus
Washington, DC 20301

20 OCT 79

C T CLINE
115 No AV
FAIRHOPE AL 36532

Dear Bidder:

Bid accepted herewith for S TRIDENT consisting of 33.3 ac incld bldgs and equip as advertised. Enclosed: title and deed.

Sinc Yrs

LT GEN H M Barnsmouth (ret)
US Govt Surplus Sales
Pentagon
Washington, DC 20301

11/3/79

Dear General Barnsmouth:

I am the new owner of Lot # 5234-1-A "S. Trident" which was bought with a bid of $5000 through U.S. Government Surplus Catalogue dated June 30, 1979. I took my deed to the courthouse in Weaverville, where we finally located the property, which I had not seen heretofore. (I made my bid sight unseen, figuring how could I go wrong at that price?) Anyway, upon arrival, we found the fence locked. Since it is a very heavy-duty 16-foot chain-link fence with four strands of barbed wire along the top, it was necessary to cut a new gate. Could you tell me where to go for the keys to the brass lock on gate # 7? Also, the electricity is on and there's a good bit of equipment still here. By the way, in a concrete pipe marked "Silo #4" there seems to be some sort of rocket. Until I hear from you, I am merely guarding the place and touching nothing.

Yours,

C. Terry Cline, Jr.

DEPARTMENT of the ARMY
Public Relations
Washington, D.C.

12-NOV-79

Dear Mr. Cline:

Your letter was forwarded to me by Gen Barnsmouth's office. Pursuant to the terms of sale as advertised in 30-June-79 Surplus of Govt Equip catalogue, having received and accepted the sum of $5000 as your bid, everything located at the site of Lot # 5234-1-A is legally yours. The electricity was an oversight and the proper authorities have been notified. It is drawn from an independent source to avoid the hazard of losing power during a possible enemy attack. According to our records the canister in Silo #4 is a decoy designed to confuse the satellite detectors of unfriendly governments. In any event, it is yours, legally. Hope this answered your questions.

Sinc Yrs

Lt Col Buck Passinque
Pentagon
WA DC 20301

11-17-79

Dear Col Passinque:

Not one to look a gift horse in the mouth, but could there be a mistake re: Lot # 5234-1-A, listed as "S. Trident"? On the fifth subterranean level there are several "live" computers, nine desks, seven locked file drawers, various typewriters, calculators, and miscellaneous other supplies. (It was necessary to have a welder cut through the doors since all were locked. Is there someplace I could get a set of keys as there are other doors on each level that are still unopened?)

My wife and son love it here! At the third level the temperature remains a pleasant 67 degrees and it is here we are setting up our little household. We plan to decorate the concrete walls with bright paint, using a modern décor and perhaps some surrealistic sculpture to break up the right angles. Come see us!

Sincerely,

C. Terry Cline, Jr.

DEPARTMENT of the ARMY
Public Relations
Washington, D.C.

30-NOV-79

Dear Mr. Cline:

It is often more expensive to reclaim equipment than to delete it. Please be assured all that is on Lot # 5234-1-A belongs to you. You may scrap it, sell it, use it—it is legally yours now. We are not the department that handles keys. It may be wise to have the locks changed, anyway.

Your plans for the décor sound a bit stark to me, but to each his own. Incidentally, the name of the location is "5" Trident, not "S" trident as you've been calling it. In future correspondence, please refer to it accordingly.

Yours,

Buck Passinque

12-8-79

Dear Col Passinque:

There appears to be a leak in the decoy in Silo # 4. I thought at first it was steam and stuck my finger in it. But the doctor said it looks more like frostbite than burn. Could it be liquid oxygen? It is very cold down there. Should this concern us?

Sincerely,

C. Terry Cline, Jr.

DEPARTMENT of the ARMY
Public Relations
Washington, D.C.

14-DEC-79

Dear Mr. Cline:

My suggestion would be, don't use Silo # 4 unless needed. If not needed, don't worry about it. If you continue to be concerned you might request a specialist from NORAD in Denver to come examine the problem.

Yours,

Buck Passinque

12-19-79

Dear Col Passinque:

With nearly 200,000 square feet of concrete bunkers underground, we don't *need* the area around the decoy. Therefore, we will stay out of Silo #4. Besides, it has quit "steaming" now. Probably part of the decoy psychology, to make it look very real to the Russian satellites.

Incidentally, my wife, Judy, says to tell you that we finished decorating the fourth level—and you were right, it was too stark. We're painting softer hues now, to go with the existing carpeting. The electricity is still on—I won't get billed for that later, will I? Merry Christmas!

Yours,

C. Terry Cline, Jr.

DEPARTMENT of the ARMY
Public Relations
Washington, D.C.

24-DEC-79

Dear Mr. Cline:

Happened to see your note when I dropped by the Pentagon on my way home for the holidays. I am so pleased your wife, Judy, has decided to go for softer tones. If I may, let me give you the benefit of a $2.8 million study undertaken by the government to learn which colors produced the least stress on men who often spend weeks underground tending the defensive nuclear weapons housed therein. The study was undertaken by an interior decorator from Ludiwici, Georgia, now teaching at Florida State University. The results were later confirmed by Sherwin-Williams. *Avoid* vermilion, purple, vivid pinks, fire engine reds, Day-Glo orange and *never* use khaki. The government learned this with your tax dollars, so I feel free to share it with you. Khaki is particularly depressing, tell her. As for the electricity, don't worry about it. Rather than fight the bureaucracy to alter it, just enjoy the free juice until somebody gets a formal cutoff order.

My best to Judy and Happy Holidays!

Buck Passinque

Jan. 3, 1980

Dear Buck:

You really ought to see level five. If I do say so myself, Judy did a great job with our limited resources. She and my son, Marc, rewired the computer to control various colored lights. So now, they can produce a soft glow, or a vivid discotheque atmosphere with the flick of a button. Marc (age 12) and a classmate have discovered that somebody programmed the computer to play chess. They haven't won any games, but it's fine for keeping them occupied. By the way, we had guests for dinner the other night (Level Three) and an interesting question popped up. Somebody asked if, in the event of war, would this site still be one of those likely to be hit in a nuclear exchange? Judy was just wondering.

You must come see us sometime, Buck. We have a great view of Battle Mountain on the one side and Gibson Peak on the other.

Yours,

Terry

DEPARTMENT of the ARMY
Public Relations
Washington, D.C.

09-JAN-80

Dear Terry:

The Joint Chiefs got a good laugh out of your question, "Would our site be targeted during a nuclear exchange?" The only *sure* answer to that would have to come from the Russkies, it's their computer! If you write them, let me know what they say.

All best,

Buck

Jan 13, 1980

Dear Buck:

How do you write the Russians about such matters? Do you have an address?

Yours,

Terry

DEPARTMENT of the ARMY
Public Relations
Washington, D.C.

16-JAN-80

Terry:

Try Kosygin, c/o Kremlin, Moscow. Don't know the zip, if any.

Best to Judy,

Buck

Jan 18, 1980

Mr. A. Kosygin
Premier
Kremlin
Moscow, U.S.S.R.

Dear Mr. Kosygin:

I recently purchased a parcel of land formerly used by the American Government as a Trident missile site. This land is located along Rural Route 3, Box 66-A, Trinity Center, California. It is officially designated (according to records I found here) as INSTALLATION CINQUEPAK 5 TRIDENT NORAD # 5234-1-A. My question is silly, I know, but since my wife, my son, and I have moved in here, we were wondering, have your military people taken this site off the strike list? It is no longer a military piece of property, and my wife, Judy, and our son, Marc, live here with me.

Thank you for your attention to this matter,

C. Terry Cline, Jr.
RR 3, Box 66-A
Trinity Center, CA 96091
U.S.A.

03MAR80

Dear Mr. Cline:

In matter of inquiry to Premier Kosygin such has been delivered to this desk of mine. The question has passed to proper authorities in which decision such resides.

Before answer can be coming, we are informed a more precise location than rural route and zip code is needed. Can you provide this and how many rubles must we pay to you for this information?

Yours for Détente and Reduction of Nuclear Weapons.

Peacefully,

Leon Petrovich Maxim
OFFICE KGB-112/ Lubyanka / g. Moskva/ USSR

March 11, 1980

Dear Mr. Maxim:

The property is listed as Parcel # 90, Page 401, County Court House Records, County of Trinity, Weaverville, California. Is that adequate?

Sincerely yours for peace, also.

C. Terry Cline, Jr.

UNION OF SOVIET SOCIALIST REPUBLICS
Komitet Gosudarstvennoi Bezopasnosti
04APR80

OCCUPANT
Latitude 41.01.16 North
Longitude 123.00.04 West
RR 3 Box 66A
Trinity Center CA 96091
USA

Dear Occupant:

It is the wish of the Union of Soviet Socialist Republics to reduce a risk of nuclear war. Our nation has peacefully ratified the Strategic Arms Limitation Talk Number One. The Soviet peoples have been disappointed by the recent American refusal to accept SALT II agreements, which have been quickly ratified by our government. The sabers rattle. Your Congress votes for more guns. New missile systems are approved. Thirsting for the commerce of continued arms sales, the American government spends more.

It is not wise to play games with something so serious as a multi-head 5 Trident missile still clearly in the firing position, prepared for launch against some helpless Soviet city and her peoples.

(signed)
Peter Bogdonovich
Asst to the Soviet Marshall
Citizens Protection from Attack Dept.
Politboro
Moscow, USSR

April 16, 1980

Dear Mr. Kosygin:

I am writing to you again because I think there has been some mistake. You may remember, I wrote about a *former* government installation that I purchased from the U.S. government. This is my land now. There are five silos, one of which has a decoy missile in it. But it is now, and always has been, a "decoy" designed to fool any adversary with satellites capable of spotting it. The land here and all equipment belong to me, and I am a private citizen with no military connection. I don't even own a pistol. I advised you of this to be sure your computers have been changed. We all know how computers are. I did not want the USSR to waste a valuable missile on a site that is now only a private residence.

Now, I have received a distinctly unfriendly letter from a Mr. Bogdonovich of the Citizens Protection Department. I am not a political person, Mr. Kosygin. I voted for Richard Nixon, then I voted for Jimmy Carter. So you can see by my voting record, I am not unfriendly to the Soviet Union. I never watch soccer. In any case, I am not a threat. Please program your computers with this information.

Sincerely,

C. Terry Cline, Jr.

P.S. Enclosed are recent photos of the interior decorating done by my wife on levels three, four, and five. You notice it is all-residential now.

SUPREME SOVIET SOCIALIST REPUBLICS
Office of Premier *Aleksei Nikolayevich* Kosygin
Red Square
USSR

30APR 80

Dear Mr. Cline:

It is against Soviet policy to correspond regarding military matters vital to the security of the USSR. However, it is refreshing to know the USSR has no enemy in you. Yet your President continues to meddle in the internal affair of others and has threatened conflict to save the world from Cuba, oil for America, and himself for office. How could you vote for this man?

Yours for Limited Arms with Honor,

Kosygin
Office of the Premier
Kreml
G Moskva
USSR

May 15, 1980

Dear Mr. Kosygin:

Something is getting lost in the translation here. I voted for Mr. Carter and that was a mistake. I'm sorry. Much of my nation is sorry. It was not a personal vote against the USSR. Personally, I like détente. Now, about my silo. Am I on your hit list or not?

Sincerely,

Terry Cline, Jr.

SUPREME SOVIET SOCIALIST REPUBLICS
Office of Premier *Aleksei Nikolayevich* Kosygin
Red Square
USSR

29MAY80

Dear Mr. Cline:

From my curiosity I ask this. Who do you think will be elected next time? Perhaps from there we may begin to discuss possible purchase of the used equipment found in the photographs you mailed to us.

Yours for European Disarmament,

A. Kosygin

June 11, 1980

Dear Mr. Kosygin:

I haven't the faintest idea who will be elected. It depends on what happens in Iran, what the Iranians do with the hostages, what the Middle East does with their oil—there doesn't seem to be much difference between the two American candidates. They both love God and want more nuclear warheads. Please—how about my silo? Am I a target? We aren't sleeping nights, worrying about this.

Sincerely,

C. Terry Cline, Jr.

UNION OF SOVIET SOCIALIST REPUBLICS
Komitet Gosudarstvennoi Bezopasnosti

07JUL80

Dear Mr. Cline:

These matters have to me been handed.

You think we are fools, Mr. Cline? We know the purpose of Lat. 41 degrees, 01 minutes, 16 seconds north, and Long 123.00 minutes, 04 seconds west. This is Quadrant nine, section six, and we play along with this poor joke of bad taste for the laugh of it. Ha ha ha. Give our finger to Jimmy Carter and his capitalistic warmongering Democrats, and to Ronald Reagan and his nuclear henchmen.

Yours for prepared defensive sites,

Leib Davidovich Tsiolkovsky
KGB Sector
Counter Intelligence
g. Moskva
USSR

August 27, 1980

Miss Elaine Bay
Nationwide Realty
San Francisco, CA 94142

Dear Ms. Bay:
Please run the following advertisement in your national listing.
Enclosed, find my check for the first month.

> FOR SALE: 33.3 Acres. Secluded. Beautiful view of mtns, near Clair Engle Lake. Quiet. Perfect getaway. Low upkeep and maintenance with plenty of storage. Something for the entire family. For details, call (251) 928-0087, Fairhope, Alabama. Price: $5,000. Terms if desired.

C. Terry Cline, Jr.
115 North Avenue
Fairhope, AL 36532

24/FEB/02

Dear Mr. Cline:

I am Peter Bogdonovich. Do you remember, I hope? It has been 22 years since I wrote to you about your rocket. Do you still own a rocket? A good joke on us. We laughed and laughed. But who is laughing now?

The world has changed, eh?

On television news I see President Vladimir Putin visit American President, George Bush in Texas. They shake hands for all to see. Our countries are friends and that is good.

President Bush took President Putin to Texas for Western music and chuckwagon food. On television, Vladimir Putin said, "I thank the American President for his hospitality. I thank him for the cowboy music. I enjoyed the four-alarm chili. It has given Putin a whole new meaning."

Americans laughed. Please to explain. Is it a joke like your rocket?

Yours for peaceful coexistence,

Leon Petrovich Maxim

My Heart's Content

(An Excerpt from *My Losing Season*)

Pat Conroy

The true things always ambush me on the road and take me by surprise when I am drifting down the light of placid days, careless about flanks and rearguard actions. I was not looking for a true thing to come upon me in the state of New Jersey. Nothing has ever happened to me in New Jersey. But come it did, and it came to stay.

In the past four years I have been interviewing my teammates on the 1966–67 basketball team at The Citadel for a book I'm writing. For the most part, this has been like buying back a part of my past that I had mislaid or shut out of my life. At first I thought I was writing about being young and frisky and able to run up and down a court all day long, but lately I realized I came to this book because I needed to come to grips with being middle-aged and having ripened into a gray-haired man you could not trust to handle the ball on a fast break.

When I visited my old teammate Al Kroboth's house in New Jersey, I spent the first hours quizzing him about his memories of games and practices and the screams of coaches that had echoed in field houses more than thirty years before. Al had been a splendid forward-center for The Citadel; at six feet five inches and carrying 220 pounds, he played with indefatigable energy and enthusiasm. For most of his senior year, he led the nation in field-goal percentage, with UCLA center Lew Alcindor hot on his trail. Al was a battler and a brawler and a scrapper from the day he first stepped in as a Green Weenie as a sophomore to the day he graduated. After we talked basketball, we came to a subject I dreaded to bring up with Al, but which lay between us and would not lie still.

"Al, you know I was a draft dodger and antiwar demonstrator."

"That's what I heard, Conroy," Al said. "I have nothing against what you did, but I did what I thought was right."

"Tell me about Vietnam, Big Al. Tell me what happened to you," I said.

On his seventh mission as a navigator in an A-6 for Major Leonard Robertson, Al was getting ready to deliver their payload when the fighter-bomber was hit by enemy fire. Though Al has no memory of it, he punched out somewhere in the middle of the ill-fated dive and lost consciousness. He doesn't know if he was unconscious for six hours or six days, nor does he know what happened to Major Robertson (whose name is engraved on the Wall in Washington and on the MIA bracelet Al wears).

When Al awoke, he couldn't move. A Viet Cong soldier held an AK-47 to his head. His back and his neck were broken, and he had shattered his left scapula in the fall. When he was well enough to get to his feet (he still can't recall how much time had passed), two armed Viet Cong led Al from the jungles of South Vietnam to a prison in Hanoi. The journey took three months. Al Kroboth walked barefooted through the most impassable terrain in Vietnam, and he did it sometimes in the dead of night. He bathed when it rained, and he slept in bomb craters with his two Viet Cong captors. As they moved farther north, infections began to erupt on his body, and his legs were covered with leeches picked up while crossing the rice paddies.

At the very time of Al's walk, I had a small role in organizing the only antiwar demonstration ever held in Beaufort, South Carolina, the home of Parris Island and the Marine Corps Air Station. In a Marine Corps town at that time, it was difficult to come up with a quorum of people who had even minor disagreements about the Vietnam War. But my small group managed to attract a crowd of about 150 to Beaufort's waterfront. With my mother and my wife on either side of me, we listened to the featured speaker, Dr. Howard Levy, suggest to the very few young enlisted Marines present that if they get sent to Vietnam, here's how they can help end this war: Roll a grenade under your officer's bunk when he's asleep in his tent. It's called fragging and is becoming more and more popular with the ground troops who know this war is bullshit. I was enraged by the suggestion: At that very moment my father, a Marine officer, was asleep in Vietnam. But in 1972, at the age of twenty-seven, I thought I was serving America's interests by pointing out what massive flaws and miscalculations and corruptions had led her to conduct a ground war in Southeast Asia.

In the meantime, Al and his captors had finally arrived in the North, and the Viet Cong traded him to North Vietnamese soldiers for the final leg of the trip to Hanoi. Many times when they stopped to rest for the night, the local villagers tried to kill him. His captors wired his hands behind his back at night, so he trained himself to sleep in the center of huts when the villagers began sticking knives and bayonets into the thin walls. Following the U.S. air raids, old women would come into the huts to excrete on him and yank out hunks of his hair. After the nightmare journey of his walk north, Al was relieved when his guards finally delivered him to the POW camp in Hanoi and the cell door locked behind him.

It was at the camp that Al began to die. He threw up every meal he ate and before long was misidentified as the oldest American soldier in the prison because his appearance was so gaunt and skeletal. But the extraordinary camaraderie among fellow prisoners that sprang up in all the POW camps caught fire in Al, and did so in time to save his life.

When I was demonstrating in America against Nixon and the Christmas bombings in Hanoi, Al and his fellow prisoners were holding hands under the full fury of those bombings, singing "God Bless America." It was those bombs that convinced Hanoi they would do well to release the American POWs, including my college teammate. When he told me about the C-141 landing in Hanoi to pick up the prisoners, Al said he felt no emotion, none at all, until he saw the giant American flag painted on the plane's tail. I stopped writing as Al wept over the memory of that flag on that plane, on that morning, during that time in the life of America.

It was that same long night, after listening to Al's story, that I began to make judgments about how I had conducted myself during the Vietnam War. In the darkness of the sleeping Kroboth household, lying in the third-floor guest bedroom, I began to assess my role as a citizen in the '60s, when my country called my name and I shot her the bird. Unlike the stupid boys who wrapped themselves in Viet Cong flags and burned the American one, I knew how to demonstrate against the war without flirting with treason or astonishingly bad taste. I had come directly from the warrior culture of this country and I knew how to act. But in the twenty-five years that have passed since South Vietnam fell, I have immersed myself in the study of totalitarianism during the unspeakable century we just left behind. I have questioned survivors of Auschwitz and Bergen-Belsen, talked to Italians who told me tales of the Nazi occupation, French partisans who had counted German tanks in the forests of Normandy, and officers who survived the Bataan Death March. I quiz journalists returning from wars in Bosnia, the Sudan, the Congo, Angola, Indonesia, Guatemala, San Salvador, Chile, Northern Ireland, Algeria. As I lay sleepless, I realized I'd done all this research to better understand my country. I now revere words like democracy, freedom, the right to vote, and the grandeur of the extraordinary vision of the founding fathers. Do I see America's flaws? Of course. But I now can honor her basic, incorruptible virtues, the ones that let me walk the streets screaming my ass off that my country had no idea what it was doing in South Vietnam. My country let me scream to my heart's content—the same country that produced both Al Kroboth and me.

Now, at this moment in New Jersey, I come to a conclusion about my actions as a young man when Vietnam was a dirty word to me. I wish I'd led a platoon of Marines in Vietnam. I would like to think I would have trained my troops well and that the Viet Cong would have had their hands full if they entered a firefight with us. From the day of my birth, I was programmed to enter the Marine Corps. I was the son of a Marine fighter pilot, and I had grown up on Marine bases where I had watched the men of the corps perform simulated war games in the forests of my childhood. That a novelist and poet bloomed darkly in the house of Santini strikes me as a remarkable irony. My mother and father had raised me to be an Al Kroboth, and during the Vietnam era they watched in horror as I metamorphosed into another breed of fanatic entirely. I understand now that I should have protested the war after my return from Vietnam, after I had done my duty for my country. I have come to a conclusion about my country that I knew then in my bones but lacked the courage to act on: America is good enough to die for even when she is wrong.

I looked for some conclusion, a summation of this trip to my team-mate's house. I wanted to come to the single right thing, a true thing that I might not like but that I could live with. After hearing Al Kroboth's story of his walk across Vietnam and his brutal imprisonment in the North, I found myself passing harrowing, remorseless judgment on myself. I had not turned out to be the man I had once envisioned myself to be. I thought I would be the kind of man that America could point to and say, "There. That's the guy. That's the one who got it right. The whole package. The one I can depend on." It had never once occurred to me that I would find myself in the position I did on that night in Al Kroboth's house in Roselle, New Jersey: an American coward spending the night with an American hero.

The Octopus Alibi

(An Excerpt)

Tom Corcoran

The air inside the taxi could've fertilized a cane field. Stale curry overwhelmed the driver's body odor and clove gum. A nicotine haze on the windows gave the sky a mustard tint. I wished I was back in Key West, packing for my weeklong photo job on Grand Cayman. I had been hired to shoot stills for a five-star resort's promo package. My southbound flight was forty-eight hours away, and I had let too many pre-trip details slide.

My wish to be elsewhere passed quickly. Sam Wheeler had done me a lifetime of favors in recent years, favors difficult to pay back. This was a chance to chip away at my debt. I needed to be right where I was, in a smelly taxi in a stamp-sized parking lot in Lauderdale. Sam, too, was doing what he had to do. In the room where Sam now stood, it was forty-five degrees colder than anywhere else in South Florida just before noon.

A GMC van departed, so the cabbie moved from open sunlight to the sparse shade of a bottle-brush tree. He shifted into Park and flipped on a small orange radio he had duct-taped to the dashboard. The box was tuned to a talk show, a meeting ground for people whose opinions outran their smarts. Someone had glued a religious icon to the dash below the radio. I wanted to invoke its powers to improve the program. I doubted that I was tuned to its wavelength.

The man tapped a fingernail on his engine temp gauge. He said, "We lose the cool, mon, or I got to go."

I watched his temp needle creep upward. He was wise to worry on a ninety-degree, late-April day. He was idling his motor with the a/c cranked to full blast. It wouldn't take long for the engine to boil over.

Sam had been inside the sand-colored building for only seven minutes. I had no idea how long he'd be in there. I slid the man twenty bucks—a third of it tip. Better I sweat in open air than melt into the

Chevy's vinyl seat covers, forced to listen to radio drivel. Sam's house-mate, Marnie Dunwoody, had loaned him her cell phone. We could call another cab when Sam was free.

A damp heat hit me as I climbed out. The driver backed away, spun his steering, went full throttle, and almost hit a sheriff's cruiser at the entrance apron. The deputy sneered, shook his head. He drove calmly to a parking slot as if near-misses happened all the time. He got out and slammed the county car's door. He was about five-eight, with a crewcut, huge muscles, a thick neck and broad chest. He wore a red polo shirt, a gold badge clipped to his belt, a weapon in a hip holster. He ignored me as he strode to the building. A lawman on a mission. I could've been dancing on stilts, juggling hand grenades. He would have ignored me.

Broward County's a tough beat.

Sam had shown up on Dredgers Lane at seven-thirty that morning. My head was under the pillow, but I heard his knock on my porch door. I knew it wasn't social. Sam never came by without calling first. He looked whipped. Puzzled. He skipped the salutations. "Alex, you got a busy day?"

I thought about my list, chores I'd put off, bills I hadn't paid, quotes I should have mailed days ago. I pictured my last-minute scramble, getting from the house to the airport two days from now.

He said, "I mean, if you're busy . . ."

"Nothing I can't ignore."

"I need to be in Lauderdale for a couple hours. I bought two tickets for a turnaround. I'll buy us a good lunch. We'll be back on the island by five."

With the constant easterlies, the past couple weeks of twenty- to thirty-knot winds starting to abate, I'd have guessed that Sam would want to spend the day catching up with his regular customers. He was dressed for work; he always wore lightweight long-sleeved shirts and long trousers. I noticed that he wore sneakers instead of his leather boat shoes. I couldn't imagine a fishing guide and Viet Nam vet needing a traveling companion. I decided to let him explain when he was ready.

I said, "Is there time to brush my teeth?"

"Take a shower. The flight's not till eight-twenty. I'll make coffee."

Sam spoke softly as he drove his antique Ford Bronco to the airport. "I got a call an hour ago from the deputy medical examiner in Broward. They found a dead woman up there, beat up bad, dumped on a tree lawn in a ritzy community. They say it's my sister Lorie. They want me to go through the formalities, sign the positive piece of paper."

"The sister you'd lost track of?"

"Since the mid-eighties." Sam paused, then said, "The same month the *Challenger* blew up, Lorie went poof, too. She'd sent me a photograph, she was holding a snook she'd caught in Chokoloskee. I called a few days later, and the phone was disconnected. My sisters and I never heard from her again." Sam went silent a moment, then added, "She had problems back then with abusive boyfriends. Strange, she was still in Lauderdale."

"How did they track you down?"

"An old picture of me in her wallet. I mailed one to each sister from Fort Benning during Jump School. Florence was about to start school. Lorie probably couldn't read yet. Ida, come to think of it, I don't know if she was born. I signed the backs of the photos, 'Love, Brother Sam,' with my service number under my name. I was one gung-ho son of a bitch."

Sam was quiet on the flight. It's not easy to talk on a droning commuter plane, anyway. We'd bought the *Key West Citizen* and the *Miami Herald* before boarding, and swapped sections during the flight. Several articles normally would have drawn comment from Sam. He'd had nothing to say. Our friendship had endured because we could survive silence in each other's company. But this deflated mood was not reflective or pissed-off quiet. In the years I had known Sam, I'd never seen a silence of sadness.

Sam nudged me and pointed as we descended over the Everglades on eastbound final into Lauderdale. Months earlier he had described the huge cloverleaf below us. The Interstate had wiped out Andytown, where Sam had grown up. He and his sisters had lost their roots to the highway planners, the graders and cement mixers.

After we touched down, Sam said, "Lorie was so damned stubborn, like my old man. She and the old man were going at it in the car one time, back when 441 was in the Everglades. He was snarling and she was snapping, arguing over nothing. He pulled over and told her he wasn't going to have her damned sass. She could change her tone or walk home. She got out and slammed the door. A mile down the highway I realized he wasn't going to stop. He was going to let a nine-year-old girl hike ten miles on a rural two-lane. I told him to let me out, too. He did, and drove away. I'd walked maybe two minutes back in Lorie's direction, the next thing I knew a big Olds sedan pulled over to pick me up. She'd thumbed herself a ride. We damn near beat the old man home."

"How did he react to that?"

"He never said a thing. She never did, either."

"Tough little girl."

"I guess not tough enough."

I found shade next to a drainage culvert, stood under a tree hung with flaming red blossoms. I checked my watch, then told myself to quit checking my watch. The cabbie was halfway back to the airport hack line. I still smelled of clove gum and curry.

I saw the building as perfect single-story bureaucracy. Some municipal architect had whipped out the Broward Medical Examiner's Lab plans on a Friday afternoon. He had been in a hurry to get to happy hour. A landscaper had saved his ass with shrubs. A trump of all flags at half-mast, an empty flagpole, stood at the entrance. The flagstaff's hoist ropes fluttered in the breeze. Hooks slapped against the hollow pole.

None of this had diddly to do with my upcoming job on Grand Cayman. But the setting brought to mind the conflict in my photo jobs. I'd had to deal with a weird blend of the beautiful and gruesome. It had bugged me for more than a year.

Three years ago I'd thought that part-time forensic work would simply boost my finances and fill unproductive time. It had started with the Key West Police Department, jobs that didn't require science or complex procedures. My name got passed around. Within months, Monroe County's detectives were calling, when their full-timers were overworked or on vacation. The only good thing was having extra bucks to put toward my bills. The bad part was how crime jobs dragged me into a realm I'd avoided most of my life. I still managed to work regularly, mostly out of town, doing journalism, or ad agency shoots, magazine features. Within the past few months, however, two ad clients had been bought out. Their assignments had vanished along with their corporate names. Even with the Grand Cayman job, this year could be as hollow as the empty flagpole. Unless I hit a jackpot, I still had seven more years of mortgage payments. My short-notice forensic gigs could make the difference between eating and going hungry.

At ten after twelve a white cab rolled into the parking lot. The woman at the wheel yelled, "Yo, Rutledge?"

I nodded. "We need to wait for the person who called you."

"You're on the clock, honey. Your buddy watched your cab leave. He called me. Damn, you're a tall one. Your buddy got a relative in there?"

"That's what they told him."

She shut off her motor, dropped the keys in her shirt pocket, and got out to fire up a Benson & Hedges. The beach or smoking had parched her skin. She'd dressed twenty years younger than her face, fighting time. "Cross your fingers," she said. She held the cigarette high so the smoke wouldn't blow my way. In her other hand she held the cigarette box and a Bic pinched between her thumb and middle fingers. She waved that hand toward the building. "They've been wrong before."

"You don't seem as freaked as the man that brought us here."

"Black man?"

"Yes."

"They're immigrants from the voodoo league of nations. They're afraid their spirits will escape inside the morgue, or their souls will be gang-banged to the sound of a hundred batá drums. Or dead people walking—zombies and fire-hags—will dance a rada in their rearview mirrors. So, this is the tissues and sympathy hack. I get sent here a lot."

"You deal with it okay?"

She waved again. "I used to work inside a door that's inside that door right there."

"For the county?"

She nodded. "I saw what came through the back, the messes they offloaded. I never got used to it, but it didn't weird me out. When I was inside, I taught myself not to react, not to have feelings. Looking back, I worry about that part of my personality. I worry about it more than ghosts or bad luck."

"So it's immigrants fighting their imaginations?"

She nodded and inhaled hard. Sucked smoke down to her knees.

I said, "Imagination can be more powerful than reality."

"They'd be shitless for sure, if they ever saw the real thing." The smoke leaked from her lungs as she spoke. She patted the taxi's roof. "The heat of the day, the nutso Gold Coast traffic, this job is heaven. Take my word."

"Heaven?"

"Well, raw heaven."

Sam stepped out of the building, flinched, and put on his sunglasses. His walk carried more resolve than before, as if he'd promised himself a course of action.

"You hungry?" he said.

"Was it bad?"

"Yep. But it wasn't her. You hungry?"

I wasn't, but I shrugged, then nodded.

Sam asked our driver to take us to Ernie's Restaurant.

"Eighteen-hundred block of South Federal," she said, then looked me in the eye. She'd told me that the people behind those doors sometimes got it wrong. She wanted to win that point.

I nodded, silently gave it to her.

Twelve minutes later, the taxi driver pulled into the restaurant lot. She turned to Sam. "Be careful, buddy," she said. "I used to work back there in that county lab. Six years, and I seen it all. The news you got sounds good, but it's not like you won the lottery. Unless you're one in a thousand, you went into the grieving process. Coming out unscathed isn't automatic. Was your sister's I.D. on the body?"

"Yep."

"Current I.D., photo of the victim?"

"Her Social Security card, a certified copy of her birth certificate, a few photos and personal papers."

"No driver's license, no unexpired credit cards?"

He shook his head.

The woman bit her upper lip. "You look like you can handle straight talk. This ain't scientific, but it's up here." She tapped her forehead. "The doctors call it empirical evidence. Your grieving might be right on. You follow me?"

Sam paid the fare and opened the door. "You mind if I ask your name?"

She pointed to the license on the passenger-side sun visor. "Irene Jones. Unique handle, eh? The assholes at the morgue used to call me 'Goodnight Irene.' I guess that's not the most sensitive thing to say to you right now."

Sam waved it off.

Just inside the restaurant's door, a dozen people waited for tables. Sam gave the greeter his name. She ignored the line behind us and led us to a remote booth in the bar. We gave her a beer order. Sam ordered us two apiece.

"Preferential treatment?" I said.

Sam said, "We've got a meeting, the local fuzz. Macho boy said he'd buy, which is unlike a cop. He said try the conch chowder."

Detective Odin Marlow showed up four minutes later. I spotted the red polo shirt and muscular build. He was the deputy I'd seen in the morgue parking lot. He clutched a box of Benson & Hedges in his left hand. The pack and a Bic, just like Irene Jones. Marlow introduced himself as "B.S.O., C.I.U.," as if initials meant big stuff to us. The greeter appeared with an iced tea, made special with two straws and two lemon slices on the rim. She put the glass down, gave the deputy a flirtatious sneer.

Marlow took his tea, then said, "Mr. Rutledge, you mind sitting over there? I'm a lefty. I'll bump your arm fifty times while I'm eating."

He didn't give a crap about arm bumping. He wanted to face us, and not worry about his gun being next to my hand. Sam slid over so I could fit on his bench. Marlow placed his cigarettes and lighter on the table as if they were ceremonial objects, and settled into the booth. He smelled like a sniff sample in a fancy magazine. He wore a diamond pinky ring and an antique Gubelin watch on a leather strap. One more piece of jewelry and his department's internal team would be on his butt. The men at the top don't like to see their boys display wealth. Perhaps Marlow had shown his supervisor a receipt for Zirconium.

The server took our food order, and Marlow started right in. "We found her out in District Eight, in what we call the I-75 Corridor, the extension of 595. You got your housing developments popping up like palmettos, your wealthy folk from south of the Gulf Stream, most of them from south of the equator. Where they come from, you know, they're kidnap targets, they can't shop, can't spend their money. It's low profile for survival. This is the comfort life. They got their Expeditions, their cable TV, slate tile floors, the built-in vacuum cleaner systems, the malls, red tile roofs. They also got public schools, no more political strife, and no more family security guards."

Sam said; "This has to do with a dumped body?"

"The last thing they want in their new neighborhood is a body. I got no proof, but I say no way this was Latino connected . . ."

Neither Sam nor I had suggested such a connection.

". . . and that improves our chances of solving this thing. Bumps it up from one percent to, say, three percent. So we know it's not your sister. All we got is fingerprints and a dental imprint, which, with women, who are less often in jail and rarely in the military, drops our chances back to two percent. Take into account, women change their names when they get married, we're back below the one percent chance."

"That relates to the victim," said Sam. "Let's go sideways. What're the odds my sister's alive?"

"I hate to use the word 'zilch,' but here's how it works. Criminals working credit scams swipe names from the living. People who want new identities grab names from the dead."

"And here we've got . . ."

"New identities go to people hiding from the law, or hiding from partners they've screwed over, or hiding from abusive spouses."

"So, if I found old dental records for my sister . . ."

"Don't even think about it. It's bad enough looking for a name to match a body. Working backward don't cut it. Hey, I know where you're coming from. The M.E.'s investigators called you in, got you all jacked up, put you on a mission. Before you knew it wasn't her, you were thinking 'eye for an eye,' to even the score. Am I correct?"

"Was it a robbery?" said Sam.

Marlow shook his head. "You'd find high-end clothing. Tan lines where the watch is missing, rings are gone. This victim, she was a Wal-Mart customer. She was small change. She was a poor target. I'd guess revenge, or she knew too much about bad people. Or, like I said, spousal abuse."

Our food arrived. Marlow shifted gears. "Tell me about that island of yours," he said. "You really like Key West?"

Sam didn't look up from his food. "Not many people live there because they're forced to."

"It's been years since I've been south of Florida City. Key West was full of fags and people smoking dope on the beach. That still the deal?"

"It's strange down there," said Sam. "You'd probably hate it. Don't waste your gas money."

The detective gave Sam a minute of silence, then said, "I'm reading your mind."

"It's blank," said Sam.

"You were thinking of ways, and don't tell me it ain't true. You're riding revenge energy. Nine times out of ten we appreciate that type of reaction. It reduces our job load. Ten times out of ten we bust you for it."

"I'm not the violent type."

"My guess, you're the right age to be a Vietnam vet. You may not be the type, but you're trained for . . . what did they call them, contingencies? So you find out it ain't her. You shift your mission, you try some freelance snooping. We like that about the same as two-bit vigilante work."

"Think what you want."

Marlow pulled a ballpoint and a tiny spiral pad from his trouser pocket. He said, "When's the last time you saw her?"

"Eighty-six."

The detective stared at Sam. "How long you lived in the same place?"

"Since eighty-one, the same place. My number's in the book."

Marlow stared at his pen, then began to snap it back and forth between the two bottles in front of Sam. The pen was not for writing. It was a prop, and the cop had taken notice of Sam's desire for two beers. "You got pictures of her?"

"Nope."

The pen went to the edge of the table, its use expended. "We wanted to let you know, ask your cooperation. We're gonna run a squib in the *Sun-Sentinel*, announce that the body was I.D.'d as your sister. I'll maybe learn something about the victim, and you'll maybe connect with a lost relative. The squib won't show up in Miami. It won't show in the Keys. We'll keep it local."

Marlow went to a vacant expression, waited for Sam's reaction. I didn't look at Sam, but I knew he wasn't showing emotion, either.

Marlow found another prop, a subtle distraction. He used a french fry to trace designs in his remaining ketchup. "Your own sister," he said, "and not a single photo? Can I ask why?"

Sam looked him in the eye. "You have your methods, I have my limits."

"Nifty answer. What's it mean?"

"You want to blow her out of the weeds. I'd like to coax her out."

"Look at it this way," said Marlow. "Her fifteen years to find you goes the other way. You've had fifteen years to find her. I take it you haven't tried."

Sam shrugged.

"And you're worried about her picture in the paper?"

Sam nudged me. "What do you think, Alex?"

I said, "I think there's more to gain than there is to lose. But if she's alive, could it put her in danger?"

Marlow leaned toward Wheeler. "This guy your roadie?"

Sam said, "No, my witness."

"You got a business card?"

Sam pulled out his wallet, laid a fifty on the lunch bill, and handed a card to the man.

The detective stood, snatched his cigarettes, fiddled with the Bic. "Do yourself a favor, Captain Wheeler," he said. "Like you've been doing since Ron and Nancy was in Washington, wait for her to call. Thanks for the club sandwich. You'll find a taxi out front in five minutes."

Marlow tensed the muscles in his chest, then walked from the table. Ten feet away he hesitated, looked back at me. "The watch was my father's," he said. "Right to the day he died, he was police chief in Greenwich, Connecticut."

Marlow exchanged patter with two waitresses as he left.

I said, "His next smoke was more important than our talk. He neglected to ask if you had other brothers or sisters."

Sam said, "Right. The type who promises what he wants you to hear and delivers what he wants you to believe."

We walked outside to find Marlow still there, leaning against his county car, having a cigarette. He said, "I'm curious, Mr. Wheeler. How's fishing in the lower Keys this month?"

Sam shook his head. "Constant east wind, just like here. Messed things up good."

Marlow agreed, "The wind blows, and fishing sucks."

"Yesterday and the day before were my first all-day charters since the third week of March."

Marlow got a distracted look in his eyes, as if he'd gotten smoke in one of them. "I was thinking of towing my Wellcraft down there this weekend. It's been eight weeks since I ran the motor."

"You need to run it more often," said Sam. "Your carb jets'll get clogged, your water pump'll go south. Anyway, the fish are hungry, but the wind's a bad enemy. If the shore trees are bending, you'll be skunked."

Marlow nodded. "Speaking of not catching fish," he said, "you decide to snoop around up here, this is not a quaint beach town. You'll get yourself in a world of hurt. Hire a private eye. We got 'em for all budgets and needs."

Sam didn't talk in the cab. He stared at the urban sprawl and reacted to nothing around us. He called Marnie from the airport, caught her before she left her office. I heard him say, "I'd rather see Lorie dead than looking like that woman must've looked when she was alive."

The flight back to Key West was bouncy. Late-afternoon heat played hell with the air mass above the heated land and cooling sea. A misty haze covered the Keys, obscured the horizon. Wispy clouds had sunk to sea level.

Sam remained quiet during the trip, consumed by another man's jargon and his own frustration. Through the past six or seven years of close friendship, Sam and I had not been constant confidants. But around me, even in his worst moods, Sam never had failed to express himself.

The engines' buzzing zoned me out. I fled to a half-hour nap, woke to find Sam staring out the window.

I said, "Was there ever a moment you wished your father was still alive?"

"Yep," said Sam. "He would unplug my radio whenever he heard 'What'd I Say?' or Buddy Holly doing 'Peggy Sue.' I wish he'd been around to see Ray Charles perform at the White House. I'd have loved to stuff that in his racist face. And I wish he could've been at that football game in Lubbock, Texas, when 49,000 people made the Guinness Book of Records by singing 'Peggy Sue' in unison."

The pilot made his seat-backs-and-tray-tables speech. Sam said, "Before I hung up, I asked Marnie to fetch us at the airport."

"Your Bronco's at the airport."

"I must be distracted. Don't tell her, maybe she won't see it. I can't have her worrying about me. She gets neurotic."

"What's happened to your memory?" I said.

"I keep forgetting to take ginkgo biloba."

"Can I ask the main distraction?"

"No cop would go to all that trouble to talk about immigrants. No big-city detective would ask me if he could plant a phony squib in the

Sun-Sentinel."

"Why lunch?" I said. "He thinks you know the dead woman?"

Sam shrugged.

"He suspects you of something? Doesn't make sense."

"That's his cop job coming through. He thinks, 'Arrest them all, and let the courts sort it out.'"

"Arrest for what?"

"He'll find something."

"What's that look in your eye?"

"I think I'll find something, too. With Marlow attached."

I Would Like to Go Back as I Am, Now, to You as You Were, Then—

Beth Ann Fennelly

Then when you bagged grit at the sandblasting factory,
loading train cars that took as much as they could stand
and got the hell out of lower Alabama, as you dreamed of doing,
watching them rumble North with your haiku on their dusty sides
written with your spit-wet finger, before changing from your coveralls
for your night school Literature class, your shame, your hope—

Or back, further, to when your mechanic father gave you
a fixed-up car—what you had asked for all through high school,
except it was the first Japanese car the county had seen, a Toyota,
and when you drove by, the boys called it "the rice burner,"
and the girls—pretty, pious, black-and-white as Dalmatians—
wouldn't get inside of it, so you paid five dollars in your empty car
to watch *Planet of the Apes* at the drive-in alone—

Or back even further to you in your plaid pajamas
sitting up half the humid night because asthma sat on your chest
and crushed no matter how you cried Uncle, so you drew
comic books bulging with muscled heroes until the blue rumble
of logging trucks signaled dawn, and better breathing,
and you could sleep, your chest heaving with its tiny
boy nipples, your legs sticking out with their leg bones—

I have loved you for your shame and for your busted body
which aches for three days after we help friends move,
because for years you were valued, like a donkey,
for how much you could carry on your back. I have loved you
for your freakishness, your exile in that homeland

where you hid your paperbacks, spoke the local language,
rose early and carried a gun if you wanted to walk in the woods.

I would like to go back as I am, now, but not as I was then—
unsure what I was prepped for in my Chicago prep school,
where girls skipped Chem to watch boys play soccer, boys
who pulled in our driveways in Benzes then beeped to have us hurry,
I wanted to be one of the thin girls dazzling in their meanness
but learned my tongue's too slow to suck that venom, I needed
to fail before meeting you, before learning myself the lucky one—

I would go back as I am, now, bend over your ribs,
lift the damp V of your pajamas and blow on your neck,
blow a breeze smelling like snow, sounding like somebody
whistling far away—I would go back for a ride in your Toyota,
beat time to your eight-track of Styx with my feet on the dash,
we'd cruise the drive-in and park, back row center,
let the girls gawk at the windows gauzy with heat—

I would go back and find you at the simmering factory
and free your wet curls from the clench of your hard hat
and unlace your boots almost lunar with red mud
and unzip your coveralls, a zipper long as lower Alabama—
go back as I am, now, and reach in, and kneel down,
and lick you to life, the life we couldn't know we were heading for,
a timely, lucky life, just beyond the margins of this poem.

The Girl from Soldier Creek

Patricia Foster

I'd just taken a bite of my hamburger when the call came. I had the night off from swimming at Earl Ray's, and I was helping Aunt Katy's little boy Henley, cutting up his hamburger into bite-size pieces and fixing the mashed potatoes the way he liked them, smooth as Dream Whip with a pat of butter melting in the center. When the phone rang, Henley put his thumb in the mashed potatoes, a big grin stirring his face.

"Oh, for goodness' sakes," Katy said as she removed his hand and wiped it off. "Now Henley, we don't do that to our food."

When the phone rang a second time, I swallowed and jumped up from the table. "I'll get it," I said, fishing a little piece of hamburger from between my teeth. I breathed into the phone.

"Guess who just *found* you?" Amanda's voice was a shock, like a voice in a dream from which I'd just awakened, but so much softer than I remembered, as if the edge had been beaten out.

"You," I said, not even bothering to say hello. My breath caught. I'd been waiting five months for this moment, planning for just how it'd be, how I'd feel, but now that it was here, I was too scared to feel a thing.

"No thanks to *you*," Amanda flared, and I could feel her anger as if she were right next to me in the room. But then the phone went quiet, and in that space I imagined something new, something hidden.

"I'm . . . I'm here with Katy," I said, sitting down on the couch, pulling the phone cord so it didn't twist into a knot.

"I know," she said. "I'm calling *you*, remember."

"Did Daddy tell you? Did he let you know I was all right?" I sank back on the couch, then hunched forward, my mind both tense and numb. I saw the letter I'd finally written Daddy a month ago, telling him why I'd run away from Soldier Creek and where I'd ended up. I saw him opening it hurriedly at his cabin on Perdido Bay, then rushing to the One-Stop and bugging Josie to call Mother.

"Well." Amanda paused, and I could imagine her narrowing her eyes, fixing them in a snake-eyed stare. She would be sitting on the wooden stool in our Alabama kitchen, the lights off, the fan whirring in the window, mosquitoes clotting the screens. I heard her breath ease out fast as if she'd been holding it in, then she was quiet, waiting.

"Well, *what?*" My own voice was charged with fear. I stared at the sun as it began to melt into the horizon, a flood of colors splashed against the blue California sky. Behind me, Henley slurped his milk and Katy said, "Hush, hush now," and wiped his mouth when he tried to protest.

"Jit," Amanda's voice went soft, edgeless, blurred into something like relief. I knew then it was trouble.

"What? What is it?"

"I don't know how to tell you," Amanda said. "I don't know . . ." Then she was silent, still, the air knotted with tension. "Jit," she whispered, "Daddy *drowned.*"

* *

The bus to Soldier Creek quivered and groaned like an old general grunting toward his grave. It stank of something awful like spoiled bologna or heat-ruined ham, but when I looked around at the dozing passengers, wondering who held the stink in their laps, all I saw was how easily they slept—knees open, hands limp, eyes twitching with the spasms of dreams. Sleep. I couldn't. Ever since I'd left Katy and Henley in Culver City, California, as I flew across country, then got on the Greyhound in Mobile, I couldn't quit thinking that word: *drowned.* I closed my eyes, trying to shut it out, and when I opened them again, I saw my first glimpse of water. Just little patches. Like islands in the land. Then a wide stretch, a giant ribbon of blue. My heart beat faster. I leaned closer as though I could breathe in its moisture through closed glass, suck it into my throat and make the words come easier. *Soldier Creek. Soldier Creek. Soldier Creek.* It was right there, threading its way beyond the thicket of pines, a pale strip of river winding sultrily into Perdido Bay, into the Gulf of Mexico, then blindly into the Atlantic Ocean.

When Daddy bought the place in 1952 it was nothing more than thick-wooded land studded with pines and water oaks and clusters of bamboo. "You could lose a fat woman in any four-foot square," Daddy used to joke, but I knew he wasn't seeing it that way. He was seeing the night mist floating low, swallowing up the water while a quietness descended inside his head, scattering the ugly thoughts. He had no intention of leaving, and there seemed no forgiveness when he did, separating—as demanded—from Mother, and moving five miles to a fishing shack on Perdido Bay.

"This is paradise," he used to say, and I'd nod because that's what it was for me, too. I could wade out in the creek, slip underwater like a woman losing her skin. Under water my eyes were sharper, the world clearer as if I'd been blind above water, following Mother and Amanda with my hands and ears, but never with sight. I think now I never did see them while I lived at Soldier Creek. No, I walked around like a sleepwalker, knowing where the danger spots were, avoiding sharp corners and slippery rugs, never fully aware of direction. Where I was going was based as much on avoidance as deliberation, so I guess it was no surprise that I turned mostly in circles. Aunt Katy said I didn't have much choice. "Honey, you were living in a minefield," she said, lying down beside me in her big double bed with its bright sunflower quilt and fluffy pillows. She stroked my head, then traced stars across my back. "You don't do much else but save yourself in a place like that."

Now I heard the hoarse, ragged barks of dogs, then saw two of them—tails wagging, mouths open—leaping at the bus as the driver stopped with a screech of brakes to let me off at the road to Soldier Creek.

"Here you are, miss," he said. People muttered in their sleep and changed their positions as the door creaked open. I hauled my bags from beneath the seat and stepped out into hot, moist air, with no breeze to speak of, the two dogs panting beside me, quivering in the heat. The bus was headed on to Pensacola, Florida, to the Miramar Hotel, and to Fort Walton Beach, where porpoises swam in blue-green water, leaping through plastic hoops to the scattered applause of the crowd. I stood there a minute after the bus thundered on down the road, wondering if I could breathe, then I shooed the dogs away and walked mechanically about fifty yards until the creek road split in a V, one leg leading to the house—to Amanda and Mother—the other right around the creek to Josie's One-Stop.

I wavered for a second, the wet air slapping my face, the sand warm on my feet, then with a pinch of guilt, I started down the road to the One-Stop. *Josie will calm me down.* I shuffled out of my shoes, walking barefoot, stuffing my shoes in my purse, everything familiar, but not quite real. I thought of Katy sitting beside me on her bed, painting my toenails, my feet lily-white because I slept during the day and swam at night in a tank inside Earl Ray's Bar. Mermaids, he called us, suiting us up in silvery blues and greens so the men sitting in the bar drinking whiskey sours and bourbon on the rocks and watching through that big picture window would see us as sexy and romantic. I took the job because swimming was the only thing I knew how to do.

I rounded the bend and there was the One-Stop, a fishing shack painted shiny gray like an oily sardine with a tin roof and a driveway of white oyster shells. I put my shoes back on and stepped onto the porch, which slanted downhill, the boards weathered to silver and warped by humidity. Through the screen I saw Josie sitting at the counter, drinking a Mountain Dew and reading the newspaper. I'd forgotten it was Sunday. Her long face looked gnarled like a piece of stripped pine, a fisherman's tan starting at her shirtsleeves and the top of her thighs. She frowned, turning a page, shaking her head as if she couldn't believe what she was reading. She didn't see me yet.

"Hello, Josie," I said, stepping inside, standing before Josie in a dress I'd borrowed from Katy, a red cotton shirtwaist with the thinnest strip of belt, buttons the size of fifty-cent pieces. Josie looked up suspiciously from her newspaper. "Three packs of Chiclets, please, one pack sugarless, any flavor," I said nervously, laying a dollar on the counter. The place was dark and cool like the inside of a cave. A ceiling fan whirred somewhere, its motor humming.

"Jesus-God," Josie smiled, "am I looking at the real thing or is the world just filling up with no-nonsense people?" Then she was up in a bound, her arms around me, one hand pinching my leg. "Where you been? I was worried and then some." She held me real close.

"California," I managed to get out.

"Loonies and fruitcakes." Josie shook her head, releasing me, but never taking her eyes off me as if I might vanish in thin air.

"I thought I'd fit in."

"Shame on you."

My eyes were adjusted now and I could see the strings of lures over my head, the fishing rods propped up against the wall, nets piled up on shelves, oars and life jackets spilling out of the corner, corks packed in buckets. I thought of Daddy picking up a can of worms, pretending to toss it to me, knowing I'd race him to the creek. Once out on the pier we'd forget all about the worms and dangle our feet in the water, making waves. "This is ours," he'd say, pointing to the water. "The Soldiers of Soldier Creek."

But when I thought of Daddy, I thought of Josie, the three of us getting up at the crack of dawn, taking Josie's boat through the channel and into the bay where we'd toss out shrimp nets, letting them drag behind us as we trolled towards shore. Daddy'd come by the creek and pick me up, then we'd maneuver the skiff across to Josie's as the sky began to lighten. He'd be in high spirits as he always was at the beginning of the day while Josie entertained us with stories about the fishing parties that came through her store. "Two old cooters don't know a trout from a flounder. Bought cigarettes and beer and I reckon they came down here to prove something about themselves."

"They're on vacation," Daddy'd say, tossing out the nets. "They won't do any harm."

"Ha! Nearly drowned themselves out there. One of 'em got drunk and fell overboard."

"Well, now they have a story to tell," Daddy laughed and turned from us to steer the boat.

When I was with Josie and Daddy, the world seemed right-side-up, alert and indestructible even though I knew our time together was stolen, slippery, never quite sanctioned. Mother didn't approve of Josie, thought she was a bad woman, or worse, a woman who'd tried to get her hooks in

Daddy. But Daddy said Josie was a character, "a real firecracker," and you could tell it tickled him to death. He admired her so much, he'd tried to move in with her once, but Josie, loving him, had put a stop to that.

Now I leaned towards Josie. "Did you see him before—?" I whispered, holding my breath, not knowing what I wanted to hear.

"Nope. You don't get around Amanda."

I felt a tightening behind my knees. *Amanda*. "Well, I've gotta see him—"

Josie nodded, locked the cash register and picked up her keys. "Let's go. I've been going by the cemetery every day since the funeral. Can't seem to say goodbye, can't seem—" But then she stopped, looked embarrassed and said softly, "Course you want to pay your respects." And she stepped out of her moccasins and put on a pair of red sneakers, the laces gone. The shoes made me smile. Her feet looked like a teenager's feet. For the first time since I'd left California, I felt a hint of relief. I was seventeen and I was here. With Josie. At the creek. Maybe it would all work out. Just me and Amanda and Mother. As if no one had ever left. As if trouble had walked further on down the road. But when I climbed into the truck and looked across the creek at the bluff, the house just visible behind the maples and pines, the white porch jutting out, the hard slant of slate roof, a stab of fear pierced my heart, followed by a sharp pain that rose in me like a tide. Already I could feel their pressure, like a foot against my chest, Amanda demanding, "Why'd you do it, run away like that?" while Mother stood beside her, remote, uninvolved, an invisible fence rising between us.

Josie rolled down her window and cool air brushed against me, lifting my hair from my neck. I closed my eyes, thought of Aunt Katy and Henley sitting in the kitchen eating popcorn, and I said what Aunt Katy told me to say, "I'll be all right, everything will be all right." As Josie drove down the narrow creek road I remembered the names of every branch and vine that hung over the front windshield, *wisteria, honeysuckle, pine*. I'd only been gone five months, but it felt like five years. The air was gentle, soft as an old blanket. We passed from the tangled brush and brambles of the land around the creek to stark, flat potato fields, the earth churned up after harvesting, combines and tractors in the fields. Then after a sudden sharp curve we pulled up into the grass behind St. Benedict's, a one-room white clapboard chapel with green shutters on the windows and wisteria vines climbing up the steeple. The grass had been mowed, the windows washed, the bushes trimmed, but I was looking beyond to the scattering of markers spread out like lost buoys at sea. A stand of trees, pines beside a few straggling oaks, their trunks thick as barrels, held the far corner.

Josie jumped out of the truck and started walking, and I followed her to it, the freshly dug dirt, the edges of the grass still separate from the rest. I couldn't help but think of birds rushing down to pick worms out of the dirt, then rising in a cloud of wild beating wings. I walked slowly, frightened. A small white cross marked the spot, and wilting flowers, roses and daffodils and even orchids spilled out like a carpet over the top. There was my daddy. Dead. Drowned in the creek while I'd been lost in Los Angeles.

I knelt down and closed my eyes, trying to find him, trying to explain why I'd had to leave. Because of Mother. Because of Amanda. And then something darker rippled across my mind. Because of me. Me. I saw Daddy as I'd seen him the night I left, drunk and sleepy, sitting in his chair facing the water, watching the tree frogs jumping at the screen door. "Jump, baby," he'd whispered. "Jump." He was alone and ill, but that wasn't what I wanted to remember. It was the other daddy, confident and sure, the one who let me ride like a surfer on his back as he swam from the pier to the island and back to the pier, the one who knew the creek like the back of his hand. *There's the sandbar*, he'd say. *Can't catch any fish on a sandbar. Watch out for the Narrows. Lots of moccasins nest there in early spring.* But the images kept getting all tangled up, and I saw him drunk and sleepy and in the water, not bothering to flutter kick, to cup the fingers of his hand, but lying inert in a dead man float. I got up quickly. "I don't want to be here anymore."

"All right," Josie said matter-of-factly. She rubbed her tennis shoes in the grass, cleaning them, then rattled her keys, found the right one.

When we came to the V in the road, Josie slowed down and looked at me, but I touched her arm and she drove on, neither of us speaking until we were back at the One-Stop. As I climbed out of the truck, I stared at the clean sweep of water, the sun falling in slow motion towards the horizon, a fiery ball about to be swallowed up by this floating cloud of land. *You can do it,* he said, holding me up, showing me how to move my arms and legs when I wanted to swim. *Trust yourself,* he said. *Let the water hold you up.*

"I've got to get into the creek, Josie."

"Fine by me."

At the store, Josie went inside, shuffling her feet and talking to her dogs while I stood on the porch undressing. Josie handed me an old bathing suit that drooped and sagged all over, but at least covered me up. The day was still hot, late May heat lingering in the trees, but without clothes, goose bumps suddenly spread up my body, etching the underside of my arms. I took off at a run, the water so shallow I had to wade quickly to my thighs, then plunge in. The coolness shocked my body until I went under. Closer to the bottom it was cooler, minnows moving by in clouds of motion. Coming up, treading water, I listened to the birds in the trees, a woodpecker not far off in the woods hammering at a maple. Seagulls ran in flurries near the shore, squawking when they landed. I lay on my back and remembered Daddy telling me, *let the water do the work, baby.* I could feel his hand under my spine, supporting me, and I felt happy seeing him in his swim trunks, his teeth gleaming, the hair on his chest bleached a silvery blond. Then as suddenly, the sun went behind a cloud and the water chilled. I knew it was time.

Josie handed me a towel and I dried quickly, putting on my clothes.

"You want a ride?" Josie asked while I toweled my hair and combed it with my fingers. It was short because of my job at Earl Ray's, and dried quickly.

"No, I'll walk.

"You've talked with Amanda?"

I nodded. "Some."

"Well, that's good. Then you already know she's mad as hell."

As I walked the creek road, dodging pyracantha branches, skirting lizards that darted across the path, I thought that Amanda had always been mad as hell. Mad at Daddy for being a reckless drunk, mad at Mother for holding on so tight, and mad at me for being stuck inside myself. "Permission for clearance," she'd say when she wanted my attention. "Reality coming in for a landing." And then she'd lie down on my bed beside me wiggling her toes, flapping her arms. "Okay, let's crack open our heads and talk." What she really meant was that *she* wanted to talk, wanted to tell me something that would startle me into life. That was the relationship we had: teacher to student, or as Amanda would say *Loudmouth to Worry Wart.*

But she wasn't what I'd run away from. I glanced up into a cloud of gnats, seeing the intensity of Amanda's searching gaze, and almost stepped on the small carcass of something no longer recognizable. Flies crowded at my feet, and, taking a deep breath, I stepped around it. No, for a long time Amanda had been my rescue. I quickened my pace, catching hold of bushes, leaves, dragging them along with me. Pussy willows grew just beyond my reach. Kudzu climbed up the body of a pine, cloaking it in a wall of green. When I saw the old scuppernong orchard that bordered our yard, my blood buzzed with pain. I felt the pull of my sister, and saw the two of us as little girls running out into the yard in our flowered nightgowns, Amanda holding my hand, saying "sshh, sshh," while we squatted down by the oak tree to look into the lighted windows where Mother and Daddy were tangled together.

Now I walked on more slowly, head down, coming into the yard so suddenly I was startled to see Mother and Amanda outside, Mother raking leaves and Amanda standing beside her, holding a big black lawn bag. They looked, for a moment, so domestic, so natural, I stopped dead still. Amanda had her back to me, her long dark hair in a loose ponytail so that I could see the pale whiteness of her neck as she bent forward, arms holding open the bag. Amanda wasn't pretty, at least not in the conventional sense—her hair a little too lank, her skin too pale, a slight hump in her nose—but there was something in the way she looked that interested people, an attitude that grabbed you and wouldn't let go. Then Mother was lifting a pile of leaves. When she saw me, she gasped, spilling the leaves all over the ground.

Amanda turned with an impatient slap of the bag, her face open, then clouded. "You've been *swimming!*" Those were Amanda's first words when she saw me standing in the driveway in my bright red dress. Instead of nodding I touched the damp curls crawling up my neck, but by then Amanda had her arms around me, hugging me, making me melt into the heat that is Amanda. Away from her, I forgot the sheer presence of her, how she could take away the air. I breathed deep, then went slack and easy in her arms, not so much hugging as being hugged.

"Goddamn you," she whispered, pulling my hair hard so I winced in pain. Then she hugged me harder as if she meant to crush something right there between us, kill it or keep it, I couldn't tell which. But when she pulled away, I saw something different in her face, a determination that hadn't been there before. I tried to touch her arm, but she shifted and my fingers caressed only air.

"I missed you," I blurted, surprised at myself. I wanted her to keep hugging me, to make this easier. I wanted to love her, to forget everything that had hurt us.

But Amanda pulled away. Her face tightened, and she looked suddenly suspicious. She put both hands on her hips. "We've been waiting for you. I'm starving and you've been swimming!"

Then Mother, hovering like a black shadow, moved forward. She came between us, almost touching my shoulder, but I stepped back, out of her reach.

"Let's go in, girls," she said as if we'd just been dawdling outside on an ordinary day.

The way I had left—rope out the window, running in the dark, dirty bus stations in Abilene, Santa Fe, and Barstow, the dry heat of the desert, then the cheap glitter of L.A.—shivered through me as I stepped back inside that house. It looked more run-down than ever, paint peeling from the doors, vines crawling up past the second-story windows and twisting into the eaves. The screen door was unhinged at the top, tilting away from the door, mesh bowed. There were no lights on in the kitchen and I saw the room as I often saw it at dusk, a trickle of light streaming through the window, shadowing the buckled linoleum floor. Our old wooden table was pushed against the opposite window, a jelly jar full of drooping wildflowers set dead center. A burst of snapdragons graced the sink. *Mother.* All along the counter there were mounds of food wrapped in aluminum foil, sour cream pound cakes, casseroles of peas and pimiento, jars of pickles and jam, Tupperware containers of chocolate-chip cookies. The wake. *Daddy's food,* I thought, and walked straight through the kitchen to the living room, where the windows opened onto the creek. Though light was leaking fast from the sky I could see the creek folding itself into the bay until there was only water and more water beyond the trees.

"I've gotta eat," Amanda said, somewhere behind me, and I couldn't help smiling. Amanda was always hungry. And suddenly I was too. I'd forgotten about lunch and had no thought about food on the bus. Tonight I hoped we'd be filled only with appetite—no scenes, no questions, no dark secrets to reveal. I wanted to sink into this place like sliding into sleep. "I'll get the chicken," Amanda said. "You get the tea."

The table was set with silverware and china, three places like it used to be before Amanda left for college. Mother brought out a platter heaped with cornbread sliced into squares and a bowl of green beans someone had left, the bacon swimming in juice on the top. She looked directly at me, but I turned as quickly away. She hadn't said anything to me nor I to her, and I wondered if we ever would. We both looked at the food until Amanda waltzed in with the chicken.

I sat where I always sat, the chair that faced the windows; Amanda sat across from me, Mother at the head of the table. It seemed almost natural until that moment after we'd unfolded our napkins, after we'd served the food and nobody knew what to say or how to say it. We were anxious and frightened, so we pretended the business of food was all that mattered. I ladled black-eyed peas and summer squash onto my plate. We ducked our heads down, eating, until Amanda clattered her fork and knife. "Jesus, I can't stand this. Come on, let's just say it. We're a mess." She laughed and put a hunk of cornbread in her mouth. Mother and I both looked up, silent, watching. I spread butter onto the crusty edge of my bread. "No, I mean it. *Say* it," Amanda said, and there was a new hardness in her voice. She glared at both of us, and for the first time I noticed that Mother looked frightened, her lips pressed together, the veins pulsing in her temples. She opened her mouth as if to speak, then shut it again. I watched all of this as if I were outside the window looking in.

"Say it," Amanda repeated, her lips tight, her eyes pinned not to me but to Mother.

"Amanda, I don't—" Mother began. She looked startled, uncertain.

"Say it," Amanda whispered, still staring at us, but now there were tears filling her eyes.

"Hey," I said, leaning towards her. I never knew how to comfort Amanda. Upset, she seemed more distant than ever. Unreachable. A shield placed between her feelings and mine. "We know we're a mess."

Mother nodded.

Amanda looked from me to Mother, and then she smiled. "Good, then we're in agreement. Just like a democracy." And she reached for the platter of fried chicken, selected the largest breast and slid it onto her plate.

For a moment I didn't eat. I didn't quite know what had happened, why Amanda was so insistent, but inside my head these words kept rotating, *we're a mess, a mess, a mess.*

* *

Night fell across the sky like a blanket. The stars reared up and sparkled as if they'd just been turned on, and the creek glowed in the moonlight, like satin, like silk, a smooth ride out to nowhere. It was so calm that anything seemed possible, a walk on water, a dive from the sky. When I was little I used to walk out onto the pier with Daddy, just the two of us, silent, serious, staring out at the creek. I would hold his hand while we sat on the pier and put our feet in the water. Always I could feel things moving beneath the water, could feel the heat of Daddy's hand, and the water seeming to creep up my feet, spreading across my thighs, rising to my waist, to my chest, and climbing up to my neck. And what I felt was an overwhelming happiness.

I walked out onto the porch, not turning on the overhead light, but staring at Josie's spotlight across the point. Mother was washing dishes. Amanda had gone into the kitchen to get ice cream for one of the many desserts still in the kitchen and I didn't hear her come back out. Bugs buzzed and thumped in the darkness beyond the screen and there was always the sound of the waves beating against the old pier. The point looked like a dark finger extending into the shivery shimmer of the creek. And I remembered why I loved it, remembered Dodo, the blue heron I used to feed from our pier, how she glided down and stood erect, waiting for me to bring the bucket of eels.

"It's beautiful sometimes," Amanda said, moving beside me in the darkness. We stood together in silence, Amanda slumping slightly, her bowl of vanilla ice cream and a chocolate brownie in her hands. I loved her then as I'd loved her as a child, without caution or restraint.

"It's the only thing I've ever wanted," I said. Even seeing the Pacific Ocean hadn't been anything like this.

"Yeah, I know." She shifted towards me and her skin touched mine.

"I missed it." For a moment I felt as if I'd never left, that Amanda and I had been staring out this window forever, two girls out in nowhere, holding on to thin air. "I mean—"

"Well, take a long look—" she interrupted, gesturing with her hand at the creek. "Because the Soldiers of Soldier Creek are coming to an end."

I could feel my breath become shallow in my throat. "Amanda, quit that. We've always lived here."

"Past perfect tense. Exactly my point." Amanda held up her spoon, and now I saw the hardness come back into her eyes.

"But Mr. Turner's always let us—"

"Mr. Turner!" Amanda snorted, plunging her spoon into the bowl. "Money's the only thing that Mr. Turner wants. Rent money. And *more* of it."

"But we once owned it . . . it's been our arrangement. Daddy always—"

Amanda was quiet, but I could feel her staring at me, judging me, and even in the dark I blushed. "Jit," she said gently, wearily, and touched my arm. "Open your eyes. We haven't got any money. Mr. Turner's throwing us out. We've got till the new year."

I didn't move. I couldn't. Daddy dead. The creek gone. A fish jumped somewhere out in the bay and we both heard the splash.

"Welcome home," Amanda said with the old hiss of anger. Then she lifted her spoon to her mouth and turned abruptly, leaving me alone on the porch.

I didn't watch her go. Instead, I put my face to the mesh, pressing it hard against the screen, listening for a change in the air, but there was nothing but the sound of crickets, the rasp of frogs in the bushes, the scuttle of squirrels. And there was me, standing here with all these breathing creatures, waiting in the dark, waiting for all this sadness to pull itself closer against my skin.

Christmas 1893

Tom Franklin

Bess was almost asleep when a wagon rolled up outside. She rose from where she'd been kneeling before the hearth, half in prayer, half for warmth. Another cold December day over, rain coming. It was dark outside, windy at intervals, the old rocker on the porch tapping against the front wall. A pair of sweet potatoes on the bricks before her was all the food they had left.

A horse nickered. She pulled her shawl around her shoulders and held it at her throat. Her four-year-old son, William, who'd been lying under a quilt on the floor beside her, got up.

"Stay here, boy," she told him, resting a hand on the top of his head. He wore a tattered shirt and pants given as charity by church women from the last county they'd lived in, just over a week before. Barefooted, he stood shivering with his back to the fire, hands behind him, the way his father liked to stand. She felt a love for him so overwhelming she nearly fainted, the things he'd seen in the world already more than she could bear.

On the porch, she pulled the latch closed behind her and peered into the weakly starred night. Movement. Then the flare of a match lighting a torch, and a man in a duster coat and derby hat seemed to form out of the fabric of darkness. He wore a white beard and spectacles that reflected the torch he held above him.

"Missus Burke?" he said.

She nodded, her knuckles cold at her throat. She heard the door open behind her and stepped in front of it to shield William.

"This is my land you're on," the man said, "and that's one of my houses y'all are camped out in."

Bess felt relief, for an instant.

He's only here about the property.

"My husband," she said. "He ain't home."

"Ma'am," the man said, "I believe I know that."

Fear again. She stepped forward on the porch, boards loose beneath her feet, and stopped on the first step. The man's horse shook its head and stamped against the cold. "Easy," he whispered. He set the brake and stepped from the seat into the back of the wagon, holding the torch aloft, a trail of cinders and sparks settling behind him, landing in the dirt yard. He bent and began pushing at something heavy. Bess came down the first step. Behind her, William slipped through the door.

The man climbed from the tailgate of the wagon and took a few steps toward her. He was shorter than she was, even with his hat and in his boots. Now she could see his eyes.

"My name is Mr. Carter," he said. "Could you walk over here, ma'am? I have something for you."

She seemed unable to move. The dirt was cold, her toes numb. Mr. Carter waited a moment, gazing past her at William. Then he looked down, shaking his head. He came toward her, and she recoiled as if he might hit her, but he only placed a gloved hand on her back and pushed her forward, not roughly, but firmly. They went that way to the wagon, where she looked in and, in the light of his torch, saw her husband.

E. J. was dead. His jacket was opened and his shirtfront red with blood. His fingers were squeezed into fists and his head thrown back, mouth opened. His hair covered his eyes.

"His hat," she whispered. "And his pistol. Where are they?"

"Ma'am, I don't know about the hat," Carter said, "but I'm gonna hold on to the gun for a while."

"What," she began, but covered first her mouth then her eyes with both hands.

"He was stealing from me," Carter said. "I seen somebody down in my smokehouse and thought it was a nigger. I yelled for him to stop but he took off running."

"Stealing what?" she asked, her voice small.

"A ham," Carter said.

Bess's knees began to give way, she grasped the wagon edge. Her shawl fell off and she stood in her thin housedress, her nipples rigid in the cold. Carter steadied her, his arm going around her shoulders. He laid the torch on the floor of the wagon, by E. J.'s boot.

"I am sorry, ma'am," Carter said, a hand now at each of her shoulders. "I wish . . ."

William appeared behind her, hugging himself, his toes curling in the dirt. "Is that Daddy?" he asked. "Is he corned again?"

Bess could only nod. "Go on inside, son," she told him. "Now." He didn't move.

"Do like your momma says," Carter ordered, and William turned and ran, up the stairs in one leap and inside, pulling the door to. His face appeared immediately in the window.

Carter led Bess back to the porch and she slumped on the steps. He retrieved her shawl and hung it across her shoulders. Then, as if he didn't know what to do with his arms, he wiggled them at his sides, opening and closing his fingers.

"My own damn fault," he said. "I knew y'all was out here. Just ain't had time to come see you. Run you off."

No longer able to hold back, Bess was sobbing into her hands, which smelled of smoke. Some fraction of her, she knew, was glad E. J. was gone, glad he'd no longer pull them from place to place only to be threatened off at gunpoint by some landowner again and again. No more of the sudden unprovoked rages or the beatings he gave her or William or some bystander. But, she thought, for all his violence, there were the nights he got only half-drunk and they slept enmeshed in each other's limbs, her gown up high where he'd pulled it and his long johns around one ankle. His quiet snoring. The marvelous lightness between her legs and the mattress wet underneath them. There were those nights. And there was the boy, her darling son, who needed a father, even if what he got was one prone to temper and meanness when he drank too much whiskey. A boy who needed a stern hand. Where would they go now, she asked herself, the two of them?

"Ma'am?" Carter tugged at his beard.

She looked up. It had begun to rain, cold drops on her face, in her eyes.

"You want me to leave him here?" Carter asked her. "I don't know what else to do with him. I'll go find the sheriff directly, tell him my side.

He'll ride out to see you tomorrow, I expect."

"Yeah," Bess said. She blinked. "Would you wait . . . ?" She looked toward the window where William's face ducked out of sight.

"Go on ahead," he said.

Inside, she told the boy to gather an armload of the pine limbs and kindling sticks they'd collected earlier and piled in the corner. She went to the fireplace and reached in and, with one hand covering her face, took with the other the end of a log and lifted it out, concave in the center and pulsing with ember. She held it away from her body as if it were a short, thick snake, hurrying through the low door into the back room, then deposited the sizzling log in the fireplace and brushed the ash from her hand. Turning, she called for the boy. He came in with his arms full of wood. She had him kneel before the hearth and feed in his limbs stick by stick. She took some straw from her pocket and tossed it in, then showed him how to blow on the fire to liven it. Told him not to leave this room, said to keep blowing on the fire until it was good and hot. "Then," she said, returning with the quilt, "go on to sleep."

Outside, Carter was wrestling E. J. to the edge of the wagon. Bess helped him and together they dragged him up the steps.

"You want to leave him on the porch?" Carter huffed. "He'll keep better."

"No," she said. "Inside."

He looked doubtful but helped her pull him into the house. They rolled him over on a torn sheet on the floor by the hearth. In the soft flickering firelight, her husband seemed somehow even more dead, a ghost, the way the shadows moved on his still features, his flat nose, the dark lines under his eyes that his father had had as well. She pushed his hair back. She touched his lower jaw and closed his mouth. Tried to remember the last thing he'd said to her when he left that afternoon but couldn't. His mouth slowly fell back open, and she put one of the sweet potatoes under his chin as a prop.

Carter was gazing around the room, still wearing his gloves, hands on his hips. She looked where he did, as if this were some kind of inspection. She'd worked hard at fixing the house up—E. J. had promised it was theirs, that he'd taken care of the arrangements. Even though she'd known it to be a lie, she and the boy had filled the cracks between the logs in the walls with mud and straw. Bess had swept the dirt and rat pellets and acorn hulls out the front door and plugged the knotholes in the floor with rags. She'd scrubbed the fireplace rocks clean, plucked the brittle wasp nests from the ceiling timbers and with a pine limb batted the dusty cobwebs out of the dark corners. Then she and the boy had disassembled the empty, crumbling trunk from the back room and fitted squares of the cardboard lining into windows with broken panes. With the salvaged nails and a rock for a hammer they'd hung pictures from newspapers found piled in a corner. An old metal washtub sat in another corner, a few inches of creek water in its bottom.

Abruptly, Carter walked across the floor and went outside, closing the door behind him. When he came back in, she jumped up and stared at him, backing away.

In one arm he held a bundle.

"This is the ham," he said, casting about for somewhere to set it. When nowhere seemed right, he knelt and laid it beside the door. "Reckon it's paid for," he said.

He waited for a few moments, his breath misting, then went outside, shutting the door behind him. She heard it latch. Heard him release the brake and heard the creak of hinges on his wagon and the horse whinny and stamp and the wheels click as Mr. Carter rolled off into the night. She went to the window and outside was only darkness. She turned.

Her fingers trembling, Bess unwrapped the cloth sack from around the ham, a good ten-pounder, the bone still in it. A pang of guilt turned in her chest when her mouth watered. Already its smoked smell filled the tiny room. She touched its cold hard surface, saw four strange pockmarks in its red skin. Horrified, she used a fingernail to dig out a pellet of buckshot. It dropped and rolled over the uneven floor. She looked at her husband's bloody shirt.

"Oh, E. J.," she whispered.

COME HOME, COME HOME, IT'S SUPPERTIME

William Gay

His dreams were serene pastoral images, white picket fences, old log barns silver in the moonlight. An ornamental tin sun set high in the eaves of a farmhouse, tinstamped rays fanning upward. When the light subtly altered he saw that the pickets were stakes sharpened for impaling, something stirred in the strawstrewn hall of the barn, and there was a persistent ringing beyond the serrated treeline the illogic of dreams imbued with dread. Then he became aware of Beth's leg flung across him in sleep, the smell of her hair, the ringing of the telephone, and he realized where he was, and that he wasn't a child after all.

He wondered how many times it had rung. Here in these clockless hours past midnight.

"Hello."

It must have rung several times, for the voice was harsh and preemptory. "I've got to have some help over here," she said.

"What is it?" He could hear the ragged hiss of her breathing.

"I'm having some kind of attack. A heart attack."

"All right. I'm on my way."

He was fumbling for his shoes. He found one sock, the other seemed to have vanished. Beth arose and he heard her stumbling toward the bathroom. Water running. He gave up on the sock and was hauling on his pants.

"Your grandmother?"

"Yes."

"Another heart attack."

He looked up. She was standing naked on the threshold of the bathroom, her face enigmatic in the dark bedroom, backlit by the bathroom light. Framed so against the yellow rectangle the light was a nimbus in her fair hair, and she seemed to be in flames.

"Do you need me?"

Stark and depthless against the light she looked like erotic statuary.

Something in her hipslung posture lent her words an ambiguity he couldn't deal with just now, everything about her lately seemed subject to various interpretations.

"I'll be back when I get back," he said. He slid his wallet and cigarettes into his pocket and went out.

He pushed the door back open. "Lock the door," he told her, but she didn't say if she would or she wouldn't.

He drove out toward the farm, off the blacktop onto a cherted road so bowered by the trees the moonlight couldn't defray the darkness, the road descended like a tunnel of black velvet, like a cleft in the earth itself he was driving off into. A whippoorwill swept up in the headlights, dark wings enormous, eyes wild and red as blood. Mailboxes, sleeping watchdogs, darkened houses shuttered against the night. Then the row of cedars, the lit farmhouse beyond them.

She was in the bentwood rocker. She sat twisted in agony. Her head in her hands, her breathing a thin panting.

"Do you need an ambulance?"

"I've called it already. It should have been here."

"Well," he said. He couldn't think of anything to say. It'd all been said before. Somewhere a clock ticked, a series of clocks deafening in the silence that stretched, stretched to a thin sharp wire. A tall grandfather clock whirred into life, gave three solemn and measured bongs.

"I can't breathe. I've got to have some oxygen. Why won't they hurry up?"

"I think I hear them," he lied.

She was clutching her chest like a parody of agony. "I'm on fire in here," she said. Behind the thick glasses her near-colorless eyes were stricken, afraid. He felt a detached and impotent pity.

"Is there anything I can do?"

"Get me a glass of orange juice. Maybe my sugar's gone down, I'm having some kind of attack."

He took a carton from the refrigerator and poured a glass of juice. He carried it to her. When she had drunk from the glass, he asked, "Are you feeling any better?"

"Maybe a little."

"Are you sure you want to go to the hospital? It never accomplished anything before. I can hire a nurse. I can stay myself."

"I've already called it," she said. "Something has got to be done. I'm not putting up with this."

He went out onto the porch. Where the porchlight tended away the yard lay silver in the moonlight, it glittered as if viewed through a veil of ice. Beyond it lay darkness, a veritable wall of insect sounds. From the ebony trees nightbirds called, cries so lost and forlorn he wondered what the configurations of such birds might be. Far up the road he could hear the whoop of the ambulance. Closer now, homing down the walls of night. Its lights pulsed against the bowering trees like heat lightning. He lit a cigarette and waited.

The ambulance backed to the edge of the porch. An attendant leaped out and threw open the rear door and hauled out a gurney. Everything seemed rehearsed, every movement preordained, they'd been here before. Déjà vu all over again, he thought.

"She needs oxygen," he said.

The driver came around and helped with the gurney. The paramedic took out a chromium oxygen bottle, a mask appended by a thin transparent tube. They seemed to have divined something unsaid from his face, for their movements had become less hurried, more studied. He held the door open and they went into the living room with the gurney.

She seemed reassured by such an authoritative presence. The paramedic was kneeling at her feet adjusting gauges. The other had immediately commenced monitoring blood pressure, heartbeat. She was reaching for the mask. He could hear a thin hissing. "Here you go, Mrs. Wildman," the attendant said. "You just relax now." She grasped the mask greedily the way a baby grasps its bottle, a drowning man a straw. As if the very essence of life itself had been distilled and concentrated in this chromium bottle, the ultimate spray can.

They were already gently helping her onto the gurney, adjusting straps. "Hand me my bag," she told Wildman. When he laid it beside her she clutched it possessively with a thin ravaged arm. They were rolling her through the doorway. "I'll see you early in the morning," he said. The door creaked to on its keeperspring. Gurney wheels skirling across the oak porch. After a moment the rear door of the ambulance closed. The ambulance pulled away, siren shrieking, particolored lights pulsing through the window, the wall across flickering in crimson neon. The wails grew faint and fainter and then he could hear whippoorwills calling one to the other.

Wildman sat in the room where he'd been a child. Where he'd crawled about the floors amongst his playthings. Images of himself at various ages adorned the walls, the tables. He leaned to study one. From across time the face seemed to be studying him back. Dark calm child with disaffected eyes. In the end time waylays you, he thought. It can outwait you, what does it care, it's got you outnumbered. There is just so damn much of it.

The room was begarbed with knickknacks, geegaws, and ceramic cats and statuary he couldn't fathom the source of. They'd just accumulated with the years, so many years, had settled like dust motes out of time. Across the room a bookcase where she kept the high school annuals. She'd been a teacher and she'd saved them all the way a traveler might save maps of places he'd been. Suddenly the room was claustrophobic, the walls were sliding inward on oiled tracks, he couldn't breathe. He put his cigarette out in a coffee cup and arose and went out into the night. Where the moon was a washed-out ghost of itself and the sky was already faint with rose-colored light, the day lying somewhere east of him.

* *

"She's a hypochondriac," Beth said.

"I guess," he said. He drank coffee.

"What are you going to do about it?"

"Do about it?"

"You can't go on like this. All these emergencies in the middle of the night. You're not sleeping, it's too hard on you working construction the way you are this summer."

"I'm used to it," he said. "I can take it."

"She ought to be thinking of you."

"She's thinking about death," he said. "It's staring her right in the face and she can't deal with it. I don't know if I could. Could you?"

"I can when I get that old," she said.

He watched her across the rim of his coffee cup. Dying seemed way down the line. She was fifteen years younger than he was. She was twenty-five years old and her skin was poreless as marble and her mouth red and bruised looking. Her green eyes were the green of still, deep waters and there was something arrogantly sexual about them, they said that she knew what she had and that she had an unlimited supply of it and it was going to last forever. He knew it wasn't and he wished he didn't.

"She's old," he said. "She can't teach anymore. She's sick and she's going to be sicker and then she's going to die. And she knows all that."

"She'll outlive us all and dance on your grave," Beth said.

He set the cup down. "Let's just give it a rest awhile," he said. "Are you going to work today?"

"It's Sunday."

"I mean are you going to write."

"I may. I don't know."

"Why don't you write us another of those thousand-dollar stories like you did that time," she said.

"Thousand-dollar stories don't grow on trees," he told her.

She smiled. "It was gibberish to me anyway," she said.

"I know. I saw your review in the paper."

"Everybody's a critic, huh?"

"Everybody's a critic."

For a moment Beth and the old woman shared a curious duality, she had been a critic, too.

"I saw that piece in *The Atlantic*," his grandmother had said. "I thought it offensive."

"They liked it," he had told her. "It was an Atlantic First Story."

"It ought to have been an Atlantic last story. It was gibberish and obscene gibberish at that."

"The world is obscene gibberish," Wildman said. "I find it offensive."

She studied him. "I liked you better as a child. You were such a lovable child."

* *

The phone rang at four o'clock in the morning and there was a nurse on the line. Wildman lay listening to the nurse and to Beth's regular breathing beside him. "She's had a rough night," the nurse said tentatively. "She didn't sleep and she's had a lot of difficulty breathing. She insisted I call, she wants you to come."

He tried to think. He was still half asleep and tatters of his strange dreams swirled about him like eddies of brackish waters. "I was just down there tonight," he said.

"Well. I don't know anything about that. I just said I'd call."

He felt like a fool. A callous fool at that. "I'm on my way," he said.

Highballing through the night at eightyfive toward the little backwater town of Clifton where she carried all her medical business. Stringing past the barren ridges and the hollows where mist pooled white and opaque as snow. All these recent midnight runs had him feeling a denizen of the night himself, one of the whippoorwills of his childhood or the whores and drunks of his youth but he alone was still on the road. Civilization had pushed the whippoorwills deeper into the timber from where their cries came to him faint and ever fainter and the hands of the clock had pushed the whores and the drunks into each other's arms and into their dark and dreamless slumber. He strung past empty allnight markets alight with cool white fluorescence and past gas stations and abandoned lumber yards and the only soul he saw was the one glancing back from the rearview mirror.

The hospital itself seemed geared down for the night, humming along on half power. He hated hospitals and went stealthily down the gleaming tilefloored hall. Past doors opened and doors closed. Beyond these doors folks with their various ailments sleeping in their antiseptic cubicles if they could sleep and if not lying in a drug-induced stupor that passed for sleep in these regions. Like the larval stage of something dread waiting to be born and loosed upon an unsuspecting world.

She herself was still wide awake. They'd moved her to the pulmonary intensive care unit and she sat by the window waiting for day to come until she heard the door open then turning her head to see. Ravaged and wildlooking in her hospital gown she fixed him with eyes so fierce he had a thought for what halfcrazy stranger was inhabiting her body. A look of utter viciousness as if she held him and him alone responsible for the predicament in which she found herself. For the wearing out of irreplaceable organs, for the slow inevitable recession of the tide of blood, for life seeping away like night sewage, drop by septic drop.

Then the face changed and he laid an arm about her thin shoulders and she grasped his other arm with a hand more claws than fingers. She hung on fiercely, you'd not expect such a grip from one so frail. Instinctively he tried to pull away, the dying would take you with them if they could, it's dark down there and cold, a little company might lighten the tone of things.

Around midmorning he talked with her doctor. This doctor was young, Wildman considered him no more than a child. Styled blond hair, thin wisp of a mustache. A preoccupied air. Wildman wondered was he competent. Perhaps he was a leech, a parasite, there was a pale vampirish look about him, a sucker of old folks' thin unhealthy blood.

"She has anxiety attacks," the doctor said. "I've tried to explain it to her. The emphysema makes it difficult for her to breathe and it scares her. The fear compounds the breathing problems and her heart trouble. Everything just compounds itself."

"Is she going to die?"

He shrugged. "Well, she thinks she is. In the past weeks she's insisted on being tested for everything terminal. There's no reason she shouldn't live another five or ten years. She seems to be willing to die. How close are you to your grandmother?"

Wildman shrugged. "She raised me from a baby when my parents were killed in an accident. I guess that's pretty close."

"Perhaps you could talk to her then. And there's no reason she has to be confined to a hospital. I'm releasing her today."

"I'll talk to her again," Wildman said. He smiled slightly. "She taught school for fifty years. She's used to doing all the talking."

"We're all going to die," the doctor said, as if this was some hot flash that hadn't caught up with Wildman yet and that he might want to make note of.

"I'll tell her," he said politely. Sometimes there were windy gulfs of distance between what he thought and what he said and there was something mildly disturbing about it. He went out into the hall. It smelled of floor wax, antiseptic. He followed it to where he could see morning sunlight through a glass door and he went through the door into it. His senses were immediately assaulted by sensations: warmth, colors, the smell of the hot light falling through the green trees. Everything looked bright and gold and new, and dying seemed very far away.

* *

He hired a practical nurse and she stayed two nights that contained no phone calls and no midnight drives toward flashing ambulances then his grandmother fired her.

The nurse came and told him about it. He paid her off and drove out to the farm to see the old woman.

"Why did you fire her," he wanted to know. "You couldn't fire her anyway. I hired her."

"She was a thief," the old woman said. "She was stealing from me."

"Stealing what?"

"My things," she said evasively. She waved an arm airily about the room. A motley of photographs, ceramic cats, plaster pickaninnies with fishing poles. "I caught her stuffing them into her purse," she said.

"Well," he said. He couldn't think of anything else to say.

"I can stay by myself. I don't need her. I don't need you."

He lifted his shoulders in a shrug of defeat. "You're three times seven. I guess you can do what you want to do."

"I'm many more times seven than that," she said caustically. "And I can't do anything I want to do. I can't even breathe God's own air like you and everyone else takes for granted. I'd give all that I own just to take a good deep breath.

* *

She was kneeling astride him, moving above him in the half-dark. Head thrown back, yellow hair all undone. She was deeply tanned but her pale breasts bobbed like flowers. Her breath came ragged, like something feeding. Yet she was somehow unreal, like a fiercely evocative dream of lust.

The telephone rang.

"Don't," she whispered urgently.

He reached for the phone and she grasped his arm and he jerked it away and the phone tipped off the nightstand. The ringing stopped and he could hear a tinny mechanical voice shrieking at him from the floor. Beth was laughing and wrestling him away from the phone and when he finally had the receiver against his ear he was still inside her and she began to move again.

"Hello?"

"I've got to have some help over here."

He didn't say anything for a time. He listened to the disembodied wheeze of her breathing, the faint pumping of her ruined lungs.

"All right," he said. "I'm coming." He laid the phone down.

Beth was laughing helplessly. She collapsed against his chest, he could feel her taut nipples against his skin, they seemed to burn him. Her hair was all in her face, it smelled of flowers. "Me, too," she said and went into another burst of laughter. She was moving harder against him. He could feel himself inside her rigid and enormous, feel the slap of her flesh against his own. She had stopped laughing. "I dare you to just take it out and go," she said. She rose above him light and graceful as smoke and he could feel her knees clamping his rib cage as if she were riding him, some succubus of the night riding him blind and full-tilt into the dark unknown, face in the wind and yellow hair strung out behind her. When she came she fell against him slack and boneless and he could feel her tiny teeth and her hot breath against his throat like a beast's.

* *

The coffin was dark rosewood, an intricate pattern of flowers and vines carved or pressed into it and he couldn't help thinking it was what she would have begrudgingly admitted was a fine piece of furniture. The woman within it on the satin pillow looked miraculously younger, no more than middle-aged. As if death had peeled away the years like layers of dead skin. Her cares had fled and the skin relaxed and smoothed itself and her face had regained the primness of the long-ago schoolteacher. Most of all she just looked not there, absolutely gone, profoundly beyond any cruelty he might do her now or any kindness. From the hard oaken mourner's bench he watched this face and there were things he might have said to her had things been different but he willed himself to turn to stone inside.

When the preacher hushed they seemed to be at some pause in the procession of things: He didn't know what was expected of him, but everything seemed preordained, dictated by ceremony. An attendant arose and closed the casket with an air of finality. He withdrew from his pocket a tool and began to tighten the screws that secured the lid. Wildman watched. It seemed to be an ordinary Allen wrench. So arcane a use for so mundane a tool. Had its inventor had this purpose in mind? The pallbearers had arisen and taken their stations.

Following the casket down the aisle of the church Beth circled his waist with an arm as if she'd steady him in his grief and he was struck with a hot flash of annoyance. Did she think he'd fall prostrate and helpless, did she think he'd fly apart like a two-dollar clock into a mass of springs and hands awry and useless unsequenced numbers?

They wound through the gravestones of older residents in this curious neighborhood of the dead toward the summit where raw earth waited. He felt tight and empty inside, his head airy and weightless, he felt as if he might go sailing up into the high thin cirrus. Folding chairs were set about and the green tent awning flapped in a sudden hot gust of summer wind.

* *

He was working that summer with a construction crew laying bricks, work he'd done in his youth. Money seemed always short and the pay was good here and it supplemented his freelance income. He was five scaffolds up helping place walkboards and Rojo was taking a bucket of mortar off the winch. Rojo said, "I've got to have some help over here."

This so startled Wildman that he stepped backward reflexively and there was nowhere to step save space. His heel caught a scaffold brace and tripped him and he was going headfirst and backward down the scaffolding. He grabbed at a brace whipping past but all it did was slow him, wrench his shoulder, half turn him in the air. He slammed into a sheet of plywood that capsized in a shower of dust and dried mortar and splintered brick. The plywood rebounded him onto the ground, then slammed down onto him.

It had all happened in an instant, but already he could hear voices, excited cries, running footsteps. He seemed to be slipping toward unconsciousness, black waters lapped at him. Man overboard, Wildman thought. Throw me one of them life preservers.

He opened his eyes. His vision was blurred. Somewhere some small critical adjustment was made, things came into focus. Colors weren't right though, everything seemed a dark muddy brown. The first thing he saw was a steeltoed work boot, the side serrated by a jagged saw cut.

He wiped blood off his forehead. Knifeblades of pain pierced his chest. There was a cut inside his mouth and he spat blood.

"This flying shit is harder than it looks."

Rojo drove him to the apartment building in a company pickup. Head bandaged, ribs tightly bound with some kind of swathing. He was beginning to hurt all over and the pills hadn't taken effect. He got out of the truck with some difficulty. He slammed the door and turned and Beth was standing on the wrought-iron stairway.

"Good God, Buddy," she said. "What happened to you?"

"He tried to fly off," Rojo called to her. "He was long on ambition but short on persistence. Just flopped his arms a time or two and give up and fell like a rock."

"Good God," she said again. Her face in the white weight of the sun was flat and unreadable.

"I'm all right, I'm all right," Wildman said.

"You don't look so all right."

"He's just bunged up some," Rojo said. "They x-rayed everything he's got and none of it's busted. Ribs stove in a little. He'll be all right in a day or two. Ain't everybody can fall five scaffolds and not break nothin."

Beth had descended the stairway and she was helping Wildman onto the first steps. Hands of gentle solicitude.

"You make it all right?" Rojo called.

"I'm all right," Wildman said. He wished he could think of something else to say. Everything he said sounded dull and half-witted.

Halfway to the second floor there was a landing.

"You want to sit down here and rest? I'll bring you a glass of iced tea."

He didn't want to say how all right he was. "I'm just a little dizzy is all," he said.

"Rest a minute."

"Oh hell. Come on, I'm all right."

He drank the iced tea on the couch. She sat across from him in an armchair waiting as if an explanation or at least an elaboration of what had happened might be forthcoming but none was. He held the cold glass against his forehead. He closed his eyes. The room seemed to be tilting on an axis, everything poised at the point of sliding across the floor and slamming against the walls.

"What made you fall?"

He opened his eyes. The highvoltage pain pills seemed to be kicking in. She was moving away from him at the speed of light, the chair telescoping backward toward the receding wall. He tried to concentrate.

"Gravity," he finally said.

* *

When he awoke it was night. He wasn't on the couch anymore. He was in bed without knowing how he got there and she was reading on a chair by the wall sconce. He watched her. She read on, oblivious to his scrutiny. You won't keep her, a friend named Avery had told him. You can't keep her at home. She's used to being on the wing. One day she'll be a high fly in the tall weeds and that'll be all she wrote. Avery had wanted her himself, however, and this could hardly be considered an objective appraisal of the situation. Wildman had caught her on the rebound so quickly it made him dizzy, she had seemed to come with the thousand-dollar story, the contract, the new agent, the dreams about the novel.

She had been with him three years but he had had to work full time at keeping her. He began to think of her as some piece of expensive and highpowered machinery he had bought on time. Some luxurious automobile loaded with options and coated with twenty coats of lacquer but the payments were eating him alive, the payments were enormous with a balloon at the end and he had begun to think he couldn't keep them current. He hadn't been trying as hard lately, he'd been slacking off, and the threat of repossession hung over his head like a guillotine on a frayed rope. Long a student of nuance he had noticed a difference in her body language when other men glanced at her, a speculative look of distance in her eyes when she studied him. He caught her appraising herself critically in a mirror as if she were evaluating herself, looking for microscopic signs of wear and tear.

After a while she seemed to feel the cool weight of his eyes and she looked up. She closed the book and laid it aside.

"How do you feel?"

"Like death warmed over," he said. "My ribs hurt. I can't take a deep breath. I can't even breathe God's own air like everybody else."

"What?"

"Nothing."

"You're acting awfully strange lately."

"Strange in what way?"

"Strange in a lot of ways. Half the time you act as if you're not even here. You don't talk to me. You talk but it's like the little things you say for your own amusement. You're off in a little world of your own. You used to act like this sometimes when you were writing but you're not writing. I don't understand you anymore."

"I don't know," he said.

"You don't know what?"

"I don't know what you're talking about. I apologize for all my short-comings. My ribs do hurt though."

"You want to go out and eat? It's early yet."

"No. I don't feel like it and anyway I'm not hungry."

"Go back to sleep then," she said. She took up the book and opened it. She sat as if she was reading but he didn't think she was. He closed his eyes.

After a while he opened them and she was watching him. "This shit is beginning to get on my nerves," she said.

"I don't know that I'm crazy about it myself," Wildman said.

* *

The next morning he sat on the sunlit balcony wearing dark glasses and watching the coming and goings of the apartment building. Across the parking lot a yellow moving van was backed up to an apartment and two men were wrestling an enormous green sofa into its belly. Folks brought out boxes, cartons, a woman carried a lamp.

So many comings and goings, folks moving in, folks moving out. There seemed little permanence left to the world. Families split and regrouped. People threw up their hands and carried their lives back to ground zero and began again. People were perpetually changing jobs, changing partners, changing lives.

His head throbbed dully. He chewed two Excedrin and swallowed them, hot sour aftertaste in the back of his mouth. The rental van pulled onto the highway, headed toward the interstate. Log trucks passed in a blue haze of diesel smoke, concrete trucks, mixer spinning slowly. They were cutting all the timber, paving the world with concrete.

"Beth," he called.

She came to the door and half opened it, he could see her, warped-looking through the glass.

"What is it?"

"You want to drive out to the farm?"

"The farm? What on earth for?"

"Just to look around a little. Anyway it's mine now. Ours."

"Ours? You can have any part of it. That place gives me the shivers. Like something walking over my grave."

"All it needs is a little work."

"All it needs is a hole dug beside it and a bulldozer to push it off in the hole and somebody to throw in the dirt. That's what it needs."

"Well. Such as it is it's mine. I thought I might clean up a little. Pack up some of her things. I don't know what I'm going to do with all that stuff."

"Dig a bigger hole," Beth said.

"I need to pick up some magazines anyhow. Is there anything I can get for you?"

"Nothing you can find in a 7-Eleven," she said. She paused. He was halfway down the wrought-iron stairway when she said, "You're even beginning to look like her."

He didn't turn.

"Buddy," she called.

He halted. "What?"

She was silent a time. "Nothing," she finally said. He went on.

* *

He sat in a welter of cardboard cartons and strewn memorabilia. It was hopeless. There was just so much of it. The room seemed time's attic, its dump heap. Finally he gave up. The old woman saturated the very walls, her spirit was not going to be exorcised by a few cardboard boxes, she was not going to be dispossessed.

She had seemed intent on absorbing him, secreting some sort of subtle chemical that was digesting him, making him part of her. Eating him alive. Every move he made came under her critical scrutiny.

"That Luna girl is no good for you," she had told him once in his junior year.

"Well. I think she is. That's for me do decide."

"I knew her whole family. There wasn't anything to any of them. None of them ever amounted to a hill of beans. She's in some of my classes. She lets the boys look up her dress."

He hadn't known what to say to that and so had said nothing at all.

He figured it'd all blow over. But she had gone over there. She had a talk with Mrs. Luna and the next time he had gone calling he was left cooling his heels on the porch fifteen minutes before Mrs. Luna even opened the door and he was turned away with polite and distant firmness.

Lynell had never spoken to him again but he had seen her whispering once to another girl and both of them were looking at him and he wondered what was being said. He never found out what his grandmother and Mrs. Luna had discussed and on some level he didn't want to know.

And yet.

She'd nursed him through all the childhood diseases, mumps and whooping cough and measles, stood between him and fire and plague and biting dogs. She sheltered him from the world.

Which at the first opportunity he'd escaped into with a vengeance, feeling that if she was so down on it it couldn't be all bad.

He sat on the sunward side of the porch in an old lounge chair, eyes closed behind the dark glasses. He didn't have to see anyway, it was all burnt into memory. Eastward lay thick timber she'd never allowed cut, a deep primeval tangle of cypress and liveoak, from this distance lush and romantic as a nineteenth-century painting. He'd wandered there as a child, alone but not lonely, spent whole days dreaming there, watched her from the rim of the wood as she walked across the stubbled field, her clothing pale and spectral in the waning day. "You Buddy," she'd call. "You get yourself over here. It's suppertime."

* *

When he returned to the apartment complex dusk had already begun to deepen and the western sky beyond the angular brick skyline was mottled red as blood. The first thing he noticed was that the canary yellow Mustang he'd bought Beth was gone. He gathered up the magazines and went up the stairs. Somehow he knew what he was going to find.

She was gone. Not only Beth but every vestige of Beth, her clothes and personal possessions, even the book she'd been reading. She was gone as completely as if she had never been, and for a dizzy moment he wondered if she had. If he'd ever smelled her hair, kissed her bruised-looking mouth. She was gone like a high fly in the tall weeds, like a bird on the wing, and search as he might there was nothing to prove she had ever been, not so much as a lipsticked cigarette butt, or a snarl of blond hair curled like a sleeping newt in the bathroom drain.

* *

In his dream he was a child being led down a winding country road. It was early morning and he could feel the dew on his bare feet and the grasses and weeds were damp. They went by grazing cows and deep woods that still held night at their center, he could see slashes of it through the trees. The hand clasping his own child's hand was gentle, the way was long but he did not tire. A hawk flew from the roadside with a flurry of wings and he glanced to the side and saw that there was no one beside him. A hand bewenned and agespotted still clutched his own and he could feel the delicate tubelike bones beneath the slack skin, feel a wedding band on the ring finger and glancing up he saw that the disembodied arm tended upward, and upward, a thin wasted arm in lavender brocade that stretched to infinity, to high thin clouds that ultimately obscured it.

The ringing phone woke him. Beth? he thought, but the voice in his ear was harsh and preemptory, curiously mechanical, like something electronic imitating a voice. It said, "I've got to have some help over here."

He felt numb, cold as ice. "Who is this?" he asked. "Is this your idea of a joke?" Yet in some curious cobwebbed corner of his mind there was a part of him that was waiting for just such a phone call, had been for days. He exhaled, he'd breathed deeper than he meant to, the sudden pain made him gasp. But some release had been negotiated, some delicate border had been broached, he was already feeling about for his shoes.

He drove through the cool summer night, everyone asleep, the highway his alone. At home with the night now, at peace. When he left the blacktop the lowering trees beckoned him into the tunnel of darkness like a vaguely erotic promise. And it was like a road that wound down through time.

Beyond the blurred cedars the farmhouse sat foursquare in the moonlight, its tin roof gleaming wetly with dew, its windows enigmatic and dark. Steeply gabled, its high eaves rose in black and silver shadows, its ornate old-fashioned tin cornicing somehow stately and dignified. A bisected tin sun was set high in the eaves, tin rays fanning upward, you hardly ever saw Victorian trim like this anymore.

He went up the brick walk to the wraparound porch, the silence was enormous, the house seemed to be listening to some sound that hadn't reached him yet. He felt for his keys. When the door was unlocked it opened silently inward on oiled hinges and he stepped into the darkness. Hot stifling darkness with compounded smells, jasmine, Vick's VapoRub, time itself. From the kitchen the refrigerator hummed, somewhere a clocked ticked with a firm strong heartbeat. He turned on the light and the first thing he looked for was the telephone. It was cradled and when he took it up all there was to hear was a dial tone.

He sat in the bentwood rocker. He lit a cigarette. She had been lying on her left side before the rocker, about where his feet were now. Beside the rocker was a table where he'd restacked the copies of *National Geographic*, the gold-rimmed bifocals. Even after all that time she had still been breathing shallowly and he had squatted there with the phone in his hand watching her. Her breath was a thin panting, like a dying kitten he remembered from childhood. Finally she had exhaled and just never took another breath.

The ramifications of what he'd done or not done were dizzying, he'd made a lifetime out of living on the edge but this time he'd slipped and fallen farther than he'd ever meant to go. "It ain't everybody can fall five scaffolds and not break nothin'," Rojo had said. What had she thought when everything began to shut down? Whole banks of memory rendered into oblivion, had she seen the little night watchman going from room to room throwing breakers, clicking his flashlight down the dark corridors, will the last one out turn out the light?

She seemed to hover the room yet, dusting the bric-a-brac, straightening the gilt-framed photograph of some ancestor whose bones had gone to dust. Most of these photographs were of Wildman though and they charted his growth from infancy to adulthood like graphs showing the evolution of a species. One of a toddler sitting in a child-size rocker, a disembodied grandmother's hand on his shoulder and all there was of the young Wildman left was the dark and haunted eyes that studied this likeness.

He went into the kitchen and turned on the light. He made a cup of instant Nescafé from the hot water tap and went with the cup in his hand through the kitchen door into what had been the living room and he saw with a stricken wonder that everything had changed forever.

The rosewood coffin on its catafalque set against the west wall where the sofa had always been. The casket and its occupant seemed to dwarf the room and were twinned by the opaque windows behind it. He approached it, stared down at the stern old woman with iron-gray hair and pince-nez. Every detail was stored in his mind with a clinical detachment. The prim pursed mouth was slacker now, a stitch had given and left a small bloodless incision, he could see the wadded cotton or whatever her mouth was packed with. Studying her so intently he saw with a dull loathing a faint blue pulse beating in her throat.

He stumbled numbly backward over a folding chair. He saw with no surprise that the room had been set about with such chairs all alike stamped McFarland Funeral Home. He righted the one he'd stumbled over and seated himself like a patient spectator awaiting the commencement of some arcane show.

He sat waiting for time to draw on. In truth time had ceased to exist, neither past nor future, all motion had slowed finally to a drugged halt and all there was at the end of the world was an old woman in a casket and a man watching with heavy-lidded eyes from a folding chair. Then there was a faint rustle of funeral silk, the smell of lemon verbena, and the old woman raised her head. Cocked slightly sidewise in an attitude of listening. Then a scarcely audible sigh, and she pillowed her head again on the quilted satin. The clock in the corner began to toll, one, two, three, twelve times in all and she raised herself again, pulling herself upright with a clawed hand on the edge of the casket, tendons pulled taut as wires with exertion. She turned toward the window, listening intently. He knew intuitively that she was listening for him, or for what he had once been, an eighteen-year-old Wildman that always had to be home by midnight.

He heard the sound of an automobile approaching, headlights slid whitely across the wall, ceased and vanished. The engine died. The old woman sank back to rest with an expression of satisfaction. The clock began to strike again, tolled on and on, turning to see he watched its hands ratcheting madly backward, he could hear the protesting grind of metal on metal, gears and pins and springs being sheared off and broken. When the hands ceased at six o'clock the old woman began to rise again and the room was saturated with the smell of brewing coffee, he could hear it singing in the glasstopped percolator, he could smell bacon sizzling in hot grease. In the kitchen pots and pans rattled, cutlery was being laid out. Outside a car door slammed, a dog dead these twenty years scrabbled up from the porch and went running to meet its master. The smells of coffee and bacon intensified, became overpowering, a corrupt stench of charred meat.

The air was tinged with greasy smoke, somewhere flames were crackling like something feeding. He turned toward the kitchen. Beyond the door was a strobic flickering like summer lightning and thick black smoke rolled along the floor. There was a step on the porch. Someone was approaching the door, he could hear the dog leaping and whining to be petted. Flames were darting up and down the wallpaper playfully and the rug beneath his feet buckled and began to smoke, ceramic cats warped and ran like melting glass, the very air was aflame.

He took a deep breath and sucked in pure fire. The flesh of his lungs seared and crackled and burst with thin hisses of steam. The last sound he heard was the screendoor opening on its keeperspring and then everything fell from him in a rush, Beth and the thousand-dollar story and the midnight runs to Clifton and every detail of his life that had made him Buddy Wildman and no other. Years reeled backward in a dizzying rush and abruptly he was on the floor, a naked child crawling about the bubbling linoleum, hair ablaze and swaddled in fire, feeling about for his playthings amongst the painted flames.

Everything Must Go

Jim Gilbert

Sounds like gunshots, I'm thinking. Sounds like some idiot, cockeyed and drunk, unloading his pistol at the high January clouds, or maybe a showdown between two nearsighted shots who squint and miss, squint and miss. It's coming from the south end of Sonny's orchard, the highest part of the ridge, where Fonder's River goes deep underground.

I'm awake now. I flip onto my back and the rusty center hinge of the sleeper-sofa I've got set up in the storeroom of the Dimestop sings like a bullfrog. I look up at the skylight. It's dark, iced-over. This is the year of the big freeze in Central. Ice covers everything, the kind of ice that seems to come out of nowhere because the air feels dry, forms patterns on things that look like mazes, with all the crooked paths doubling back on themselves. Hard to look out of a window all frozen over like that and still be able to concentrate on whatever might be outside. Your eyes just come unfocused, staring at the patterns.

Next morning, Sonny's on the phone, trying to recruit me to help keep his bonfires lit. Last night I lost thirty-five trees on the south end, he tells me. The rough lemons, the big bushy ones. The trunks are freezing all the way through to the center rings, popping open like cans of biscuits.

I heard, I say.

The weather service, says Sonny, predicts the weather will continue. Supposed to be so cold, it's like the sun won't even be out.

What's the wind chill factor? I ask.

Sonny snorts. Let me tell you about wind chill factor. You only worry about wind chill when you're shipping produce cross-country on a flatbed truck.

Sonny always goes off on that.

Wind chill, he says, it's just some way for the weathermen at Channel Six to make the temperatures sound exciting. It'll be such-and-such, but it'll *feel* like minus such-and-such. Cold is cold, says Sonny, and cold is bad.

Which is about what you'd expect to hear from a citrus farmer.

I tell him I can't. I tell him I've got too much else to do. I tell him I've got to get over to the Franklin Street house, crawl under there and double-wrap the pipes. Check the pilot light, see if it's blown out again. Cover Dorina's yellow rosebushes with plastic bags, even though I know they're already dead, just in case she comes back, and can see that at least I tried. Or on the off chance somebody actually stops by to look at the house, so things won't look like shit.

When you gonna open the Dimestop again? Sonny asks.

I look at the empty brown shelves. Sometime, I say.

People still stop by occasionally, the brave soul who'd rather take a narrow state highway in search of sights than the shiny new four-lane that drones on through the pines, over the land Sonny's dad used to own, before Sonny sold it. They come in looking for a fill-up and a clean windshield, potato chips and Cokes, same thing they can get on the off-ramps, but they want to see the locals. I've got a Miller or two back in my fridge I'll sell you, I always offer, but I got no gas. They nod to be friendly and scratch their heads. They don't stay long. I guess I ought to put a sign in the window, Out of Business or Temporarily Closed, but I just never get around to it. Besides, there's enough grime on the front windows already, even without a sign, and I need all the light I can get.

Old Griff died last winter, used to own this place, not long after they opened new 32. His will provided for practically nothing. Nobody seemed to mind when I set up camp in the back of the store. Dorina was gone by then, gone to live at the university, and had taken most of the furniture with her. Griff's only living kin is an invalid sister in a Beaumont nursing home and his daughter Stacy, living with a cult up in Montana, who nobody's heard from, not even when Griff died. He used to brag to me about a steamer trunk full of money he'd stashed in a crawlspace at the back of the store. Once he was gone I dug through the walls to find it, this oblong wooden box with a rusty lock, easily enough broken. Inside was about seventy thousand dollars in crumbly, moldy

Confederate money. The only person interested in the store was Sonny himself, who thought he might like to buy the several square miles along the railroad tracks as they ran through town, where he could plant another orange grove. Which would have meant demolishing the Dimestop. But the town voted him down—Sonny was about the last person they would be giving a ninety-nine-year land lease to at this point.

I get on my boots and start climbing into the parka I found in the meat cooler, when there's Blake tapping on the back window of the storeroom, wanting to be let in the loader's entrance. I don't even get the door a quarter the way up, he scuttles under like a crab. Hide me, hide me, he's saying.

Now what the hell is it with you? I say. He smells like a brewery and his hands are shaking.

We killed Conroy, he says.

Normally this would be a joke, but the skin under his eyes is as white as the eyeballs would be, if they weren't so bloodshot. So I don't say anything else. The wind outside pushes against the walls of the building, trying to make more ice. I lead Blake by the shoulders, then push him down until he's balancing on the edge of the bed. His knees stick out funny and his feet are angled under the sagging mattress. His eyes are pointed at me, but he's not looking. I get us both a beer from my fridge and he drinks his all in one go and just keeps sitting there.

Conroy owns the dirt pit located off old 32, between Central and Go Junction, which is about now the only major source of commerce in the area. Southern Dirt and Shale has been just about everybody's employer at one time or another. Since the Dimestop closed it's been my main source of revenue, going down there two, three times a week to oil the loaders, check under the hoods of the bulldozers, grease the hydraulics on the shovels. Good to see you, Conroy says every morning my face shows up at the gate, but I'll be damned if I know why you're staying.

It's a vigil, I say.

Not that I think I'm the greatest mechanic in the world, but I know you wouldn't find another one in a two-hundred-mile radius that understands the particular grit that attaches itself to the machines down in the pit.

Conroy wheezes, takes a blast from his inhaler and shakes until the medicine gets to his lungs, says to me, Well, we gotta push like hell today, boys. (As if I'm more than one, or maybe indicating I need to be doing the work of two or three men today.) With this cold the ground's harder than a four-week-old turd. Then he turns, begins his long slow walk up the sloping cliff, towards the Airstream trailer that serves as the main office, perched like a giant silver tick on the highest ridge. From there he looks down on the whole operation, all day standing before the big side window, his nose almost to the glass.

Conroy used to shag ass down in the pit with the rest of us, chomping cigars and manning the loaders, until the time he made that run up to Eagle Pass, carrying a double load of dirt for some subdivision foundations. Conroy pushes the contract deadline right down to the final hours, doesn't leave till after midnight of the morning due. Sometime past three he's about ten miles north of Laredo and begins moving through this heavy fog. Fogs don't usually vex Conroy, he figures it's just low-lying and he'll be out of it in a minute. But that Laredo fog gets thicker as the truck gains momentum, starts playing tricks on his eyes, light from the landscape spilling in all directions, and he loses the road for a second, bumping hard over the gravel shoulder, getting a close look at a deep drop-off, jerking at the wheel to keep the rig from jackknifing. Close, he thinks, pumping the brakes.

About ten miles down the road, he sees pale blue and red lights in his sideview. They stick long enough, Conroy knows they're for him, so he eases over to the side. The trooper is pale, and his face is all folded down, like he's eaten some bad bacon. Trouble, Officer? Conroy asks. The trooper shines his Q-beam along the underside of the trailer until the light uncovers shiny folds of red metal, flapping torn ragtop, splintered glass and the headless body of a man named David Vinson. The head they find back up the road, ear to the center line like he's listening for Indians coming over the hill.

No criminal charges were filed, no punishment decreed—in a fog like that who knows what happened? But two weeks later Conroy comes down with a double pneumonia that lays him up for nearly a month. He has fever dreams about that head lying in the middle of the road, talking to him in a language he can't understand. His young wife Judith waits on him night and day, spoonfeeding him warm applesauce and milk, whispering over his shivering form. So now he supervises from above, consulting with Tommy, the foreman, with the new cellular phones, or calling out orders over a PA bullhorn, affixed to the top of the trailer.

And that was how Blake found himself in trouble. Blake's been at Southern Dirt for two years, can find a vein of quartz like a mystic, a vein so pure they almost won't have to wash and sieve the stuff. So he decides to ask Conroy about a little more paid vacation time this year, but comes up on the losing end of the haggle. Later, explaining all this to the boys in the pit, he raises a ceremonious middle finger at the trailer. Conroy of course sees the gesture and, using the bullhorn, announces to everyone how Blake has just won himself a three-day dock in pay. I don't put up with vulgar bullshit like that, Conroy's voice echoes down the red pit walls.

You killed him over vacation time? I ask.

No, you jackass, Blake hisses. We just got drunk, is all. Me and Bucky McFearson. That was later, after everybody knocked off. Sure, I was pissed, but you know, I figured a good drunk would cure that.

He tells me what happened.

Zonkers closed at two o'clock, and Blake and Bucky found themselves in Bucky's car with a fair amount of party left in them. At Blake's suggestion, they went to 7-Eleven, got a twelve-pack of Bud and a couple bottles Mad Dog 20/20. Blake wanted to drive out on new 32, shoot highway signs with the .38 he discovered in the glove compartment of Bucky's car, but Bucky thought it would be a better idea if they parked themselves someplace solid. They agreed on Blake's apartment, since the best idea of all would be not to wake Bucky's wife, considering their condition.

On the way there they passed the lot where Conroy's double-wide was parked. Let's see if he's home, Blake suggested.

He wasn't sure if the door was open or if they forced the lock, which all things considered was certainly possible. However they did it, they managed to make enough noise to bring Conroy shuffling down the hallway into the living room. Goddamn a bear, what the hell is this, Conroy said.

We having a party, Blake declared, dropping the beer at the foot of the sleeper-sofa, since I don't get no vacation time. Thought you might like to join us.

You drunk bastards, that's five days' pay now for the both of you. You lucky Judith is out working the late shift. She'd kill you both before I had time to explain how you broke and entered.

Bucky spotted the Bowie knife in Conroy's fist.

Hey now, watch that knife.

Don't come near me, I thought you was burglars.

Conroy lifted his left hand, palm up, and brought out his right, holding the knife, a position Blake recognized as one not unlike those he'd seen late nights on Kung Fu Theater. But Bucky reacted first, charging low at Conroy's knees. Blake caught him as he came down, grabbing the knife arm and twisting it. Conroy let out a wheeze but did not drop his weapon.

They ended up pinning Conroy facedown on the couch, still gripping the knife.

Now you promise not to use that knife on us, we let you up?

Goddamn you boys, get my face out of this pillow. His straining shoulders shone pink in the light drifting in from the hall. I'll kill you, get off me, get off me.

They decided he was still a threat.

We just having a little party, Conroy. If you don't want to party, we'll leave but you got to promise not to kill us, we let you up.

You dumbass bastards, let me go I swear to God, get off me, you crazy sumbitches, my med'cine.

Blake sat down in the middle of Conroy's back.

We can't let him up, with that knife. That's a big knife. He'll kill us.

Bucky nodded and opened a beer, passing it to Blake. Blake chugged a quarter of the beer, chased it with some Mad Dog.

Now Conroy, we'll just hold you down nice and easy here until you stop kicking like a good boy, quit being violent and we'll let you right up.

Conroy by now had stopped cussing at the two of them, was just thrashing and kicking soundlessly.

Bucky, sit on his legs, will you, before he kicks me in the head? That's it, Conroy, be still and we'll leave you alone. Here, let's watch some TV. You like *Matlock*?

The next thing Blake knew there were headlamps from outside, flashing across his face and down the wall, into the kitchen. The static light from the TV showed Bucky at the other end of the couch, snoring with his head back and mouth wide open, a stain of spilled beer puddling over his leg. Blake's own hand rested against Conroy's cold neck. Footfalls on the steps outside. Just enough time to duck through the kitchen, kicking empty beer cans out of his way, into the laundry room, and, after dealing with a troublesome deadbolt, out the back door.

I been running since before dawn, he tells me. Running like a bat out of hell. Think my lungs are all burnt up, this cold air.

He's got his arms rested on his knees and he lowers his head. What am I gonna do, Steve? What am I gonna do?

Blake and I have been in Central for a long time. Me, all my life. I guess Blake too, but I don't remember him much before we had homeroom together, at junior high. That was a bad time, after Andrew died, so it was a good piece of luck for me and Blake to take to each other the way we did. We'd known each other before then, but really got to be friends afterwards. He even got me out to Cripple Creek the next season, hunting deer with our .22 rifles, which seemed like a miracle. Even though I haven't shot anything since, it was good just to go up to the camp, build fires and play poker and have some laughs with somebody.

We used to stop traffic out on old 32 by putting on rubber Halloween masks and costumes from the previous years, kept in a box under the bathroom sink at Blake's parents house. I was always the Wolfman and Blake was the Phantom of the Opera. We'd go out at night and hide in the darkness of the ditches until we could see approaching headlights. At just the right moment we'd leap up, stagger across the road, and shake our horror-glove paws at the approaching vehicle, then disappear into the weeds of Pittman's field on the other side. This would only work with out-of-towners, of course, the locals being used to seeing weird shit cross the road in front of them on hot summer nights. In fact, sometimes cars would speed up, as like to hit us, or we'd hear gunshots and have to hit the deck. But for the most part it was just fun, getting people to slam on the brakes. We were always safely hidden in the weeds, giggling quietly just forty or fifty feet from the road. If there really was a monster, nobody ever waded into the weeds to find it.

This game changed only slightly as we got older. We took to lying splayed out on the side of the road in broad daylight, next to an old bicycle we'd retrieved from the county dump and smashed up at the dirt pit, and our faces covered in ketchup. Boy, that would stop traffic. That was the funniest ever. Sometimes people would slam on the brakes so hard their cars would skid and we'd have to roll out of the way or really be hurt. It was funny until somebody would send the sheriff out, or the ants would come, attracted by the ketchup.

Even now, we might be jumping boxcars to Brownsville, with back-packs full of beer, if the trains hadn't stopped running five years ago. We might be driving to Rook Mountain, like we used to in his Chevy Nova, sitting on the hood and drinking, singing along with the tape deck, So put me on a highway and show me a sign and take it to the limit one more time, if Blake hadn't run his Bronco into a telephone pole last spring. I guess we might even go back to Central High to play craps and smoke cigarettes in the bathroom if it wouldn't make us look like complete fools, with our five-day beards and our beer guts hanging over our belt buckles. So instead we play nickel poker or blackjack on the counter of the Dimestop, waving away customers, bullshitting like we used to about running across the border, holing up in some Mexican whorehouse for a week, moving down the landscape like a couple of bandits, ending up down on some isolated beach in an abandoned bungalow, some convenient place to store our plunder.

I say to Blake, like I might say to Judith, I reckon Conroy's better off.

Yeah, says Blake. But I ain't.

Did Judith see you?

Jesus. I don't know. I heard her start yelling right as I hit the ground.

Will Bucky say you were with him?

Why wouldn't he?

Blue light leaks down from the skylight.

Sonny called me this morning, I say.

Goddamn Sonny, says Blake.

No, this is good, listen. I tell him about Sonny's bind. I know for sure that he's been calling all over Central about his cordwood fires, and that nobody is moving one finger to help him. He'll be grateful to see Blake's face, to hide Blake in one of his greenhouses, be grateful to ask no questions at all. Assign him to the back forty, all by himself. Just keep your head down, I say.

When I see Sonny at the funeral three days later he gives me a quick nod, smiles off one side of his mouth. It occurs to me that pretty soon I'll have to approach him for myself. The iron gates at the front of Southern Dirt are staying locked, the only sign explaining why is the No Trespassing sign, which has been there forever and is no news to me. All the machines are clustered at the bottom center of the pit, like dropped toys. I'm not fooled by the fact they haven't been running. They attract that grit all the same. All the same.

Delivering the eulogy, Father Hollingsworth goes on and on about the ascension of Conroy Southern, a man who spent his whole life with his hands in the dirt. I mean to sneak out in the middle, but the colored light shafting in from the tall stained glass windows is like the saints and angels come to life, shapeless blue and yellow and red ghosts floating above the pews, liberated from their glassy prisons, waiting to tell us some new story, if only the wind outside will give them voice.

Out in the churchyard everything is gray. Bats scatter from the steeple when they ring the funeral bell. Judith stands beside the circular wreath planted on three green wire legs where Conroy's headstone will go. She keeps her hands clasped in front of her and her head bowed. From where I stand I hear the ropes creak as they lower Conroy into the ground. The outside service is quick, on account of the cold. Most people leave even before Father Hollingsworth throws the first handful of dirt on the casket, dirt from the pit no doubt.

I wander the rows of tombstones, the uneven cryptmarkers, slabs grown dull over the years now glimmering with a veneer of new ice. My boots grind fresh tracks over the graves. There's Griff's wife Marion, been dead twenty years. I only know her by name. Griff's name and dates are carved on the cryptstone beside hers, but he's not under there, decided he'd rather be cremated and have his ashes scattered over the railroad tracks in front of the Dimestop. There's Sonny's dad, Marshall. In big letters above his name it reads Father.

I pause briefly at Melanie's grave, Blake's wife. She was stung in the crook of her elbow by a scorpion, and the venom went right into her bloodstream, to her heart. She was shaking out her running shoes, and the damn thing fell out and landed on her arm. Shortly after they installed Melanie's headstone Dorina and I came to visit. It was afternoon, late spring sun way up in the trees. She set down some flowers and had a little cry and then tugged at the collar of my shirt. Here, she said, pulling me down behind the headstone. This is a graveyard, I said. The dead don't mind, was her answer. Sometimes I wish she had a tombstone here too. At least that way I'd know exactly what I'd be dealing with.

Now the stumpy white marker with the cross and empty urn on top, which would be under shade except the shuddering limbs above are bare. Andrew Stuart Henley. Our Son, it says, above the name. I crouch down, balancing on the balls of my feet. The headstone cuts a little of the wind.

I don't know how long I'm there like that. All I can think is, I don't come here often enough.

Terrible, I hear.

There's a shadow over Andrew's headstone. Judith stands black-coated and sober, hair blowing back and forth in front of her eyes. She tilts her head, staring sharply at the etched dates, says, He wasn't even ten.

No, I say.

Andrew's body was so light, as Mr. Fiske and I carried him to the pickup, Papa trying to keep a scarf tied around his neck. He was still breathing then, but had bled a telltale pool into the seat of the truck by the time we got to the emergency room twenty minutes later. The doctors didn't bother to pick even half the buckshot out of his neck. How many men were hunting in those woods this morning? one surgeon asked Papa as he peeled off his stained rubber gloves, Do you even know? Papa just kept shrugging, staring at the large round clock at the end of the hall, as if when a certain amount of time had elapsed he would be free to go, back home, back into the life he knew, where his youngest son was still alive, or perhaps into another life entirely.

Must have been really hard on you, Judith says.

Why do you say that?

Well, being young and all.

Yes, I say. Must be hard on you too.

She nods, walks over to the side of Andrew's tombstone. Hard, she says, mostly because of how it happened and everything. I expect you know all about it?

I've read everything they printed in the paper, which is this: Judith Southern came home to find her husband dead of asphyxiation, a drunk man sitting on top of him. Bucky McFearson, at the county dock, is in an alcoholic blackout, remembers being at Zonkers after work with a bunch of guys, but nothing after that. Doesn't know how he got to Conroy's. Sheriff Fowler and his deputies are still investigating, but the circumstantial evidence is pretty strong.

I reckon that's all there is to know.

Well, she says, taking one long hand to move a swatch of hair out of her eye. We both know there's always more to a story than what they print in the papers.

Then real slow she kneels down, starts running her finger along the grooves of Andrew's name, saying, Isn't that right, Andy? Sometimes people don't take the blame that's coming to them.

I stand up. I don't figure exactly what it is you want.

Judith's fingertips never leave the streaked marble. I want Blake Kessler, she says. I know him and Conroy had a falling out earlier that day. And I know nobody in the world drinks blueberry-flavor Mad Dog but Blake and there was one spilled in the crack of the couch.

I shrug. Call the cops.

I don't want the cops. At this point, with cops there'd just be a whole lot more questions. I don't want questions. I want this handled by people who—and she pauses, takes the time to look from me to the lettering on Andrew's headstone, thinking for a second before looking back to me—people who understand. Blake ain't come forward on his own. That tells me everything I want to know about him, and everything I want to know about how it needs to be dealt with.

I say, Maybe he's just afraid.

He's got good reason.

She comes up from the tombstone to stand at my side. I don't look at her. She touches my cheek. Her hand is cold.

Do it for Andrew, she says. Andrew says you know what to do.

Up the hill, the wind goes blowing through Conroy's wreath, flapping leaves on the inside of the hole, the sound of a ghost.

There's a shadow over Andy's tombstone. She leans closer, whispering.

"Conroy was in the woods that day, too. He never said nothing to nobody but me."

I can't see anything but the sunken letters spelling out Andrew's name, where she touched them. That's what's real. But even now, when I wake up for no reason in the middle of the night, I'm thinking about him. Not about what happened on the day he died, but about how he used to wake me up to tell me about his dream. He'd reach across between our beds to shake my shoulder. I had it again, he'd say. I'd roll over onto my back, tilt my head so I could see out the window at the pines edging our property, shining blue under the moon.

Always in the back of our parents' car, a metallic gold Plymouth Fury III, at night. Powerlines roping reflections across the back window. Andrew is playing, sometimes coloring in a color book when the moon comes out enough for him to see the lines, sometimes rolling his Hot Wheels over the warm hump in the floorboard. I'm there, hunched over reading *Hunters Monthly* by flashlight, holding it close to the paper so the light won't distract Papa's driving. Andrew got his first pellet gun last

Christmas, and Papa promises him a .410 when he turns eight. He wants to be like me when he's a teenager, wants to go up to the hunting camp with me and Papa this season, even though he's only six. But then all of a sudden I'm not there, the backseat is empty, just the pale blue shadows tracing over the vinyl upholstery as the car moves along.

Andrew drops his toy cars. They thump solidly against the thin floorboard carpet. He scrambles onto the backseat, looks out the rear window. The car is moving slowly through downtown Go Junction. In the curve of the window, the Candyland Theater warps into view, the red and white and green marquee straightening out as the car inches away. Andrew can't make out what movie is playing, but he thinks it's that Disney flick Papa took him to see, *Bedknobs and Broomsticks*, the one where he got too scared by the suits of armor moving with nobody inside and had to leave before it was over, but thinks he could watch now.

He turns, straddling the hump in the seat. There's nobody driving. He's alone in the car. The steering wheel makes little movements to the left and right, like it's being remote controlled.

Andrew doesn't cry. He stays calm enough, just turns back to the window and watches Go Junction pass by. There's the Salvation Army store with the big red-and-white badge painted on the front window. There's Miller's Hardware, where Papa buys new rubber washers for our leaky bathroom taps. Andrew can see clearly into the stores, past the gloom and glare and grime on the glass storefronts, as if he's light itself, passing through. He can see how barren the shelves are. There are signs taped in all the windows, some sagging or peeling down from the corners. They all say the same thing, no matter if it's Sivil's Department Store or Delay's Style Shop or Miles Drug or Griffin Cleaners or the office of Elkin's Used Cars. They all say Going Out of Business. They all say Clearance Liquidation. They all say Everything Must Go. Blank papers float down the sidewalks, hang momentarily against a fire hydrant or telephone pole before drifting on.

Nowadays I guess that's more my dream than his.

Exactly what are we talking about here? I ask.

Plenty, Judith says.

I say, Okay.

We stand there not moving and not saying anything, with the gray tombstones scattered all around us, like we've been there forever and they've just been dropped from above.

A cashier's check is delivered to the Dimestop the next day. Computer made out to me, from Southern Dirt and Shale. For parts and services, previously rendered, it says. Twenty-five thousand. Not much for a man's life, I'm thinking, but what the hell.

I take it to the credit union in Go Junction, where they don't know me, to get it cashed. In fifties and hundreds. This takes about an hour, since I have no account with them, and they have to pre-approve the check or something. The package with the gun I find when I get back, brown wrapped and strapped with twine. It's a .38, and loaded.

I call Sonny. Think I need some work, I say.

One man's bane, says Sonny. I been getting a lot of calls from you guys today. And just in time, too. Another front's moving in this afternoon, it'll be colder than a witch's tit here by midnight.

Wind chill factor? I ask.

I got your wind chill factor, says Sonny.

Too cold for snow, but the trouble that night does indeed turn out to be the wind. Strong enough to snuff out small fires. But oddly enough, when I arrive shortly after dusk my first task is to help Sonny and a Mexican named Bones douse a two-tree fire on the north side.

Sonny spits. Well, I reckon I can write those two off. Bones here does his job too well. Thaws out the trees enough, they catch fire.

I watch ash piles sputter as they transform into black nests of ice crystals. Up the ridge, a tree explodes. This close, it sounds like a double-barrel shotgun.

Keep your fires low, Sonny advises. What I mainly need is to keep the roots and the lower parts of the trunk alive. Likely enough, most of the fruit-bearing parts on the scions are dead already. I can graft those back to health. But if the roots die, that's a whole mature tree that'll take years to replace. Five, to be exact. He jumps in his pickup, flicks the ignition. Okay, boys, he says, you know what they say about the home fires. Then he's rumbling down the ridge to deliver cordwood to men in other sections of the orchard, and with his headlights, so goes the last of the daylight. The darkness, beneath the full canopy of orange-bearing branches, is near total. The wind rushes at us.

Jack Frost get lost, I say.

Fire and ice, says Bones, fire and ice. His eyes and teeth are luminous, tracing his movements as he begins stacking wood in the center of a four-tree quadrant. I move two rows over and do the same.

One of my more successful fires thaws some of the frozen fruit hanging above my head. Oranges go off like little grenades, spraying ice in all directions. Bones laughs, retrieves a chunk of crystallized fruit. It disappears into his mouth, or at least into his scraggly beard, which glitters with ice.

Didn't your mama ever tell you not to eat no yellow snow? I ask.

I ain't got no mama, says Bones.

Next time he turns his back, I scuttle down the dark side of the ridge. These low-lying areas are where Sonny is having most of his problems. As I start moving laterally through the rows, I hear another tree crack open, and then another. One of them I hear fall and the other I do not. Clumps of orange flame sputter weakly in the wind, the forms of men moving back and forth between them. Flashlight beams swing through columns of rising smoke. Burning wood sizzles as the frost from above melts into silver drops, drips down. In the holes left in the canopy by fallen trees, ruddy clouds of smoke graze the stars. I step over the splintered remains of one tree, kicking away frozen oranges and brittle leaves. I pass muttering voices without answering. Fire and ice, I'm thinking, Fire and ice.

I skid across a frozen pond, the low-hanging branches I try to grab for balance breaking off in my hands. I fight blindly through an opaque copse of brambles and wild pines, a break in the orchard that Fonder's River doesn't covertly touch, then find Blake almost by accident as I stumble out of the darkness, on the other side. The one fire he seems to have been able to keep lit is a steady beacon, though the light it sheds extends barely beyond the scope of its heat, just enough to outline

Blake's face. He's sitting hunkered down, his nose almost in the flame.

I remember this story I read as a kid, about how to catch goblins in the woods. You hang a lantern from a low branch, turn the flame up high, then hide yourself behind a bush. Goblins are irresistibly attracted to flame, just like moths. Sooner or later they'll come, unfolding out of the shadows, to gather round the lantern and stare and stare at the flame until they're mesmerized, and their eyes grow wide and round. Then you can sneak up behind them and throw a net over them.

Blake raises a bottle to his lips. I see the label as the flat underside tilts toward the firelight. Blueberry.

A tree explodes nearby—in front of us, behind us, to the left or right, I don't know. The echo of the ridge and the sheer volume of the report conspire to dislocate the sound.

My left hand is in the deep side pocket of the parka, where the brown paper bag is wrapped around the twenty-five thousand. Sonny saw it earlier, I told him it was my lunch. Careful it doesn't freeze, he warned. I told him it was cold cuts anyway.

I pull the bag of money out of my pocket, toss it onto the frozen ground between us. It lands with a short spray of ice.

Blake swivels on the balls of his feet. I'm all in the shadows, except for my right hand, holding the gun towards him, a shaped metal reflection in the hollow light. He drops the bottle, puts up his hands like he's being robbed.

Take it, I say. Go, I say.

Going Back to the Bridge in Berlin

W.E.B. Griffin

"What happened to the church?" the wife asked, looking up at the still fire-scarred ruins of what once had been the Kaiser Wilhelm Kirche on the Kurfurstendamm.

"We bombed it," he told her. "Either we did, at night, or the Brits did in the daytime."

He gestured around the area. "This was all bombed out," he went on. "It used to be what you would now call a flea market. Except the currency was cigarettes and coffee."

She was younger than he was, and an Argentine, he thought, and it would be unreasonable of him to expect her to understand.

"This is where I bought the chess set," he said. "The one on the coffee table in my office in the house?"

She knew the chess set and nodded.

"I paid two cartons of cigarettes for it," he said. "You could buy a carton and a half of cigarettes a week, for eighty cents a carton."

"Really?" she asked.

He did not tell her that for a carton of cigarettes you could also rent for a night a stunning blonde, or a gorgeous redhead.

"I parked my jeep over there," he said, pointing. "The way you locked it was with a chain and padlock around the steering wheel."

"Really?" she asked.

"Really," he said.

He had won the right in a raffle to buy for $830 the rebuilt jeep from the Army. It had been painted black. For a time, it bore the legend "Miss Begotten" neatly painted just below the windshield. Then a major's wife had complained to her husband that it was vulgar, and he had found out who owned the jeep and telephoned The Colonel, and The Colonel had called the man—the boy—in and said that while the major was obviously an asshole, it would probably be smarter to just paint over "Miss

Begotten" than to tell the major to tell his wife to attempt a physiologically impossible act of self-impregnation.

Two days later, General Lucius D. Clay stopped the boy—who was really a sergeant, but whose uniform bore blue and white triangles with the letters US in them, so that people would think he was a civilian—outside the PX and asked him what had happened to the "Miss Begotten" legend.

"Mrs. Clay thought it was clever," the U.S. Military Governor of Germany added.

"Sir, some major's wife complained that it was vulgar."

General Clay shook his head in disbelief and walked away, and the boy sergeant considered having Miss Begotten painted back on. But he didn't, because he heard all the time that people in his line of work should not draw attention to themselves.

In the morning at precisely 9:30 the hired Mercedes and driver were waiting outside the Hotel Kempinski. The wife was impressed by the punctuality. The man was not surprised. When the train from Munich had arrived the night before, it came to a stop as the sweep second hand on the platform clock touched 12, and it was 8:25:00 precisely.

"Is this your first time in Berlin?" the driver asked, in flawless English.

"Yes," the wife said. "I want to see Sans Souci."

"On the way," the man said, in rusty German. "Go through Zehlendorf."

"Anyplace special in Zehlendorf?"

"Forty-four forty-six Beerenstrasse. It's near the U-Bahnstation."

The house was unchanged, except there was now a basketball hoop and a crescent of macadam in the garden.

The house had been the official quarters of a senior member of the Office of Military Government, U.S., who for purposes of protocol carried the assimilated rank of brigadier general. He was twenty-six years old. He had been captured at sixteen in 1940 while serving with the French Foreign Legion. He had been released at Hitler's personal order as a goodwill gesture and had become a war correspondent. He had won the

Pulitzer Prize for Journalism before he was old enough to vote, and then had returned to Berlin when the B-17 in which he was flying was shot down. That time, he stayed in the POW camp.

In 1946 or 1947—*God, is it that long ago?*—he had offered the boy-sergeant the hospitality of his home because they had had the same French teacher in high school, and she had written the senior official that the boy was also in Berlin. And because the senior official was not married and was lonely in the fourteen-room house.

They shared the house with a female spider monkey who used to swing from the chandelier in the foyer and scream at female guests of the senior official and the boy, of whom she was jealous.

She also used to escape from the house and break into nearby houses and pass out in people's living rooms and bedrooms from drinking too much of anything with alcohol in it, preferring cognac, but perfectly happy to settle for perfume.

"I used to live here," the man said.

"Nice house," the wife said. "When are we going to Sans Souci?"

"Just as soon as we swing by Sven Hedin Strasse," the man said, as much to the driver as to the wife.

The house on Sven Hedin Strasse, where the boy had worked, was deserted. A bored German policeman sat in a shack guarding it.

"You Americans gave everything back," the driver explained. "But they don't know what to do with places like that. The property of Nazis—I think that house belonged to Martin Bormann . . ."

"No," the man corrected him. "Willy Ley."

"One of the Nazi officials, anyway. So it's supposed to have been forfeited, but the relatives are suing to get it back."

"Why was it forfeited?" the wife asked.

"Sort of a fine, honey," the man said.

It didn't take nearly as long to get to Potsdam as he remembered it did.

"This is the Unity Bridge," the driver announced. "Potsdam and Sans Souci are just the other side."

"Stop the car," the man said.

"Why?" the wife asked.

"Get out the video camera," the man said. "I want a picture of me walking across the bridge."

"It's just a bridge," the wife said, but she started getting the camera from its bag.

The Colonel had called the boy one night just before midnight, at the house on 4446 Beerenstrasse, and told him to come, *mach schnell*, to the house on Sven Hedin Strasse, and to wear an Ike jacket with stripes and parachute boots with white laces, and to bring the rest of the MP crap, the Sam Browne belt and the MP brassard. And the Thompson.

Something had come up, and someone was sick, or unavailable, and the boy was going to have to fill in—as contingency plans made provision for him to do—for him in the MP Platoon.

The boy got in the jeep that had once been named Miss Begotten and drove to Sven Hedin Strasse. The GMC six-by-six truck carrying the real MPs was there when he got there. As were two MP jeeps and two black Opel Kapitan sedans.

The Colonel went over again with the two MP officers what was expected of them, and then the boy and three others from Sven Hedin Strasse all dressed up as MPs got in the back of the six-by-six with the real MPs. The Colonel got in one of the Opel Kapitans and tooted the horn and the convoy set out for the Unity Bridge.

The Engineer platoon with their generator and floodlights was at the bridge when the convoy arrived.

The Colonel got out of the Opel Kapitan and started to walk across the bridge.

The men in the back of the six-by-six got out and were lined up in ranks.

The Colonel came back off the bridge, nodded at a captain from Sven Hedin Strasse, and then went to the second Opel Kapitan and opened the rear door. Two men got out, one of them awkwardly. The second man out of the Kapitan removed handcuffs from the first man, and then put his hand on his arm.

A captain walked down the line of real and counterfeit MPs and passed out magazines loaded with dully glistening brass .45 .ACP cartridges. The bolts of the Thompsons were pulled back, the safeties put on, and then the magazines slammed into the actions.

The captain called the platoon of MPs to attention.

The Engineer platoon's generators roared under the increased load as the floodlights were switched on.

One of the MP lieutenants called, "Detail, 'ten'hut. For-ward, har-ch. Column left, march!"

The MPs marched on the bridge, splitting the column left and right and lining up, as they had practiced, on both sides, with men every ten feet up to the middle of the bridge, where a heavy steel barrier was suspended across the road.

"Detail, halt! Present h'arms!" the MP lieutenant called when he had reached the barrier and was looking into the face of his Volkspolizei counterpart.

For this purpose, the command "present arms" meant unslinging the Thompson from one's shoulder, and then holding it resting on one's hip, with one's hand on the trigger assembly, the trigger finger carefully kept *off* the trigger.

The boy was on the left on the bridge, immediately behind the MP lieutenant, within six feet of the barrier, looking into the face of his Volkspolizei counterpart.

Their platoon, the boy had been briefed, although they were wearing the enlisted men's uniforms, was made up entirely of commissioned officers.

Behind *their* platoon the boy could see three men in civilian clothing walking toward the barrier, in a line.

As they got within ten feet of the barrier, the three men stopped. One of them gave the man in the middle a little shove, and he started walking alone toward the barrier.

As the boy realized the barrier was being raised, he became aware that another man had come from behind him and was walking toward the dividing line.

The two walking men did not look at each other as they passed one another.

As soon as the two men had passed the barrier it came down.

The boy saw the face of the man who had come from Potsdam as he walked past him. He was licking his lips nervously, and he had been, to judge by the bruises on his face, really worked over.

The MP platoon stayed at Present Arms for perhaps two minutes, which seemed like much longer. Then the MP lieutenant ordered, "Sling h'arms. About face! Forward h'arch!"

By the time they marched off the bridge, the two Opel Kapitans were no longer there.

The captain came by and collected the Thompson magazines, and checked each piece to make sure it was *really* unloaded, and then the MP Platoon got back on the six-by-six.

When they got back to Sven Hedin Strasse, the boy got back in the jeep once known as Miss Begotten and returned to the house at 4446 Beerenstrasse. When he walked into the foyer, the spider monkey dropped onto him from the chandelier, where she had been waiting for him, causing him to drop the Thompson onto the floor.

"What's so special about this bridge?" the wife asked.

"It used to be where they exchanged spies," the man said.

"Exchanged *spies?*" the wife asked, not understanding.

"It's not important, honey. Let's go see if we can find something to eat before we go to Sans Souci."

Just a Little Closer to the Lord

Winston Groom

There is a tiny town along the coast of the Carolinas called Widgeville. It is situated between a river and a swamp, and the land around it is very flat and good for growing rice, which is what the people in Widgeville do, grow rice, and when they are not growing rice they keep to themselves and go to church and do not have much to do with the outside world.

Two types of people live in Widgeville, black people and white people, and they have lived there for hundreds of years. The white people are short and squat and have blue eyes and blond hair and speak in a dialect that is not like any dialect heard in that part of the country—or, for that matter, in any other part of the world. It is said that they are descendants of Englishmen who survived a mysterious shipwreck off Cape Hatteras in 1652.

The black people are tall and thin and fiercely black, and they talk with an accent that is clipped and short and very difficult to understand, and it is said that their ancestors were of an ancient and powerful tribe that was kidnapped from a remote mountain region in Africa and sold into slavery. But black and white alike, the Widgeville people live together in harmony, growing rice, going to church, and speaking in their peculiar accents.

All but one.

His name is Walking Hand, and he is very old and does not speak at all, and some people believe that he is the Devil.

Walking Hand simply appeared one day and began roaming the streets and highways around Widgeville, carrying a preposterously battered black suitcase. Sometimes, early in the morning, he would materialize at the head of the little main street, follow it to the end, and turn off down a lane to the highway near the river. Later, near sunset, he would return by the same route and go off down a dirt road that ended near the swamp. Occasionally, his journey would be made at night, a tall, stark figure shuffling quietly down the streets, which would scare the bejesus out of anyone who happened upon him unexpectedly.

It had been nearly a year since he came, and in all that time he had never said a word to anyone.

Just how this Devil business got started nobody could remember exactly. Perhaps, seeing him on the street, someone commented that he certainly "looked like the devil," which was interpreted in different ways until it finally became the consensus that if Walking Hand wasn't exactly the Devil, he was at least under the Devil's spell—doomed for the rest of his days to roam in silence, without apparent food or shelter.

In fact, he did present a frightening appearance.

He was gaunt and tall, with sunken, amber eyes that stared straight ahead and did not blink. He had a long, slack jaw and a large, bulbous nose. He might have been bald, or white-haired, but no one knew because he always wore a dark slouch hat.

And he never, ever, smiled.

Now, whether by coincidence or by design, the Widgeville rice crop was experiencing an awful setback that year; there wasn't enough water in the river to flood the fields, and the tender green shoots began to wither and die under the summer sun. Since the rice crop supported the town, its loss could mean the end of everything, and the Widgeville people were anxious and afraid. They began to go to church more often, both to pray and to discuss their problem, since the churches, black and white alike, served as meeting houses as well as places of worship.

It was during one of these meetings that someone remembered the river had begun to fall at almost precisely the same time that Walking Hand had appeared in their town.

A low and uneasy murmur ran through the Widgeville community during the next few days. If before they had believed that Walking Hand was in some way in league with the Devil, this feeling was all the stronger now, and the discussions began to center on him, and what role he might be playing in the drought.

"He is cursed by Satan, and we are cursed by him!" cried Ebenezer

Gooch, alderman in the black church.

"You can see the Devil in his eyes," declared Jonathan Boswell, deacon of the white church.

But they were afraid and confused about what to do next. Of course, the Devil was certainly not as powerful as God, but he was certainly not to be trifled with by mere mortal men. And if Walking Hand was indeed the Devil's disciple, then he most assuredly had some of the Devil's powers. If, for instance, they ordered him to leave town, or tried to overpower him, and failed, he might very well place an even meaner curse on them.

Then they discovered that Walking Hand actually *was* the Devil, for who else would live in the swamp?

The swamp was a dark and forbidding place at the outskirts of town, and the closest most of the Widgeville people ever came to it was when they went to dump their garbage at the trash heap at its edge. It was covered in brown, tea-colored water, out of which rose fallen branches and rotting stumps and choking green water plants. Beneath all of this, in the muck and quicksand, lived snakes, alligators, snapping turtles, and the Lord (and the Devil as well) only knew what else. Tall stark trees grew in the swamp, their branches gnarled like terrible fingers in the sky. Many of them were draped with huge clumps of Spanish moss, some so large and deformed that they resembled ghostlike, human forms.

But the eeriest thing of all was the opossums.

The opossums hung by their tails from the branches of the trees, upside-down, and at night their eyes could be seen shining like myriad tiny lights, sometimes a dozen in a single tree, slowly consuming the foliage, hanging like bats and looking like rats.

The Widgeville people hated the opossums and feared them.

Since they were nocturnal creatures by inclination, whenever an opossum was seen in the daylight it was assumed that it was rabid or mad—and at the very least a bad omen.

One evening, three of the village boys followed Walking Hand on his sunset return, hiding behind him in the bushes and shrubs, and reported back in gasping breaths that he had disappeared into the darkest and most remote regions of the swamp. If there had been doubt about his identity before, this news made it all the more certain because the swamp was unquestionably the Devil's lair.

That same night, a meeting was called in Widgeville. It was held in the white church, which was a little larger than the black church, and it was packed to the last row with black and white people alike.

"The Devil is in our midst," said Percival Widge, for whose ancestors the town had been named. (Actually, there were only six family names in the entire village: Widge, Boswell, and Slocum were the white names; Gooch, Cantwell, and James were the black names. Everybody else was kin to them.)

"What shall we do?" the others cried.

Ebenezer Gooch raised his finger into the air. "We must rid ourselves of him. It is the only way."

Much discussion followed, a vote was taken, and it was decided that the following Sunday the town would approach Walking Hand and politely ask him to leave. These were good, God-fearing people in Widgeville, and they would not seek to harm him, but if he refused, other steps would have to be taken, for God-fearing people could not tolerate the Devil in their midst.

During the next few days, Walking Hand was shunned like an awful disease. People who saw him coming down the street would immediately cross to the other side. Mothers would shuttle their children inside when he passed by, and lock the doors and pull the shades. By the time Sunday arrived, an electric sense of excitement and anticipation had filled the town.

Then there came an omen. One of the Widge boys saw it first.

High atop a telephone pole in the center of town a large opossum had perched.

In broad daylight, no less.

It was gripping the pole with its clawed feet. Its skinny white tail was wrapped snakelike around the glass insulator, and its pointed snout opened and closed rhythmically, baring a set of sharp, gleaming teeth.

The Widge boy shouted and ran for his house. Other people, on their way to church, began to gather around.

Mothers clutched their children to their skirts in case the opossum decided to leap upon them. The men wore strong, dark frowns and muttered among themselves as to what it might mean. Plainly it was an omen, but what kind of omen, no one could say.

"Why is it so ugly, Mama?" cried Martin Gooch.

"Can I have its skin?" said one of the Slocum boys.

"I get it, I saw him first!" exclaimed Tommy Widge.

"Be quiet, all of you!" Mrs. Gooch said.

Without warning, from behind the crowd, a stone sailed up toward the opossum. It missed by several feet and fell with a clatter on the roof of a house across the street. Eyes turned. One of the Slocum boys was preparing for another throw.

"Don't! Don't do that!" exclaimed Ebenezer Gooch. "We must all of us decide."

"Let's get rid of it," one of the men said. "We must stand firm."

"It might have the rabies!" another cried. "It might jump down and bite someone."

A second rock flew up at the telephone pole, bouncing off a foot or so below the opossum's perch—and then another, and another, whistling by its head. The opossum did not jump or flinch, but remained frozen in the same position, facing in the direction of the swamp. From that height it could probably see the trees and the dark sloughs and perhaps even smell the musky, damp odor.

Now there was no stopping them. Everyone—men, women, and children—was picking up rocks and throwing them. Some missed only by inches, others by yards, but none yet had actually struck the opossum. Then from the back of the mob a voice rang out like a clap of thunder.

"Stop!" the voice commanded.

The people spun around. There was Walking Hand, looking as fearsome and devilish as ever. A gasp ran through the crowd. He was standing ramrod straight, his black suitcase on the ground beside him. Some of the people began to back away, and others fingered the rocks in their hands menacingly.

Behind them, high on the pole, the opossum remained motionless except for an intense working of its beady eyes. The warm summer breeze ruffled its matted fur, and it looked tired and sad, as though it knew it was never meant for telephone poles and streetlamps and automobiles.

Walking Hand strode through the crowd. He seized a rung on the telephone pole and began to climb. When he neared the top, he reached out, and the opossum neatly curled its tail around his wrist. Then, slowly, he came down, each step taken carefully, his arm held out level with the ground, the opossum hanging from it by its tail, upside-down.

When he reached the ground, the crowd was facing Walking Hand. Ebenezer Gooch, with Jonathan Boswell at his side, stepped forward and confronted him.

"Sir," said Ebenezer Gooch, "you have caused a great deal of trouble. From the day you came to our town we have had no water for our crops. The rice is dying and we will all be poor. We do not know what you want, or why you are here, but we must ask you to leave."

Walking Hand did not reply. His eyes were fixed on Ebenezer Gooch and Jonathan Boswell, and they glowed in his head like two hot coals.

"If you do not go," Jonathan Boswell said, "we will be forced to take steps. You roam our roads and streets, you frighten our children . . ." He was about to continue when a cry from the back of the crowd interrupted him.

"Hey, look at this!" said an excited voice. They turned, and the crowd parted. Several of the children were kneeling around the battered black suitcase. They had opened it and spread the contents on the ground.

There was a neatly folded brownish shirt that had obviously been washed in swamp water. There was also a handkerchief and a pair of socks. There was a bag of mulberries and a sack of wild rice and a bottle of water. There was also an ancient and well-worn Bible. Pressed, dried leaves marked places in the Book of Psalms.

At the very bottom of the suitcase was a box of watercolors and brushes. The watercolors had been made from swamp berries and herbs and the brushes carefully woven of dried swamp grass. Beneath all of this was a stack of several dozen flat, thin layers of tree bark, each about a foot square.

"Hey! That's me!" exclaimed one of the Widge boys, "and you, too, sister, and mother and father!" He could hardly contain his excitement. He held the bark high for all to see. "It's our house, too." Sure enough, it was the Widge house, with the entire family posed in front behind a little white picket fence—even the Widge dog was in the painting. Everyone gathered in close and began examining the other pieces of bark. On each one was a portrait of a Widgeville family in front of their own house.

"Oh, that's us!" someone said. "They're so real. They almost look like photographs."

And slowly, as each family looked at the painting of itself, a hush fell over the crowd, for each saw in his or her own face a deep and radiant beauty that they had never recognized was there before. The fact was that the Widgeville people had always believed they were ugly—the whites because they were short and squat and different from people in other towns around them, and the blacks merely because they were black. But here in the portraits they saw themselves for the first time as an outsider might see them, each face framed in a glow of hope and love- liness that bloomed almost magically from the paintings.

There was one piece of bark left in the suitcase. It was not a portrait of anyone but a drawing of the town and the rice fields as they might have appeared from the sky. And there were strange markings on this drawing, in the rice fields, that did not in fact exist on the ground.

They turned back toward Walking Hand. The opossum had uncurled its tail from his arm and crawled along it to his shoulder, where it sat comfortably, gently nuzzling his ear.

"But what does this mean?" Jonathan Boswell asked haltingly. "Are you trying to mark us . . . for something?" He searched for words. "First you ruin our crops . . . and then the omen . . . and now *these*." He gestured at the paintings and the drawings of the fields. "Are you making records of us?"

Walking Hand spoke for the second time.

"I am a painter," he said, "and I came here because I admired your lovely town. I have ruined no crops, but I believe I have a solution that can save them. Every day I have walked from the swamp to the river and taken measurements. I believe that if your men will dig a canal across the rice fields, you will be able to irrigate your land and no longer have to depend on the uncertainties of the tides. I intended to leave all of this with you. The drawing shows how the canal might be dug."

The people of Widgeville began to shift uneasily and lower their heads in shame, and there was a long silence, except for the rustling of the warm summer wind in the trees. Then a tiny voice came from the front of the crowd. It was Martin Gooch.

"But . . . we thought you were the Devil," he said hesitantly, and with a touch of disappointment, "because you live in the swamp. And then the omen . . . why did it come? Why did he climb up there?"

Walking Hand spoke for the third and final time.

"I am only a painter and a lover of God's creatures. And this," he said, petting the opossum's fur, "is not an omen. He came because he wanted to see the town, or he might have been hungry.

"Why he climbed, I do not know. Perhaps he wanted to get a little closer to the Lord."

With that, Walking Hand strode down the main street toward the swamp, leaving the suitcase and the paintings behind. They all watched until he had vanished down the path, and the only sound was the soft sighing of the wind in the trees.

Later, near sunset, the people of Widgeville went down to the edge of the swamp and sat on the bank, waiting for dark. Night fell like a hundred midnights, and with it the opossums came out to feed in the trees. In the blackness, their eyes glowed and twinkled like fireflies.

Then, at precisely the stroke of twelve, a large, orange pair of eyes appeared high in the tallest tree in the swamp. These eyes did not blink; instead, they stared out ferociously at the Widgeville people, but with a certain inquisitiveness—the better to watch them, perhaps, or just to get a little closer to the Lord—no one ever knew, and no one ever would.

LOVE LIKE A BULLET

Melinda Haynes

Jesse died underneath a neon sign with three burned-out tubes. During the day the sign spells out Star Lite Motel just like it's supposed to do, but at night the first, fifth, and eighth letters stay dark and each time that sign lights up, it spells 'tar it' against the backdrop of the raceway across the street. And that's how I'm beginning to feel— tarred and feathered and like God was waiting with a big stick to run me out of town before I'd left the womb good. I watched Daddy last night while he leaned against our truck and prayed that same old worn-out prayer—that each of us would be granted a dignified death when our time rolled around, thanking God and paying proper respect while his hand stroked the cracked, pebbled cover of his brown Scofield Bible. The pavement's still damp over there underneath that crippled sign and so far I've counted nine stores here in Saint Elmo with backward letters in their hand-painted titles. It took me a while, but now I know God ain't never heard a damn word my daddy said.

Our pickup hit a bump and threw Jesse into the grillwork of a white Peterbilt. That would've been the end of it if there hadn't been a TV crew parked over at the raceway interviewing Clevon Clemons, this year's short-track winner, Saint Elmo's home-grown Rusty Wallace minus corporate sponsorship but with what looked like a truckload of girl-friends. That red car of his was dangling from a crane plastered with advertisements for Valvoline and Jiffy Lube and wearing a taped-on number 69. The interview stopped short when the fat guy eating a Butterfingers threw Clevon the microphone and hauled ass across Highway 90 to film us all—eleven of us, some standing, some hovering in the middle of all those rolling Coke cans and blowing paper napkins from the cab of that semi—a whale of a rig with a contoured top that climbed like a mountain.

While Jesse bled, I peered through an opened door and saw an eighteen-inch color television set built into a walnut console and stereo speakers mounted all over the place and a tag that read GOD IS MY CO-PILOT. I remember thinking, Well, shit, God ain't Mario Andretti after all, and wishing I could've warned Jesse to grab his ass cause God was behind the wheel gunning for him. I was thinking this as Jesse's blood filled up dry cracks and crevices in the motel's faded asphalt.

Sarah pointed to stepped-on gum on the bottom of her sandals and screamed while some guy named Buzz yelled into a handheld telephone, "A kid's dying here at the Star Lite, you mother-fucker! Whaddaya mean, calm down!"

Mama chased white bats. That's what those napkins looked like. She ran, this way and that, her Keds changing colors, growing a nasty new red tread each time she made a pass, running from truck tire to truck tire, hurrying back to stop a while, then running for one more bat, steady crying and looking up at me while I studied that truck tag.

"Levi! Help me, baby—Scrape that gum off Sarah's shoe!—"

A blond girl, wearing short-shorts and a red bow as big as the moon grabbed my arm and pulled me toward Jesse. I felt long fingernails cut into my upper arm, the whole while she was screaming up into my face, "Get over there and do what your mama says!" Buzz and Clevon and just about everybody around that place knew her. They called out—"Bullet, run get some towels, baby!" and "Bullet, grab that kid and shush her up!" And she did those things. She fetched and carried, scraped gum and picked up napkins, even grabbed the grillwork of the Peterbilt and hauled herself up, scaling that thing like a mountain climber, looking for the flashing lights of the ambulance. The blond girl was everywhere at once, doing those things just like Jesse was hers or at least a part of hers. She got her hands bloody just like the rest of us, just like she was family.

The TV man was behind me, breathing chocolate across the top of my head and talking into a headset. He kept mumbling, "This is great, man, great . . . Man, oh man, this is great . . ."

Bullet said the reason the rest of the media showed up was because we looked like a page out of *The Grapes of Wrath*. I've never liked Steinbeck, never could stomach more than a couple of chapters at most and now that I know there's something deeper in on a dusty page that looked like us, I know the reason why.

* *

We ended up here because we blew a tire on our way back toward Brownsville day before yesterday. There's a field next to the Star Lite where we've always camped and waited for the soybeans. Daddy got sick in Loxley, coughed blood solid for three weeks straight, so we're later this year. Leftover cotton's gone, so are the pecans, nothing much left here except freeze-burned collards and turnips. But motel pools need cleaning, including this one, and Daddy made a deal that paid for the tire and bought us some food.

I've scraped away green crops of algae in concrete swim holes from Destin to Gulfport, and the smell of chlorine hangs in my clothes and hair and burns the skin inside my nose. Two things I hate about this: the smell of chlorine climbing into my food, and me having to hide my bleached-out hands deep in my pockets every time we make a piss stop just to keep people from staring. Sometimes we're clear to Brownsville before I can taste food again.

We map our existence by towns—Wilmer, Irvington, Grand Bay—for leftover cotton, Theodore—for stubborn pecans that don't want to leave their trees; Silverhill—when the turnips come in, which means it's winter and time to slow down a bit; then on to Myrtle Grove and the warm neck of Florida for pole beans and Pink-eyed Purple Hulls.

Around March we head back toward Texas if the rains are slow and lately they have been, and even through thick truck exhaust, I notice things, queer changes that make me wish for the ordinary—fresh paint on run-down buildings, palm trees next to the Pizza Hut in Lucedale, a Sonic Drive-in next to a Laundromat in New Augusta. I see red and white and sleek chrome blazing against faded Mississippi silos while country girls who've never owned a pair try to look normal on roller skates.

* *

In Saint Elmo, the night before Jesse died, Daddy read to us and I felt safe from changes. I sat leaning against the truck, watching those blinking motel lights missing their letters and felt Jesse against me. He'd had pizza from a convenience store for supper and all I could smell was garlic on top of chlorine so I shrugged away from him. This bothers me now, the way I moved away from him. But that night it was just one brother moving upwind, no harm intended and truth told, even though I decided somewhere near Brownsville there ain't a true word on one single page, I still wanted to listen. I've always liked the story and the way Daddy reads it and Jesse's shoulder against me was a distraction.

That night Daddy's voice seemed deep as a Pentecostal preacher's. He knew the story by heart so he moved around our camp like the Tin Man, stretching out his hands against the fire, throwing shadows that made the girls squeal.

This was one of King James's best, from the time the judges ruled, when there was a famine in the land and a certain man of Bethlehemjudah went to sojourn in the country of Moab, he and his wife and his two sons. The man's name was Elimelech, and the name of his wife was Naomi, and for a short season they were happy as fresh Jews on Miami Beach in wintertime.

I followed Daddy's words with pictures behind my eyes, adding my own colors and smells. He always skipped over the names of those sons, too, but I didn't care. They died early on anyway, shortly after they married two Moab beauty queens. It's Naomi and her daughters-in-law that finished off my pictures: Ruth and Orpah, both Moabites. Dark. Mysterious. Beautiful.

Jesse was nodding and I moved closer and gave his head a prop while Daddy gleaned Ruth, chapter one, verse three. He put a cry in his voice and stood up straight like an undertaker. He read and read, almost an hour's worth. Elimelech and the boys are dead and all the women left alone, no bedmates, no comfort, no kinsmen to lean on. And to make matters worse, to pour salt all over that open sore, Moab's struck by famine now. It seemed God picked that year to piss east and kiss west.

Daddy paused and looked across the fire at me, "What's this telling you, Levi?"

"Pussy ain't worth shit, if you're starvin'." Mama was dozing and I got away with it.

Daddy always got a kick out of that one. Even though he'd been sick, he slapped his leg and laughed deep until he coughed old blood and woke up Mama. She shook his shoulder and patted his back like he was a baby while he wiped his mouth and pointed with his handkerchief to the rest of us. In a strangled voice he said, "We'll finish tomorrow. Levi. You shake Jesse and make him wash before he crawls in the sack. I swear to Jesus, he smells like a goddamn wop."

I fell asleep that Tuesday night watching a blinking motel sign and dreaming of Ruth and thinking Saint Elmo was a slow-changer, not too queer at all, so it seemed, a place better than most to have a blowout.

* *

Bullet's sitting next to me out by the clean pool and stroking the middle finger of my right hand when the Butterfingers man shows up again. It's barely nine a.m. and his pants look slept in. He's muttering he needs more footage while he wanders here and there making a box out of his hands and looking foolish while he peers through it. Seems his station's working on a follow-up piece because our story drew a thirty-nine in the overnight ratings.

There's a dark-haired girl standing over there in the shade holding a can of hair spray and practicing her lines. She's putting on pink lipstick and fluffing her hair. Every now and then, she bends at the waist and shakes her head like it's full of water. From the waist up, she's neat as a pin, all pressed and starched and buttoned-down, but from the waist down she's another story, like one of those books you can turn upside down and read again. She's wearing beat-up Reeboks with no socks and a wrinkled pair of plaid boxers over lime-green nylon running pants.

The cameraman walks by and sizes me up through his box, then moves on. I'm not pitiful enough this morning, I guess. Maybe my jeans are too clean or maybe it's because my socks match. He pulls a candy bar from his back pocket and splits that yellow paper straight down the middle with a long fingernail, and devours it in two bites. Then he sniffs the paper, looking for scraps. I'm forgotten, but he's watching Bullet. The sun's in her eyes, so he moves until she's sitting in his shadow and can't miss him. When she looks up he licks that candy wrapper from top to bottom with a fat, chocolate tongue. Before he turns he winks, and even though I'm slow witted, I know he's sent that girl some mail. She turns to me, tucking tiny feet in enormous red shoes under her bottom.

"Levi, you really seventeen? Y'all really named from the Bible?"

This is just my second day of knowing her but I've already figured out she asks double questions. I watch her. Underneath all that makeup, there's fresh pink baby skin that can't be hid or made old-looking and tiny fluffs of hair sprouting along her widow's peak. I'd be willing to bet that underneath that armor, she's as clean as rubbed-down Ruth. I try to pull my hand away because honest to God, it's annoying and kinda painful.

"Seventeen last December and yes."

"Jeezus. Tell me again."

I don't feel like it, but I do it anyway, "There's Sarah, she's six. David's seven. Then there's the twins Jacob and Esau, ten and a half. Those two hate each other with a passion." I'd pull a joke from Genesis, chapter twenty-five about birthrights and stew and how God does seem to love a cheater, but somehow I know it'd go clean over that blond head. "There's Jesse . . ." My throat closes and I hurry on. "He was fourteen. Leah's nine. Michael's eleven. Seth's sixteen . . ." I trail off, tired of talking.

"Jeezus. I never knew such a thing . . ."

Of course she didn't. Nobody did till Jesse lost his grip and we ended up on all four local stations. The trucks from St. Vincent de Paul and Salvation Army started pulling in at dawn. Now there's a motel room full of boxes of clothes and shoes and an envelope full of eat-till-you-shit gift certificates to Shoney's and Godfather's Pizza.

"I bet you'd look like James Dean if you had a haircut." She crosses her legs and smacks her gum. Juicy Fruit.

She still owns my finger and she must hate the candy bar man because she just flipped him the bird. Finally she lets go and I can breathe again. She's doing her nails. Ravishing Red with glitter sprinkles. She's got her whole kit spread out on her lap and the manicure balls, red now with old polish, are rolling across the concrete like bloody cotton. The pool's looking real good, though, for such a fast job. Jesse took the shallow end and I scrubbed past the six-foot mark because I grew tall this past summer. My hands still stink but not so much as yesterday and it don't seem to bother Bullet.

I study my beat-up sneakers. They're a mess for sure. Bullet blows a bubble the size of Sarah's new goldfish bowl and I cross my legs, wondering if there's a pair of Nikes that just might fit me hiding in one of those boxes from Salvation Army. Her bubble pops and she looks at me, smiling, while she blows her fingers, then waves them in the air, catching a breeze. I turn away embarrassed and look down Highway 90 past Gulf Lumberyard, where I think I saw a barbershop.

* *

We glean, at least that's what Daddy calls it. We travel in a truck he traded something for somewhere outside of Houston. It needed a new engine, but he's a wizard with a wrench and we've been sailing down the road ever since. We follow the combines, those huge monsters with tinted windows and loose teeth. They hoe down thirty acres in no time flat but they leave a wake of leftovers that's ripe for the picking. I know this to be true because we live off of them.

We watch from the side of the road, drinking Kool-Aid, eating potato chips and waiting, the girls stretched out in the back of the truck underneath a canvas tarp, sleeping or maybe reading. We stand there, pretending we're farmers, and work the math in our heads. You figure three hundred a bale for cotton. One and a half acres yields a bale, and most farms carry sixty or so acres. Enough to make a farmer sweat blood when the time comes for sure. Enough to make even a pagan believe in sweet Jesus.

While we wait our turn we lean against the truck, all seven of us boys, watching those machines make their sweep, and we hoot and holler because the brand-new International Harvester's got a missing tooth for sure. We yell at them as they pass, "Get a move on! Moon's gonna get you!" or "While you're draggin ass, your wife's givin blow jobs down at Hardee's!" Daddy started this yelling business. Most drivers laugh with it and fly us the bird. When they do this, it's like raising a fist and making a trucker blow his horn. Daddy slaps his leg and yells and then goes into a coughing fit that, more often than not, turns scary real fast.

The drivers turn the switches off at dusk and climb out of their air-conditioned cubicles where tape decks play everything from "Canon in D" to George Jones. "It's all yours, boys!" some of them yell. We grab our bags and set out and work all night, all eleven of us, Mama and Daddy making a game out of it. We glean those acres and if the moon is full, it's like picking up warm snow. We've got good gloves, too. Wells Lamont. Daddy sees to that. And we stop and drink and rest and holler jokes across the rows, harmless ones about elephants in trees near the smaller kids, shadier limericks about dead whores in caves down the longer rows where us older ones like to pick. I've heard Daddy tell some nasty tales in my time and I laugh as loud as Jesse and Seth, but I'd rather be reading a good book and waiting to fall into a dream.

Some years at the end of a run we make close to three hundred dol-lars from leftover cotton alone. We work solid for weeks at a time. Pecans are harder and don't bring as much, but we time it so's we land near Theodore, Alabama, around Thanksgiving and the holidays, because even though there ain't much cash involved, Mama makes the best damn pecan dressing a person ever put in their mouth. After the gleaning times, it's on to swimming pools with their own nasty crops, and if it's a really bad year, we pick up trash along the fairgrounds and raceways. Life is hard, always has been, but today feels harder than most because the Seventh Day Adventists and the Catholics are fighting over Jesse. Seems they all want him to rest in their burial plots. I sit in a lawn chair and watch Mama and Daddy mull it over down by the Coke machine— Daddy, arms folded over a chest that looks more and more like it's caving in on itself and Mama patting at her hair and wishing for a mirror for the first time that I can ever remember.

* *

Bullet is bouncing back from her twelve o'clock john, who wore a braided ponytail and never even turned off his truck. That red thing spit diesel fumes the whole while and wore a tag on the back stating, *Old truckers never die, they just get a new Peterbilt.* The curtains to her room fluttered once when Sarah and David bumped into her door on their way to the Coke machine at the corner, Sarah wearing a "Spoiled Rotten" T-shirt Bullet found buried in one of those boxes and David, his head down, playing a Game Boy somebody left for us at the front desk.

"Say, David, you think it's Christmas? You somebody's Christmas angel?" Her voice is high-pitched, baby-talk style. Bullet hands them each a piece of gum and fluffs their hair like they're two puppies.

David puts his thumb in his mouth and looks at Sarah, who answers for him, "Yes ma'am. Miss Bullet."

"Jeezus! You kids are cute as hell!"

Jacob and Esau are playing basketball without a hoop. They drew a spot up on the back wall of the restaurant with a piece of chalk and every time the ball comes close to the mark, they do a high five and practice their dance. They're both wearing shoes two sizes too big for them and they've pulled off their shirts and tied them around their heads 'cause it's hot as hell, even here in early March. They look as natural flapping around that makeshift court as a monkey fucking a football.

She's still laughing when she grabs my hand over by the swimming pool. She's wearing glitter see-through plastic heels now instead of those huge ugly red things and there's a green Mardi Gras barrette in her hair.

"I've got a surprise for you, Levi!" She's out of breath from running on top of those cigarettes and her cheeks are flushed. "Had to go clean to the Bookmobile for it. But that don't matter." She's not wearing rouge now and against the backdrop of the swimming pool, she's kinda pretty.

"Come see."

I stand up slow and follow her to her room, hands deep in my pockets, nervous because she lives here and answers to some guy named Buzz who sits at the front desk and picks his teeth with a matchstick. But truth be told, I really don't know who answers to who, cause the day Jesse died she walked up to him and said big as you please, "Take care of them, or I'll cut you off for sure." He swallowed hard and scratched his nose and said, "Okay—but I ain't likin this, Bullet. I ain't likin this at all." I was holding Sarah up in my arms and watching the ambulance pull away, all flashing lights, but silent. Behind me I could hear Bullet whispering and planning and Buzz complaining but seeming to give in.

Her room is next to mine, room thirteen, with a door that's painted pink and trimmed out in turquoise with a big wooden heart for a door knocker. Inside she's got Aladdin curtains from Wal-Mart hanging over the tiny window, and she's thrown at least a two full bolts of blue-green gauzy material over the lamps and draped it down from the ceiling to the head of her bed. There's also a microwave and something she calls an espresso machine sitting on a table and right next to it a video player and a tape. She points to it.

"Know what that is? Ain't you excited?"

No, I'm not. The outside of the black case reads *The Grapes of Wrath*, and there's a red sticker on the side with day after tomorrow's date on it. Now, I'm familiar with videotapes. I don't like them, but I am familiar with them.

* *

Wednesday night, four hours after Jesse had been sealed and zippered and carted away in a body bag, while we were huddled down by the truck trying to find our rhythm again, Bullet wandered down in her nightie and began to circle us like a cat.

She spied out the portable grill, the sleeping bags, our stowed boxes of cans. Her eyes found the books I keep in the copper-colored bread box: *Strong's Concordance. Catch-22. Testimony of Two Men.* Then, with no invitation from anyone, she sat down on a broken cinder block and crossed her legs. I watched her garters run up and disappear into black lace. There were twin strips of white flesh above those stockings that had no place to go and in the moonlight and against the fire they looked like velvet. I watched so hard it made me dizzy. I watched so hard I heard Mama clear her throat three times and even then I couldn't stop myself.

Seth spit in the fire and made it sizzle, and I forced my eyes up to the red satin bow tying back her hair. Daddy saw it too. The garters I mean, not the bow. He's always been a below-the-waist man. He watches cooks and whores and 7-Eleven clerks and even old women hitching up the highway with a gas can, and his eyes never see their faces. I can always tell he's been watchin because at night he tries to make Mama kiss him out in the truck cab or he reads King James harder. That's what he did then. He cleared his throat, pulled out the Scofield, and turned his back to Bullet, and even though everything had changed from one day to the next, he picked it up right where he left off the night before when my brother sat next to me stinking to high heaven.

Seems that back in Moab Naomi decided to give her daughters-in-law a way out. "Go, return each to your mother's house; and the Lord deal kindly with you, as you have dealt with the dead, and with me." He paused, stretching his arms out over the fire showing off, even with Jesse only four hours dead, showing off because of those garters. "Then she kissed them good-bye and those two dark girls lifted up their voices and wept—"

He stopped for a long minute and I thought he was going to cry, but he began to cough instead. A part of me wanted to say "Turn around and chase those garters, Pop. Get your mind off your lungs," but another part of me, a queer new part, wanted a gun so I could shoot him and put him out of his misery. I crossed my arms and glared at Bullet.

After he spit a not-so-large wad out into the dark, he read hard again, "And then Ruth said to Naomi, 'Entreat me not to leave thee, or to return from following after thee; for whither thou goest, I will go; and where thou lodgest, I will lodge; thy people shall be my people, and thy God my God—' "

"Holy shit! You mean them is two women talking? To each other? Holy shit." Bullet was up off her cinder block and leaning against Daddy, peering over his shoulder down at his Scofield. She looked up, her eyes round like quarters. "Somebody ought to sue these goddamn preachers! They use this shit at weddings for Christ's sake! They make it seem like it's a couple sayin these things." He looked over at me then, like I owned this girl, like he never saw those garters at all and I did the only thing I could think to do, I stood up and moved around the fire and stood by her ear.

"Bullet, why are you botherin us?" I hissed it through my teeth because acting hateful felt good right then.

She cleared her throat and stepped back. "It was on at six o'clock, but I set my timer. Thought you folks might want to see it." We all looked at one another, waiting, not understanding what we were supposed to want to see. Daddy finally nodded his head, shut his Bible and moved forward, following her while she clicked across the parking lot, looking over her shoulder every once and a while, making sure we were still there.

We went into a strange room that smelled like strawberries and sat on her bed and all over her floor and watched a family of scarecrows moving in slow motion on the television set. There's Daddy, head down, hands clasped together under his chin, crying. Mama chasing napkins trying to stop Jesse's bleeding. The rest of us looking like we never learned how to keep our mouths from gaping open. Then there was Jesse, facedown, his chest still moving. Once. Twice. I could almost swear he pulled in a third breath. Then stupid stuff: breakaway footage of the truck and the driver, who was shaking his head and trying to light a cigarette; the voice-over: "Here in Saint Elmo, tragedy strikes"; something else about homelessness and hard times. And finally, the name of the bank where concerned viewers could send their cash.

Bullet clapped her hands together and squealed and stretched out the remote and the whole thing began again.

It was a cruel thing, but somewhere a part of me knew she saw it as some sort of kindness, some sort of favor. So I watched again and again, even after Mama and the rest of the family drifted out the door, quiet like worn-out ghosts. I watched, not because I cared about seeing how we looked to the rest of this county, but because I wanted to watch Jesse's chest move up and down one more time. I sat there on the edge of a strange girl's bed and watched, remembering how his shoulder felt leaning into me, how he liked to pick on Esau till he made him cry, how his favorite was Sarah. I remembered his hair and his eyes and how he always laughed the loudest, even if he didn't get it. I sat still, barely moving, just watching, because somewhere deep inside that black video case, Jesse was still breathing.

When I finally left her room I saw Daddy standing over by the truck holding his Bible and praying. I wanted to go up to him and tell him not to bother, God ain't listening, but I couldn't do it. I was wishing I could though; all the way across the parking lot I was wishing I could say that thing. I stood in front of him full of large words and realized for the first time I was looking down, I was taller than him for the first time ever, and this sealed it. I sat down hard and leaned my head back against the truck. He was to my side, his old chinos worn thin in places and smelling like motor oil.

"Finish the story, Pop. Don't leave me hangin."

Mama wandered out of her motel room then, and all the rest of the clan trickled out too, and there on that hard place underneath a tarp stretched out by the side of the truck we listened while he finished the story. For almost an hour it was camp again, just like Tuesday night when life was ordinary. The light blinked and buzzed over our heads and each time it spelled "tar it" out against the raceway, that damp spot in the middle of us all would shine for a while.

The way those words rolled off his tongue, I swear I felt their grief—not ours, but Naomi's, and those two dark girls. Actually only one dark girl now, Ruth. Orpah didn't have the stomach for queerness in a strange land.

"And so Naomi returned, and Ruth the Moabitess, her daughter-in-law, with her, which returned out of the country of Moab; and they came to Bethlehemjudah in the beginning of barley harvest . . ."

I shut my eyes and watched them chase hope whose name was Boaz. Boaz, luckily a man with a few bucks and a lot of land and hopefully not too old to remember how to fuck a woman . . .

Daddy's words poured over me and I saw the colors, even with Jesse dead I saw them.

There was Ruth when she found his field, tired after days and days of walking. She circled for a while, unsure, spying out the land, curious as a cat. She was wearing lavender and loose cloth that draped from her hair the same way that blue-green gauze hangs from Bullet's ceiling. She followed those workers, hanging back out of politeness, picking up scraps, working all day, stopping only once to sip some water.

I watched her mouth open as it moved to the cup. Boys were hiding back a ways in the shadows, watching, groping for pockets, ashamed their hands were bleached out and smelly from scraping algae out of swimming pools. I saw Boaz from inside my shadow, sitting a tall horse with spangling reins. He was watching me watching her. He used to be a warrior and his shadow's so large it ate us both up. She stood up because she lost the sun and put a hand over her eyes, straining to see. Before she catches a glimpse, though, he pulled at his horse and rode away. As he passed his workers he yelled and whistled, "Leave a little extra grain in the field, boys," and "Get a move on, you lazy fools! While you're draggin ass, your wife's givin blow jobs down at Hardee's!—"

His workers smiled and flipped him the bird. They got away with it that time because Boaz was in love. They got away with it that time because the man on the horse had seen Ruth. Beautiful Ruth, dark, draped, and sweet. He was smiling again, for the first time in years.

Daddy read on and on, tired and paraphrasing now. The girls were asleep in the truck bed and David and the twins piled up next to Mama. Just me and Michael and Seth left.

"Seems Naomi was so impressed with what that gal brought home from gleaning that it set her to thinking. She opens up a chest she's kept locked for years and pulls out oils and spices from Egypt and the Chaldeans. Precious oils that rode the back of a camel for ten or so years to find her. Inside those corked bottles is a smell so large it could fill the sky. Naomi takes Ruth by the hand"—and holds her middle finger—"while she heats water over an open fire. She tells her secret things: to bathe herself and rub her skin down good and proper till she smells like a young woman again; to go to the threshing room with a handheld lantern, to find Boaz. who's been winnowing there. He's been tossing grain all day and into the night, watching the chaff break away and fly into the fire. He'll be happy. It's a good harvest." Daddy's voice was bigger than ever because Jesse always slept through this part.

My ass was numb but behind my eyes I saw everything—
Ruth, standing naked in a sea of steam. Clouds curling around her
ankles and down to the floor like the fog does sometimes when we cross
Jubilee Parkway at midnight. She looked over her shoulder at her
mother-in-law, who was standing near the door watching her, knowing
what she was sending this dark girl to do, knowing she's making a whore
of her in order to buy some grits, but doing it anyway, doing it because
some things in life stay true no matter what you wish for, doing it anyway
because pussy ain't worth shit if you're starvin.

Ruth rubs silky oil up and down her arms, answering back that it's
okay, she don't mind doing this thing. She watches Naomi while she
slides a thick gold bracelet up one arm and then she bends low and rubs
oil up one leg, slow, like it's got its own map and knows how fast it wants
to get there. She set a dark bottle of spicy oil on the black video case by
the bathtub. The wind was soft and even though her Aladdin curtains
are pulled down low, they began to stir. I lost my breath then, because
that Moabite girl was naked, naked and dark except for a red bow as big
as the moon that's tying back her hair—

I pulled my legs up and hugged them tight because even with that
motel sign blinking and buzzing and reminding me I'm marked, even
with Jesse dead barely six hours now and Daddy coughing blood and
smelling like used-up Valvoline, King James just gave me a hard-on.

* *

That was two nights ago. Tonight I'm older. Tonight I'm watching
The Grapes of Wrath.

The movie is all right, I guess. I don't think Daddy looks much like
Henry Fonda, but I could see how a person would make the comparison
to their way of living and ours. Bullet's cooked up some popcorn in her
microwave and she's propped up the pillows so I can have a back rest.
She's kicked off her shoes and I can tell her feet are soft as a baby's, or at
least a toddler's—one who ain't walked much yet. Her back is to me and
she's stretched out long at the foot of the bed watching Mama Joad ask
Tommy if prison made a mean man of him. Grandpa says he ain't going

to California and while they get him drunk enough to toss in the back of the truck, I'm thinking of Boaz.

While a black-and-white Dust Bowl spreads over me like the flu, on the backside of my eyelids I can feel those warm colors. I see Boaz sleeping. I watch him tonight through Ruth's eyes. He's an older man with lots of land and a barn full of horses. He's not that great-looking either, maybe a little thick around the middle even, and after all these years, he's just about decided it's hand jobs from here on out. But he's a good man and he used to be a soldier. He cashed his best years gleaning a noble cause. He's spent his later years worrying over thinning hair while he sat at the gate of the city and watched pretty women. He sat on his ass and sniffed their wake and yearned like a schoolboy.

Fonda's just buried Grandpappy Joad out beside some highway in the middle of a gray-filled world while inside my head a gas lamp full of fragrant oil burns near a threshing room door. Dust motes fight then drift and float on a night breeze and the light's so soft it shoots through Ruth like a cotton arrow. When she stands still and straight and holds her arms up over her head, her shadow swallows him, this older man, and she sees him, sees the lines along his eyes and his nose for the first time. She sees his arm wound up over his head with his fingers relaxed and curled in a little, like a baby's. She sees the shape to his legs, open and relaxed under the cover, the way his feet turn out slightly. She watches him, really sees him now, and her stomach jumps, like it's full of grasshoppers. She clutches her robe to herself and wills herself not to cry, but she can't help herself. She looks over her shoulder into dark crevices, shuddering, remembering those boys in the shadow, the way they licked that yellow paper from top to bottom, the way they tried to force their mail on her—

Bullet reaches up and presses the rewind button for the seventeenth time. She loves this part. The "wrath in the grape part," she calls it. She's got her a fresh box of Kleenex and she's plumped up her pillow. Fonda's sitting by Mama Joad holding her hand, telling her he's gotta leave, but he'll still be everywhere at once—empty, stupid, words, words of a coward. Once a person leaves, they're gone forever, just like Jesse. Fonda's hauling ass and trying to smell sweet while he does it. He's scram-

bling for a piece of dignity to hide behind while he heads away from worrying about who's got enough to eat, or whether or not Rosa Sharon will
have milk for her baby or if there's really twenty full days of work waiting
for them up in all those peach orchards. Fonda ain't afraid of the law.
Fonda ain't "gotta" leave. Fonda's just sick of dragging nine people across
kingdom come in a raggedy-ass truck. He's baling out and serving up this
shitty speech to Mama Joad because he can't leave unless it's dignified and
it sounds pretty. He can't call what they do "beggin," or "stealin leftovers,"
he's gotta call it "gleaning." Like givin it a name out of King James makes
the whole thing fly. It's his pretending there's something noble about it all
that I hate. I have to turn my face from all he's saying, cause they're my
words and somebody's already used them up and beat me to it. Mama Joad
hates it too. She says "Tommy, we ain't the kissin kind, but come here and
kiss me." When she turns her face away from him so he can kiss her cheek,
she looks right through me and I have to shut my eyes.

Ruth is gliding toward Boaz while Bullet hits the play button.
They're loading a limp, sickly Rosa Sharon into the back of the truck
while Bullet scratches her big toe. I see her back. I see black and white
cut through her and I watch her fingers move against baby skin and it
makes my stomach hurt, just like it's full of grasshoppers. Just like Ruth's.
Inside a huge barn that smells like a promise this Moabite widow is
weaving a velvet harness. Bags of barley line the walls and bales of hay
and bins of corn stack nearly to the ceiling, but she's not afraid—

"You watchin, Levi? Your eyes are shut and it don't look like you're
watchin—"

I crack my eyes and mumble, "Yeah, Ruth, I'm watchin," before I can
stop myself but Bullet missed it and rolls over again and when she does
her skirt rides up and I see a scar on the backside of her knee, white and
grown over, like she cut herself shaving. I shut my eyes and go back to
the threshing room. I stretch my arm over my head and make a point of
relaxing my fingers, just like a baby's, just like Boaz's.

—She's lowering herself to the floor. First one knee, then the other.
She tucks her feet wearing enormous red shoes under her bottom and
reaches out like a timid nymph and pulls at his covering. While she

uncovers her kinsman, she prays for coolness and this time she lets herself cry. She frees those grasshoppers once and for all. But her last thought before she falls into her dream is of what she has left, who she has left. Ruth turns her head toward Bethlehemjudah because she knows a woman is standing alone in a shadow, crying against an open window, and she wishes she could comfort her and thank her for her insight and tell her one more time that she don't mind doing this thing—

The bed bounces and my head bumps the wall.

"Well, whaddya think? Wasn't it great?" Bullet's double question is softer this time, not so bossy as before.

* *

Earlier in the day, right after I got back from the barbershop, she pulled me into her room and showed me pictures she dug up from the library archives down on Government Street, Dust Bowl death pictures from *Life* magazine. Sure enough there we were. Gaunt. Tense. Tired. She fanned them out on her bed and pointed, excited. "Do you see it, Levi? I swear. I wonder if y'all might be time travelers or something. Jeezus!"

One picture showed a room with a single bulb and newspaper on the wall. Four babies were piled on a bed wearing snotty noses and caked eyes that ain't seen nothing but hard times and wantin. Their mother had her legs crossed trying to look proper for this queer camera and this strange man who wanted to take her picture. The cut of her chin looked just like Mama's and I can't help wondering if the man taking the picture bothered to pay them for their trouble or if he just snapped it and flew out the door, on the prowl for the pitiful.

Bullet had her arms crossed, smiling, pleased as punch with her discovery.

Another picture showed a man standing by a truck. The man's chest was caving in on itself, he held his hat in his hands, and his face looked like a picked-over field.

I felt the vomit coming up into my throat while I stormed toward her pink door, throwing it open, knocking her Aladdin curtains clean out of the Sheetrock. Buzz was out there in the sunlight next to the swimming pool eating some banana pudding Mama whipped up in the motel's restaurant. She talked about those big stainless steel pots and deep sinks for most of an hour last night. I said over my shoulder in a strangled, Daddy-sounding voice, "If we'd wanted a mirror, Bullet, we would've asked for one."

Buzz was staring with meringue on his wide-open mouth as I ran past him through the parking lot and straight across the two-lane into the field by the raceway. While the Butterfingers man finished the interview Jesse's death interrupted, I stood in tall grass underneath a red car dangling from a crane and cried like a baby.

* *

I'm over it now. That was four hours earlier when I was still sitting at the gate of the city like an old soldier, sniffing the air and dreaming. Tonight's full of queer changes and not wantin it to be so don't mean it ain't gonna happen. I know this now. There are other things, too. I know I ain't Boaz and I know Bullet ain't Ruth and I know God ain't never heard a damn word anybody's said.

She's watching me, waiting for an answer to whatever she asked me a few seconds earlier.

"I think tomorrow's gonna be a long day, Bullet, and I need some sleep."

We've decided to bury Jesse with the Catholics, in sacred ground next to a trio of pine trees. Back beyond their cemetery is a covered picnic area and an outdoor shower and a basketball court with not-too-bad asphalt.

There's new clothes from Stein Mart for all of us, and Daddy has himself a new pair of shoes, black wingtips, the kind like a preacher might wear. Buzz says there's work for Mama here at the Star Lite if she wants it. Seems those truckers want the restaurant fired up and running again and damn! your mama sure can cook. And the raceway needs a good, steady wizard with a wrench and Daddy seems able to wear that hat, for a while at least, till his lungs give out. It seems we're set, thanks to Bullet and the local news.

I'm suddenly embarrassed because I'm in her room close to tears for the second time in one day and I'm sick to death of smelling strawberries. I stand up and turn to straighten her pillows out of politeness, and feel a hand at my waist, behind me, a strange hand, a kinsman redeemer hand.

"I like the way your daddy reads, Levi. I wish you'd finish that story."

For a second, I'm frozen, lost, then her hand is up underneath my shirt rubbing my side and I swear to Jesus I think I'm having a heart attack.

I turn to her, reaching for her hand to move it away, and accidentally touch the front of her shirt. "Bullet. Don't. I can't."

"Why not? 'Cause Jesse's dead?"

When I look down at her I see a piece of popcorn glued to her lip, a tiny piece that looks big as the sky. Ruth would've wiped her mouth. I know this, but Bullet's hand, warm and moving in circular motions, is up near my left nipple saying things, reading a new story to me that's chasing Ruth clean out of the barn.

I've never kissed a girl and I don't want to kiss this one but I can't help it. The TV's gone dark and grainy, and the static sounds like a storm in my ears. Through a break in her Aladdin curtains I watch the motel sign sputter and blink, and even though I know my brother died there, just days ago, I can't help but kiss her. And that's not all I want to do, either. I want to reach down inside where Ruth lives with Boaz. I want to crawl onto that threshing room floor and praise Naomi for her insight. I want to travel to a strange land where colors run hot and old men really do sit at the gate of the city and smile because sometimes they get to see them. I want to do these things and this is what I'm thinking while I watch my hands, like strangers, pull up her blouse and touch her breasts and sweep up alongside her neck, searching for those fine, baby hairs. I'm willing myself not to cry, but that's just one more thing that I can't help.

Left Behind

Frank Turner Hollon

Edward Tuttle sat perfectly still in the chair on the wooden porch behind his trailer. It was a warm morning, and the sixty-three-year-old man wore a light blue terrycloth robe and brown bedroom slippers. He leaned forward slightly in the chair with his right arm cocked, holding a hammer, the metal resting lightly against his unshaven cheek. The small black-and-white cat peered from her place beside the wheel of the trailer. A bowl of cat food waited at the old man's feet.

Three months earlier Deloris Tuttle had packed her shit and left. For thirty-three years she had awakened every morning in Edward's bed, but when the time came to make the decision to leave, she was unnaturally swift. In less than one hour she was completely gone—clothes, kitchen utensils, photographs, and twelve of her thirteen cats, in the car, out the driveway, gone away. As he watched his wife gather her possessions, Edward felt as though he were watching a television show. At the end he actually said, "Don't let the door hit you in the ass on the way out." He said it too late. Deloris Tuttle was already gone.

She'd left before, but this time was different. This time she took the cats. Through the years, no matter where they moved, or what financial crisis they faced, there was one constant. The cats. They were always there, underfoot, swarming across the kitchen floor. A choking cloud of cat urine hovered around their home. And hair. Cat hair. Everywhere. Edward could rub his hand across the couch and fill his fingers full.

A cat door was installed. The beasts came and went as they pleased, their pink noses high in the air, with the never-ending ungodly whining. For years Edward tried to round up the females and have them fixed in a futile effort to control the sheer numbers. It couldn't be done. New cats would appear, breed, and then disappear. One time, many years earlier, when Deloris had left him on Christmas Eve, Edward had loaded the cats in the trunk of the car and dropped them two miles away at Stilton's barn. The next morning, Christmas Day, one by one the cats returned, and later that night, so did Deloris. This time was different though. This time she took her cats away with her. Except for one: black and white, skinny, about half-grown, somehow left behind.

On the first day Edward chased the frightened creature across the yard with his shovel, but the cat managed to escape. Each night the cat would sit alone on the back porch completely quiet, waiting for food. Edward watched her curiously through the window of the back door. It was a standoff. Some evenings he would sit outside and call the little cat to him. She would stand away, coy, stepping forward and then back again, Edward's fingers allowed to brush the fur lightly before the cat would circle away, lie down, and flick her white-tipped tail.

The phone never rang. Edward would pick it up from time to time and make sure it still had a dial tone. The days passed, and Edward Tuttle imagined his wife, head held high, fixing her hair in another man's mirror. He pretended to enjoy his freedom from the constant complaining, the roar of the vacuum, the stink of cats. She had taken every hairbrush, every bottle of shampoo. At night, lying alone in bed, Edward had to struggle against the feeling that Deloris was in the next room and would come to bed soon, like always. Anger and loneliness combined to form a new, completely separate, emotion.

On one certain day, without giving it much thought, Edward threw a chicken bone out the back door to the starving cat. He watched the cat crunch the bone, gnawing the marrow and gristle, not leaving a single morsel behind, nothing. After that, sometimes he would toss out a biscuit or a handful of Cheetos.

In the back of the refrigerator Edward found an old mayonnaise jar half-full of leftover brown gravy. He unscrewed the top, knelt down at the door, and rolled the open jar across the wooden back porch towards the hungry little cat. The cat was cautious, watching the jar and Edward at the same time, until it came to a stop a few feet away and the smell of the jellied gravy was too much temptation. She sniffed the opening, hesitated, and then shoved her muzzle into the jar, ears folded tightly back, lapping at the gravy. Eventually the cat's entire head was inside, tongue stretching for the farthest taste, until the glass was licked clean. And then the trouble began. The cat's head was trapped. It had gone inside easily enough, seeking the sweet taste of brown gravy, but now it wouldn't come out. Edward watched from the door. The cat panicked and then stopped, dead still. She could see Edward through the glass jar step forward onto the porch. The cat swung her head wildly, spinning backwards, with the jar crashing against a cement cinder block on the edge of the porch. The glass exploded leaving a jagged collar around her neck as she darted away to the safety of the wheel of the trailer. The sharp edges of the glass cut the skin under her chin and behind the ears. Edward stood in his pajamas, cigarette hanging between his fingers, his arms limp. He tried to figure out how he felt about what he had just seen.

When the coast was clear, the pitiful cat eventually came back to the porch. Edward stood at the back door, and they stared at each other in total silence. Blood trickled from the cuts and scratches around the cat's neck, fresh red and matted, but she sat anyway, and waited for something. Edward Tuttle smoked his cigarette and wondered how he ever ended up in such a place staring at a goddamned cat with a jagged glass collar. He listened for the sound of a car coming up the dirt driveway, but there was nothing. No one was coming.

The next morning, early, Edward Tuttle positioned his chair in the middle of the porch. At his feet he placed a fresh bowl of cat food, and in his hand he held a hammer. It was a warm morning. He knew what a hammer could do. Edward concentrated on remaining still, feet wide apart on either side of the bowl, hammer raised at exactly the right angle. The cat watched from her spot by the tire, smelling the food on the porch, seeing the old man in his light blue terrycloth robe and brown slippers, sitting without motion in a chair. She stepped forward, stretching, with an ache in her empty belly and a burning sensation under her chin. Closer she came, and closer, smelling the fishy cat food, watching the man, until hunger overcame fear and the cat found herself face down crunching big mouthfuls. Edward steadied himself, drew his aim in his mind, and swung the hammer downward with the necessary force, eyes square on the target. It was the first thing he felt good about since the day that bitch walked out the door. Edward stood, flung the hammer in the yard, and walked inside the trailer.

The Last Days

Silas House

Evans.

For the second time in his life, Evans had been taken from his home in the middle of the night. The first time he had not awakened until he was in a different state, with a different last name. Even his mother was changed in such a way that he did not recognize her at first, her face distinctly more flat and square, as if life had simply hissed out and made her a deflated thing.

This time he awoke shortly after she packed him out to the car. He was seven now, and too big for her to carry easily. She had a hard time opening the car door with him in her arms, so he woke up. He drifted in that place between sleep and awareness for a moment before sitting up and realizing that they were in a car, going down the interstate. Tall, skinny streetlights made stripes of silver slide around in the car for a time, then suddenly the road was black and desolate. They passed no other cars, only an occasional eighteen-wheeler. He saw no signs of houses or stores or any light at all.

"Where we going?" he asked.

"Home," his mother, Nadine, said. She was sitting up very straight, as if giving an example of perfect posture. Her hands clung to the steering wheel. The only things that moved about her were her lips with the single word. She did not even blink.

"But we're going the wrong way," Evans said.

"Back to where we come from," Nadine said. "Our real home."

"How long we staying?"

"From now on," she said, and only then did she reach her hand out. She tousled his hair, the way he had seen television mothers do when a television child scored a home run or presented an excellent report card. In the brief light from an oncoming semi, he saw that she was wearing makeup. He had never seen her with it on before. Nadine always worked and took care of him. This was all she ever did, and never took the time to fix up. He could not remember ever being away from her—they were always together, every minute of every day.

"I like it here, though," Evans said. He was used to his mother making sudden decisions—they had moved six times in the last three years—but this was the first time she had not told him first. Except for that very first time, which he could barely remember anyway. His father had been mean to them and they had left. They had to hide from him. That's what his mother had told him, the one time he had asked.

"I know you like it, but—"

"For good? Forever?" Evans said. His window was rolled down and the wind whistled in hot and loud. He rolled it up so roughly that the glass clattered against the door. "I don't want to move again."

"Well, I'm sorry, baby." She put her hand atop his, but he pulled away. "Sometimes things don't seem fair. I know all about that."

Nadine.

Since stealing her baby away, Nadine had had amazing luck finding work at motels. She thought working in motels was the best possible plan for someone in hiding. People you saw at motels were traveling, on the go, in too big a hurry to notice a woman and her little boy. They would not be around long enough to memorize the faces of Nadine or Evans. They would not connect them to posters that were in the interstate rest stops or pictures that were on those little cards that came with the grocery papers every Tuesday.

Nadine and Evans had appeared on one of those cards not two months ago. Below the caption *Can You Help Find Me?* there was a picture of Evans looking surprised and full of questions. What upset Nadine most about the picture was not the fear of being caught, but the fact that she had been the one who had taken the picture in the first place. Now it was being used against her. Her ex-husband, Robert, would have laughed at the idea of picking up a camera to preserve a memory.

She thought a lot about the day she had taken that picture. It was a memory that bordered on obsession. The freedom of that day, the white light, the clean smell of air and laundry on the line, the way their legs had taken great strides, their hands pushing against the air as they walked. Evans had been three years old, and she had taken him up on the ridge for a walk. She was always taking pictures of him, as if some part of her knew that he would someday be taken away from her. That day Evans had snatched up a dried dandelion and blew the fluff away. Just as he had brought the stem down to his side and looked up at her, she had snapped the picture. "That boy is all eyes," Nadine's mother-in-law, Evelyn, had said upon looking at the picture. And it was true. Even then he had seemed too old for his age. His face had shown that of a baby, but those big eyes possessed a secret knowledge.

God, the memory of that day haunted her. She often thought that if she hadn't taken that picture, they couldn't have used it in the missing persons posters. This was ridiculous, of course. They would have used any photo available, but this particular picture was perfect. Evans' inquisitive gaze would make anyone want to help find him, to keep him from danger.

When she found the missing persons card in the motel mail, she looked at it for a long time. She folded it in half and carried it in her pocket for most of the day so that she could pull it out and study it occasionally. That evening, she burned it in the ashtray on the desk of the motel office.

It wasn't being caught that bothered her so much. And it wasn't just that she had taken the picture. Being made out to be the bad guy was what burned her up. She was the kidnapper, the crazy mother. People would say she took her child just to spite his father, things like that. She couldn't stand the thought of Evans thinking she was a bad person. If she did get caught, that would be the hardest thing. Not going on trial or being put in prison, but having Evans think that she was in the wrong.

After taking Evans, Nadine had started out being a motel maid. Her plan was to travel to every busy tourist spot in America until Robert either stopped looking for them (he wasn't very determined, but he was malevolent enough not to give up easily) or until she knew that it was safe to stop running.

First she had gone to Myrtle Beach. She had never seen the ocean, and when she finally did, she was disappointed. When she stood on the beach and looked out at the black water, she felt nothing but fear. The water came in and went out, in and out, a redundant act that reminded her of how all things can become trapped. She did not even take a job there because she knew she could not stand the salt air, the beautiful people in their yellow swimsuits, the old men with their white legs and black socks.

Next she went to Georgia and found work at a motel near the Six Flags theme park. The manager agreed to trade her work for a room. It was easy to talk people into this kind of arrangement. She slowly realized that it had more to do with fooling the IRS than simple compassion. She felt the need to move on quickly and went on to Orlando, but she couldn't stand it there, either. The heat made tourists mean and they were so drained by Disney that they never left a tip.

They stayed longest at Biloxi, where she became a manager in a small motel that claimed to be the only one right on the beach. She liked the Gulf—it was a good mix of strangeness and familiarity. The water was unbelievably big, yet there on the Mississippi coast, behind a string of barrier islands, there were no tides and very few waves, so that it almost seemed like a huge lake.

At night Nadine and Evans sat in the courtyard by the pool, or went down to the pier and sat with their feet hanging off the edge. There was a casino just down the beach that was always lit in purple lights. It was in the shape of a pirate ship and seemed eerie and foreign. Sometimes they could hear the laughter of drunks stumbling out of the casino.

She felt safe in Biloxi, where there were mostly men on gambling sprees who were too absorbed in their sweaty worlds to notice kidnapping bulletins or a woman who neither wore lipstick nor smiled in a sly way. But she and Evans had to leave Biloxi after Nadine saw somebody from home, a doctor from Black Banks who was in town for gambling and anonymity, as he was having an affair with his short, owly receptionist. She didn't think either of them had seen her, but she packed up and left an hour after they came in and rented a room.

They made a short stop in New Orleans—which seemed like great madness to her—and then to Memphis. She worked for a time in a big hotel near the river. The Mississippi was so wide it amazed her. The river inexplicably smelled of rotten watermelon. Her coworkers kept telling her she needed to go down to Beale Street but when she did she didn't stay long, as it was no place for Evans. There were boys who did back flips all the way down the street and a woman who breastfed her child while she read fortunes on the sidewalk. There were all manners of drunks and protesters, and people on the tops of buildings waving American flags, as the war had just started.

For reasons she could not name, she kept moving until they got to Nashville. They had stayed in Nashville now for nearly six months. Nashville was actually quite close to home, but it happened to be one of those cities which people from her home region shunned—in the mountains where she came from, people were so surrounded by country music that they certainly did not want to vacation in its capital.

Now they were leaving Nashville and it was beginning to rain. Evans had fallen back to sleep. He was like his father in this regard—he could awaken, carry on a whole conversation, and then simply fall back into dreams in an instant. Nadine herself could sit up for two days without getting sleepy. She had done it plenty of times. Tired, yes—she stayed tired—but never sleepy. Sleep was too still and wasteful for her. She had to use every moment she was given to learn how to keep her child.

At least she once had. Now she was taking him back home. She would have to face her ex-husband and his family. She had to give her baby back and she would most likely never see him again. She kept driving.

When full morning came, it bloomed like an impossibly perfect summer day. Nadine rolled down all of the windows and memorized the day. She breathed it in very deeply, letting her eyes linger on everything they passed. She tried to think of what all she would want to file away if she were dying. She took in the sky, the soft movement of the trees, the rise and fall of Evans' chest.

Evans awoke hungry, as always. When they got to Knoxville, she stopped at a restaurant just off the interstate. In the parking lot, she felt absolutely free at her realization that she didn't have to eye everyone with suspicion now. She didn't have to search faces for signs of recognition or curiosity. She didn't have to dread the newspaper stand, expecting to see herself on the front page, above the fold. She was on her way home, and she didn't have to hide anymore.

When they had ordered their food, Nadine put both hands around her coffee cup and sat that way for a long time, as if she needed warming. She studied Evans as he walked back from the bathroom. She looked at the way he held his shoulders high, the cowlick caused by his double crowns. She stared at his hands, which seemed fitting for an adult, even though they weren't particularly large. When he saw that she was looking at him, he smiled sheepishly. In that moment she saw the man that he would become and felt certain that she would never get to know him. She took a long drink of the coffee to keep from crying or screaming—she didn't know which she wanted to do the most.

"I want to know why we're leaving," he said as he sat down.

"I told you, honey. It's time for us to go home."

"But it's not my home," he said. "I don't remember nothing about it."

Her palms were clammy and she wiped them on the lap of her skirt. "Well, you were just turned four when we left."

Evans stared at her, as if he expected her to say more. A whole crew of teenagers filed into the restaurant, noisy and full of movement, but he didn't even turn to look at them.

"Do you remember your daddy at all?"

"He smoked," Evans said, as if this recollection had just come to him. "And he was mean to us."

Nadine leaned across the table as if she didn't want anyone to hear. The act of hiding in public was a habit now, and hard to break. "What makes you say that?"

"You told me."

"I didn't," she said, but she wasn't sure. Those days just after they ran off were a blur—a wild mess of images and loud voices. She could not even remember driving to Atlanta. It seemed that she simply left the house and suddenly arrived in Georgia. "Did I?"

"You said that he was mean to us and you couldn't let me stay there."

Robert had not been mean to them in the way she could explain to people in a courtroom. He had not beaten them or forced them to do anything wrong, but he had terrified her. He had never even raised his voice to Evans, never drawn his hand back to slap him, but still, he frightened Nadine in a way that she found impossible to articulate.

Shortly after they had married, a puppy started hanging around their house and eventually Nadine began to feed it and play with it. One evening when Robert came home from work, she was sitting on the porch with the dog in her lap. She had stroked its fur so long it had folded itself up on her legs and fallen to sleep. Robert bounded across the porch, taking great steps like a man stepping over rows of beans in a garden, snatched the puppy from her hands, and held it by the nape of its neck. The puppy's eyes popped open and it began to whine quietly.

Robert didn't say a word, which scared her all the more. He stood there, holding the puppy straight out.

She tried to get the dog away from him, reaching out, begging to him, but he kept pulling it back. Finally, he took it by the neck and stran-. gled it. It did not take long to die.

He would not even let her go anywhere with her own brother, whom she had always been very close to before her marriage. Robert had been completely consumed by this quiet sort of madness, so much so that when she became pregnant, she was afraid that he would envy the baby any affection she showed it. But when Evans was born, Robert did not react the way she had thought. Instead of being jealous, he took over. When the baby awoke in the middle of the night, he wouldn't let her go to Evans. He ran to the nursery and rocked him back to sleep. He held Evans on his knee while they ate supper. He refused to let Nadine bathe him or carry him when they went anywhere. He would not allow her to be close to her own child.

She had not been able to explain to anyone why she had left him. There was too much to spell out. When she decided to leave him, she should have known that he would take Evans from her. Robert's father was the county judge, and in a town as small as Black Banks, this meant he had huge connections. They went to court and Robert won full custody. She was given supervised visits. That was all there was to it and there was nothing she could do.

One night when Robert's mother was watching Evans, Nadine went to the old woman's house. When Evelyn opened the door, Nadine pulled out a little .22 revolver. "I want my baby. Right now, Evelyn," she said.

Evelyn tried to fight her, but she was too old. Nadine pushed her down—breaking her hip, Nadine would later find out in the paper. Nadine went into Evans' room very quietly. She gathered him up, wrapped a quilt around him, and drove away for what she thought was forever.

She felt awful about hurting Evelyn—her mother-in-law had always been good to her, and was the only who tried to talk Robert out of taking Evans from her. A month after arriving in Atlanta, Nadine drove three hours to Montgomery, Alabama, just to mail a letter to Evelyn. It read: "I didn't mean to hurt you. Please forgive me."

The waitress slammed their food down onto the table, apologizing all the while. The group of teenagers had only been a prelude—a school bus had stopped at the restaurant and now it was full. All the waitresses and cooks were running about as if a bomb had just been dropped.

"I shouldn't have told you that," Nadine said. "Your daddy loved you. He never was mean to you, but he does have problems, Evans."

She wanted to explain everything to Evans, but he was only seven years old. She couldn't even get her own best friend to understand, so she didn't know a way to tell Evans.

"You're going to be living with him now," she said. The words seemed to hang in front of her face after they escaped her mouth, pulsating and hovering on the air. "I'm taking you back there."

"We're all going to be together, then?" Evans said. There was neither delight nor disapproval in his voice.

"No, you'll be living with your daddy. And your granny. She'll be good to you."

"But what about you?" Evans laid his hands flat on the table. The eyes from the missing persons photograph burned into her face.

Nadine glanced down at her plate and knew that she could not eat. "You'll see me every once in a while. We just won't be together all the time."

Evans didn't say any more, and ate everything on his plate.

EVANS.

Evans had come to know that his mother had kidnapped him. He even knew why she was taking him back.

The day before they left Nashville, he made a friend at the motel swimming pool. He was a boy about Evans' age and they swam and played together all day long. Evans was fascinated by the boy's nasal, Northern way of speaking. Nadine watched from her little plastic chair that sat right outside the office door. The boy's mother watched with one eye over her Danielle Steel novel.

When the boy's mother said it was time to go in, the boy begged for Evans to come along. They were going to the putt-putt course across the street. It was a great, monstrous thing with fiberglass dinosaurs and food-coloring waterfalls.

"It's fine if he wants to," the woman said, lighting an abnormally long cigarette. "They play so well together. I'll keep an eye on him."

"No," Nadine said, too loudly.

Evans jumped at the sound of her voice. He had never heard this tone before. The woman flicked her ash into the swimming pool. "I certainly didn't mean to offend you," she said.

"No, no, it's fine," Nadine said, putting her hands on Evans' shoulders and steering him toward the office. "I'm sorry," she said, looking back. "He just can't go. It was nice to meet you all, though."

Nadine sat down then and put her elbows on her desk, her face in her hands. He didn't ask why he couldn't go because he knew. The same reason they had to be very careful all the time. The same reason he was only allowed to play in the pool when there was hardly anyone else around. The same reason Nadine had a boy from the grocery deliver what they needed.

She was taking him back because she wanted him to live. Neither of them had been doing that in the last three years.

NADINE.

Upon leaving Knoxville, Nadine realized that she could not take Evans back home today. Home was only two hours away, but she did not possess the power to do it. She needed a little more time. Maybe if she just drove on toward home, someone would see her and the law would pull her over and she wouldn't even have to take him back. They would take him instead.

"I'm going to take you to where I was raised before we go back to Black Banks," Nadine said when they crossed the state line.

"Where's that?"

"The town before Black Banks."

When Nadine turned onto the main street of the town, she said, "Lord, there ain't nothing here no more." Then she realized that there never had been anything in this place. When she was a child, it had only seemed that there was existence here. But it was nothing more than a post office and a little store, a bank that was housed in a mobile home and two cigarette stores with neon lights in the windows.

She turned from street to street without thinking. She turned onto country lanes and finally a long dirt driveway that was flanked by pine trees that her father had planted.

Halfway down the driveway, she put the car in park, but left it running. The sun was high in the top of the sky and heat bugs were screaming. The car's air-conditioning pushed out a steady stream of cool air that made no real impact.

"Let's get out, Evans," she said, and opened her door. "I want to walk up to where the house sat."

The driveway was rutted with twin ditches now that all the gravel had been washed away. Instead of walking up the drive, she took Evans' hand and led him through a pine thicket. The air was heavy and damp here, like sweat hanging from the sky. It seemed to her that there had once been coolness beneath the pines, but it was not present on this day.

She was incredibly aware of the presence of Evans's hand in her own and longed to just squat down and put his palm to her face.

The thicket abruptly opened onto the wide field. It was high with grass gone to seed. There were wildflowers that Nadine could not name, but they were dulled in the heat and harsh light and gave no color.

"See way up there?" she said, pointing with her free hand. There was nothing to see but more of the field. It ran for yards and yards until it met a steep hillside populated by straight white trees. "Our house sat up there."

"What happened to it?" Evans asked quietly.

"It burnt down when I was in high school. A heater turned over and burned it down. My daddy died in the fire, and that's why I had to move to Black Banks, to live with my aunt."

"You had plenty of room to play," he said.

She looked down at him and felt sick. The world shifted and blurred and then through the numbness she willed herself into a state of clarity.

"I did," she said. "I used to run these fields all day long. Daddy took a bush-hog to them back then. It was an all-day job, every other week. Sometimes he let me ride on the tractor. I'd sit there with him forever. Too much noise to talk, just watching. I had a good daddy."

A scattering of crows flew overhead, heckling and cawing. Their shadows ran over Nadine and Evans. The birds descended upon the field in a noisy racket and disappeared in the high grass near the house-seat.

Nadine put her arm around Evans' shoulders and caught his earlobe between her fingers. He had always liked this, and giggled softly against her side. She let him go and slowly began to turn round and round in the great field, the way she had done as a child.

"When we get home, you'll remember our yard," she said, stretching her arms out. "There's a ridge round back. It's a hard climb but once you get there, you can look down at all the little houses." Her words went loud, then soft with each revolution she made. "You can watch people without them knowing. The woods are clear and you can run there. You can spin around, like this."

As a child, she had spun and then let herself fall onto the ground, the way people make snow angels. She did this now, giving herself to gravity. It didn't hurt when her back met the earth with all her weight. She put her hands on her belly and laughed uncontrollably. An observer might have thought her insane.

Evans squatted down next to her, smiling.

"That's the best thing about being little," she said. Behind him the sky was a cloudless blue. "Running. Spinning around. I hope you always do that."

EVANS.

He watched his mother as they entered Black Banks. She kept her head busy, looking at everyone they passed. When they got into town, she looked at the people walking down the sidewalks and those sitting in the cars next to them at stoplights. When a police cruiser went slowly by, she did not flinch.

It was nearing dusk, but it was a summer evening and everyone was out. Twilight gave some comfort and it seemed that everybody had come out onto their porches or walked down the road to enjoy the dampness settling itself out over the valley. As it began to get dark, Evans watched children catching lightning bugs in their yards. It seemed that every other house they passed had a whole gang of kids scampering around the yard, trying to find light on the graying air. Their legs were all very long and tan, unlike his.

His mother took him to her homeplace, her high school, the restaurant where she had had her first job. In Black Banks she pointed to the movie theater where she had first gone out on a date with his father. She told him the name of the movie that had been showing that night, but he had never heard of it.

She drove up a high black mountain to the hospital where he had been born. There was a statue of Jesus in the parking lot, his arms stretched out over the length of three or four cars. Nadine said on clear nights you could see Jesus all lit up on Hospital Hill from the road that wound around the mountains across the valley. Sitting in the parking lot, she told him all about the night he was born.

Evans listened to her closely. He took in each word as if it were a bit of air he might use later when breathing became scarce. He liked to hear her talk. He liked the way she talked about these things, especially. The way she told about how it felt when she gave birth to him, the feelings she had when he was first put into her arms. When she talked about this, there was a look on her face that he had never seen before. He liked seeing her like this. Her smile seemed to change everything about her: it gave her eyes a new sort of beauty and her voice a tenderness he had not heard in a long while.

Now she was talking about when he was little. All the special things he had done, things she had dog-eared and kept for herself. It was dark now.

"Let's roll down all the windows and just drive," she said. "All right?"

He cranked down his window and the air came in moist and cool when they passed under the mountains. He could smell separately the river and honeysuckle and the leaves of all the trees. He was not used to these scents, but she named them all to him. Summer smelled different here.

It had been a long day. He undid his seat belt without asking and stretched himself out on the seat. He put his head into her lap. She put her hand on his head and stroked his hair, keeping her eyes set on the winding road. Before long, he went to sleep with all the new smells on his face, her hand upon his head.

NADINE.

She watched Evans awaken. A flutter of eyelashes, a short-limbed stretch. A yawn, and then his big eyes came open slowly.

She had not slept. She had pulled over on the side of the road and sat there with his head in her lap all night. She had not cried, either. She had not allowed herself this pleasure because she was afraid that she wouldn't be able to stop. There hadn't been much traffic and no one had stopped to see why she was sitting on the shoulder of the highway. She had looked away from Evans only long enough to see daylight melt onto the sky.

"Where we at?" Evans said. "Did we sleep in the car?"

"I couldn't stand to spend another night in a motel," she said. "You slept good, though, didn't you? Like the dead."

"I'm hungry," he said. These were his usual first words of the day.

"I'll get you something to eat as soon as I make a phone call," she said.

She started the car and drove back toward town. At the first gas station, she pulled into the parking lot and got out at a payphone. The station had just opened. Miners and factory workers were stopping for cigarettes and coffee. No one even glanced at her. In the wide plate-glass windows of the station, amongst the big American flag and the signs announcing the lottery, she saw a faded rectangular placard that bore a picture of herself and Evans. Across the top it read ABDUCTED.

She picked up the receiver and dialed Evelyn's number. It was answered on the first ring. "Hello," Evelyn said loudly, as if aggravated.

"Evelyn, it's me."

In the long silence that followed, Nadine could picture her former mother-in-law sitting at her kitchen table before a steaming cup of coffee. Bacon was probably frying on the stove. Evelyn's house was always warm and smelled of grease and lemon Joy.

"Nadine? My Lord."

"I'm home. In Black Banks. Robert ain't there, is he?"

"He's done gone to work," Evelyn said. Her voice was shaky. She had already started crying.

"Listen to me, now. I've brought Evans back. I can't let him live this way. Hiding out. I'm going to give him back, but you have to promise me something. I know your word is good."

"Anything, Nadine," Evelyn said. "You know I always loved you like my own. I'd give anything in this world if all this hadn't happened. But I'm just stuck in the middle—"

"Evelyn, I want you to promise me that you'll raise Evans. You know well as I do that Robert ain't fit to. I've messed up. Bad. I know that. If I hadn't run off, maybe I could have got him back eventually. But they'll put me in jail. I know that, and I'm trusting you with my baby."

Evelyn broke down crying. She couldn't speak. Nadine could picture her great bosom heaving, her large arms jiggling beneath the thin sleeves of her housedress.

"I'll bring him there and leave him with you. Then I'm going to go to the police and serve my time until I can get back to him. But don't call Robert. I can't bear seeing him. You know it'll all lead to trouble. Let me get gone first."

"I promise it, Nadine."

"I'll be there in ten minutes." She held on to the receiver a long time after hanging up the phone. She felt unsure of her legs, and rushed back to the car, where she sat down behind the steering wheel and breathed as if she had just run for miles.

The girl at the Dairy Queen eyed Nadine when she pulled up to the drive-through. She was just a shadow of a girl, not more than sixteen, with brown liner around her maple-colored lips and a ponytail pulled up so tightly that her eyes rose at the corners like teardrops. Nadine could see that the girl dimly recognized her. The realization would hit the girl as soon as she handed Nadine the bag of food. She would probably start hollering for the manager.

Nadine drove away fast while Evans devoured his BLT.

Evelyn's house had not changed, of course. It still sat in the curve of the road, tucked in a U-shaped bend of the river. Willows stood in the yard. Nadine drove over the rickety bridge and turned off the car. She saw Evelyn step out onto the porch, wringing her hands.

"Evans, do you see that woman?"

"Why yeah," he said.

"Do you remember her?"

Evans studied Evelyn a moment as she stood there on the porch, peering out at the car like she didn't know who it was. Evelyn looked as if she wanted to jump off the porch and run down to them.

"It's my mamaw," he said, and then his whole body changed. He seemed to crumble in on himself. His eyes spoke before his mouth. "Don't leave me here. I want to go with you."

"Evans, please don't do this. You have to stay with her, now. She loves you better than anything. You'll see me in a day or two."

"Where you going?"

Nadine had nothing but the truth. She was denying herself grief—she wanted to scream, to cry, to pull her hair out by handfuls and watch it float down in front of her. She didn't know what else to do except be honest. "I'll be in jail, Evans. I broke the law, but it'll all work out. It'll be all right in the end. I promise you that."

"I want to go with you."

"Do this for me, now," she said. She was aware of time running out. There was no time for a long, drawn-out goodbye now. She had spent these last days doing that, and that was enough. It would have to be. "Stay here with your mamaw."

Nadine watched him for a moment. He was going to do as she asked. He had always been so cooperative, always so eager to please her. She had to force herself to move. It seemed opening the car door was a great act, like lifting the entire vehicle. She had to lean against the car as she made her way around to get Evans out. She put him on her hip. His legs dangled to the backs of her knees, but she held him very close, the way she had always done when she had been alone with him at home, when Robert wasn't there to take him from her. She put her hand on the back of his neck and he laid his head on her shoulder.

Evelyn stepped close to the edge of the porch. "Thank the Lord!" she cried, and Nadine felt a momentary urge to slap her face.

Nadine let out blocks of breath as she spoke, the way a child will do after crying for a long time. "Take good care of him, Evelyn."

Evelyn nodded her head furiously. She ran her hands up and down her crossed arms as if her fingers ached to touch Evans.

Nadine put him down on the porch. Although he had always seemed so much more grown up than other children his age, now she was intensely aware of his smallness. He shoved his hands into his pockets and looked at Evelyn, then Nadine.

"Remember what I said," Nadine whispered. "And don't cry after me."

Evelyn reached her hand out. "Me and you are going to have a big time."

Nadine wanted to fall on her knees on the porch, pull him to her and tell him over and over how much she loved him. She wanted to kiss his face and say "Goodbye" aloud with each kiss. But she couldn't. She had to leave while she was still able to make her legs move.

She turned and scrambled down the steps. Before she got to the car, the state police cruisers came around the curve. Their blue lights were flashing but their sirens were silent. They roared across the bridge and parked haphazardly in the yard.

Nadine looked back at Evelyn, there on the porch, as if the house might offer some sanctuary.

"I never called them!" Evelyn cried. Her face was a great mess of confusion and sorrow.

"Get him in the house!" Nadine screamed. Her voice came from deep within, tearing at her throat. She watched with relief as Evelyn pulled him onto her hip and hustled into the house.

The state troopers actually had their guns drawn. Nadine was stunned by their seriousness. They hesitated behind the open doors of their clean, shining cars. There were five of them. All of them wore sunglasses and their shirts were perfectly pressed.

Nadine sank down in the yard and stretched her arms out straight in front of her, as if offering them to be handcuffed. The ground was damp beneath her knees and left watery mud on her bare kneecaps. Finally, she bowed her head and cried. The tears washed out of her with such force that she felt as if she had thrown up.

The policemen moved toward her with great caution, only putting away their pistols when they were close enough to touch. She knew the men felt her anguish spreading out across the yard.

When the first cop put his hand on her shoulder, she did not move. A large stillness came over her, as if she had been soothed by a mother's hand. She kept her head bowed and although none of them could decipher her voice through her grief, she spoke his name.

The Fall of the Nixon Administration

Suzanne Hudson

In light of my current situation with the law, I suppose it's a good thing I did not shoot Will Luckie in the back of the head when I had the chance. After all, if folks are going to get all tore up over the demise of a few pullets, then there surely would have been a mighty hue and cry over Will's departure from this life—even though he is no better than any of the yard fowl I exploded with my DD's—that's the Calhoun family abbreviation for "Dead Daddy's"—Remington Model 1100 12-gauge automatic. And I refuse to say otherwise, even if they put hot lights in my face, interrogate me for days on end, or attempt to beat any endearing words out of me. Will Luckie has single-handedly brought down the Calhouns and I will never forgive him.

First of all, you have to know that Will Luckie is a descendent of the mouth breathers who live out the Pipeline Road, where they pass their beer-ridden days hauling pulpwood, screwing one another's wives, and having an occasional trailer burning to collect enough insurance money to buy more beer and pulpwood trucks. He is through and through Florida Panhandle white trash—pure cair'n—and I have been subjected to his low-class ways ever since my mother took up with him. For one example among the myriad, he keeps a pouch of Beechnut in the front pocket of his double-knit shorts, which makes for a rather unnerving bulge that is, at best, in bad taste, and, at worst, just plain lewd. And he knows it. To be thoroughly honest, he rarely, if ever, wears underwear. I can safely say this because of the revealing nature of sand-colored double-knit; it just does not afford the barrier that, denim, say, does or heavy cotton. And when the heightened level of sexual arousal that has settled upon my mother's abode is thrown into the mix—well, let me just say that I am quite certain—and I apologize for being so graphic—but it is more than obvious that the smarmy little gigolo is not even circumcised.

Plus, he spits. He spits that stinking concoction between his index and third finger, pulling his lips taut and skeeting that mess out in high, arching streaks of amber. At present there are tobacco juice stains dotted across Mother's patios, in puddles next to the ornamental urns, down the back walkway that once wound so pleasantly among the pines, and all around the swimming pool where he passes the days sunning and sipping fruity drinks of gin bearing paper umbrellas. Hell, at this precise second three of mother's Waterford crystal tumblers hold a few ounces of that nauseating-looking, tobacco-infused saliva; I even found one of Grandma Lucie's sterling silver goblets perched on the toilet tank, floating those little black flecks across a phlegm-glazed surface of bubbly brown spit. I have told Will Luckie repeatedly how repugnant it looks. He laughs every time. "Tell it to Bob Haldeman," he says, laughing.

My God, how he laughs! He laughed when I told him to wear a shirt to Mother's sixty-first birthday luncheon last month. Knowing that the leading citizens of Pollard would be there, taking mental notes on the progress of Mother's debauched incapacitation. He laughed and said that if he was going to stand around the pool nibbling cocktail weenies with a bunch of tight-assed holy rollers, he had to be prepared to bail at any second. Thus, the aforementioned double-knit shorts (bathing suits do not occupy a place in his wardrobe). And the chest hair with those hideous gold chains garlanded in it like some kind of pornographic Christmas tree. And yes, he did at one point do a cannonball into the water, which soaked the fondue table and Mayor Burgess's wife Kathryn's silk skirt. It also soaked the famous nude shorts, which subsequently displayed yet another level of phallic information we did not require; the energy that went into avoiding eye contact with his vile, blue-veined interloper would be enough to fuel all the paper mills in this county. I have never been more mortified. That should show you how much he cares about making the right impression with influential people. Plus, he threatened to invite John and Martha Mitchell to the party to strew feathers hither and yon. Instead, he rounded up Charles Colson, his favorite, and, as an encore, proceeded to introduce him to the guests, all the while stroking him and making absurd little kissy noises at him.

The thing that absolutely stuns me is that people—even well-bred ones—seem to like him, up to a point, contrary to all personal moral codes, as they surely must object to his pulpwood ancestry and his flim-flamming of my mother. Maybe it is because he drags out that cheap guitar and sings country music with a disturbingly rich voice or tells those "humorous anecdotes" that always eventually descend into the blue depths of hard-core porn. Maybe it is that subtle layer of pansexuality that seems to intrigue both genders in spite of themselves. Maybe it is the Newman-blue eyes, the dimply smile or the lacquered-in-a-tan physique of one who has spent the past two decades in the Marine Corps. No matter. I consider him an idiot savant of a Svengali who tapped into Mother's sense of herself as a poet who should have lived the life of an artistic expatriate rather than "atrophying" here in Pollard. She never did appreciate her status.

Status. The state of us. There is the crux of it, as far as I am concerned. Mother has called me shallow, but civic responsibility should never, in my opinion, be taken for granted. You cannot fully appreciate this whole fiasco unless you understand that the Calhouns are one of the three most prominent families in Pollard, which is prominent in itself as the county seat. Because of this, and out of a sheer sense of civic duty, I am President of the Ladies' Club, parliamentarian of the DAR, Brownie scout troop leader at the Methodist Church, Sunday School class coordinator at the Baptist Church, and I would have beat out Bitsy Burgess, Kathryn's evil daughter, as president of the Daughters of the Confederacy if not for the shame of Will Luckie. As it is, I feel that my genetic destiny as a community leader has slipped; if I had chosen to do nothing it could have taken years to rebuild the family name. So I did something about it, albeit apparently too much to ever hope to repair the Calhoun name now. And Mother? Mother simply fails to care one whit about the shambled legacy she has foisted upon me.

You see, my DD's DD was a circuit judge who survived the Crash and three bouts of cancer before he died of age, and naturally he knew everybody and their legal business. My DD was a banker with the foresight to buy all the timberland and mineral rights he could get his hands on, so naturally he knew everybody's financial business. He was a philanderer and died of gallstones. My husband, Winston Dozier (though try as I might, I can only contextualize myself as a Calhoun), is a physician—the only one in town besides Dr. BobEddie, who is ancient—and he knows everybody's personal business so it does not matter that he is a tad prissy for a man. And my mother is from an extremely well regarded political family in Birmingham, Alabama. Did you know that right this second her brother is some Big Ike in the Nixon administration? And she acts like it is no big deal that the Nixon administration is falling into a mangled heap, running around like a bunch of decapitated biddies. So you see, she could know everybody's political business if she had the inclination. On top of that, it is said that she is the wealthiest woman in three counties, thanks to her DD and my DD. And what does she do, after just eight months of mourning my daddy? She takes herself a boyfriend twenty-two years and seven months her junior—making him four months younger than *me*—and sets all the town's tongues to wagging about my own family's familial business. Are you beginning to fathom why Will Luckie might be so intrigued with my withering up old mama? And why I have so much to lose?

Of course I have attempted to be fair where Will Luckie is concerned. It simply would not be Christ-like to do otherwise. I am the first to concede that Mother is not ordinary. She is a bit of an eccentric, as so many of the wealthy are, and she has always been fond of drama. She is not above pressing a palm to her chest or the back of a hand to her forehead and uttering plaintive little bleats of suffering peppered with curses. Mother can swear with the fluency of a wounded sailor. Of course, her dramas and her imminent death are all in her head. Dr. BobEddie has been giving her sugar pills for years. And me? Well, I am the devoted daughter, childless, without siblings, with only a limp-wristed Baptist husband to help with my mother and her shiftless little slut of a boyfriend. Now don't get me wrong—I heartily embrace my daughterly duties. Heaven knows, I have never failed to be at her side when she was mid-crisis, even throughout the hypochondriacal frenzy of her golden years, living with my husband in the cottage next to Mother's big white-columned three-story. Many are the times I have delivered satin bed jackets and Merle Norman cosmetics to her hospital rooms, spoon-fed her while that popping jaw of hers nearly sent me over the precipice and into a ranting, maniacal conniption fit, and taken all the verbal abuse I should have to stomach in five lifetimes.

"CeCe, I cannot bear the thought of dying without seeing you living your life," she will say. "Run off to Nepal, for God's sake! Go to a goddamn nude beach in Europe. Have an affair in Lisbon and breakfast in Madrid. Do not fester and stagnate as I have." Or: "Cecelia LaRue, you have no hunger for life. Where is the passion you should have inherited from me? Jumping Jesus, if you would just come alive you would begin to claw at this provincial little coffin of a town." Which is precisely the point, you see. She just wants to live through me—or at least she did BWL (Before Will Luckie).

"She overshadows you," my DD used to say. "You've got to learn to talk louder, act meaner, and cuss dirtier than she does." Easy for him to say, with his bourbons and baseball. With his hunting camp whores and wooded weekends. But it simply is not in my nature to be overbearing, like Mother. On the contrary, I feel that I should project an image of calm competence and ladylike deference what with my position and all. Hell, I have even been called a saint by some who have observed my devotion to Mother.

Our maid Lindia only calls me a fool. She thinks I should get a new husband, "one that don't swish," she says, leave Pollard, and let the chips fall, insisting that Mother would be just fine. She even thinks Mother should be allowed to have her way with this—character of hers. "She deserve it. She went long years not getting none from your running around daddy. Well, she damn sure getting plenty now."

But I cannot let it go. Not when the whole town is watching and talking and looking at me with the false pity of peons who just eat up a good high-society scandal with the same sticky spoon. Not when Mother and Will Luckie go on trips to India and Morocco, come back loaded down with expensive trinkets, ivory, rich fur pillows, hand-woven rugs—hell, her home decor has become a bohemian ode to fucking. And of course you know who is paying for these trips and trinkets. Yours truly. I am not only paying with my birthright, I am paying with my once impeccable reputation. Just listen at a few of the other things that piece of filth has done to cause an avalanche of shame to come cascading down on the Calhoun family:

First of all, he moved in with her after just two movie dates and one dinner date to Rosie O'Grady's in Pensacola. Swept her right off her chubby little size five feet (mine are size nine; she refers to them as "Jesus-Christ-walk-on-water skis"). I believe the off-color line he wooed her with was, "Baby, you sure do make my rat crawl." At least, that's how she tells it, delighting at the gag-reflex-inducing reaction she gets from me and any other listener of character. No marriage has ever been discussed (as if I could ever allow that!)—just a craven union of depraved lust and musked-up sin, which in and of itself is all the town ever needed to justify looking down on me.

Second of all, he buys lubricating jelly and female hygiene spray at Mr. Cleo Williams's pharmacy, and I don't have to tell you the lurid tales that swarm around Billy's Barber Shop and the House of Hair in the wake of that. Don't even ask me about the handheld muscle massager.

Thirdly, I think I already mentioned he laughs at me and runs me down both to my face and behind my back. He calls me a "social-climbing flippy-tailed prissite" just because I care what certain people think. He says the crudest things to me, obviously intended to provoke, but I usually manage to hold in, just as I have always done with Mother. "You need to loosen up, girl," he will say. "You got the biggest bug up your butt I ever seen. Must be one of them dung beetles. You need a dose of Uncle Luckie's Root Treatment." Or he leans in close and flirtatious and whispers, "So who's cutting your stove wood? Cause I know your old man ain't got the ax for it."

Winston has even witnessed him toying with me, insulting me, yet my own husband refuses to take up for me. All he will do is bring me samples of knockout pills to settle my nerves, then turn around and give Will Luckie all the free medical attention he needs, and then some. Knowing that "Uncle Luckie" doesn't think Winston has any testosterone, all the time asking why Winston and me don't have any babies after eight years of marriage. Then, when I try to tell him something like I guess Jesus isn't ready, he says, right in front of Winston, "More like Winston ain't ready. And Winnie won't be ready unless you get yourself a dildo. Maybe that would turn him on." Then he laughs while Winston blushes. Of course. "Bet I could take care of Winnie's retreads if he made a little pit stop on my turn." The gall. My mother's boyfriend flirting with my husband! "Hey, Doc," he says. "My dick stays harder than Chinese arithmetic. I need to come in and get it de-pressurized, all right? Just drain off a little fluid."

I swear I am not exaggerating. He continues his slimy talk and his questioning of Winston's virility just because he knows crude behavior is one of my Achilles' heels and my husband's effete demeanor is the other. I already told you Winston is a touch feminine, but that is just the way of some folks with superior breeding. Plus, I have always said that there's more to a successful marriage than wallowing around in bed linens. But don't try telling that to Mother or Will Luckie. Their sordid little soiree goes on in front of all of Pollard. Here's what I mean:

In recent years Mother has taken to routinely calling the police department, fire department, or ambulance company when she needs little errands done. Once, at the conclusion of one of her extended hospitalization-slash-vacations, she even phoned up Cheatham Jackson at the colored funeral parlor to drive her the three blocks home, just because the hospital ambulance was out on a call and she simply *had* to get home right that very minute to set up for *mah-jongg*. Yet this town's three bored cops—plus assorted paramedics and firemen—seem to get a kick out of it, driving up to the big house, sirens blaring and lights ablaze, to see what the eccentric socialite wants this time. This behavior never used to bother me too much BWL, as it was quite harmless then. Hell, I used to sometimes be there to enjoy the company, when Mother would wave the back of her hand at Grady Fortner, a semi-winded paramedic. "No, darling," she would chirp from her multi-pillowed perch beneath the yellow dotted Swiss canopy. "I'm just fine. Really. All I need you to do is run to the kitchen and pour a little Tab over ice."

And he would.

"Run to the liquor store for me, sweetie pie, and pick me up a fifth of Crown. I'm all out and I'm parched as a goddamn nun's drawers."

After a two a.m. call the honeyed command might go something like, "Be a sugar-doll, won't you, and run downstairs to the garage. I woke up with this feeling of dread that I forgot to extinguish the lights on my automobile. Oh—and if it's necessary, be my precious and check the battery."

But after the arrival of Will Luckie the visitors became more like customers at a peep show in a Bourbon Street sex salon. Hell, they can't get to Mother's fast enough to gather material for the next tale they will share at the barbershop, and she never lets them down. Just a few months ago, when Mother's hairdresser accidentally fried the hair he was supposed to be touching up with henna highlights, it turned into yet another show for the P.C.P.D.

When I laid eyes on Mother, all done up to perfection except for the frizzled tufts of hair zigging and zagging from her scalp, I briefly hoped it would be the death knell for Will Luckie, scare him off, maybe. After all, she looked like Bozo the Clown with a singed afro. And mother's looks, which I did not inherit, by the way (I only inherited my place in the pecking order of Pollard), are known to be strikingly beautiful, even at her age and poundage.

I sat with her in the study, in the dark, waiting for her Man, struck by the strobe of firelight hitting her face, playing upon the burned out barbs of frazzed hair. She held a cigarette in her left hand, a scotch rocks in her right, smoking and sipping in the slow silence. Her pearl-handled Derringer lay in her lap.

When the doorknob rattled to his touch, Mother simply sat, smoked, sipped, inhaled. When the slat of light fell across the room she exhaled.

He flipped on the study light, jumped, and uttered, "Sheee-it."

Mother drew on her Virginia Slim, blew a cool plume of smoke. "Will, darling." Pause. "This is the new me." Pause. "Like it?" Such timing would be a thing of beauty if not for the circumstances.

That man regrouped quicker than any man I have ever encountered. "Mmmm, baby," he said, all the while unsnapping that hideous pink cowboy shirt he is so fond of. "That is hot. You kind of look like a soul sister."

"Good," Mother said. "Because if you didn't like it I was reconciled to the idea of putting a bullet into my feeble brain." She picked up the pistol with a dainty little flourish. "Here, sexy. Do something with this instrument of death."

He took the gun, steady slurping at her neck while my lunch wanted to be upchucked. Of course, I might as well have been invisible, and he kept on lapping at her like a horny mutt, talking about how he always wanted a taste of dark meat.

"Ooooh, darling," Mother squealed. "You know that makes me want to give in to wild abandon. It's absolutely criminal!"

He grunted. He still had not acknowledged me, you will note, intent as he was upon whipping my elderly mother into a hedonistic frenzy. Well, she went into a frenzy all right, and she shared it with the town of Pollard. While that man licked her neck like it was the last lollipop on the planet, she called the police. As was the routine, an officer—this night it was Paul Baggett—let himself in with the spare key Mother had given the department to keep in their one and only squad car. Baggett just stood there, smirking. I was overcome by a paralysis of shame.

Mother stood and swept an accusing arm at Will Luckie, who was mixing himself a fruity gin drink at the bar. "Officer," she panted, "arrest this man!"

Will laughed. I felt denuded.

"Arrest this man on the grounds that he's too goddamned sexy!"

Paul Baggett, too, began to chuckle, salivating, I am certain, at the prospect of playing barbershop raconteur the next day.

"Oh, you think I am funning with you?" Ice cubes clinked in Mother's favorite scotch glass. "Well, if you don't arrest this man immediately, I am going to have to tear off my clothes and make love to him with the ardent fervor of a sixteen-year-old. And God help your conscience if I have a stroke from it."

Paul Baggett ended up having a beer with them. I went home to Winston.

You know, my DD always told me I would never have to work, that the money would take me into old age, a plush casket, and a choice plot overlooking the Conecuh River, with plenty left over for a dozen children. Of course, here I am, childless, because Winston has such difficulty with The Act that we've taken to separate bedrooms over the years, making blundering attempts only when he's had enough merlot, which is difficult for a teetotaler. And Daddy certainly never figured on Mother having a geriatric fuck-fest with a redneck cowboy swinger who is as low-down as gulley dirt, talks to chickens, and has his eye and his fist on my inheritance.

Oh, Lord, the chickens. I *must* tell you about the chickens. They were the deserving objects of my rage after Will placed the absolute last straw across my load-weary back. He brought three hens and a rooster when he moved in with Mother last fall, then had the nerve to convert the gardener's shed—which sits near my own yard—into a chicken coop. It sends that chicken-yard odor across both our back lawns, not to mention the pre-dawn rooster wails and nonstop clucking and flapping. The half-assed fence Will put up routinely fails to contain them at all times, so they end up wandering over to the pool and even into Mother's kitchen just last week. Of course you know what Will Luckie did, and Mother and Lindia, for that matter. They laughed. Here you have a yard hen, filthy, full of parasites and histoplasmosis, meandering about the place where food is prepared, and those fools thought it was just about the most humorous occurrence of the decade. I spent the evening Cloroxing Mother's kitchen floor, an already festering resentment building toward those damned birds, whose numbers have grown considerably.

You see, he kept on adding more of the feathered beasts throughout the months of his cohabitation with Mother. A few more pullets, another rooster, a couple of Domineckers, all slick-feathered in rust and green, and then the guineas that got into my winter garden and landed us all in court (the judge, of course, who was utterly taken in, would not allow me to sue the guineas or Will Luckie). He even brought Mother a peacock, which she adores because it is so flamboyant, like her. It is even named

for her—Maureen. Will Luckie named it, of course. He said he could justify using her name because it fit in with the whole Watergate setting of
the chicken yard. Oh, did I forget to mention that he put a sign on the
chicken coop that said "Watergate Hotel" and named each chicken after
that whole Nixon bunch? And with no regard whatsoever to gender.
Well that is precisely what the no-count fool did. It started out as a cyn-
ical joke, as Will Luckie makes no secret of the fact that he believes he
fought in a great big con job (i.e., Vietnam) and spends a great deal of
time belittling Republican politicians (of course, my DD is turning in the
grave at the prospect of Mother copulating with a Yellow Dog Demo-
crat). But the chicken project took on a deeper meaning for him when
he began keeping a daily log, entitled "The Chicken Sheet," in which he
records each bird's name, egg production, idiosyncrasies and infirmities.
The shell-shocked buffoon began to see the ornithological specimens in
a new light. They took on the characteristics of *homo sapiens* in his
deranged mind.

"Martha Mitchell looks peaked today," he writes in the log, or "G.
Gordon has been spurring Haldeman all afternoon. Haldeman won't
even look him in the eye," or "McGruder—three eggs but little enthusiasm—perhaps constipated?" and on and on. It is the only thing near a
job I ever witnessed him doing, so you can see right there how useless and
sorry that man is. And I am here to tell you he takes that job seriously. J.
Dean, Erlichman, J. Mitchell, R. Secord, E. H. Hunt—these are their
names. There is even an Egil Krogh, which he spells E-a-g-l-e C-r-o-w.
And the fastidious detail that goes into the recording of the daily lives of
the yard fowl is quite disturbing. He acts as if they are evolved even
beyond pet-dom, as if they are his bosom buddies, chatting with them as
he inventories the nests, caressing that slimy-looking plumage. Chuck
Colson grew so tame from the attention that he let Will Luckie loop a
chain dangling a diminutive gold crucifix about his gullet, which he has
worn for going on a month now. But it gets even more insane. Yesterday,
Staff Sergeant Luckie added a bit of green cloth to the chain. He then
pinned to the cloth some kind of ridiculous war medal he supposedly
earned, making that absurd chicken look like the military dictator of the

Watergate Hen House. I swear, I sometimes think that his tours of duty in the jungles of Southeast Asia effectively booby-trapped his little bird-brain.

When a raccoon got into the shed last month and assassinated Tricky-D, that inbred idiot actually got teary-eyed and planned a funeral for the mangled carcass. Then insisted that the family attend. He strummed his guitar and sang "Amazing Grace," all weepy-like. I had not known until that incident just how attached to the poultry he had become. This display of emotion was something far and away different from his randy romancing of my aged mother. And this realization of mine undoubtedly saved Will Luckie's life this morning. Let me tell you how it all unfolded:

Winston said he had to stay at the hospital late last night delivering a baby, so I took a knockout pill and went to bed early. Sometime before midnight, however, I was awakened by the horrific screams of one who was surely being murdered very, very slowly. When finally, through a fog of cabernet and Valium, it dawned upon me that the peacock, Maureen, was the source of the utterances, I was quite relieved, yet could not go back to sleep with those howls punctuating the night. I made my way down to the kitchen and out the back door, which had been left standing wide open. Of course, I assumed that Winston had come in and was reassured to see his Cadillac parked in the driveway. But something felt odd. The night seemed a trifle off center, and the scuffling sound coming from around the chicken coop, accompanied by an occasional peacock shriek, drew me to take a silent stroll that would be the terrible undoing of all that I have grown accustomed to.

This is so very difficult, putting into words what I saw there in the moonlight that glowed through the gauze of leaves above. Those garlands of gold (some purchased by my own mother), the ones that were always nestled in the chest curls of Will Luckie, caught the cast of the full moon. He leaned against the outer wall of the old gardener's shed, his breathing was a purring moan, fingers were playing across his bare Marine Corps stomach muscles. He was caught up in the most intense display of sexual pleasure I have ever witnessed, and I have to confess that some of that pleasure spilled into my own psyche. I felt a mesmerized longing, a huge gulp of desire such as I have never known, until it dawned on me that the kneeling figure causing Will Luckie's pleasure was my own husband.

I have told you about our conjugal difficulties, so it was outside of my frame of reference to see Winston, kneeling there, so caught up in such a perverted act, so absorbed by what he was doing, so oblivious to his surroundings, emitting muffled groans quite unlike the twitters of counterfeit passion he has offered me over the years. I could not move until the lunar light revealed Will Luckie's gaze upon me. And he—you will not begin to believe this, I know. He actually grinned, raised his right hand, extended his index finger, and crooked it at me three times. Can you imagine? Here he is being carnally devoured by my husband, and he has the egomaniacal nerve to invite me to the party! Have you ever in all your life?

The strangest part of this perverse scene, and I can barely admit it to myself, is that I came within a hairbreadth of walking over, surrendering to God knows what. It was hypnotic, and the stirrings within me were so white-hot and demanding. All I knew was a feverish desperation for some implied promise of satisfaction, something I know very little of, unfortunately; but, just as I started forward, Will Luckie let out a gasping moan that sent me headlong toward the sensuous safety of my own bedroom.

Needless to say, I did not sleep at all that night. My bewildered arousal and shock gave way to a mulling inventory of wrongs done unto me until, as dawn broke, I found myself in the throes of a righteous rage that wanted only to be visited upon Will Luckie. That is when I made my way to Mother's garage and loaded my DD's shotgun.

I paused at the door to the study, where Mother's man-whore had apparently passed out, and contemplated his murder. There is no doubt that I will roast in hellfire for all eternity behind the homicidal inklings that rustled about my brain, but at this point I fail to give a shit. You see, when earthly anguish (as in the form of one's lunatic mother, her sexually ambiguous leech of a boyfriend, and my cheating impostor of a husband) becomes infused within the pores of one's flesh so that Lucifer's den looks to be a relief, then the time to act has arrived. And so I acted. And I did Will Luckie one better.

I acted upon those goddamned yard birds of his. Chuck Colson met me at the gate, having been taught to hold high expectations of those humans who serve him. I laid the stock on my hip, got my palm beneath the barrel, and fired, silently thanking my DD for teaching me to shoot. It struck me that a shotgun went a long way toward obliterating coop fowl, effectively blowing them to smithereens, as it were. You have never seen such a tornado of feathers in your life, a maelstrom of beaks, guts, gristle and feet. A few wings in the throes of dancing nerves, jitterbugging against dirt-grained blood in the chicken yard, slinging dots of bright red against the shed. I managed to annihilate Erlichman, Secord, Krogh, and Liddy before folks came running. Trying to hit Martha Mitchell, who had flapped over to the patio thinking I would not notice her there among the white begonias, I accidentally fired into the bay window of Mother's kitchen, and the sound of breaking glass tinkled like wind chimes into the hurricane of squawks, screeches and staccatoing wings on Mother's dewy green lawn. I got John Dean and Haldeman, vaguely aware of Will Luckie's stream of curses, his moan of anguish as he raked through meaty feathers for his Bronze Star and crucifix, a moan quite distinct from his orgasmic utterance of the previous midnight. My mother's profane shrieks of hysteria against the tableau of sounds grated against my very last nerve and I admit to a flash of a desire to turn the gun on her. That was when Angus Stevens from across the street wrestled my DD's gun away from me. Of course the P.C.P.D. was absolutely thrilled to wheel up to a real emergency—a bona fide chicken massacre—at Miss Maureen's.

Mother was in her vicious-tongued mode. "CeCe, you have lost every bit of your goddamn mind!" she screamed, as down snowflaked upon the wig she still wore behind the hair-burning. "Is this what you foresaw when you gave your heart to Jesus? Murdering sweet creatures that give us our morning nourishment?"

"Oh, the humanity!" Officer Baggett murmured.

"If you had only lived a life, you could not be capable of such lunatic

rage!" Mother went on. "And didn't I always try to get you to live a goddamn life? Didn't I?" She quieted a moment and actually took a deep
breath. "If you could only learn to live and laugh. Laugh at yourself.
Laugh at this absurd life! Then you could never be so vicious as to murder
poor Will's friends. You have no idea what you have done to him. Goddamn, I need a Bloody fucking Mary."

Of course I did not argue with her, not in front of the police and the
neighbors. It would only encourage her to provide more drama for the
townspeople to view. And I certainly did not tell her about Winston and
Will Luckie. I can never do that! Lord, what would folks think of me
then? I don't believe there has ever been a homosexual incident in Pollard, and I am not about to go down as a witness to the first homosexual
incident on record.

As I climbed into the police car—Baggett insisted that I sit up front
with him—I spied Will Luckie by the pool. He had that little net he uses
to clean leaves and bugs out of the chlorined water, but on this landmark
morning he was dipping at some of the feathers, still drifting on currents
of air like ashes from a barrel burning, that had landed in the pool. His
shoulders were hunched and shaking. He was sobbing as he netted the
remnants of the Watergate conspirators. I was able to take a little satisfaction in that. Hell, he is probably having a huge funeral for them even
as we speak. I wouldn't be surprised if he went out and bought marble
slabs and headstones with more of my inheritance money to create a
memorial garden for the Watergate gang, with an air-conditioned vault
for Chuck's remains, of course.

Anyway, here I am. Mother is not pressing charges, of course, but
James Caffey, her attorney, says that the state might have to, because
firing into a residence is a felony. I imagine that Mr. Caffey is working on
bailing me out right this minute.

I suppose jail is quite uncomfortable in a bigger town than Pollard,
but here it is quite homey. Baggett, Trent Givens, and Rita, that sweet
little dispatcher who does the wake-up call service, brought me lunch
from the Jitney Jungle, let me use the phone to cancel the Ladies' Club
meeting for this evening, and even rolled a TV into my cell so I could

watch the Watergate hearings. That John Dean is testifying. He is kind of a squirrelly little man, but have you seen his wife? Maureen? She is gorgeous, not a blond hair out of place. Perfect skin. Big eyes and big earbobs. She has style. Even a stylish nickname—"Mo." I almost feel bad about shooting her husband.

I must insist upon one thing. You cannot tell a *soul* about Winston's indiscretion. Surely I can trust you people. Surely I have nothing to worry about where you all are concerned. Hell, we don't even know any of the same people I'll bet. Moreover, we understand our status, one to the other.

You know, after lo these many months of Will Luckie's ill-mannered, low-life ways, it is a relief to have this sense of clarity about the state of us—*n'est-ce pas?*

A Modern Tragedy

Douglas Kelley

Thomas Foley poured himself a second shot of bourbon and set it on the table by his easy chair, next to his glass of water. Then he sat down to watch CNN for a few minutes and see what was going on in this world before he went off to his other one. No matter how important the anchor tried to make it sound, though, there was nothing newsworthy. Gasoline prices were rising, the stock market was down, and there was still a drought in Africa.

The first shot went down quickly and easily, and Thomas waited the customary time, enjoying the warmth flooding through his chest, before having the second. He sat back, melding into the chair, forearms languid on the armrests, one hand idly fingering the television remote.

He had intended to write his sister today. Much like yesterday. He had put it off for weeks, right from the moment he had decided that he should contact her. He could call, but that would be too sudden after all these years. While telling himself he would write tomorrow, he knew he would not.

On TV, the President was standing at a podium. Probably reciting what the people wanted to hear, Thomas thought. Telling us that things are about to get better.

Now there was a reporter speaking into the camera from the White House lawn. Thomas paid him no more attention than he had the president. He let his mind coast. That was all right. This was his own time. Later he would be thinking someone else's thoughts.

Thomas Foley was an actor, and had been for more than twenty years. Ever since he had been told by his high school drama teacher that he had talent, and ever since he had gone to NYU to learn how it was really done, he had considered himself an actor.

Whenever anyone asked, that was the occupation he gave. It made no difference if at the time he was doing yard work or selling shoes or, that most actor-like of all day jobs, waiting tables.

"I'm an actor," he would say, as he fitted a Florsheim on a foot or cleared away the soup. And so he was.

The drama teacher taught him how to deliver lines, to project his thin high school voice out across the audience. The instructors in New York taught him how much more there was to learn, how inadequate his Indiana upbringing had been. They also instilled the belief that it was not too late, that there was indeed latent talent there, that the Hoosier in him could be cast away, or at least kept skillfully hidden.

So Thomas ceased telling those just met that he was from Indiana, certainly never mentioned Muncie, and visits back home where he was again just Tom became rare events.

He stayed in New York, determined to belong in that place. And he acted, accepting every offer, every role. He appeared in small theaters, playing small parts, proving himself as one who could be depended upon to make his character deliver just what the playwright or the director had in mind.

In time he was invited to audition at larger venues, landing more important roles. With each new play, he dedicated himself wholly to the part, working to become, for a few hours each night, the very person in the script. If asked to play a butler, no actor ever held a tray with more aplomb. If playing an aristocrat, no one would guess he was not born a Rockefeller. If playing a homosexual dancer, as he did in A Chorus Line, he plainly had not an ounce of masculinity. But through it all, over all the years, he knew he was best at playing an actor.

Because that is what he was.

No matter how big the part, and no matter how big the play, he always knew he was just acting. Even after he made it to Broadway, getting the headlining roles on the big marquee shows, he knew that he was not really the character out on the stage. He was just the actor.

And that was sufficient. He knew that his duty was to merely pretend. Even though he was classically trained and was best known for Shakespearean roles, he had no desire to actually be Hamlet or Macbeth or the more modern Willie Loman. Such tragic figures anyway.

He remembered the early days, still at the university or during those lean years when six struggling actors shared an apartment, when they would all go out drinking at some dive bar where the drinks were cheap and get drunk and laugh at the characters they played. They would talk about how much better off they were, starving actors having to share a window to throw their piss out, when fate could have dealt them the hand of Othello, and who needed friends like his?

And that was how it continued to be. Every morning they worked their day jobs, every evening they pretended to be someone else, and every night, after the play, they went to the Lakeside Lounge in the East Village and drunkenly praised themselves.

It was a glorious life.

But after twenty-five years, and maybe a thousand stages in a thousand nameless towns, the glory he drove himself to attain had begun to pale. Sometimes, usually after a night when the play had not gone well, when someone dropped a line or a prop failed, revealing that what was on stage was not real after all, he felt a lack of purpose in all the pretending. On those nights he wondered if perhaps he should have done something different with his life. Perhaps he should have actually built for himself something that lasted longer than the applause.

He often professed a desire to do something, only to let it slip away by his own inactivity. Like calling his sister. Or he could have painted, and had art as the result. Then he would at least have something to hang on the wall. He could have written a book, or perhaps a play. Something to hold in his hands, something that came from himself. Instead, he had spent his life pretending to be someone else. Now he would soon be fifty, and had accumulated nothing of Thomas Foley.

Sometimes the feeling came upon him as soon as the curtain fell. Sometimes it came long after the house went dark, after the fifth or sixth shot of post-performance bourbon. Sometimes it was after coming down from the occasional cocaine-laced high, for it was only in the cocaine that he could still find the old euphoria.

Sometimes the nagging feeling that the play was not the thing lasted until he slept, and even sleep did not erase the doubt.

But the next day, in a clearer light, he would dismiss his thoughts of the night before as a postpartum-type depression, a result of leaving the stage while the adrenaline still flowed. It happened to many actors. That was why so many went out afterwards, trying to maintain the on-stage rush, and finding it in a bottle. Or in a line of powder or in a needle and a spoon. Thomas knew that the larger mistake was taking it home with him, where alone in his apartment more bourbon or more coke had the opposite effect. He knew the mistake, but awareness of the danger did not stop him.

His customary two shots before a performance were for a different purpose. They put him into the cosmopolitan mood needed to leave his quiet apartment and go into the bustle of the city streets, arriving at the theater ready to slip into his role and leave Thomas Foley behind. By the time he left the dressing room, and until he returned after the last curtain, he was the character he played.

It was nearly four, so he reached for the second shot, downed the bourbon, and chased it with water. This time he savored the sensation for only a few seconds, and as the warmth inside him faded he stood up and slipped on his coat. "Off to the show," he said aloud, but only to himself.

Tonight was the closing night of *Julius Caesar* at the Majestic. The play had been on for fourteen weeks, a long run for Shakespeare on Broadway with these modern audiences. Give them a beauty and a beast any day. Thomas was sorry to see it end. Every serious actor felt the fire of wanting to do Shakespeare. After four hundred years, his plays were still the best. Who else could claim such memorable lines? Thomas had no other role lined up and, besides, would have been content to play Brutus from now on.

Ah, Brutus. Arguably the best-known character in any play without billing in the title. When Caesar groans, "*Et tu, Brute?*" the whole world knows what has happened.

The theater three hours before the audience arrives is a magical place. It is large and dark and quiet, with only the passing muted voices of stagehands and cleaning people to disturb the peace. Thomas Foley liked to arrive early. The resounding echo of footsteps across an empty stage spoke of the power of the place, of the implied force of what would come later.

He stepped out from the wings, stage right, and walked in turn to his marks for the coming night. Here is where he would make his first appearance, early in Act I, when Caesar is warned to beware the ides of March.

And here, a few steps toward stage left, is where Brutus opens Act II in his orchard, wandering in the night. And then center stage, where Caesar falls to the floor of the Senate, conspirators all around him. But it is Brutus he calls by name, exclaiming in the Latin.

This pacing about the stage was wholly unnecessary for learning the part. Thomas knew his marks as well as he knew his lines, and he knew his lines as if they were his own words. It was all part of the preparation. If it was for him to thrust the dagger under the cloak of Julius Caesar, then he would do it so perfectly that everyone in the audience would swear they saw the knife pierce the emperor's side.

Thomas Foley, at that moment, had a thought. It was such an extraordinarily radical notion that he stopped in mid-stride, halfway to his next mark, so struck was he by the possible consequence of the idea. He turned to look back at the spot where Caesar would fall, just as he had every night for the last three and a half months.

He went back to where in a few short hours Brutus would kill his emperor and onetime ally. He stood in the spot as the idea developed fully in his mind, coalescing from abstract thought to concrete plan. He marveled at the possibility. Such showmanship. The idea had come so unexpectedly, it would take time to think through. Yet he was amazed at how plausible it seemed.

It was perfect, though. What if, on this last night of the run, when tomorrow was not important, Brutus actually did kill Caesar? Or more correctly, what if Thomas Foley, playing Brutus, produced from the folds of his tunic a real knife, not the usual stage prop, and stepped into a real murder plot? It would be one hell of a way to close out the play.

"Caesar assassinated by Brutus," the newspapers would say. It would probably even make CNN, take everyone's mind off that drought in

Africa. Thomas's mind whirled. Could he make it work?

Up in the balcony, workers were checking for trash around the seats, and he heard other activity backstage. The others were beginning to arrive. Thomas, still thinking his plan over, left the stage and went toward his dressing room. On the way, he ducked into the prop room to see what his choices were for a weapon capable of drawing real blood. The usual collapsing dagger would not do.

Then he went to dress.

* *

The curtain came up to less than a full house. There were empty seats scattered about the theater. Entire rows were vacant in the back. Thomas was pleased to see that the balcony, however, was nearly full. Those in the cheap seats, those least able to afford admission, were in for a special performance.

He watched the opening scene from the wings, waiting for his entrance. As Scene Two opened, he followed Caesar onstage with the rest of the emperor's entourage. As he prepared to step up and deliver his first line of the night, he felt an uncommon thrill, as this performance, starting just like countless others, promised to end so much more dramatically. When the actor playing the soothsayer, a minor part but of immense importance, spoke his line, "Beware the ides of March," Thomas took a deep breath. From now on, he would *be* Brutus.

Hearing the warning, Caesar says: "What man is that?"

Brutus: "A soothsayer bids you beware the ides of March."

Caesar blanches slightly, and covers his uneasiness by turning away. The crowd follows, except for Brutus, who remains on stage and for the moment is left alone, brooding and thoughtful. If played correctly, the pause is, without a word spoken, a very telling scene. It is performed perfectly.

When Brutus opens Act Two, in the predawn darkness of his orchard, he is restless and awake, despite the hour. In the distance, lightning still flashes from a receding storm, and the lingering clouds hide the stars, so he does not know how near day is. In his solitude, he justifiies to himself what he is about to do. The assassination of an emperor is not undertaken lightly, especially when he has been a lifelong friend. Still, Brutus convinces himself that Caesar's ambitions must be stopped, for the good of the country, before it is too late: "And therefore think him as a serpent's egg, and kill him in the shell."

Finally, the scene comes. The crowd is gathered in the Senate. Caesar is in the middle, center stage. Brutus and the rest of the conspirators move close to him.

A study of Brutus's eyes reveals nothing of his thoughts or emotions. It is time.

Now.

The assassins press in, daggers flash. Caesar sees Brutus among them: "Et tu, Brute? Then fall, Caesar!"

And he does.

Caesar's body lies crumpled on the floor as all around justify their act and defend their motives to an angry Mark Antony, who has entered from stage left. After much back-and-forth, the scene ends with Caesar's limp form carried off stage.

In the wings, once out of view of the audience, the actor playing Caesar stands up and dusts himself off, congratulating his fellows on a scene well done.

Brutus, just as he had acted on stage, stands aside. He does not seem pleased with the performance. In the end, he has decided that he cannot commit murder.

But now there is another plan, and he feels a tingle of exhilaration. The play goes on.

Brutus reenters to face the stunned Senate. His resolve is strong, the actor bringing a sublime presence to the stage. He delivers his lines flawlessly: "Not that I loved Caesar less, but that I loved Rome more."

At intermission, the audience talks of the wonderful performance. Thomas Foley as Brutus, they say, is at the top of his form. Reviewers are already working on their dispatches to the papers. It is too bad, they will say, that the play has ended its run.

Backstage, Brutus girds himself for the show's finale.

Acts Four and Five, taking place months after the assassination, have the armies of Brutus and Cassius on the field of battle against those of Antony and Octavius. After a long war, they meet in a final assault on the plains of Philippi, where Brutus makes a final error in judgment. He had erred in not killing Mark Antony when he killed Caesar, and he had erred in allowing Antony to make his "Friends, Romans, countrymen," speech at Caesar's funeral, which was the beginning of Antony's rise to power. Now, in the heat of battle, Brutus fails to cover the flank of his ally Cassius's army, allowing Antony's forces to win the day and win the war.

Brutus withdraws, barely escaping under the cover of darkness. He and his remaining supporters meet and discuss their situation. Brutus says the end is near: "The ghost of Caesar hath appeared to me two times by night; at Sardis once, and, this last night, here in Philippi fields: I know my hour is come."

Then he announces his decision: "Our enemies have beat us to the pit. It is more worthy to leap in ourselves than to tarry until they push us."

To his aide Strato: "Stay thou by thy lord. Thou art a fellow of good respect. Hold my sword, and turn away thy face, while I do run upon it. Wilt thou, Strato?"

Strato: "Give me your hand first. Fare you well, my lord."

This, then, is the moment.

Brutus: "Farewell, good Strato." He falls on the glinting steel of the upturned sword. Within the body of Brutus, the actor Thomas Foley feels a rush of euphoria. He knows he is putting forth the best performance of his career, for just this once it is not a performance. The actor and the action are united in truth. Just as quickly, he becomes disoriented, and the floor of the stage rushes up at him. He is on his knees. Feeling weak, he makes certain to consciously project the words, just as he had long been trained to do.

Brutus: "Caesar, now be still. I killed not thee with half so good a will."

Antony and Octavius enter. Antony kneels by Brutus and sees what has happened. The actor starts, but suppresses his reaction, save to look pleadingly to the wing. Offstage, someone rushes to a phone. Antony remains kneeling by Brutus, hesitant. Octavius turns his face from the audience and whispers, "Go on. Say your lines."

Antony nods. Recovering, for the show goes on, he stands up and continues the performance. His voice falters at first, but after a few words he rises to the role: "This was the noblest Roman of them all. All the conspirators, save only he, did that they did in envy of great Caesar. He only in common good to all, was made one of them. His life was gentle, and the elements so mixed in him that Nature might stand up and say to all the world, 'This was a man!' "

At his feet, Brutus lies bleeding. A moment later the curtain falls to great applause.

Payback

Tom Kelly

Everything in life seems to go in cycles and it is apparent that turkey hunting, in an effort not to be left out, is caught up in the throes of a brand-new phase. In the past few years it has become fashionable for more and more people to spend time flying back and forth across the country in search of what has come to be known as the Grand Slam.

The Grand Slam is the name we have chosen for our current fixation on the act of killing one each of the Eastern, Rio Grande, Merriam's and Osceola subspecies of turkey in a single year. I have no particular feeling about this, one way or another, as long as I am not expected to join the club. Because in at least two respects, my own situation is completely different from that of these far-ranging turkey hunters.

First of all, I am not at all convinced there is very much difference between the subspecies.

I know there are turkeys in Missouri that weigh more than twenty pounds on a regular basis. The deer in Maine outweigh the deer in Alabama by fifty to seventy-five pounds, which seems to excite nobody at all. I know that western turkeys have a white tip to the tail feathers and that eastern species have tail feathers with chestnut tips, none of which makes me wake up in a cold sweat. Nor does any bit of it cause me to wonder if perhaps the heavier turkeys in Missouri ought to be a subspecies, *Meleagris gallopavo gigantius* perhaps, and the deer in Maine thrown into some special classification.

I have killed, in central Florida, a turkey that I was assured was an Osceola and he may very well have been. But he could have been put down in the middle of a string of Alabama turkeys forty feet long and no man on earth could have told the difference, or picked him out without a crib sheet.

I say this neither to proselytize nor to condemn. You are perfectly at liberty to believe in your soul that there are four species in the continental U.S. and that there is a Gould's in central Mexico for a fifth. I am absolutely confident that the Ocellated turkey, in Yucatan, is a separate species and if you want to throw him into your own personal slam and raise it to six or take him out and leave things as they are, I am indifferent.

If the snipe hunters can have fourteen or fifteen species of snipe and at least three of pseudo-snipe, then we can have four or five species of turkeys. You can have any number that makes you happy.

I am perfectly content with the one we have here on the Gulf Coast, even to the extent of being content to have taxonomists keep saying that ours in south Alabama is an Intergrade, a mixture between Eastern and Osceola. Only on the South Carolina coast does the purity of the strain of Eastern turkeys seem to be of overriding importance to anyone. The Carolina coast, as a matter of fact, concerns itself with the purity of a lot of things, to a degree uncommon in the rest of the country. For example.

It is my understanding that the newspapers never publish a list of the attendees at the St. Cecilia's Ball in Charleston. It being assumed that anyone who was there saw you there, assuming you went, and people who were not there are so unimportant that it does not matter what they think.

I also understand that no divorced woman has ever been invited to attend this function, which does not surprise me in the least, since South Carolinians have always had some unusual marital regulations.

I was married in that state, many years ago. At that time the fee charged for a marriage license was two dollars, the lady in question did not have to appear at the courthouse at the time the license was issued, and the state recognized no grounds for divorce whatsoever. Clearly, this was a society that made the state of matrimony as easy to get into and as difficult to get out of as possible.

The prohibition of the attendance of formerly married persons at social functions may be a case of inadvertently confusing the definitions of chastity and purity, although the city of Charleston has never asked for my opinion on the matter.

The thought does occur to me, as a person wandering out here in the rural jungles of social unacceptability, since no list of attendees at the St. Cecilia's Ball is kept, how can anyone be positive that a divorced woman has not at some time or other managed to elude the purity patrol and slip in the back door?

The thought also occurs to me that we may have wandered somewhat far afield in our discussion of the Grand Slam.

Secondly, wrapped in the error of my closed-minded ignorance that a turkey is a turkey, is the fact that never in all these years have I ever found it necessary to give my business to strangers. The turkeys here at home have been perfectly capable of hurting my feelings and crushing my spirit with the greatest of ease. I have never had to drive five hundred miles to search out cruel and unusual varieties of pain and tragedy, because within fifty miles or so there has always been a turkey that was delighted to inflict the homegrown variety upon me.

Not only was he delighted to inflict it, he was perfectly willing to run uphill across half a township and stand in line for two hours after he got there to do it.

But it has come to my attention just very recently that there is a most unusual relationship now existing between the turkeys in the State of Florida and myself. A relationship that slipped up and caught the both of us unawares.

In a hunting career that began in 1938, a matter now of sixty-two years, I have almost exclusively stayed at home. In all of that time I have hunted turkeys outside of the borders of my home state for a grand total of six days. All six of these days have been within the past five years, and all six have been in the State of Florida. Six days in sixty-two years is clearly a prime example of what must be considered an extreme case of provincialism. So much so that there are probably Trappist monks, who entered the monastery as a novice at the age of fourteen, who have had more experience of the outside world than I have.

In the six days I have spent in Florida, I have called up and killed five turkeys, all of whom were three years old or older, and one of them, the second to the last one, was called up with a turkey call that is 122 years old. The single day of the six that I hunted in Florida and did not kill a turkey could hardly be considered dull. That day I called two turkeys from the roost, three minutes apart. Each of them flew over my head at a height you could reach with a fishing pole of moderate length. Both birds then landed in a road so close behind me I could hear their feet thump down on the surface of the gravel when they lit.

Add to this situation the fact that in two of the other instances I called up two turkeys and shot only one of them, and you are forced to the obvious conclusion that my experiences in Florida are completely off the normal probability scale.

In summary then, in six days of hunting in Florida I have called nine turkeys into gunshot range, killed five of them, and passed up legitimate shots at two of the survivors. A statement which, unless you believe that the hunts were conducted within the boundaries of a poultry farm, or that I am a congenital liar, would seem to suggest only two reasonable courses of action.

First, and best of all, would be for me to deny the whole thing, or as an alternative, modify it until it becomes completely unrecognizable.

Admit to going down to Florida one time, years ago. Admit to jumping a twelve-pound yearling gobbler from a brush top at the side of the road just after I stepped out of the car and loaded the gun. Confess to shooting him neatly up the ass as he flew off, and let the whole matter die right there.

This is not a viable alternative because the entire series of affairs, all six of the instances are factual. They all really happened. They were all done in front of witnesses. Witnesses who, to a man, are reliable and responsible observers, impervious to either bribery or intimidation.

In short, I can't deny any part of the series because every bit of it was done in front of too many people.

The second choice would be to firmly resolve never to hunt another turkey in the State of Florida for all the rest of my life and to hold to the resolution.

This, of course, is the obvious and most intelligent solution. It leaves me not only a clear winner, but a winner with a remarkably favorable story to tell. A winner, furthermore, who is able to go into honorable retirement at the peak of his game. Like Bobby Jones dropping golf the year after he won both the U. S. and British, Amateurs and Opens in the same year, or Ted Williams retiring the afternoon he hit his 521st home run in his last time at bat.

I could initiate brandy and cigar reminiscences all the rest of the way to the bone yard, on the strength of this resignation, with the opening statement,

"Ah, Son, you ought to have been there in the spring of Double-Ought! Hardly a man is now alive who etc., etc., etc," and then sit back and let the howling gales of rhetoric move the ship along at twenty knots.

But you and I and every other turkey hunter who happens to read these lines knows in his soul that no such thing is ever going to happen because it violates every normal principle of human behavior.

Turkey hunters simply have to take that final pick at the scab. They cannot refrain from that one last tentative step. The pitcher simply has got to go back to the well, one more time.

No turkey hunter, living or dead, could get up and leave the performance at this juncture because the temptation to stay and see how the string comes to an end is absolutely overpowering.

There truly are temptations so strong that no man can resist them. There really are boxes that positively shriek to have the lid removed, no matter how much the box trembles, no matter how much colored smoke is leaking through the cracks around the hinges and regardless of how many troubles may be liable to escape when the lid comes off.

I have been tempted and I have succumbed. We will press on from here.

In casting up the dread balance of the amount I already owe to the percentage tables, it becomes necessary to establish my normal batting average if, for no other reason, than to calculate how long it is going to take to amortize the debt.

In a normal forty-two-day season in any given year, I will go to something like eight to ten turkeys gobbling on the roost, make no spectacularly stupid mistakes either during the approach march or occupation of position, sit down and call up two of them. During the same season, on no special schedule, I will make eight to ten turkeys gobble on the ground after they have been off the roost for some time, hide quickly and call up four or five of these. In the normal course of events I will kill a total of three out of both groups combined. On averages, therefore, three turkeys bagged, out of this many chances year after year, represents a fair assessment of my level of skill and expertise.

This is what I hit. This is the average that will go in the final listing of my career statistics at the close, unless I grow blind or deaf in my declining years.

If you will divide three by forty-two, the number of turkeys bagged divided by season length in days, the constant produced is .0714 turkeys per day.

Take the five Florida turkeys I have already killed, divide it by the .0714 which is my personal average, and you will find that in order to kill that many turkeys I should have hunted 70.02 days. Since my hunts in Florida average two per year, and since I can be credited with the six days I have already spent there, it becomes obvious that in order to square the account, I owe the State of Florida an additional sixty-four days. The debt will therefore be satisfied in only thirty-two more years, the year I turn a hundred and five.

Nobody in his right mind really wants to live to be a hundred and five. At that age all your friends are dead. Your doctor, your lawyer, and your stockbroker are not only all dead but you have very probably outlasted most of their grandchildren. Your own lovely, lissome daughters have turned into arthritic old ladies, and nobody is left alive from any of your wars.

When you finally do get to that last muster, that Great Battalion Party in the Sky, all your friends will already have been there for years, and you will be such a late arrival at the function that, to quote an ex-saw hand friend of mine.

"All the fish sammiches will be gone and all the lovin' spoke for."

Fortunately, debts owed at the time a person stacks arms can be handled by the estate. In the case of something like money, payment can be handled in specie or in kind. Debts that can be handled by heirs or assigns are open and shut and can be covered by instructions. Debts that can only be handled by personal attention are somewhat more difficult and tend to require special arrangements.

Mark Twain, in *Life on the Mississippi*, talks about the tradition connected with the old Raccourci cutoff, a natural cutoff that shortened the length of the river by twenty-eight miles. After the old river bend had begun to fill up, a steamboat took the wrong turn in the enormous elbow and got confused by the vague and distorted shapes in the changed channel. They began to run into mysterious reefs, and the heads of islands, and finally the frustrated pilots, in sheer perplexity, uttered the wish that they hoped they might never get out.

In accordance with the immutable laws that govern all the hoary traditions of the sea, this is exactly what happened.

To this day that phantom steamer is still butting around in that deserted river, trying to get out. Twain reports that more than one grave watchman had sworn to him that on rainy, dismal nights, the watchman had "glanced down that forgotten river and seen the faint glow of the spectral steamer's lights drifting through the dismal gloom, and heard the muffled cough of her 'scape pipes and the plaintive cry of her leadsmen."

I will never get to be a hundred and five, thank God, but that is no matter. Arrangements have already been made.

If you happen to be a young man in the early stages of your career, it is entirely possible that you will still be here and you will be hunting early one morning in the spring of 2032. If the area of your operations happens to be that part of Florida between the St. Mary's and the Apalachicola Rivers and north of Latitude 30, you may witness what appears to be a ghostly form, wearing seriously old-fashioned hunting gear, working the area a quarter-mile ahead of you. You should not worry.

What you see will not be a poacher, nor will it be someone who is hunting on your territory without authorization.

It will be nothing but the tattered apparition of a tattered old man, thirty-two years after the fact, faithfully paying the last installment of his debt to the State of Florida.

KILLING STONEWALL JACKSON

Michael Knight

Ghost Story won't tell you his real name. He's been shot fourteen times, still has lead in his kneecap and in the bones of his thighs and in two of his ribs. Pink scars pock his chest like extra nipples. There is a tumorous lump on his collarbone where he was nicked at Front Royal. He claims he is thirty-four years old, but when he wakes this morning, coughing blood onto the back of his hand and limping around in dingy long johns, you'd swear he'd been alive a hundred years.

At Cedar Mountain, you see Eustace Wilson cut in half by a chain. The enemy has run out of artillery and is loading whatever they can find into cannons: horse manure, broken-up slivers of wagon wheel. The chain makes a sound like a little boy whistling and takes Eustace apart just below his privates. His legs loll away to either side like a puppet's legs. His trunk thumps to the ground at your feet. His eyes are wide with surprise, his mouth gaping open and closed like he can't catch his breath. This is what they call the monkey show.

Ghost Story smokes tobacco rolled in corn husks. His best friend is a dwarf named Walpole. Walpole has a beard that drapes to his ankles, knotted with burrs and stained black around his mouth. When the army stops long enough, he makes whiskey from pine bark and lamp oil and rotted meat. He carries canteens of his concoction on the march instead of water. His hands and shoulders shake with palsy. His breath smells like kerosene.

The men tell stories about Stonewall Jackson. He keeps a colored whore and reads the Bible to her while she holds him in her mouth. He chews lemons even in the heat of battle. The day he earned his nickname he shot two dozen of his own men for attempting to flee the field.

He sleeps standing, like a horse. You see him up close one time, rounding a bend in the road with a group of officers, the horses dancing and blowing and bumping flanks. You are resting beside the road watching a hawk turn figure eights in the sky, and the general himself pulls up short and shouts, *We are an army of the living God!* Then he spurs his mount, drawing the glittering officers in his wake, the horses giving rise to spirits of dust as they pass.

Every night Walpole breaks for the freedom of the woods and every night Ghost Story brings him back. Ghost Story waits until he thinks you are asleep, then glides over you in the tent, smelling vaguely of camphor and sweat. You can hear cicadas ringing in the trees and the droning of a thousand snores. If there's been a fight that day, you can hear the terrible voices from the field, the abandoned and speaking dead. Finally, Ghost Story's shadow reappears against the side of the tent and you close your eyes, pretending sleep, and listen to him nestling down beside you in the dark. Before he comes to bed, he lashes Walpole's beard to a tent post to keep him from escaping again. Each morning, his memory wiped clean by drink, Walpole is amazed anew to find himself unable to stand.

In a cornfield at Sharpsburg, you fight McClellan to a standstill. The crop is shaved to stubble, bodies lined up in rows exactly where they fell. There is a whitewashed church beside the field. The September leaves are just beginning to change. The men gather in the church before falling back and write their names on the wall: Gellar The Jew and Henry Cotton, Ugly Joe Noon and Watkins Price. Even little Walpole climbs on Ghost Story's shoulders and scratches his name above the rest. When he's finished, Ghost Story sets him down and pats his head. You watch Ghost Story as he runs his hands across the plaster, hoping he will add his name as well, but he says the wall looks like a tombstone to his eyes.

Winter brings stragglers to camp, country women and slaves with no place else to go. You are squatting in the woods, pouring your insides out, when this girl appears beside you like an apparition. She wrinkles her nose and says, *Are you sick?* You smuggle hardtack from camp to feed her, take her down to the river and pull her nightgown over her head and wash her hair in bone-cold water. Before the war, miners worked these rocks and panned this river for gold. The girl can't be more than twelve, thirteen years old. You watch the water running over her hands and bare ankles, the two of you wading in the shallows, looking for bits of gold the miners might have forgotten.

Gellar The Jew carries a bag of teeth for good luck. His father is a dentist. He has two long curls of coal-black hair dangling from beneath his infantry cap. Ugly Joe Noon writes letters and poems to a woman no one believes exists. On the march, you catalog the names Ghost Story has denied. At night, you dream of Eustace Wilson playing cards. He's drinking Walpole's whiskey and winning all your money. His disembodied legs skitter from shadow to shadow just beyond the reach of the firelight. You wake screaming and Ghost Story smacks your head. He tells you to shut your damfool mouth.

You beat them back at Fredericksburg, hunkering in the sunken road, giving them canister and shot, watching their lines melt away like snow in the rain. It's so cold the wounded freeze before they bleed to death. The Aurora Borealis shows itself as far south as Black Mountain that night, the sky tracked red with streamers, running brighter than shooting stars. Watkins Price says that must be a good omen. Ghost Story says it's just spirits of the dead hurrying from the field.

No one will share a tent with Walpole. He vomits black bile all the time. He is a belligerent drunk. His feet are blistered and rotten, and even he can't stand the smell. At night, when Ghost Story brings him back to camp, he arranges Walpole's feet outside the tent, wipes them down with water from his canteen, and smears them with bacon grease. These are serious feet, big enough for a man twice Walpole's size. His toenails are yellow and hard as rail spikes. Ghost Story has to cut them down with his bayonet once or twice a week.

Sundays, now and then, General Jackson presides over the chapel service. He mounts the podium like he's going to ride it into battle, and he is strictly Old Testament in his preaching. Henry Cotton, who is in charge of trimming the general's beard, says that God himself told Stonewall how to turn Nathaniel Banks at Port Republic. Jackson's beard is always well-groomed and shiny, edged at his chin with a dignified sprinkling of gray, his hair swept back beneath his hat with pomade. You see him mornings turning his face side to side before a mirror, while Henry Cotton knots a gold sash around his waist.

The army is bivouacked near Zion Crossroads when the girl turns up again. It's evening, all fragile February light and woodsmoke, old songs and musty Bibles and letters home. You see her standing at the tree line, her nightgown breezing against her calves. You bring her rice, and she finds a worm as long as your finger in the bowl. She says, *We'll just eat acorns and live in the woods like squirrels.* When you ask if she is real, she laughs and slips out of her nightgown and lies back on the brittle grass. You kneel between her legs and take her in before nightfall—her pale hair spread like a wing around her head, her boyish nipples, so skinny you can count her ribs. You tell her that she's just a girl, this isn't what you want. You close your mind to thoughts of other men in other camps not so generous as you.

Ugly Joe Noon produces a letter from his woman at mail call. He crouches by the fire and reads it out loud. *I'll wait for you, Joe,* the letter says, *no matter what happens. If you are killed in battle,* the letter says, *I will keep myself pure until we meet again in Heaven.* The men fall quiet, loneliness settling over the morning like a fog. Ugly Joe sifts through the pages again and again, as if he can hardly believe what he's holding in his hands. The fire crackles and spits, dark birds turn circles in the sky. Somewhere, way off, the orderly patter of rifles. Then Gellar The Jew says, *I'll bet his sister wrote it.* All around the fire, men pick up the joke. Ugly Joe has his sister writing him letters. Ugly Joe couldn't get a woman in a whorehouse. Joe leaps to his feet, denies everything, takes a swing at Gellar The Jew, but the men laugh even harder. After a while, Joe gives up trying to change their minds and consigns the pages to the fire.

Stonewall Jackson has blue eyes. He wears a bright yellow plume in his hat and keeps a lady's underdrawers in his campaign chest, but they turn up missing when a thief follows spring into camp. There are new blooms and frightened grouse. Gellar The Jew loses a pocket watch, and one of his sidelocks is snipped from his head while he sleeps. Watkins Price loses the brass buttons from his uniform. He has to tie his coat with strips of boot leather until he can scavenge a new one from a dead man. Henry Cotton loses a gold tooth. Briefly reinspired, Ugly Joe Noon swears that the thief has stolen the rest of his beautiful love letters. Ghost Story sleeps with his bayonet even though he has nothing to lose. From his map table, General Jackson scrawls out a bounty: twenty Confederate dollars for the identity of the brigand.

One night you hear voices from Walpole's tent. He and Ghost Story are just back from their nightly cat and mouse. You sit in the darkness and eavesdrop. There's Walpole mumbling like his mouth is full of mud. You've never heard him speak a single coherent word, but Ghost Story understands him. He says, *That's right. We'll be up to our armpits in island girls. Hell, you'll be over your head. They'll have round bellies and skin as brown as baseball gloves. Just let me get your beard tied. There now. That's right. You sleep now, Walpole.* For a long time after he returns to the tent, he shifts his legs, trying to get comfortable against the ground.

The white canvas glows in the moonlight like you are bedded down inside a Chinese lantern. Finally, when you can't stand the quiet any more, you ask Ghost Story if he has ever been in love. After a moment he says, *Yes*, and that is all. The wind pushes leaves against the tent. You open the flap and look out at the night, all the sleeping men, death close upon them in their dreams. You can hear horses snuffling and tugging at the grass, the faint tinkling of armaments like silverware on a dinner plate. Then you say, *Tell me your name, Ghost Story. Someone should know your name in case something happens.* He rolls over so the two of you are back to back. Softly he says, *The army knows my name.*

Ugly Joe Noon is killed in a skirmish at Kelly's Ford. Gellar The Jew salvages his pack and searches it for evidence of the mystery woman. He finds a tattered daguerreotype of a girl with the same sloping forehead and crooked teeth as Ugly Joe, the same harelip and weak chin and shovel nose. He shows you the picture and says, *Has to be his sister, don't you think? No way Ugly Joe had a woman.* He takes the picture from your hands, folds it carefully, and hides it in the leather pouch with his lucky teeth.

The girl finds you on sentry duty. The woods are dark, crazy with insect chatter, and you don't hear her slipping up behind you, running her arms around your waist. She tells you it's fine that there is no food tonight. She came here to see you. She eases you back against a warm flat rock and pushes herself down over you, her hair swinging at her cheeks. When you protest, she covers your mouth with her hand. You tell her this means she'll have to marry you when the war is over. You tell her that you want to meet her family, and she says they're all dead, mother and father, four brothers and eight sisters. When you close your eyes, you see Ghost Story chasing Walpole through the woods, his breath huffing in and out, his eyes bright in the moonlight, his stride cantered and smooth like some nameless animal. You want to tell the girl to stop, but it's too late for that.

You dream of Ugly Joe Noon dancing with his sister, Eustace Wilson reunited with his legs. Walpole is eleven feet tall, his eyes clear, his hair neatly combed and dyed with bootblack. Ghost Story is bathing in a swiftly running river, shedding scars and tumors like snakeskins, and you wish you could find a place for yourself in this dream of restoration.

Sometimes Walpole trips over his beard. Ghost Story breaks rank and hauls him up by the collar, carries him under his arm until the order comes to halt. The line bumps to a stop, like rail cars. His beard is too thick to be cut by scissors or knives, so, after dinner, Ghost Story holds Walpole over the fire by his ankles, lets the hair catch and burn a few inches toward his face, then pinches it out with his fingers. Walpole blusters and fights, twists his body like a snake, but Ghost Story refuses to let him go. Moths flicker in the firelight. Ghost Story keeps burning it back until Walpole stinks like poison and the beard is nothing more than a singed goatee. He scrubs his face with whiskey and water, runs a wire brush under his fingernails, dunks his head in a pot of scalding water. When he's finished, Walpole shimmers pinkly in the darkness, glowing like a new June bride.

The thief returns before Easter. Gellar The Jew loses his boots and his second curl. Henry Cotton loses twenty-seven pounds to dysentery. Watkins Price loses his right eye when his rifle backfires on the parade ground. And you begin to lose your memory of the girl. It's been a month since her last appearance, and somehow you know you're not going to see her again. You try to think of her at night so she won't slip away completely, how you groped along the bottom of the creek and warmed her cold fingers in your mouth, how you fed each other acorns like grapes and whispered promises against her neck. Walpole sees you moping and offers you a swig from his canteen.

These days, Walpole's beard is too short for lashing him to the post, so Ghost Story is up and down all night. He asks do you mind if he sleeps nearest the tent flap. You listen to him slipping into the night and listen when he returns. He ties Walpole with strips of bedding, but Walpole gnaws through the cloth with his rotten teeth. Once he tries bringing Walpole into the tent with the two of you, but Walpole farts and grumbles like he's speaking backward, and eventually Ghost Story picks him up by the belt and pitches him outside. *You're on your own, jackass,* he says. But when Walpole has had a chance to go scurrying away, his footsteps tiny, almost soundless in the grass, Ghost Story lumbers painfully to his feet and is on the trail again. Finally, after nearly two weeks, Ghost

Story returns alone. He drops at the mouth of the tent, lights a husk of rolled tobacco without lifting his head. *I'm too tired,* he says, his voice blue smoke. In the distance is the deep bass note of cannon fire. You say, *I never figured why you didn't just let him go before.* Ghost Story sighs, drapes an arm across his face. He says, *Walpole won't last a minute on his own.* You say, *Maybe he'll surprise you,* and he says, *Yes, that's right, maybe he will.*

Letters mark the days that you have lived. You write to the girl, but you tear the letters up before they are finished, not only because you have no place to send them, but because the right words, all full of reverence and apology, are impossible to say. Gellar The Jew writes to Joe's sister, tells her that Ugly Joe was brave and honest and talked about her all the time. His last words were of his dear sister, Gellar writes, though you were there and you know this not to be the case. The sister writes back and Gellar writes again and so on. In the evening, with all the sad harmonicas blowing, Gellar The Jew unfolds her picture and holds it to the setting sun. He says, *She's not so ugly. Do you think?* You give him an eyebrow raise, and he says, *No, really. Look. You just have to see her in the right light.* He holds the picture up again and tilts it back and forth. *Look here,* he says. *Look here.*

Nine men are shot for desertion on nine successive days, lashed to a wagon wheel and made heavier with lead. Each time the bugler calls you to formation, Ghost Story's face goes pale. You hurry to the parade ground, form up, and watch General Jackson lift his hat above his head, then let it drop, a lemon wedge clutched between his teeth, but the dead man is never Walpole. Stonewall watches without emotion, slips a hand under his coat, and adjusts the wire on his corset. The air is rich with echoes. Sometimes Ghost Story creeps outside at night and vanishes for hours. But more often than not, he lies beside you and fails at sleeping, his limp growing more pronounced every day, his back bending into a stoop, all the old wounds refusing to let him rest.

You dream Walpole chasing island girls across packed sand, his feet jeweled with salt water, his beard flying over his shoulder like a cape. He offers them gifts to pry their legs apart, a matching pair of sidelocks and a gold tooth, brass buttons and your memory of the girl. Walpole must have ten children in the dream, each of them hobbling around on their father's stubby legs, calling out to him with unpronounceable words.

When you have marched fourteen miles in an afternoon and routed the enemy at Chancellorsville, General Jackson rides out along the front to survey his position. The wounded are pleading on the field because someone didn't do a proper job of killing. Ghost Story has been sent to the picket line without supper. Gellar The Jew starts another letter to Joe's sister. He says, *Would you read this for me? I've never been very good at saying things right.* Just as he is handing over the pages, you hear the report of a single rifle, and six days later old Stonewall is dead, his amputated arm buried in a separate grave. *We were scared,* Ghost Story says with a shrug. *Someone must have mistaken him for the enemy.* He winks and roots around in his pack, comes out with a canteen of whiskey that you didn't know he'd saved. He gets himself drunk enough to sleep. *Popskull,* he says, raising his tin cup. *Oh, Be Joyful.*

Sometimes, when new prisoners have been taken, you ask them if they've seen a girl in the woods. *She's always hungry,* you say. *I knew her a long time ago.* They have haircuts, these men, and their uniforms are clean. They are happy to be done with fighting. They cross their boots at the ankle and link their fingers behind their heads and say that if they had found a girl in the woods, the army wouldn't have seemed so bad.

Watkins Price sees Stonewall with his blind eye. Henry Cotton hears him in his sleep. They talk strategy and women's clothes. He saves the hair from General Jackson's comb, sprinkles it in the furrows of a tobacco field, hoping that Stonewall will sprout from the ground with the summer crop. Gellar The Jew believes that Stonewall is still alive, that he's been sent west in secret to remedy the situation along the Mississippi. Once you catch Ghost Story humming while he shaves, his jawbone lathered with soap. You ask him why he's so pleased, and he tells you that the days are growing longer now.

The army moves north without Stonewall, as though nothing has changed, through Maryland and Pennsylvania, then back across the Rappahannock toward home. You run through names for Ghost Story to pass the time: Saul, Jacob, Daniel, John. You have an idea that you won't be allowed many more guesses before he puts an end to the discussion altogether. So you study him quietly, trying to match a name to his features. There is a burn scar on his cheek shaped like a thumb, a lint bandage on his neck where he was grazed at Little Round Top. Gellar The Jew weighs in with Edgar. Henry Cotton thinks it's Richard, and you have to agree there is a Richardly curve to his broken nose. But Ghost Story shakes his head when you suggest that particular name. You are digging graves, the worst duty in the army, and he stops for a second to wipe the sweat from his brow. He rests a heel on the butt of his shovel. Crows are hopping on the new mounds, dawn skimming on the bottoms of the clouds. Ghost Story mutters to himself, a string of words that you don't understand, then shades his eyes and lets his gaze wander, as always, to the shadowy woods.

White Sugar and Red Clay

Bev Marshall

J.P. and Bob were headed down Enterprise Road on their way to Johnny Moore's Store when they saw Luther's car in the distance. J.P. watched the cloud of orange dust grow larger as the ten-year-old 1947 black Ford bounced toward them on the rutted road. Luther slowed and stopped the car alongside them. "Where you going to, J.P.?" he called from the window.

J.P. moved closer and leaned into the car. "Mama sent me to the store for sugar. She's making cake for Memphis's laying out."

Luther patted his son's cheek, and then in a much gentler voice than J.P. was used to hearing from his father, he said, "Well, get on home soon as you can. I'm helping with Deke's chores and you got to slop the hogs fore dark."

J.P. stepped back. "Okay, Daddy. Me and Bob be back quick." He stood for a moment in the road waiting until the Ford was out of sight. Then, he reached down and scratched behind Bob's ear. Straightening up, he waved the dog on toward Mr. Moore's store. Bob hadn't left his side all day. The bulldog seemed to know he was needed more than ever, and he had left his usual shady spot beneath the oak tree to accompany J.P. on all his errands and chores this hot, sunny day. J.P. did need Bob's company today. He'd awakened forgetting about the events of the night before, and throwing on his overalls, he'd run to the kitchen to grab a biscuit before meeting Memphis on his porch. But when he'd seen his mother's broad back standing at the stove, he'd remembered. Memphis wouldn't be meeting him today. He was lying in a box in the front room of his Mama's house. Without a word, J.P. had backed out of the kitchen and returned to his room to think. There, lying on his cot, arms crossed behind his head, he'd relived all the events of the night before. He remembered teasing Memphis, who had been afraid to slip out of his house at night.

"You're nothin' but a big baby," J.P. had said to him. "When you gets to be seven like me, maybe you won't be such a scary cat." And Memphis had hung his head and later changed his mind about sneaking out of his house after everyone was asleep. They had heard that the sheriff was going to be on a stakeout at the Parsons' Place, looking for robbers who had taken valuables from several houses in the area. J.P. had convinced Memphis to go when he pointed out that, if they caught the thieves, they'd be heroes and maybe get some money, or even a medal. But they hadn't seen any robbers or Sheriff Patterson, and J.P. had finally said they might as well go home. Turning around, they headed back across the pasture toward their homes until they came to the barbed wire fence. They ran along the fence line in the dark, and J.P. raced on across the space where the gate hung open, but Memphis had hopped upon the gate to swing across.

J.P. turned on his side in his narrow bed. "If only he hadn't climbed up on that gate," J.P. whispered. "If only, if only . . ." He covered his eyes with his forearm. His misery was too deep for tears, and he wondered at the emotion he felt bottled up just under his ribs. Physically, he felt sort of like he had when he'd contracted the mumps. He felt swollen and stiff and achy, and when Tee Wee called to him and sent him outside to gather the hen eggs, he'd felt as if his legs were swinging on metal hinges that needing oiling.

Bob had come along with him to the hen house, and with his protruding round eyes, he'd watched J.P.'s every movement. Even now, the dog looked sideways at him as he waddled along in the heat. His wrinkled white skin quivered in waves as he walked; his long pink tongue hung down in the dust that billowed up beneath J.P.'s feet. He had lived with J.P. for six years, and he seemed to understand that J.P. derived some comfort in the feel of him brushing occasionally against his leg.

J.P. and Bob usually meandered off the road into the ditch that ran beside the packed red clay on which they walked, collecting grasshoppers and slugs, bottle caps, and shiny round pebbles. But today J.P. walked with purpose, keeping his eyes focused on his destination. J.P. felt the mid-afternoon sun beating down on his head, adding to the weight of his sorrow. Occasionally, he lifted his forearm to his brow to wipe the beads of sweat which formed around his cropped hair. He stayed in the center of the road, unaware of passing the Thompsons' place, the Keppers', the Tates' pasture land. He heard a mockingbird's cry, a cricket in the tall grass that lined the ditch, a Jersey cow's bellow to its calf. No other sounds intruded on J.P.'s thoughts as he continued on his mile walk to the little store which sat in a wedge of pie-shaped land where Enterprise Road and Smithdale Road forked.

The store was a white wooden building standing in the middle of the vee between the roads. It was narrow at the entrance with a center door opening into a long rectangular room. Mr. Moore's daddy had added on the store before Enterprise Road was widened for cars, and when Johnny Moore had included a single gas pump to his business, he had placed it in the vee, precariously close to both roads. Traffic was usually light, but when cars passed the store, dust clouded the pump and billowed through the screen door into the interior of the dark store, coating the merchandise with a fine layer of red powder. Whenever a customer handed over his purchase (whether it be a can of soup, a bag of tobacco, or a stick of peppermint), Johnny would lift the merchandise to his mouth and automatically blow off the dust before ringing up the amount on his big gold metal register.

Today Johnny Moore was sitting outside his store in one of the three cane rockers lined up close behind the gas pump. The two other rockers were occupied by Mr. Whittington and Mr. Kepper, whose heads were wreathed in clouds of smoke billowing up from the cigars stuck in the sides of their mouths. J.P. and Bob slowed their steps as they approached the men. Ducking his head, J.P. whispered to Bob. "You lays down quiet. White men don't like for dogs and coloreds to disturb their talking." Bob obediently ambled over to the shade offered from a pine on the side of the store and lay down, closing his eyes, but lifting his ears to follow J.P.'s steps. J.P. slowly and quietly walked toward the front door. He needed sugar and the peppermint Tee Wee had told him he could buy with the change from the wrinkled dollar he had stuffed in the pocket of his overalls.

Ten feet from the men, J.P. stopped and waited until he was noticed. Mr. Moore looked over at him first. He was, after all, a businessman and colored money spent the same as white money. "You needing something today, boy?" he asked.

J.P. nodded his head up and down.

Mr. Whittington motioned him forward. J.P. could see little brown dribble spots on his shirt from the cigar he was chewing. Ducking his head, J.P. looked over at Mr. Kepper's big brown boots. "You Luther and Tee Wee's boy? The one that was with Deke and Icey's boy last night that got hisself killed?" J.P. nodded again. He could sense the quickening interest of all three of these white men, and he felt his heart thumping with fear. He hadn't done anything, had he? Heaving his shoulders, he breathed in the white scent. These men smelled differently from the big white men in town. Their aroma was more familiar because they were farmers who carried the pungent odors of manure and molasses-based feed, and the acrid pesticide which never completely left the skin.

Mr. Moore rocked back in his chair. "Sit down, boy, tell us about what happened. What'd you see? How bad was he mashed up?"

Looking around, J.P. didn't see another chair, so he sat a few feet back on the ground in front of the dust-coated red pump. He didn't know exactly what was expected of him; his face immobile, he waited. Mr. Kepper leaned forward. "Sheriff Patterson I heard run right over the middle of him, squished him flat. That what you saw?"

Still J.P. couldn't find his tongue. He looked across the yard at Bob lying in the dirt, ears lifted. Bob's presence was a comfort, but J.P. couldn't make himself put on the smile like he usually tried to wear when talking to white people.

Mr. Moore was growing impatient. "Well, boy? What you got to say? Cat got your tongue?"

Now J.P. succeeded in managing a small smile for the men. "No, sir. Memphis, he laying out at his house. Ain't squashed none I could see. Got on a white burying suit Mrs. Parsons brought his mama this morning."

"Nigger doctor was out, patched him up, I bet," Mr. Kepper said.

J.P. nodded. "Doc was to the house last night. We knowed he were dead though, but Mama she sent for him anyhows. Sheriff Patterson wanted the white man to come to see to Mrs. Parsons and them all, and he did that I reckon. I ain't seen none of them today." J.P., rounding his back, hunching his shoulders, drew back into himself. He'd never spoken for so long to so many white men.

"Boy, was you there when they pulled him out beneath the truck? I heard that truck was so gunked up with blood and guts they had to wash out the underside fore it'd run."

J.P. shook his head. "I weren't there long. Sheriff sent me to the house to get Memphis's daddy and my mama."

Mr. Whittington spat out some more tobacco juice, which landed only a foot away from where J.P. sat. "What about his mama? Why didn't you get her?"

"Oh, she was already there," J.P. said, and beginning to understand now that all the attention of these three men was directed on him and that he was expected to give a performance, he continued on. Sitting up straighter, his voice took on a louder, more lively tone. "Yessiree, I was right in front of Memphis when he jumped on the gate, and I turned back and seen Memphis's mama running up jest when Memphis fell off the gate, and the truck were skidding, and there was a thump. Then she screamed such a scream it was to make your blood go cold in your body and I was feeling I gonna freeze to death just hearing that awful screaming." Checking the men's faces, J.P. now realized he was giving them what they wanted. " 'God, Lord Jesus,' she said. Sheriff Patterson, he jumped out of the truck and he seen his shoes covering with the blood of Memphis and he puked in the bushes, and I says, 'Somebody got to help this woman and this here white man.' And I starts to run for help, but I seen Memphis's leg sticking out from underneath the truck and I smells the blood and I knowed God done took my best friend, and . . ." These last words brought J.P. back to himself, and now he remembered his loss. He fell silent. J.P. glanced over at the men. They were staring at him with an intensity he'd never seen in white men's eyes. He thought perhaps this was the way they looked at their own children, and he began to experience for the first time an emotion he'd never had before. Although he couldn't quite identify it, J.P. knew that the respectful listening these men had given him wasn't something even his daddy would know about. And then he did something he'd never done before. He violated his mother's taboo. He lifted his eyes and stared right back into the faces of these men. When his eyes met Mr. Moore's, he saw the tightening muscles at the corners, the lift of the brow. Instantly, he realized he'd been too bold. The spell he'd bound was broken. Quickly, J.P. tucked his chin in and lowered his eyes. He heard Mr. Moore rising from his chair, opening the screen door. "You wanting something to buy? Come on in and get it and be off."

J.P. scrambled up and followed him into the dark room. He couldn't make out anything for a minute or so, but when his eyes adjusted, he roamed them over the shelves of tinned goods, dry goods, barrels of nails and pickles, jars of licorice and peppermint. Back to himself now, he lowered his head and mumbled, "I needs sugar for my mama, and I got money to pay." He drew out his rumpled dollar bill and laid it on the counter.

Mr. Moore lifted a brown one-pound paper bag, blew on it, and snatched the dollar from the counter. Opening the cash register, he drew out some change and slapped it on the varnished wood. J.P. scooped up the coins and dropped them into his overalls pocket. Then, taking the bag, he silently backed out of the door.

Bob was waiting for him, keeping one eye on the men in the rockers. That he was nervous showed only in his continual tail twitching. J.P. slapped him on the head to turn toward home. Trying not to run, he walked as fast as he could away from the store and he kept the pace until he knew he was out of sight of the white men who had somehow won something from him he didn't understand.

As J.P. and Bob walked on more slowly, J.P. began to talk to Bob in a low voice. "I feels like I done something wrong back there. We ain't gonna say nothing to Mama. She told me to jest say yes to whites, don't go telling nothing to 'em. But I done told about Memphis, and now I feels like Memphis would be mad at me for it."

Bob banged against J.P.'s leg. Hearing the tremor in his master's voice, he began to quicken his pace toward home. They were passing the Kepper place now which meant they were nearly half way there, and J.P. stopping talking, thinking now that he'd forgotten to buy a peppermint for himself, and feeling somehow glad that he at least hadn't rewarded himself for his disloyalty. He didn't notice the blue tick hound sitting in the Keppers' yard.

Bob lifted his head, sniffing the dog's proximity. The blue tick rose up and, standing on his long sturdy legs, watched them move toward him. Out of the corner of his eye, J.P. saw a shiny object lying on the other side of the ditch which served as a boundary to the Keppers' property. J.P. jumped the ditch and squatted down to pick up the bottle cap to add to his collection at home. He heard the hound's growls and Bob's bark at the same time. Quickly, J.P., dropping his sugar and bottle cap, turned to run back to the road, but he slipped on the loose gravel and fell in the ditch.

Nothing had seemed normal all day and now Bob let all his anxieties work their way out in this natural savage urge he felt toward this enemy bearing down on his master. He bounded across the ditch and met the dog with his wide jaws open. Although the blue tick was faster than Bob, he was no match for the strength of a bulldog. Pushing his way underneath the hound, Bob's strong teeth tore into soft flesh.

J.P. scrambled out of the ditch. Frantically, he forced himself to move toward the melee. He tried to grab Bob's back legs but he wasn't strong enough to budge them. When he tried to pull the blue tick away from Bob, the enraged dog tried to sink his teeth into J.P.'s arm. "Stop. Stop, Bob," he yelled over and over as he continued to try and separate the dogs with his trembling hands. But Bob was oblivious to his commands. In only a few minutes the fight was suddenly over. The blue tick fell on its side. His throat was torn open.

The dogs' and J.P.'s shouts had brought Mrs. Kepper out of her house, and when she saw what had happened on the road, she too began screaming, running toward them. Grabbing Bob behind his neck, J.P. dragged him backwards away from the dead hound. Mrs. Kepper swooped by them, and knelt on the ground beside her dog. Then she looked over at Bob. His folded face and squared white paws were covered with blood. His mouth was parted, showing cherry-stained teeth. Panting heavily, Bob sat docilely beside J.P.'s feet, and when J.P. didn't reach his hand down to stroke him as he usually did, the dog looked up at him, seeming to wonder why he hadn't been praised for saving his master.

Mrs. Kepper lifted a shaking arm toward Bob. When Bob lifted his head to her, J.P. held him tighter by the heavy folds of skin around his neck. "Stay, boy. Don't move," he said, wanting to run away as fast as he could himself. But running wouldn't change anything, and he stood holding the dog, waiting.

She walked a few steps closer to J.P. Her yellow and white hair, knotted on top of her head, fell around her perspiring face. Her face was red, splotched with blemishes, the ugliest white face J.P. had ever seen. She squinted her colorless eyes at him. Her mouth twisted into a squiggly line. "Boy, this here was a prime huntin' dog. Blue tick. You know that?"

J.P. shook his head. He hadn't had time to notice what kind of dog Bob had fought.

Mrs. Kepper swung her finger at Bob. "You got a killer dog there."

J.P. opened his mouth. He ain't no killer, that dog just came at him too suddenlike, he wanted to say. But he knew better. A dog that had killed another dog would do it again. As young as he was, he knew that.

Mrs. Kepper drew herself up, the setting sun behind her back. "Here come Mr. Kepper. He'll deal with this."

J.P. wheeled around and was surprised to see Mr. Kepper getting out of his truck. He hadn't seen or heard the truck pass behind him. He watched as Mr. Kepper walked toward his wife. J.P. nearly felt relieved for a moment thinking this was the man who had wanted to hear his tale about Memphis, but then he saw the outraged look on Mr. Kepper's face when he saw the dead hound, and J.P. knew that he was only the owner of a killer dog now.

Mrs. Kepper grabbed her husband's arm. When she had blurted out her version of the massacre, she turned around to J.P. and said, "There's the dog that done it. I saw it with my own eyes. Blood all over him. See for yourself."

Mr. Kepper walked over to where Bob and J.P. waited, and with his boot, he kicked the dog hard on his right flank. Bob yelped, looked up to J.P. for help. "I said that was a mean dog when I seen him back at Johnny Moore's." He turned to J.P. "You know how much money your dog just chewed up with his ugly face?"

J.P. shook his head. "He scared him," he whispered.

"What's that?" Mr. Kepper yelled.

J.P. shook his head again. There wasn't any use pleading Bob's case, especially to a white man.

"Wait here," Mr. Kepper said, walking off toward his house. Mrs. Kepper opened her mouth to say more, closed it, and silently followed her husband across the yard.

J.P. thought about running, but there wasn't any use in that. The Keppers would find him, and they'd find Bob, too. Still, he looked longingly down the road toward home. The sun seemed to be running down the sky now, escaping with its light beyond the fields. It shot out beams of reddish-orange light over the tops of the scrub oaks in front of the Keppers' house, and behind the trees the house took on an unnatural golden glow. In the dimming light, J.P. squatted down beside Bob. He stroked his head, scratched behind his drooping ears. "You done wrong, Bob," he whispered. "I know you didn't know no better, but you gonna have to pay for it now." Bob nudged his head into J.P.'s leg, hiding his face, as if he knew what the tone of the voice meant. "You was always a good . . ." J.P.'s voice broke off. He stood up. He heard Memphis's small voice rising across the space between them. Last night, frightened of the dark, Memphis had said the only prayers he knew. "Now I lay me down to sleep. Thank you for this food." J.P. heard the crunch of gravel beneath Mr. Kepper's boots.

"Step out of the way, boy." Mr. Kepper said, raising the tip of the big double barrel shotgun.

J.P. jumped across the ditch, and stood in the road. Bob rose up from the ground and turned to follow him. "Stay," J.P. commanded. And Bob stopped. He stood still, looking confused, as if he were unsure of what he was supposed to do next. J.P. looked away from him, stared at Mr.

Kepper's stubbled chin, then at the hairy knuckles that held the gun. He watched the puffy index finger crook around the trigger. The knuckle whitened a split second before the explosion.

Without looking at Bob or Mr. Kepper, J.P. moved forward, picked up his sugar, and began the half-mile walk home. He thought about his mama. She was gonna be waiting for the sugar she needed for Memphis's funeral cake. And, as he walked on in the twilight down the newly widened road, J.P. felt he was coming home from a very long journey from a distant land. He began to quicken his pace, walking faster and faster. When he finally saw the silhouette of his house outlined in the pink sky, his bare feet were skimming over the ground so fast, it seemed to J.P. he may have lifted off the ground and flown through the open doorway into his mama's arms.

BLACKBIRD

Barbara Robinette Moss

Rodney Wood got run over and killed on his bicycle two days ago. He was six like me, but in the second grade with my brother instead of in the first grade with me. I think he started to school early to get away from his mama. But he might of started early just so he could get free lunch at school. Nearly everybody living on this side of Trafford thinks it's worth learning to write all those words for hotdogs on Wednesdays and macaroni and cheese on Fridays.

Rodney was crossing Fulton Street to talk to Viola. Viola was walking home from work, holding a red umbrella to keep the sun out of her eyes, but she still saw what happened. She told the sheriff it was a brand-new Cadillac with Alabama plates from the next county over. A slick black 1957 Cadillac, going real fast. She said the driver didn't slow down, even after he hit Rodney. Viola told my mama she thought Rodney saw the car coming. Said he popped his front tire up and rode straight into that fast-moving car.

Whenever my mama goes in the hospital to have another baby, Viola keeps us kids. She don't like girls, so I stay out of her way. But she just loves my brother, Stephen. And Rodney Wood. He's my brother's best friend in second grade. But not now because he's dead.

When Viola keeps us kids, she smiles at Rodney and Stephen. "You boys behave," she says, and smiles and smiles. She reaches out with her black wrinkled hands and messes up their hair. She don't smile at me, but I don't care. She's old and only got four teeth and they're the same color as her skin from chewing tobacco. Viola carries around a tin can to spit in. She misses a lot, and tobacco juice drips all over her fingers and the sides of the can. I think she ought to just smoke, like Daddy does. Smoking don't make puddles in the corner of your mouth like chewing. Viola wears stockings rolled down below her knees with tobacco juice spots on them, and she wears the same blue dress every day, but it never looks dirty.

Viola liked Rodney because he'd steal stockings for her. He'd steal them from Sandlin's Store. One time he stole Viola some stockings and a pair a socks for hisself. When he got home there was only one sock. Viola took the one sock over to the store and told Mr. Sandlin she got cheated and he gave her the other sock. Rodney wore them and wore them, and they laughed and laughed.

Every time Rodney visited our house, he'd come through the screen door, and say, "I got on my stole socks today." He'd roll the bottom of his jeans way up high so we could see them. They was nice socks, too. Blue with black diamonds on the side. I looked in the casket to see if he had on his stole socks today, but the top of that casket was cut in half, and the part that covered up Rodney's legs and feet was closed.

Mrs. Wood had the funeral home bring Rodney's casket over and put it right in the living room where his bed used to be. He slept on a crib mattress. He had to stuff it behind the couch every morning before he went off to school. My daddy lifted me up so I could see Rodney in his casket. Everybody talked about how nice he looked, but he didn't look nice to me. If that flat scar on his forehead didn't show, I'd bet it was some other kid. I'd never seen the white shirt Rodney had on. The preacher's wife must have bought it. She should have bought him a blue shirt. That white one made Rodney's blond hair look gray, like an old person's hair. Somebody cut Rodney's hair, too. Seemed kind of silly to cut Rodney's hair if he's dead. He won't get to see it and brag about it. Preacher's wife must have done that, too.

Preacher's wife is pretty nice. She gives us penny candy and prays for our souls not to rot in hell, and for us to be forgiven for everything we done, and sometimes for stuff we didn't do. She gave us seashells and little metal crosses with a fish carved on it. She told us to carry those crosses in our pocket and the Lord would protect us. Rodney had one, but I ain't sure he had it with him when he got hisself killed. Rodney might of lost his cross, or traded it to Sam Butterworth for a dip of snuff.

Sam Butterworth loves snuff. "It'll make your babies be born naked," he jokes when he pushes a pinch in his lip. He's got a smile like a suckerfish with that snuff in his lip. Sam told me he'd been dipping since he was my age. That's a long time. He told me he'd be thirty-three on his next birthday, and that's almost as old as my daddy. Sam's got lines around his eyes, but he still likes to play. Sam makes us laugh.

One time he tried to teach us to fly by flapping our arms. We couldn't fly but it sure was fun to try. We'd been watching a bunch of blackbirds in the soybean fields. They'd fly down from the trees and peck around, soar around in the sky, then land on the tree branches again. Sam told us that birds hold on to the souls of dead people. Some souls can't make up their minds whether they want to be in heaven with God or on earth with us, so they take up in birds and fly back and forth. I like Sam. Some people are afraid of him. Mrs. Wood said Sam is touched in the head, but he seems all right to me. And he was always sweet to his mama. He painted sunflowers and a flock of red-winged blackbirds on the wall in her kitchen.

In our coloring book, my little sister colored a picture of a man. She made one eye blue and one eye purple. I told her that was wrong. But Sam's got one brown eye and one green eye, so I guess it's not wrong after all. Sometimes I color one brown and one green myself. I color most everything green anyway. It's my favorite color and we've got two green crayons because Rodney traded Stephen a green crayon for a locust skin.

Last year locusts came through Trafford buzzing like a million chain-saws. Stripped the corn down to the soft cob and left the soybeans nothing but cockleburs. They even ate the leaves off the trees. They stuck around long enough to shed out of their skins, then they flew away, making a cloud like a twister in the sky.

Everybody cussed about them locusts. My daddy called them hornets from Hell. Their tiny legs hold tight on to a piece of bark and they split out of the back, just peel away from their own skin, leaving it stuck to the tree. Even the skin over their eyes peels off and leaves a shell like a crunchy brown monster. Us kids pulled all the locust skins off of the tree trunks. Nelda Wood, Rodney's little sister, squealed when she pulled them off the tree. I'm not scared of them one bit. All us kids collected locust skins and put them in cigar boxes we bought for a penny at Sand-lin's Store.

Rodney Wood had more locust skins than anybody did, but he traded real good stuff to get more. He was crazy about them little things. I traded him my cigar box with ten locust skins for two of Miss Thiweet's pears. My mama thought Miss Thiweet gave me them pears. She wouldn't of let me keep them if she'd known I got them from Rodney. She knows he steals them. Miss Thiweet would never give Rodney's family any pears. Rodney's daddy drinks real bad and cusses and smokes and chews and cusses. His mama, too. Rodney's mama has got lots of children but she don't like them much. I go over to play with Nelda sometimes, and Mrs. Wood'll holler, "You kids get your ass outside." She feeds her babies corn bread broke up in coffee and hardly ever changes their diapers. She was meanest to Rodney. Hit him with a fly swatter. Sometimes his bare legs had red welts on them from that fly swatter, but it didn't leave scars. Rodney liked scars. He had them on his forehead and elbows and knees. He got all those scars from riding his bicycle into trees. He'd ride as fast as he could right into the trunk. One time he hit his forehead and cut a big gash in it. He said he wanted lots of scars so he'd look mean. Mrs. Wood said he looked a fright. My daddy said the same thing about her.

"That woman's hair never sees a comb," my daddy said, but he smiles at her when Mama ain't around. I think he likes the way she feeds that newest baby. Just pulls out her nipple and lets it suck right in front of folks.

My mama watched Mrs. Wood's babies at the funeral so Mrs. Wood could spend her last time with Rodney before he got buried. Mrs. Wood wailed all afternoon. She said, "Lord, bring back my child. I'll go to that church on the hill every day, every single day." She fell down by Rodney's casket and beat on the floor with her fists. I saw her look to see if the preacher was watching. Everybody knows she don't mean that talk. Mrs. Wood never goes to church. Last week, when me and Nelda was playing house and going to pretend church, Mrs. Wood yelled, "Them's a bunch a hippocats, and they're all going to hell." She took a draw on her cigarette and said, "I ain't never stepping foot in that barn full a snake-handling, holy-rolling hippocats, and ain't none a my kids neither!" Then she went back to feeding them babies corn bread broke up in coffee. She put her cigarette on the edge of the table instead of in the jelly jar lid. Her table has got long burns all over it where she forgets about them. Long black burns. I can always tell Mrs. Wood's cigarette butts from my daddy's by the red from her lips. Sometimes I find her cigarette butts and they're old and flat and rained on, but they're still red on the ends.

Miss Thiweet said Mrs. Wood is going to hell because of her red lips and the stuff she puts on her hair. She likes her hair to be that blond color, like Rodney's. One time, when I was over at their house, Mrs. Wood said, "My hair was just like Rodney's when I was a girl. All the boys just loved my hair."

Miss Thiweet never puts nothing on her hair. She wears it in a ball on her head. She wears white gloves and lace-up shoes. Stephen said she's ugly. Miss Thiweet was his Vacation Bible School teacher before she got too old. Now she just visits people—only good people—and puts up pears from her tree, and gives away little white Bibles with red words on the pages. She gave all us kids a Bible: Stephen and our baby brother and baby sister and me. Stephen traded one of our Bibles to Rodney because Miss Thiweet wouldn't give him one.

"No sense giving good Bibles to the Woods. They're on their way to Hell," Miss Thiweet said. She ought to know. She goes to Blinded Light Baptist Church every Sunday and Sunday night and Wednesday night. She has her Bible in a homemade pink cover with lace around the edges, and can tell you anything you want to know about Jesus. Anything. Miss Thiweet always looks clean and smells like lye soap.

Viola smells like tobacco, and Mrs. Wood smells like dirty diapers. Mrs. Wood says Viola's all right for a nigger, and Viola says Mrs. Wood is a whore and a no-account. Viola won't keep Mrs. Wood's children, but Mrs. Wood don't know it because she never goes nowhere to need a sitter. She had her last two babies at home with Doc Flint's nurse helping. Viola wishes Mrs. Wood would ask her to keep her children, so she can say no. But Viola liked Rodney Wood anyway. She said he was a sweet boy, which wasn't so, and a precious soul, which wasn't true neither. Rodney would hit you, and he didn't care if your brother was his best friend. Rodney killed one of our kittens one time, too. Shut its head in the icebox. Killed it dead. Mama said it was an accident and she was sure Rodney wouldn't kill the kitten on purpose. But he did. It was the only white kitten. All the rest was black or gray.

I told my daddy about Rodney killing one of our kittens, and he said, "Only one?" My daddy hates them cats. Last night when he come in from work, he sat on the front steps to drink his beer. He threw his hardhat at Tiger. "Jesus Christ," he said, "who's feeding all these damn cats."

Mama was sitting on the front porch rocking her newest baby. "They keep away the rats," she said.

"Well, it don't take a damn army of cats to keep away a few mice," Daddy said. He got up and went for another beer, and Mama said, "Rats, not mice."

My mama don't say much unless we do stuff we ain't got no business doing. She just sits on the porch holding her babies, and watches the trains go by. The railroad tracks run along our house. The trains make it shake just enough to rock the babies to sleep. We put pennies on the tracks and the train pounds them flat. One of my pennies came out shaped like a heart. I've still got it. I slide it between the boards in the kitchen wall, under the table where the water bucket sits. Stephen can't find it there. I get it out sometimes to carry in my pocket. It taps against the cross with the fish carved on the front and makes a fine music.

Stephen and Rodney threw rocks into the train cars when it flew by, but I couldn't throw hard enough. One time Rodney hit me with a rock. "You're sissified! You throw like a girl!" Which is a stupid thing to say since I am a girl. But after he said that, I tried to throw more like a boy. Rodney hit me with a dry corncob one time and made a purple place on my leg. My mama got mad and said we couldn't play with the corncobs no more. But the bruise was kind of pretty. It was deep blue, like Mrs. Wood's eyes after Mr. Wood hits her.

Viola said Mrs. Wood deserves to be hit. "That woman needs her ass beat twice a day." Viola don't like Mrs. Wood. This morning, right in front of everybody, Viola said it was Mrs. Wood's fault Rodney was dead because she's a no-account woman. Mrs. Wood said it was Sam Butterworth's fault Rodney was dead for giving him that bicycle.

Even though folks told him not to, Sam Butterworth showed up at the Woods' house for Rodney's funeral. Everybody stopped talking. Sam didn't dress up. He had on blue jeans with grease on the front and a long john shirt with the arms cut out. He always wears his work boots, but he don't lace them up, just walks all over the strings. He had on his fishing cap with lures stuck in the bill, and he had a bottle in a brown paper bag stuffed down in his belt.

Mrs. Wood saw Sam Butterworth come in, and threw a whatnot at him. It was a china blackbird. Sam ducked, and the blackbird crashed into the wall, and its wings broke off. Rodney bought that bird for five cents at the Shining Light Baptist Church rummage sale. He gave it to his mama. I wanted to buy that blackbird real bad, but I didn't have five cents.

Sam Butterworth picked up those wings like he was gonna throw them back at her, but instead he ran outside. Everybody started talking at once. I'd been standing by Rodney's casket, trying to be good, but Mrs. Wood breaking that blackbird scared me, and I ran for my mama.

"Moonshine gonna kill Sam Butterworth someday," Miss Thiweet said, sliding a plate of ham and mashed potatoes onto the coffee table for Mama. "It's evil, downright evil working in that boy. The very idea, bringing such a thing to Rodney's funeral. Moonshine's what caused that boy so much grief in the past. His poor mama. God rest her soul. It's Pandora's Bag, that's what it is, Pandora's Bag." Miss Thiweet patted my brother Stephen on the head and walked off.

I crawled up on the couch. "What's Pandora's Bag?" I asked.

Mama was leaning over the couch to change my baby sister and one of Mrs. Wood's babies at the same time. She took a safety pin out of her mouth and pushed it into the diaper. "It's Pandora's Box," she said, looking over her shoulder to make sure Miss Thiweet couldn't hear her. She took the last safety pin from her mouth. "It's a myth, a story, about a box that was given to a woman named Pandora. It was full of all the evils that trouble mankind. When Pandora opened the box the evils flew out."

"What kind of evils?" I asked, handing her a clean undershirt.

"Oh, let's see . . . sickness, locusts, drought. That kind of thing." She picked up both babies at once and sat on the couch between Stephen and me. Stephen had been right beside Mama all day. He wouldn't even look at Rodney in his casket. I tickled my baby sister and made her laugh.

"Miss Thiweet believes the whiskey Sam brought with him is one of the evils from Pandora's Box," Mama said.

"Well is it?" I asked.

"I suppose it's an evil all right, so I guess it could be."

"How did the evils get in the box?"

"Oh, I don't remember anymore," Mama said. "It's been a long time since I read about it."

I thought about this a minute, then scooted off the couch and went looking for Sam Butterworth. I wanted to be close in case Sam cried. I wanted to see if Sam's different-color eyes cried different-color tears. I walked out the screen door and onto the porch. Mrs. Wood followed me outside. She wiped her mouth with the back of her hand and smeared red lipstick all over her face. Then she started yelling at Sam.

"You're just a damn killer is what you are. A killer! And everybody knew that before you killed Rodney!"

Sam shouted, "I gave Rodney that bicycle because he's my friend."

But Mrs. Wood wouldn't listen. She started crying real loud.

Sam shouted again. "Rodney was my friend."

Mrs. Wood closed her eyes, put her hands over her ears, and whined like a hurt mule so she couldn't hear what Sam was saying. While her eyes were closed, Sam walked up closer. Mrs. Wood was on the porch, and Sam was on the ground right under her nose. Mrs. Wood stopped bawling and opened her eyes. She saw Sam and spit right in his face.

"You killer!" she screamed at him. "Look at you! Look what you done to your own mama. Your own mama! Shot her with a sawed-off shotgun, then burned the house down around her!"

Sam dropped his face into his hands and started to cry.

"You killed your own mama, and now you got Rodney killed, too!"

I couldn't stand to hear Sam cry. Mrs. Wood was just being mean! I walked right up to her and patted her arm. "That ain't so," I said. "Sam didn't kill his mama. That ain't so."

My daddy come out the door and grabbed my hand. "Come on, Whistle Britches, let's leave them be."

"But it ain't so!" I tried to pull away from Daddy. Miss Thiweet, Viola and the preacher stood just inside the screen door, watching.

"Oh, it's so, all right!" Mrs. Wood screamed. "Shot her with a shotgun right in the heart. Killed his own mama! Tell them the truth! Tell them the truth what happened!"

The preacher and several women came out on the porch and pulled Mrs. Wood back inside. "It'll be all right," they said, and patted her on the back. My mama leaned out the screen door. She bounced two babies in her arms. She nodded to my daddy, and he made me sit on the top step. He sat beside me.

"Sam's mama was very sick," Daddy said, looking over his shoulder at Mama. He reached out and pulled Sam down onto the step in front of us. He put an arm around me, and one around Sam. "She couldn't walk anymore and she was hurting real bad. The Preacher said she'd been begging Sam to shoot her for a long time."

"No, Daddy! Sam's mama burned up in the house fire," I said.

"Well, yes, she did," my daddy said, "but she was already dead by then, you see?"

"But the house burned down, and it burned the trees all the way to the mouth of the creek!"

"I know," Daddy said, "but Sam's mama was already dead."

Tears got in my eyes. "Sam killed his mama?"

"Yes," Daddy said.

"Is that why people are afraid of Sam? Why they say he's crazy?"

Daddy put his finger over his lips. "Shh." Sam covered his face again.

"Well . . ." Daddy said. He shook his head. Finally he reached into his shirt pocket. "Looky here." He opened his hand and the china blackbird was perched right on his palm. "I bet Sam can glue those wings back on and nobody'd ever know it got broke."

Sam took his hands away from his face. He looked like he was gonna cry again, but I didn't want him to cry. I blinked back my tears, took the bird from Daddy, and held it out to Sam. He took the little bird, pulled the wings from his pocket, and fit them together. His eyes filled up with tears.

"Just forget it, Sam," Daddy said. "Ain't nothing you can do. She's got to have somebody to blame it on, or she'll go crazy."

We sat on the steps and looked at the blackbird for a while. Sam gave Daddy the bottle of moonshine. He took a sip and gave it back.

Sam wiped his nose on his arm, took another sip of moonshine, and handed it back to Daddy. They passed the bottle back and forth a couple of times, then Sam got up to leave. I guess Daddy figured visiting Sam was better than watching Mrs. Wood cry. He took my hand and we followed Sam down the trail by the creek.

A few days ago, me and Stephen and Rodney came down to the creek. We covered our ears and shouted to see if we could shout as loud as the creek roared. We saw Sam Butterworth down on the bank running a trotline. Stringed the line all the way across the river with chicken livers for bait. He caught a lot of fish, too. Catfish. He gave Rodney catfish all the time, enough for everybody at his house to get a whole one for supper.

Sam lives in the Gypsies' house now. It belongs to Mr. Sandlin. He rented it out to the Gypsies last year. But them Gypsies just disappeared a while back, and left all their furniture, three cats and a bunch of birds. Mr. Sandlin said a year of rent had been paid, so Sam is staying there and taking care of all the Gypsies' stuff. He ain't got nowhere else to go because his house is burnt down. He likes the Gypsies' red table and chairs and wind chimes hanging everywhere. He made some more wind chimes out of old rusty pipes and hung them in the trees.

The Gypsy house is so small it looks like a dollhouse. It's pink with short, fat poles holding up the front porch. Even the porch is pink.

We broke through the woods to Sam's backyard, and Daddy said, "Why don't you get Sandlin to paint that damn house, Sam?"

"Oh, I don't mind pink," Sam said. "Besides, them Gypsies might be back soon."

"Hell, Sam, them Gypsies ain't coming back. They been gone nigh on to four months. If they was coming back, they'd be back by now."

Daddy kicked red mud from his boots.

"They left an awful lot of stuff not to be coming back," Sam said, scraping his boots on the steps, his shoestrings all covered with red mud.

"Well, I grant you, there ain't nothing in this house they needed or they wouldn't of left it. It's all yours now, Sam. As far as I can see you got yourself a bunch of junk furniture and a bunch of caged birds to care for. Not to mention these damn cats." Daddy booted a calico off the porch and walked inside the house. "I'd just drag about half this stuff out back and burn it, Sam." Daddy shook his head. He wished he hadn't said nothing about burning stuff. He pretended to look at a picture of Jesus on the wall.

A picture of Jesus sitting at a table with a bunch of other men. An electric picture. When you plug it in, everybody looks like they're moving and talking. I wanted to plug it in for Daddy, but I didn't want him to know I'd been over there before. Daddy told us to stay away from them Gypsies.

The Gypsy house had two rooms, kitchen and living room. The living room had a green couch and a coffee table made out of Coca-Cola crates. Bright blue curtains hung from the windows, and pink scarves had been tied around the bottom of the birdcages. I found a red scarf with dark red hearts and wrapped it around my shoulders. Sonja used to wear that red scarf to school before she up and left. She's older than me, and even older than Stephen, but she was still in my class. She told me she'd missed so much school from moving that she never got to finish a year. She'd been in the first grade three times. I liked her black hair and big eyes and her skin the color of brown eggs. I walked home from school every day with Sonja and her grandmama. Her grandmama talked in tongues like the preacher on Easter Sunday.

As soon as we went inside, Sam got a tube of glue and smeared some on the blackbird. He fit the wings back on and put it on the windowsill to dry.

Daddy looked at the kitchen doorway. No door, just strings of colored beads hanging to the floor.

"What the hell are these?" Daddy asked, picking up a string of beads like it was a snake. "They don't keep nobody in or out and you can see slam through, so what good are they?" He dropped the beads and looked at a wind chime.

"Why did the Gypsies leave anyway?" I asked Daddy.

"Who knows why anybody does anything," Daddy said, shaking his head again. He touched the wind chime and made it ring.

Sam took a long drink of moonshine. "The Gypsy people made the spikes used to crucify Jesus," he said. "Their punishment was to walk the earth with no real home to call their own."

"Is that a fact," Daddy said, taking the bottle from Sam.

Daddy don't like to talk about Jesus. He took a sip of moonshine and started looking at the birds. The Gypsies left five birdcages with different birds in each one. Two little yellow birds sat on a stick inside one of the cages. The next cage had a green parakeet looking at hisself in a small mirror. Daddy looked at a big blackbird.

"What the hell kind a bird is this?" Daddy said. "Is this a crow, Sam?"

"Is this a crow, Sam?" the blackbird said, hopping up on the pole in his cage.

Daddy stood up and slapped his leg. "Well I'll be John Brown! This here's a talking bird!" Daddy looked over at me, and smiled. "Come look at this here bird, Whistle Britches."

I acted surprised and laughed, but I'd talked to that bird before. Daddy don't know. He told us kids to keep away from the Gypsies because they steal children and make them work. There was a bunch of them Gypsies living in this house, but none of them looked stole. They all looked just alike: Dark hair, dark eyes, and brown skin. Daddy looked real close at the blackbird and tried to get it to talk again.

"Say hello," Daddy said to the blackbird. The bird jumped down to the bottom of the cage and looked up at Daddy.

"Say hello," Daddy said.

The blackbird flapped its wings and said, "Sam's a good man." Daddy looked over at Sam and raised his eyebrow like he does sometimes.

Sam smiled. "I taught him that." He took a sip of moonshine and handed the bottle to Daddy. Sam and Daddy started laughing. Just a little at first. Short little laughs. Then they laughed a lot. Just laughed and laughed and laughed.

The blackbird flapped its wings again and said, "Sam's a good man."

AND WHEN I SHOULD FEEL SOMETHING

Jennifer Paddock

I call my parents to see how everything is in Arkansas. It's the first nice spring day in New York, and I want to tell my father about jogging through Central Park. My mother answers the phone and sounds different, distracted, and says she'll call me back. I read the paper, watch television, and when my mother calls, she says my father has killed himself.

My mom has arranged for a friend's son to take me to the airport. He lives in New Brunswick, New Jersey, and will be here in an hour. He will buy my ticket, and my mother will reimburse his father.

I'm not ready when he buzzes my apartment, but I let him up anyway and try to finish packing before he gets upstairs. I open the door and see a guy and girl, about my age, twenty-four, and hold my hand out to the guy, trying to be polite, and say, "I'm Chandler." He shakes my hand and says his name, then he introduces his girlfriend, but I don't listen. I apologize for not being ready. They ask if they can help me pack, but I say, "No. Thank you. I'll just be a minute."

They watch me, and they look around. They look at my bedroom, at my bookshelf, at the small kitchen that is part of the living room.

Driving to the airport, there is traffic, and I wish he had taken the tunnel. We don't talk much, except about the traffic. I wish I were in a cab.

At the American Airlines counter, he buys my ticket home. "Twelve hundred dollars to Fort Smith, Arkansas," he says, handing it to me. "I'm glad Dad's the one who's buying it." His girlfriend gives him a look, and I say, "Thank you. I really appreciate everything." I don't want to be indebted to him, but I am. I give him and his girlfriend an awkward hug goodbye.

Waiting in line to board the plane, a woman asks me what time it is. I pause too long. The woman says, "My watch stopped." I tell her two-thirty. Once seated, I cry. I don't want to make a scene. I don't want anyone to ask me what's wrong. I put my book in the pocket of the seat in front of me, then I look for it, thinking I put it in my bag. My face is hot and streaked with tears.

At home, people turn and look at me and whisper. My mother doesn't seem right. She's acting light-headed, in a fluttering way, like she's at a party. "Oh, Chandler," she says when she sees me.

Flowers are everywhere, and my mother tells me that there are some for me by the fireplace. My best friend, Sarah, who is also from Fort Smith and living in New York, sent a huge, flashy bouquet, gladiolas and Easter lilies.

A childhood friend of mine is here, my first boyfriend in the sixth grade, and I motion for him to follow me upstairs. "I'm glad you're here," I tell him.

He says, "New York sure has been good to you. Man, oh man."

"What do you mean?" I ask.

"You look so good," he says. "You look really hot."

In a pleasant way, I say that I'm exhausted and ask him to leave, but I feel angry and lie in bed. Various friends of my mother's poke their heads into my room and try to say something. Mostly, they say, "Oh, Chandler."

That night, after everyone has left, my mom gives me two sleeping pills. She has already taken two herself and is drowsy. She climbs into bed with me and holds my arm and says, "He did this for you and for me. It was an act of love." She runs a hand through my hair. "We'll never have to worry about money again."

The next morning I read a photocopy of my father's suicide letter. The police have the original. It's written only to my mother and says that he loves her and me, but he cannot face financial ruin. He says that his insurance policy will pay a million dollars, and that she can pay the bank the four hundred thousand owed, and that the house will be free and clear with six hundred thousand left over, which should be enough for us to be all right. He says that his body will be in the warehouse and for my mother to call Phil Conti, a friend of my father's who is also a lawyer, and for my mother—*You do not go down there.* He says that at his office will be instructions regarding the policy and the will and that Phil Conti will handle everything.

The warehouse used to belong to my grandfather, who made his money from real estate, and it's an enormous place divided into sections that are rented out to various businesses for storage. The clearest memory I have of my grandfather is watching him play the eighteenth hole at the country club. I'm walking past the golf course toward the tennis courts with my friends, and I tell them, "Watch this. That's my grandfather, but he won't recognize me." I yell over and wave at him, and he looks back at me with no recollection. I laugh and my friends laugh, and we keep walking.

There is an office right as you go into the warehouse, and I keep picturing my father walking in, sitting in a chair, placing the butt of a shotgun on the floor and the barrel in his mouth and pulling the trigger.

The funeral plans have been made, but there is still the matter of picking out a casket. I go down to the cemetery with Phil Conti, and it was his son, I learn now, who drove me to the airport. I have only met Phil Conti a couple of times and don't remember that he's from New York. He tells me about growing up in Brooklyn and ending up in Arkansas because of his wife. We talk about Manhattan, and he says that his mother is in a nursing home in the Village on Hudson Street, close to where I live. Phil Conti has a terrific Brooklyn accent. I love Phil Conti, feel grateful to him, and think I will go visit his mother.

There is a brochure with different caskets at different prices. I'm almost certain that I remember my father saying he wanted to be cremated, but I don't say anything. Phil Conti picks out a mid-priced coffin. The funeral director asks if I want to reserve a plot for myself, so that the Carey family can all be buried together.

"No, thanks," I say.

The funeral director says there's not much space left in the mausoleum, which holds Louis Carey, Marie Carey, Ann Carey, and Don Carey, my father's parents, sister, and brother. "Maybe you would like to start another family area outside by some trees," he says. "Or if you like, you could be cremated, and space would be saved because we could put an urn in the same slot, and that's a lot cheaper."

I ask if they could cremate my father, but he says that it's too late, the mortician is already working on him, and of course, it will be a closed casket. Phil Conti tells the guy that we will stick with what we have, and the mausoleum is fine, and thank you very much.

"God, that was horrible," I say in the car home, and Phil Conti smiles, and I laugh a little.

Later that day, Phil Conti brings over the clothes my father was wearing when he shot himself. He got them from the police station. They are in a brown paper bag—a plaid shirt, tan pants, black socks, Nike tennis shoes, and a Timex watch. They have a certain smell to them. It isn't the smell of blood, or of something rotten. It is the smell of guns, and the smell my father had after he went hunting and was cleaning quail.

My mother reminds me that I must send the airline a copy of the death certificate to get some credit for the twelve-hundred-dollar ticket home. She says, "Phil Conti has been so nice to us, and we must get this taken care of right away." I nod. "And from now on," my mother says, "we're going to be smart about money."

Even though there is a full house with friends and people from the church with casseroles, my mother and I go down to my father's law office. Mom says we should start cleaning it out, but I know what we are really doing is looking for clues. My mom looks through his files. I look in his desk drawers and find his life insurance policy with a highlighted section that confirms it will pay off on a suicide if the policy is held for three years. His policy is twenty years old. He got it when he was thirty-six, after surviving a heart attack. I remember growing up all we ever ate were chicken and fish and skim milk and margarine and wheat germ and cantaloupe. I remember my dad getting heart medicine delivered every week and meditating with a special word that he wouldn't tell anyone, doing whatever he could to stay alive.

The next morning, my mother and I ride to the funeral in the back of a limousine, and she points out to me all the prominent people of the community. She even rolls down the window and waves at some of them.

I bow my head and put my hand over my eyes.

"Can you believe all these people are here for Ben?" my mother says. "I don't think he had any idea how many people loved him."

The chapel is packed, and there isn't enough room for everyone. "I hope they all sign the guest book," my mother says. "Oh, I sure hope so, too," I say. My mother gives me a look.

During the service, the minister lists off my father's accomplishments, but then focuses on his suicide, before saying that we should not remember his death but his life.

At the cemetery, outside the mausoleum, there is a receiving line with my mother and me shaking hands and thanking everyone for coming. There are people I know and people I don't know and don't want to know. What a performance I'm giving and giving. I meet the mayor. "Thanks for coming," I say. I meet my mother's book club friends. "Thanks for coming," I say. "Thanks for coming." I meet cousins of my father's whom I've heard of but have never seen, and when I look into their faces and speak, I can see my father and myself, and I want so badly to be back home in Manhattan.

* *

In New York at night, in the darkness before sleep, I lie in bed and look through the bedroom door for my father. It seems as likely a place as any he would show up. He could peer around the corner, say good night, or hello, or everything all right? If I squint my eyes, I can see an outline of him in the pajamas, robe, and tennis shoes he wore around the house when I was growing up. He normally wore a suit to work, but he thought that when you were at home and with your family, you should be comfortable.

Several months ago, during Christmas break, when I was home in Arkansas, my father and I played a lot of gin rummy. He would say, "Cut them thin, so Ben can win." It was something he said when I was young and first learning to play cards. Yesterday I heard the word gin on television and fell apart. Something like that, and I fall into tears, and another day passes.

On television and in movies, there are always people threatening to kill themselves. There are jokes and storylines about insurance policies not paying off on suicides. I know that they do. I want to scream out that they do. And my friends say, "I wanted to kill myself," and don't realize what they've said. They have no idea what is inside me.

When we talk on the phone, my mother makes me promise that I will not kill myself. My mother says if I won't, then she won't either. My mother says, "Now, let's keep our promise to each other." I agree, but it seems crazy that we would say this at all.

My father is the reason that I'm in New York and in law school, and his money will make it easier for me to stay. But it's hard to go to class. I make myself. I can sit through lectures fine. If I get called on, I say, "I don't know." I spend afternoons wandering around Times Square, among tourists, everyone unsure of where to walk next.

I walk to the Ambassador Theater where *Bring in 'Da Noise, Bring in 'Da Funk* is playing. It stars Savion Glover. I've seen him dance before, when I was twelve years old, on a trip here with my father.

The musical is in previews, and I am able to buy a matinee ticket, a good one in the orchestra, maybe because I'm by myself. I wander back into Times Square and wait for the show to begin.

The theater is old with an orchestra and mezzanine. The ceiling is a gray-blue, and a glass chandelier hangs down. The seats are violet. I'm on the fourth row. The curtain is deep red. The beginning isn't seen but heard. There are taps, and it is dark, and then there is light on the dancer's feet, more taps that grow faster, and then there are other sounds, other feet, other dancers. There are drummers. There is a singer. There is a speaker. And being here so close to the dancer, Savion, I feel a charge, and a current runs through my heart, and I am happy, and I won't let myself look at anyone but him because I don't want my happiness to leave.

Some days I fall into fits of hard crying. My shoulders shake, and I scream and feel out of breath. Then I stop myself, even though I'm alone, because somehow I feel like a fake. I am carrying on this big act of grief, and I feel ashamed for putting on such a show. I know I am sad, but the sadness sometimes reaches an evenness. It isn't always outrage.

The week before my father died, I called home to talk to my mother. My father answered the phone, and I hung up. I felt startled. He never answered the phone. Whenever I was home visiting and the phone would ring, neither of us would answer. It drove my mom crazy, but my father and I would look at each other and smile, coconspirators.

I remembered right when he said "hello" that it was my mother's book club night, and that she wouldn't be there. I know he would have had fun talking to me, once we started talking, but always, in the beginning of conversations, we didn't know what to say to each other, as if we were anyone else we'd meet in the course of a day.

I want to go back to that phone call. I want to say, "Don't do it. Don't leave me yet. You are more than money." I at least want to speak this time.

How did he feel that early morning, walking down the stairs, leaving our house, the house he also grew up in, for the last time? Was he crying? Did he pet our cocker spaniel on the way out like he did every other morning?

* *

Savion pushes up on one toe and stays. I don't even know where his other foot is. Normally he's on one toe and the other is tapping around him. What I like most about coming here is seeing the differences in each performance. He dances in front of a bank of mirrors, and this time he is louder, his taps heavier. He does different steps. At the end of the solo, he falls to the floor in exhaustion. A woman from the mezzanine yells, "Oh, Savion." He stands up quickly and looks in her direction and grins.

Savion is changing tap dancing, changing Broadway. He will be remembered. He matters.

When Savion taps he hardly looks at or faces the audience. He wears loose black pants, an old T-shirt. His shoulders slump a little. He is in control when he dances, not only with movement, but with sound, and somehow with emotion. When I'm watching, and hearing the taps, I'm right with him, and I feel like I can do, am doing, what he's doing. We are in this together, and he knows I need him. He must know that.

Seeing the musical is helping me. It is because of Savion that I get out of bed, leave my room, talk to anyone. It is because I know I can see him dance again. I can see him Tuesday night and then again Saturday matinee. He is someone I have come to depend on.

My father used to send me checks in the mail and write, "To cover a few matinees." He would say that if you see a good musical, you walk out feeling like a million bucks. Despite everything, I still like that expression because my father said it.

The tears are light and slow, but they are always near. They come to me now as I'm sitting in the back of a cab, watching out the windows, looking at buildings and people on Sixth Avenue. I am envious of girls with fathers, of families, of any two people walking together.

I reach into my purse for the picture of my father I carry with me. It was taken when he was twenty-six here in New York at a law firm party. I hold it in my hand, a beautiful faded color with a white jagged border. My father stands in a circle with the other young associates. He looks strong and handsome and happy to be where he is.

The cab takes me past Macy's and Bryant Park, moving closer to the familiar turn on West Forty-ninth Street. I put the picture back in my purse, and I don't feel as sad because I know he was good, and was alive, and was my father.

People say I am like my father. I am smart and kind. I am a good tennis player. I am nice looking. I also like staying home. I like to wear pajamas any time of the day.

When I go to see Savion, I prefer to go alone. When I went once with friends, they said, "Oh, it was good. Have you seen this other play? It's good, too." Even my best friend, Sarah, wasn't visibly moved, and I felt lost that even she could not understand that what we were witnessing was amazing.

The cab drops me at Forty-ninth and Broadway, and I walk the half block west to the Ambassador. I always get a thrill walking this small stretch, seeing others dressed up, rushing to the same theater. I'm not alone at all, and I don't have to speak or shake a hand.

My seat is on the third row center, four from the aisle. There is no one next to me yet, and I begin to feel awkward and obvious. It is not until the lights dim and the orchestra begins playing that the usher leads several people down the aisle. Even in the dark, the whole audience sees who they are. A bodyguard, a beautiful woman, and a movie star. I have seen the movie star before, but I don't know his name, but those around me do, and they whisper. At first, I have to make myself not look at the movie star, but then I get caught up in Savion's dancing.

During intermission everyone wants the movie star's autograph, and I feel almost sorry for him. He doesn't know how to respond. To get away from the crowd, I think, he turns to me and asks how I like the show. I say with all the enthusiasm I've ever spoken with that the dancer is the greatest tap dancer in the world, and this play is better than any book I've read or film I've seen.

"Yes, yes," he says.

We are looking at each other and nodding. I say, "I've seen it five times." I hate to say I've seen it more.

"This is my second time," he says.

I smile.

"It's fantastic," he says.

"It's the only thing that makes me feel better," I say.

"Yeah," he says. "Yeah."

On my first trip to New York, my dad had gotten two rooms at the Waldorf that were connected, so I could have my own room. I was only twelve. At night, I would sit in front of the window in my pajamas and lean against the glass, and listen to the cars, the sirens, the subway, people talking and laughing, the doorman whistling for a taxi. My parents would watch me and say, "What are you doing?" and I'd answer, "Listening."

We had already seen *Big River* and *Biloxi Blues*, and for our last night, we had tickets to *Cats*. I did not want to see *Cats* no matter how much my mother did or how often she told me they were T. S. Eliot's cat poems. I wanted to see *The Tap Dance Kid* with Savion Glover. I had seen an ad for it, and at the time, I was a Michael Jackson freak, and Savion reminded me of Michael as a kid. Savion was about my age and on Broadway, and I wanted to see him. My dad, without too much persuasion, gave up our *Cats* tickets and bought three tickets for *The Tap Dance Kid*. He even got a limousine to take us to the play. Our driver was named Mannie, and I kept his company card on my bulletin board at home for a long time after.

I remember we were three of the very few white people in the audience. The kid on stage was smiling and playing music with his feet. All the dancers had on tuxedos, which I thought was nice. I kept nudging my parents, saying, "Did you see that?" and "This is incredible." They would smile and look at each other. My father was wearing wire-rimmed glasses, and they moved a little as he smiled and nodded in agreement with me. I knew he didn't like it the way I did, but I was smart enough to let him know that I loved it, and that was all he needed.

After the show, I bought three *Tap Dance Kid* sweatshirts. At school, I wore one and gave the other two to my friends. There was the proof all over the school that I had been to New York City.

* *

I moved to New York two years ago for law school at NYU. I had no money to come here, and my father didn't have it to give to me.

We all sat in the den to discuss my going to school. My father put on his glasses. "I can't take care of my family," he said.

"Everyone takes out loans," I said.

He sat with a legal pad in his lap, writing down figures, adding what he could afford to pay. "I have these two cases," he said. "One of them has to pay big."

The two cases involved personal injury. He was not used to that type of work, waiting for a settlement or a judgment before he could get paid. He was used to billing hours to a corporation and getting paid each month.

When he finally admitted that his law practice was failing and that we were running out of money, my mother found him these cases. The plaintiffs were two of her acquaintances who quickly became good friends. My father didn't have the money or experience to try the cases, so he got the help of a personal injury firm in St. Louis. He felt if they were willing to put up millions of dollars on behalf of his cases, he was sure to win. My father felt his luck was changing. He felt like the cases just fell in his lap.

My mother was sitting next to me, and she said in a pleading voice, "What will we do if they don't? How are we going to live?"

My father's eyes narrowed, and he shook his head. "Don't say that. I can't stand it when you say that."

"How did this happen to us?" my mother said.

I didn't understand that either. We were rich when I was young. My father was a corporate lawyer. When he was in his twenties, he had worked for a prestigious firm on Wall Street. In Arkansas, he'd worked for the same corporation for twenty years. When it was taken over, he lost his only client. He had one interview to work with a firm in New Orleans, and when he didn't get the job, that was it. He didn't send his resume out again. He told us that he didn't want to move and that he would figure things out. "I can get clients. I don't mind doing wills and divorces. Not to worry," he said. "I'm a winner. Everything will be fine." So for years, my mother and I thought everything was fine.

My mother, who had always lived in Arkansas, said, "I blame you for her wanting to go to New York City. It is all your fault."

At that, my father looked at me and smiled, and I knew we were in this together, and I would be able to go.

* *

I love the freedom of New York. I can walk around, and no one knows me. No one knows or cares what has happened to me. I can't imagine how my mother is making it back in Arkansas, how she's able to go to the grocery store or the bank, where she is certain to see someone who knows. I feel so lucky to live in Manhattan, and sometimes I even say out loud to my father, "Thank you." Then I feel ashamed. I only think about myself, about being a daughter who has lost her father, not about my mother and what she has lost.

I decide to call and apologize and ask how she is, but when my mother answers, I don't say anything and hang up.

Back in the fall, months before my father died, I walked to The Public Theater hoping to see Savion dance. I already knew the musical was sold out. When I had called earlier about a ticket, a woman told me the show was moving to Broadway, and I could see it in April. I walked down to the Public anyway. I wasn't sure why. I knew I didn't have a chance of getting in. And then I saw Savion. He was leaning against the outside brick of the theater, staring out into the street and the sky, smoking a cigarette. I looked at him as if he were a painting, something to be studied. The white of his shirt, his dark hair compared to his lighter skin, his black pants, and his shoes.

I like Times Square. I like the bright lights of the electric signs. I don't mind walking past Peepland or Runway 69. To me, the neon X's from strip clubs and the yellow arches from McDonald's somehow add to the beauty. My mother was always afraid of walking through Times Square and I was, too, when I first moved here. And it probably isn't entirely smart now, walking around without reason, away from Times Square and into Hell's Kitchen, as day turns to night. But since my father died, I don't feel like anyone can hurt me.

Without intention, I walk down Forty-ninth, past Broadway, to the Ambassador. A scalper sees me, walks up to me like he knows me, and offers a ticket. I reach into my purse and pay him. I walk to the side door, the one with fewer people, only one ticket taker, and pray the ticket is not fake. Then, at once, I feel someone brush against me, and I look back and see the white T-shirt, and I look up and see the hair, almost in dreads, and I am at his shoulders, and he passes me, and I'm not sure I am appreciating the good fortune of brushing next to the dancer, this man who I believe is saving me.

I don't feel nervous or excited. I don't want to talk to him. I don't feel anything. And when I should feel something, some kind of gratitude, it is too late, and my chance to feel what I should have felt has passed.

After seeing the musical as many times as I have, I want to skip through certain parts. My mind wanders during the songs and the words. Only when the dancer who brushed against me is dancing is my mind where I wish it to be. Only when he is making music with his tap, notes I have never heard, as if he is inventing them at every performance.

What I feel is the smooth slide, tap, scrape, tap, tap, tap, scrape, and I remember looking up at the dancer, and his face is serious and almost sad, tired, not different from mine.

How This Song Ends

Judith Richards

Emma slammed the front door as she went out—the old-fashioned front door with the wavy glass—Jack's prize door. Not so hard as to break the antique glass, but hard enough to signal that she was angry. Jack Hardy wouldn't be coming after her. He'd already abandoned her. She was in no danger of saying ugly things to him, or worse, of having to apologize.

Emma intended to wallow in her anger. She'd walk to her favorite place on the bluff overlooking the bay, lie down on the pine needles, and stare at the clouds.

She breathed in the scent of pine. It was a warm day for November, with a cool light breeze from the south. Butterflies moved from flower to flower—monarch, yellow sulfur, and a small one she couldn't identify. Bees were busy, too, but Emma couldn't hear them. Instead there was the drone of an airplane, and a high buzz of an electric saw from a nearby construction site, punctuated by the echo of a hammer. Distant voices rose from the beach park. She strained to hear the lap of water at the shore. That damn saw! Or was it one of those Jet Skis roaring by? She hurt. Head. Middle back. And she was so tired.

The first time Jack Hardy put his arms around her, he slipped from an embrace to long strokes down her spine. He spread his hands on either side and slowly slid them down to the curve of her buttocks. "I've wanted to do that since the first time I saw you," he said. She'd been so young then, and in spite of having been married, inexperienced.

Emma wished for those hands now.

She and Jack had married years after their son was born. He had wanted to marry her right away but she said no. No, she'd tried that before, briefly. Emma's memory of the first marriage still hurt. Lonely to the bone, isolated, afraid of displeasing the man she was pledged to live with "till death do us part," she decided that the marriage was death itself, and the time to leave was as soon as possible. Emma started saving quarters, dimes, dollars when she could, until she had enough money to buy a bus ticket to someplace far away. She left a note telling her husband where to find his clean underwear and that was it, she was gone. She rode the bus for twenty-four hours before getting off in a medium-sized Southern city. She'd taken a job as a waitress and rented a tiny apartment in an old hotel while she looked for something better. Better came right away. Her first job interview was with Jack Hardy.

Emma would have said she was a social person before meeting Jack, but in his company, reticent was a more apt description. Jack was courtly in the Southern manner, leaping up to pull out a chair for her, holding the door, guiding her by the elbow as they entered a restaurant or theater. He smiled, complimented, offered a witticism—not just for Emma, but for every person he encountered. Traversing a crowded room required that she be patient. His open manner and willingness to listen to other people's stories delayed him.

Emma tried to emulate him, awkwardly at first. Jack called her his rosebud, "about to bloom." He insisted that people "just loved her." It wasn't true, of course, but she adored him for the lie.

Wearily, she stood up and stretched her arms as high as possible, pulling herself taller. She could feel the tug on the scar where her left breast had been. She slipped a hand under her shirt and stroked the raised skin following the trail of the incision.

When Emma first noticed the lump in her breast, she'd told Jack. "Go to a doctor now," he'd commanded. This from a man who resisted yielding to the ministrations of a physician for himself. Artists with no health insurance could hardly afford to run to a doctor on a whim. She said she'd wait. She'd had lumps before.

After several weeks of worrying about a growth in her breast, Emma had gone for a mammogram, then a series of tests. Jack blanched when he saw the bills, said he hoped to hell they knew what they were doing. Then he caught himself and hugged her. "Of course they do," he said. "Don't mind my bitching." Months later, she awoke before dawn to a strange sound and a light from the office. Jack was at his desk bent over a mound of medical bills, sobbing.

They had taken a second mortgage on the house to pay for her sur-gery and chemotherapy. Emma felt guilty for putting them in financial jeopardy, but she sometimes thought Jack worried more about money than her well-being. He'd always said he loved her more than his life. She'd saved him, he said. Wasn't she still the most important person in his life?

At their first meeting, Jack hired her to answer mail and the phone, pay bills and deal with galleries so that he could concentrate on painting. Within a week he'd asked her to pose for him. She was riveted to the intensity of those blue eyes as he painted. He wasn't handsome. His skin was pale and freckled, hair shaggy over prominent ears and the color of new copper. She watched his hands. Rugged working hands with short nails and reddened skin. Suddenly he was beautiful, and she was in love. Three months later they were sharing a bed. She'd held him off until then, not knowing how to separate work and sex, afraid of losing her job.

Jack saved her, not the other way around. He'd saved her from a life of tedium. He began to ask her opinion on his paintings, on promotional ideas he was considering. For the first time in her adult life, she felt valu-able.

The night Emma found him weeping at his desk, she waited, then slipped into the studio. Jack looked up, shoved the papers into a drawer and pulled her into his arms. He gave her a little smile and began softly singing the Randy Travis song he said was theirs.

> *If you wonder how long I'll be faithful*
> *Just listen to how this song ends*
> *I'm going to love you forever and ever*
> *Forever and ever, Amen.*

He spread his hands along her spine and stroked, stroked, until she dozed on his lap. Even then he knew he would be leaving her.

As Emma healed, Jack became more distant, as if he bore the weight of the world and could not share it with her. Would not. He painted more in three months than he had in a year and his work reflected an energy she'd not seen before. Because of the changes in him, Emma wondered if he was having an affair. Jack would leave the house without notice and return offering no explanation. Emma asked vague questions, hoping he would tell her he'd been on some urgent errand. Something important to both of them.

There were also sweet memories, filling Emma with reassurance that Jack still cared for her. They would make love, and reminisce about their wonderful life together. Twice he surprised her with gifts. Once, as if money were unimportant, he gave her a pair of expensive earrings. Another time, a painting of her and their son, Jackie, when he was a toddler, eighteen years ago.

The sun was lower now, huge and orange, and the bottom rim had already dipped into the bay. Fiery light flared along the horizon and across the water—a beautiful hell. Emma turned toward home, walking past old cottages that were being transformed into mansions by wealthy people who'd been attracted to the neighborhood because it was quaint and arty. Her own house came into view at the end of the street. Gray with peeling white trim; a roof with shingles so old, dry and curled a passerby had remarked on the unusual style.

Emma paused under the cedar tree at the edge of their yard. They should have cut it down years ago, knowing it would be overwhelmed by the magnolia. Instead, she and Jack spent many summer afternoons sipping iced tea in the fragrant shade.

A figure appeared at the front door of the house. Anger melted and tears filled her eyes. She blinked and wiped her cheek.

The door swung open and her son hugged her to him. "Mom," he said. "I was getting worried. We'll be late for Dad's wake. What would he think?"

Emma tried to smile but a sob escaped her. "He'd know," she said, "how this song ends."

From Tucson to Tucumcari, From Tehachapi to Tonopah

Richard Shackelford

He was seventy years old when they made him go to the doctor. Until the year before, he had driven an over-the-road semi-tractor trailer truck, but he had come home, restless and agitated, to spread the wide vistas of his emotional swings through the already fixed and angry lives of his relatives, a mixed bag of in-laws, outlaws, sons, daughters, their husbands and wives, and his own ex-wife, now widowed for the second time, which made three runs at marriage for her. The truck driver had been pushing his rig when the other two husbands died.

Home, such as the trucker knew, was upcountry Alabama, midstate, no more than forty miles from the Mississippi line. The name of the town was Reform . . . pronounced REE-form, something like the way PO-lice is dragged out by Southerners. The old man had never taken to heart the suggestion the town's name made.

In any case, his youngest daughter, Jolene, literally put him out in the pasture, almost a quarter mile down the slope, in a trailer . . . as if moving into a wheeled home, he had just moved from the front cab to the rear, but would keep on driving.

Within the week the daughter and her husband, twice married apiece, had started talking like it would soon be twice divorced. The old man had a knack for starting a flap. He had a knack, too, for becoming wildly emotional, sometimes weeping bitterly at the portion life had meted out to him.

Sometimes his children thought of him as having only two gears, low and compound low . . . no hill too steep; he could, and did, plow straight up the field along whichever row his inner sealed beams lit up for him.

When they'd made the old man, who was "feeling poorly," go to the doctor, the family called his eldest son, Eugene. Jolene said on the phone that the old man had an aortic aneurysm.

Eugene had to look it up.

What it amounted to was this: The old man's aorta, the major artery leading from his heart, had a bulge in it, like an old inner tube. The old man was about to have the big flat on the freeway of life.

Eugene asked Jolene, "When?" It was the kind of dumb thing Eugene would often say, knowing better, but filling spaces with words while his mind was sorting. Before Jolene could answer he changed his question to "What'd the doctor say?" Eugene's daddy had kept a boot on little Eugene for so many years, he'd grown into a man who watched his mouth. Wrong words in the little boy's mouth had come to sting his ass.

Jolene told Eugene that the doctor, true to weathercasters of all sort, in every day and clime, had said: "It could happen anytime."

"Well?" Eugene asked, waiting for the balance of the prognostication.

"Well, what?" Jolene said. "He needs to have an operation or he's going to die."

"What's *Daddy* say?" Eugene asked, already assuming that the old bastard had told the doctor and everyone else to fuck off. How many times had Eugene heard the old man say he'd rather die stepping over a log in the woods and fill the belly of a fat-ass buzzard than die under the fluorescent glare in a hospital room, breathing in disinfectant and some doctor's aftershave.

"He doesn't want to die," she said, stating the obvious.

Who does? Eugene thought. "What's going to happen? Is he going to have the operation, or what?"

"We're all trying to talk him into it," she said.

"*We all*" meant "*the family.*" Blood family, stepfamily, in-law family. Up the country it was all one big hodgepodge of *family.* Ranks closed. The old trucker's route was being highlighted and shoved onto his dashboard.

"What do the doctors say about his chances?" Eugene asked, pointedly.

"At his age?"

What other? Eugene thought. He said: "Y'all ought to let him be."

The upshot of it all, finally, was that Eugene got in his post-divorce ten-year-old Volvo station wagon and drove to Tuscaloosa, where his daddy had been checked into the hospital.

Everyone else cleared out of the room, glad to be relieved of their watch duty. Eugene sat there looking at the old trucker, sedated, appearing to be asleep. He watched the rise and fall of that barrel chest. Eugene sat trying to imagine the soft pumping of his heart and a ballooned artery. He recalled deep needs never quite fulfilled, love and hate. He remembered how he would line up when Daddy was supposed to be coming home, watching up the long, thin backcountry asphalt road for the truck and for the trucker who would bring home various trinkets of the roadside, from far-off places with names like Tonopah or Tucson or Tucumcari, names he knew from the ballad that was still played on the radio.

He remembered, too, that time he'd called his daddy because he needed seventy-five dollars, or he'd be thrown out of his college room at the university. And Daddy, after cussing about giving goddamn hard-earned money to somebody who ought to be making his own instead of fucking around forever in school, said he'd be at the Parade Truck Stop on Highway 82 west of Tuscaloosa at noon. "And don't by-God be late." So Eugene went out and sat, from late morning just in case the truck rolled in early, and then all day, until it got darker and darker, plainer and plainer that this would be a no-show. He'd moved in with a friend for a few weeks, until he could do otherwise. There was more than enough hurt there.

Like the time he was playing wild in the house when he was seven, like he knew not to do, because he had been told not to, and broke *the* lamp. "This one I won in a poker game and hauled two thousand miles to my wife and kids." Eugene flogged his own legs until he left blood and welts there, hoping his daddy would think he'd been whipped enough, but it hadn't held the old man back.

Oh, Daddy, he thought, *what in the hell are you doing here . . . What am I doing here?*

"Eugene? Is that you?"

"Yes, sir," he answered promptly, as if the voice and a little boy's yesterday were all one voice and day.

"I've just been hanging on till you got here, boy."

Eugene knew that was just more of the old man's bullshit. The old trucker was a long way from dead. Death was hovering somewhere in these corridors, but he knew that the man on the bed figured he'd have a chance if he could just see the bastard coming. This damn artificial sleep was the real threat.

"I've been a hard man, son . . ."

"Yes, sir."

"I did it all for you, you're my oldest boy."

"Yes, sir," he said, remembering how when he was small, and the only blue-eyed child in the trucker's bunch, all the rest with his father's dark eyes, his pale and bright as the sky, the old man looked at him strange, as if he weren't even his own flesh . . . treated him so, and the other children sometimes saying, too, he wasn't one of them, until time, and nature, brought him on until, but for the age and eyes, they could have been two out of the same womb, and both knew it. It just hurt to remember those days before they both knew it, and he wished he hadn't come to this hospital.

"All the others, they want me to let that damned doctor cut on me . . . say I'll die if I don't. Might die if I do."

"I can't say," Eugene said, looking away, because whatever else there was, his daddy's voice and presence still had the power to move him back in time.

"Can't say? You can't say?" Eugene could almost hear the long, wide, heavy-buckled truckers belt sliding silkily through its loops.

"No sir," he said. He wanted to say: *Go home, damn you, go home and sit still, take it easy, or jump over fucking logs, let God pick the time, but you keep driving, old man.* But he stayed silent.

"We ain't talked much." The voice from the bed was quieter, thin.

Eugene sat there then while the old trucker took the old roads, talked the old talks, and eventually drifted into the gentle amnesia of narcosis. Eugene got up and went out in the hallway. He hated the hospital smells out there, but it wasn't as bad as sitting in the room.

They took his father into surgery early the next morning and went at it until early afternoon. The old trucker survived that and Eugene saw him again . . . literally, watched him sleep for a full hour, before heading back to the coast, blinking away the miles home in the silence of the car.

But the day after he had gotten back to the coast, and shortly after he arrived at the magazine offices where he was working part-time as an editor, Jolene called. There were complications, serious complications. The old man had lost circulation in his legs and was getting gangrene . . . they had taken him back into surgery. His legs had to come off, no saving him otherwise.

His father was not long out of surgery when Eugene got back to Tuscaloosa in the late afternoon. This time the breathing was hard and labored and the sheets lay flat down at the end of the bed. Eugene just sat there staring at the floor, wishing he had told his daddy to go home before all this started. He could see into the small closet where his daddy's clothes were dangling. A pair of worn trucker-cowboy boots leaned over together on the floor, useless and obscene.

He got up and took the boots out of the room, out of the hospital, until he was out back by a Dumpster. He threw them in the trash. Throwing away the boots broke him down. He wept as bitterly as he had when he was a boy.

When he got back to the room the old trucker was stirring, twisting under the sheet, clutching the edges of the mattress. "Eugene," he bel- lowed. Then the wide, dark, flashing eyes saw him. "My damned feet are itching, boy, you got to scratch them."

"I can't, Daddy," Eugene said, and shook his head, helpless to soothe the horror growing in the old man's eyes as he apprehended the sheer flatness of the bed before him. It was then that the old man bellowed with an awful rage, trying to get unstrapped from the bed where they had tried to immobilize his hips. It was a hoarse, angry howling that rose up until the stitches ripped open all across the old man's chest and he died in a flap, angry, toiling in compound low uphill with an entourage of cursing motorists behind him, then up and over the top, downhill, hard on the horn, the hounds of hell on his tail.

Eugene was shaking so bad he had to sit in the chair, hands trying to hold each other still until he could look over at the awful scene in the bed. And, wishing he had said it before, he said: "You are the meanest sonofabitch I ever knew, but I love you. I always loved you." He got up and touched the old man's eyelids, closing them.

When the others came in and all the crying and pleading with God started, he got up and went out in the hall. Jolene came out.

"What happened?" she asked, her eyes red and wild.

"He wanted me to scratch his feet," he said.

They buried the old trucker two days later in a small cemetery near Reform.

Not long after that his mother and Jolene gave Eugene a gold watch chain with a small penknife on the end of it that had been his father's, and a little case that held a bottle of Jack Daniel's and four tumblers having the same squarish shape as the bottle. Eugene went out and bought a wafer-thin gold pocket watch, attached it to the chain, put the knife in his back pocket, the watch in his front, and threw away his wrist-watch.

He went down to the ancient thirty-foot wooden Chris Craft he had about half-restored before stopping the work to watch his wife pack up and leave. He had never turned his hand back to the boat, and it sat moored and listing on the edge of Fly Creek, near Mobile Bay. He'd lived on it for about a month, right after the divorce. For all he knew, the boat might have caused the divorce, she complained so bitterly about his expenditures on it.

From where he stood on deck he could see creek and bay, seagulls and a few pelicans. He could smell the clean brackish water, hear the waterfront sounds lifting and falling on the Southern breeze. It came back to him why he'd bought the boat. He ducked into the main salon and dragged out a deck chair onto what he had called the "the back porch" when he lived aboard. He sat down with the whiskey case, opened it, and took out the Jack Daniels and one tumbler. He poured himself half a glass, drank it, poured another half tumbler and set it beside him on the bulkhead-mounted fold-up table.

Then he took from his shirt pocket the last letter his daddy had written to him. It was an old letter, had arrived at a time when he was too pissed at the old man to even open it. He wondered what had made him save it. Now he began to read it, and tried to measure his own tight-fisted life by the lives, the many lives, that lay beneath the surface of the words.

It was slow going, because sometimes he wept. Someone listening would have said he whimpered, like a child might, alone in a room, scared in a passing storm, afraid to call out, afraid to wake his daddy.

The letter was signed: "Your loving father, Casey."

When he'd finished, he drank the other shot of whiskey, wiped the glass out with his shirttail, and put the bottle and tumbler back in its case, carefully, as if afraid he might break it. And he thought, *Oh Daddy, now I am the meanest sonofabitch in the valley,* and he wondered what to do about it.

VIETNAM

George Singleton

When Big Jim Shorts lectured to garden clubs, watercolor societies, and educational groups around the Southeast about the roots of his artistic vision and habits, he always mentioned God, Ronald Reagan, and a bottle of cheap wine he drank before walking into the Goodwill thrift store in Opelika, Alabama. Later on he would acknowledge that I was the sole reason he quit altogether. Big Jim had about a seventh-grade education. He worked in North Carolina cotton mills up until he got laid off in 1984. That's where Reagan came into his artistic roots story. Within the year, for reasons not clearly explained, Big Jim began hitchhiking toward Texas. He got stuck in Opelika, drank the best part of a half-gallon of Burgundy, and went into the Goodwill to find some new eyeglasses. From that point on, according to some critics, the primitive art world changed.

"I picked me up some good spectacles with plastic frames and plastic lenses, you know, and they set on my nose right, which is uncommon. I ain't sure what my eyesight was or is, but I can't imagine it ever so bad I couldn't make out a micrometer's reading somewhere between arm's length and a foot from my face."

My wife, Ava, and I sat in an auditorium at Wally Preston College outside of Asheville, thirty miles from our house, surrounded by rich northeastern retirees, local craftswomen, and a few students. I looked down at my program and read that Big Jim Shorts worked solely with gourds because of a gospel song he once heard in his head that involved harvested gourds and the Lord's sword. Ava leaned over and said, "He's the real thing." She made a living tracking down primitive artists, buying up their works, and selling them to people who owned second houses. She worked as both agent and finder.

I wondered how obvious it would be if I pulled out my flask.

"I'm not sure what happened, but I set my specs down on the

counter, and something distracted me. I looked up. Maybe I heard a voice call my name, I don't know. People been writing in the art magazines that I heard the voice of God come down and tell me to pick up another pair, but that's just rumor. What happened was, this other old boy set his free eyeglasses down, he picked up mine and I picked up his. Well, as it ended up, that old man must've been blind, 'cause when I went outside and put the things on, I damn near could see the tip end of Florida."

Inside the program it pointed out that, "The free glasses' strength was similar to two jeweler's loupes." At the time I didn't think Big Jim Shorts wrote his own biography. He looked a lot like that guy Junior Samples on *Hee-Haw*. I pulled out my flask and bubbled it twice.

"I'd picked up one a them free newspapers and wanted to see if they was any work in Opelika, you know, like cleaning up a construction site, or gofering—just enough so I could make some change and not feel guilty about leaving unannounced for Galveston, or Blanco. Well, I picked up the paper, and they was this picture of that year's senior class on the front page. With regular sight you couldn't make out a face. But with my new glasses you could not only recognize every single high school graduate, you could distinguish the tiny black dots that make up print."

People in the audience nodded. I'm not lying when I say a bunch of people did that "Ahh" thing that's always seemed a little melodramatic to me in the movies and sitcoms.

Big Jim Shorts didn't wear a suit. He didn't wear overalls, either, like someone trying to feign primitive art status before a crowd of admirers. He wore regular khakis and a bowling shirt. "Big Jim" was stitched above the right pocket. I had a shirt just like it, except mine said plain Warren. I'd thought about putting a peace sign after it, but figured I'd get my ass kicked somewhere—either in a bowling alley or at one of these lectures Ava said I needed to attend so I might get another idea.

My latest idea was the Obituary Channel—kind of like the Weather Channel. I hadn't thought it through yet, though, and couldn't approach investors.

"So finally I decided to use my new glasses, and etch little pictures on the outside of gourds," Big Jim Shorts said. "There's something about angels on a pinhead, and I believed in it. I started right off by doing the Last Supper. Then I figured out I had enough room to paint Adam and Eve, and Noah's ark. I had all the pairs of animals and everything. Then when I got done with that I saw where I had room still for parting the Red Sea, and Moses coming down the mountain, and the crucifixion scene. I did the burning bush, and made up my own little joke—if you look close, it's a burning gourd." A slide of Big Jim's first gourd appeared behind him on a pull-down screen. Drunken Noah appeared outside of a cave, reflecting on Big Jim's forehead.

I didn't laugh when my wife leaned over and said, "He sold that piece for ten grand." I got up, went out to my car, filled my flask, and looked up at the clear stars to see if they spelled out anything for once.

* *

"I understand how God and the Goodwill store influenced your becoming an artist," some woman stood up and said. She wore a shirt that read Decoupage Artists Reunion. "How did the wine come to play? I thought maybe you were drunk, put on the bad glasses, and thought you could see better." There were actual chortles throughout the audience. I'd never heard a chortle before, and knew I'd have nightmares later.

"The whole reason I went in Goodwill was to get a new shirt so I could go look for day jobs," Big Jim said. "I'd spilt wine all down the front of what I wore, which was my best shirt with buttons."

I had to pee. My wife sat on the edge of her auditorium chair. I thought of things I'd spilled before and had come up with everything normal like hotdog chili on up to gunpowder when I said to Ava, "I had a friend growing up who took the arms off his sister's Barbies and glued them onto G.I. Joe's crotch. I could find him if you want me to, if that's art."

My wife said, "Shut up."

The woman who asked about Big Jim's wine held her hand to her heart. She said, "Everything just fell into place, didn't it."

Big Jim didn't answer. One of the students—I should mention that there were microphones set up in either aisle, just like on some kind of national talk show program—stepped forward and said, "You must have had some kind of artistic training before. I mean, I know you're basically self-taught, but why miniature art instead of, say, music, or poetry?"

I looked at my wife. I said, "Now we're thinking. That's a valid question. Big Jim's going to have to get existential on this one."

Big Jim didn't look like he wanted to yell, but he did. He bellowed. "Music? I can't write a song about everybody living in Opelika, Alabama—or Macon, Georgia, and everywhere else I've drawn every human being alive on top of my gourds. It's my job to have people feel remembered. That's it, boy."

I looked back to the night's program. Big Jim served in the early days of Vietnam. His bio jumped straight from, "Born in Greensboro in 1948, Big Jim Shorts spent two tours of duty in Vietnam." Then, evidently, he came back to North Carolina, and worked as a doffer in the cotton mills, a carpenter for a construction outfit, and a security guard inside the vacant cotton mill once it closed. Then there was another gap, followed by the Opelika story, the gourds, and so on. He decided to stay in Alabama because of the vision.

I stood up and raised my hand before Ava could hold me back. "Seeing as no one seems to understand our involvement in Vietnam, or the repercussions our soldiers suffered, I was wondering if you've depicted the war on one of your gourds."

Shorts stared at me two minutes. The folks in the lecture hall who had been nodding the entire time I asked my question now turned their heads my way as if I'd asked the length of Big Jim's pecker. He said, "I've tried. I got me one gourd with the events that took place at Dem Dot Doh Dey—where me and my platoon spent seventy-two hours holed up against enemy fire—but I can't figure out how to put the faces in between all the trees. We never seen them, so I kind of feel like it'd be cheating."

Everyone started nodding again, smiling, clapping their hands together a few times. Let me say this: I wasn't in Vietnam. And I'm no scholar when it comes to history, but I felt certain that there was no Dem Dot Doh Dey. It sounded like Morse Code or pig Latin. When I sat back down Ava whispered, "Don't ask him about that town. Promise me. It doesn't matter. In his head, I'd be willing to bet, that's where he was. Maybe he doesn't pronounce Vietnamese words very well."

I didn't say, "Well, we'll find out soon enough," seeing as Big Jim would be staying at our house after his talk and the reception scheduled afterward.

* *

The regular art department at Wally Preston College brought in their regular guest artists. Over the years, normal old post-post-Impressionists, expressionists, and realists came in, spent a week at the school, worked with the students, et cetera. To be honest, no one from the community ever showed up for the free lectures.

Fortunately for Ava, the president of Wally Preston was a woman named Dr. Wanda McGaha. She wasn't really the president, seeing as the college was founded on those idealistic "no one is above another"—this came from the second commandment about graven images—principles so that instructors had to take turns serving five-year terms conducting PR, raising money, shuffling papers, greeting visitors, and scolding over-the-top instructors. Wanda McGaha had received her undergraduate degree from Berea College, where she double-majored in philosophy and Appalachian heritage. She may have been the only college president in America who could weave a basket, carve out a bread bowl, operate a still, and quote Schopenhauer.

My wife and Dr. Wanda McGaha met at an auction. They fought over a set of picture frames braided out of Clove, Juicy Fruit, and Wrigley's spearmint chewing gum wrappers. As only women can do, they got to talking later, intuited each other's lives in a couple minutes, and became instant soul mates. Soon thereafter Ava became an advisor to the Wally Preston College Cultural Life Program series. Maybe once a month Wanda would come over to our vertical house two mountaintops away, drink Manhattans with me, and talk about whomever Ava had recently discovered who painted signs of the apocalypse on hubcaps, or carved peach pits into Jesus, or wove creels from loaf bread twist ties.

"He's it," Wanda said to me at the reception. She held a glass of white wine. "How long's he going to stay with y'all? I wouldn't mind coming over and listening to him tell stories."

We stood in the gallery adjacent to the auditorium. Poor male art students got stuck pouring wine. I watched them take turns on break, their sports coats bulging with lifted liters.

Ava walked around with Big Jim, introducing him to people who stood in front of his etched gourds. I said to Wanda McGaha, "There ain't no Dem Dot Doh Dey in Vietnam. This guy's making some things up. I understand how people need to create their own backgrounds and reputations in order to survive in the art world—hell, in any world—but I wouldn't go so far as to say that this guy's the real thing. Unless the real thing means people who make up their own history." I pulled out my flask and offered it to Wanda. I knew she wouldn't take it unless it included some vermouth and a cherry.

"You sound jealous," she said. "Goddamn, Warren, ease up. They're only gourds with depictions of what every high-school student knows."

I looked over at my wife leading Big Jim. She held him by the right elbow, as if he were blind. *Con man. Grifter.* "It's not jealousy. It's patriotism, by God. If you had friends and relatives who suffered and died in Vietnam you wouldn't want someone getting a bunch of glory by faking it, would you?"

Wanda McGaha shook her head no. She said, "Did you have a bunch of friends and relatives over there?"

I said, "No. Well, I've met some people." I saw Ava put a red dot next to a gourd Big Jim Shorts had etched of The Battle of Franklin, Tennessee. I couldn't tell who bought it, and only hoped it wasn't my wife, seeing as I didn't want any Civil War paraphernalia inside our house. That's me.

"How's the invention business coming along?"

I looked over Wanda's shoulder. My wife tousled Big Jim's hair. He laughed and reciprocated. I'm not sure if it was the bourbon I drank, or my new need for bifocals, but Ava's red, red hair sparked showers a foot higher than her six-foot frame. "After I finish my work with the Obituary Channel I'm going to invent a tic-tac-toe kind of game called Dem-Dot-

Doh-Dey. Each player has to go into the jungle and come out with an M-16." Wanda wasn't even listening when I said, "Plus, a rice paddy hat with a pictorial of the entire history of southeast Asia."

Wanda said, "Do you mean, like, a channel that just keeps showing who died?"

I cared about Wanda McGaha. Out of all the friends a man's wife could have, Wanda McGaha was the best. I said, "Why don't you come on over tonight. Big Jim's following us home in his weird truck and you can follow him. Or *go* with him. Live dangerously, Wanda. You'll end up on a gourd."

* *

Here's our house on top of Fob Mountain: The bottom floor's six hundred square feet of cement-floored glassed-in space. It could hold a bar, pool table, dartboard area, foosball table, putting green, and fancy poker table, but it doesn't. There is a bar, only because I built a one-by-twelve shelf at elbow level on the southeast corner, overlooking Lake Fob. I set up six barstools, and stocked knee-high shelves with whiskey. Ava uses the rest of the room for storage space, although she calls it a gallery. Every whittled, latex-painted, or hand-built piece of folk art she can't part with ends up there. I would bet that there are thirty portraits apiece depicting Jesus and Elvis—in various stages of their careers—in the glass room.

The second floor is another six hundred square feet of kitchen, bedroom, bathroom, and half-den. This is where we watch TV and where Ava works. A spiral staircase leads up to four hundred square feet of what was supposed to be my workroom—a place where I could sit at the computer and work up new ideas to pitch to money men—but ended up being another storage space for primitive art. Luckily, Ava lets me pick what goes up there, so the top floor's pretty much filled with snakes, dogs, face jugs, and tramp art built from cigar boxes, bottle caps, Popsicle sticks, and wooden matches. Upstairs holds the collection of Walter Dean's work—he killed field rats down in South Carolina, boiled the carcasses, then painted pictures of Republican presidents and senators on the rats' blanched skulls.

Out back by the creek were three ten-by-ten outbuildings filled with leftovers that Ava hadn't sold yet—Dot Cammer's carved rolling pins with Eat Me or Taste My Pie scrawled in bas relief, for example.

Although I may bitch and moan to Ava nonstop about the walls moving inward, I love the place. Outside of nearly stepping on copperheads and timber rattlers every five feet in the yard, our home offers unmatched tranquility. None of Ava's folk artists have the talent to paint portraits wherein the eyes follow a person across the room, is what I'm saying.

"I still think that the works of Mitchell Mitchell will end up in the art history books," Dr. Wanda McGaha said when she and Big Jim came inside the glassed-in room. I went straight to the bar and didn't look back. Mitchell Mitchell had a fascination with tobacco products. He made chimes out of snuff cans, and an entire thermos out of cigarette butts.

I held up a quart of Old Crow to Big Jim, making the international sign for "Would you like about four fingers of this stuff?"

Ava said, "It's hard to say what'll happen to Mitchell Mitchell's work. With all this backlash against the tobacco industry, he'll either skyrocket in price or flounder completely. From what I can tell from my buyers, they're still all waiting to see, too."

I put a Dillards CD on and skipped ahead to "Dooley." Big Jim Shorts—and this proved my point—said, "You wouldn't happen to have any Disaronno Originale? It's an amaretto. I hate to be picky, but if you ain't got that, how's about a nice dark cognac?"

I turned and stared at him in the same way any man stares at a good coon dog gone feral. "I don't think we have anything like that. You must've acquired a taste for brandy and whatnot over in Dem Dot Doh Dey or wherever." My wife pretended not to listen. She showed one of Po Munn's clay bedpans adorned with bull's-eyes and fire extinguishers to Wanda. I poured myself the drink, turned some bottle labels around, and said, "The best I got close to what you're talking is single-malt Scotch."

Big Jim, fake primitive artist, said, "That'll do. Neat."

"Dem Dot Doh Dey," I said. "That must've been something." I

wanted to go upstairs, get on the Internet, and check out the entire history of Vietnam. Somewhere, probably, was a list of every man who shipped over.

"I met Mitchell Mitchell one time. I believe he's queer," Big Jim said.

"He probably wasn't in the war, then," I said.

Ava said, "Let's go upstairs. I made some crab cakes earlier."

The Dillards sang about slipping through the woods.

* *

Ava gave me that look she normally reserves for workmen explaining why they didn't show up the day before. Wanda McGaha went into the bathroom. Big Jim and I sat down in front of the television, but I didn't turn it on. Listen: This was toward the end of the 1999 baseball season and the Braves were playing the Mets. I feared that Big Jim would want me to turn on PBS, and the only thing worse than not watching a big-time baseball game altogether is watching opera while a big-time baseball game airs two channels away.

I pulled out my little Mead notebook and wrote down *Baseball or Opera?* There was a board game in there somewhere. Wagner—you got either Honus or Richard, baseball or opera. There's a question there, somewhere.

Big Jim leaned my way. "You seem to have a problem with me. I understand that. It doesn't bother me. I guess maybe you expected someone like me to come in ordering moonshine, or telling stories about killing deer with my bare hands."

Wanda came out of the bathroom. She said, "I love what you did with the pine needle motif in there, Ava. Who makes those soap dishes?"

I leaned Big Jim's way. "I could care less how a man makes his living. But I care about people lying about their military record. I ain't got one to brag about, so I don't. I feel guilty enough."

Shorts looked back toward my wife. He sipped his drink and leaned in closer. "Your wife's doing me some good. I don't want to lose my new lifestyle, understand. And I imagine she don't want me taking hers away neither."

Our goddamn foreheads nearly touched. I said quietly, "I figured that much out."

"I'm Big Jim Shorts now. People know me from San Francisco to Baltimore. Before I told people I went to Dem Dot Doh Dey I lived in a snailback trailer on my folks' land down in Gig, South Carolina. They farmed land until the Savannah River Nuclear Plant waters came up and turned their soil sour. It's one of those things. I had already gone off to college to study agriculture. Then I came back to nothing. It's not a whole lot different than going to 'Nam, man. I figured if the government could change the way I was supposed to live, then I could change the way I saw myself. It was my Vietnam, goddamn it."

I could only nod and feel sorry for him. I didn't ask if Greensboro and all the cotton mill work was a lie, too. Downstairs, muffled, came the Dillards singing something about Ebo Walker's daddy saying "Durn your hide." No movie soundtrack could've fit better.

Wanda yelled from upstairs, "Hey, Warren. I changed my mind. I want a salty dog."

I said, "I got you," to Big Jim.

He said, "Hot damn—I bet the same could be said about you and the president of the college, for that matter. I don't know about Ava, but I bet Dr. McGaha didn't grow up saying what she's said so far tonight."

I said, "If you ever etch a gourd that shows a man doing everything he can possibly do to hang himself, I'll buy it."

* *

For the most part, I've learned, primitive artists only act in extremes. They'll either want a dollar bill for their works, or they'll demand a few thousand. When Ava and I show up at, say, Selma Weedman's house— she paints only on old washboards, and her subjects are pretty wavy— she'll either open the door and greet us immediately, or play some kind of hide-and-seek from behind the blanket-covered porch window. Ava and I have left the property of about every primitive artist under shotgun fire at one time, but the next meeting might end with a basket full of scuppernongs as a gift.

I prepared myself for Big Jim Shorts's transformation. I figured fifteen minutes after his first Scotch and he'd get defensive about Dem Dot Doh Dey. Or he would break down crying, full of apologies. By the time Ava finished cooking, and Wanda McGaha quit touching everything on our walls, Big Jim took a seat and said, "I meant to go to Vietnam. I signed up and everything. It just ended up that I didn't have to go. Y'all called me on that one. I knew I should've said My Lai or some such place."

I poured him another drink. Ava said, "Do not go around confessing what you just told us, Big Jim. If you want to stay in business with your gourds, just shut up. For all I care you can print up little business cards saying you lost your larynx in the war."

Ava got twenty-five percent when she sold his art. The least she ever took in was $250, and that was for one of those miniature pumpkins.

President Wanda McGaha said, "That'd put a damper on the lecture tours. I say you go further. I'd say that you went to Vietnam, and then you got orders to work for Nixon in some capacity. You got fired for plotting to kill the son of a bitch. And then you became a heroin addict." She looked at me and shrugged her shoulders. "You used to be a better host, Warren. Where's my goddamn drink?"

I didn't want to be the cause of Big Jim's last gourd. I got up and found a bottle of sour mash in the cupboard. Ava handed out paper plates. "What I should be doing is taking my gourds and etching the faces of every boy who ever lost his life in the war. That wouldn't be so hard. I could go to that wall in Washington and copy down names, then travel around to where the boys went to high school, look them up in their yearbooks, you know. That sort of thing. Hell, I bet I could get a grant to do something like that."

I handed Wanda a Manhattan instead of a salty dog. She said, "I have friends at the South Carolina Arts Commission. You might be too good to get money from them. You have to be really, really primitive for money down there. If you can pretend to be a blind artist who wants to paint murals, they'll give you ten grand."

I said, "You ought to quit altogether, Big Jim. Then write a book about the idiots who bought into your story."

"Shut up. Warren, just stay out of this," my wife said. She had tartar sauce on her chin, though, and I laughed.

"I can write a story," Big Jim said. "That's not a bad idea. Except I don't know who's bought all my work. And I don't want anybody tracking me down and killing me 'cause their works went from priceless to flea market."

Ava looked at me across our small handmade table. She shook her head and gave an incredulous smile. I said, "This isn't my fault, Ava. It would've happened before long anyway."

"If you write a book about your life and all of your adventures I can promise you a spot on the faculty as our resident nonfiction writer," said Wanda. "We don't have one at present, outside of some guy who wrote a book about the life and times of Wally Preston."

"A professor!" Big Jim Shorts hit me on the back hard. "All right, Warren. You ought to get a job at a placement service. You ought to get a job with one of those agencies that place people where they belong best. There's your calling."

Ava said, "He ought to get a job," under her breath, almost.

* *

There's a cot upstairs and a fold-out couch downstairs. Wanda McGaha promised that she would go upstairs and fall asleep immediately, but that wasn't the case. Ava and I went to bed. We heard Big Jim and the president of Wally Preston College downstairs, mostly clinking through my liquor bottles. My wife put on sweatpants and a T-shirt from Dirty Dick's Legless Wonders, a barbecue joint up in Norwell, Massachusetts—as if people from New England knew good pig, chicken, or groundhog. I said, "Hey, don't get mad at me. I'm not drunk. This whole thing started because your folk artist claimed he was some kind of war hero. That's it."

We pretended not to hear glasses banging together and the muffled laughter downstairs. Both of us concentrated—we compared notes later—on not envisioning Big Shorts naked. As it turned out, though, they weren't amorous. Big Jim didn't pin and grope the president up against one of Gene Hucks's carved telephone poles depicting John the Baptist, with his head way up high away from his body.

We heard music. I said, "I should've hidden the CD player."

"You shouldn't have bought all those Tony Bennett and Dean Martin discs."

Here's Ava: She rigged a collapsible periscope and kept it in the closet so when I was on the first or third floors she could check me out from where she worked the telephones daily on the second floor. She wanted to see if I drank nonstop or actually did my best to conceptualize. I knew all about it.

I went and got the thing out, dropped it from our bedroom window, and peered into the compact-sized mirror on my end, tilted at forty-five degrees. "They're dancing," I said to my wife.

She got out of bed. "Let me look."

Listen, this was real, old-fashioned, mannered dancing—Big Jim held Wanda McGaha with a two-foot space between them. They box-stepped as Dino sang that song about the moon hitting your eye like a big pizza pie. When Ava gave the periscope back to me, I swiveled around and checked the rest of the bottom floor, expecting to see the Gold Diggers or something.

"I'll be damned," I said.

"You ruined him." She pulled her periscope up in sections. "In ruining Big Jim Shorts you've also ruined me. There's no way I can take the guy seriously now. It'd be like asking people to buy stock from a man whose favorite game is hopscotch."

My wife and I got back in bed. She didn't move. We listened to another few Dean Martin songs. Two minutes after the music stopped—and this is when we had to work the hardest not to imagine them naked—we heard Big Jim start up his Alabama pickup truck. Two doors shut. I couldn't decide on whether I respected Wanda McGaha more or less. I couldn't decide whether I held no hope for higher education, or saw her as a maverick administrator who could appreciate hormonal drives in regular college sophomores and whatnot.

"They have to come back. Wanda's car's still here," I said to Ava. I got up and looked out the window. "Maybe they're just going for a drive to talk about art."

Ava rolled over toward me now standing naked at the glass. "Come back here," she said. "Sometimes I think you don't realize that there's a difference between normal and visionary art. Or between trained artists and primitive artists."

Whenever we made love over the next couple years one of us would yell out "Dem Dot Doh Dey," and the other would laugh out loud. My wife never mentioned Big Jim Shorts again, at least in my presence, and whenever Wanda McGaha came over for parties she made a point not to look at the one gourd my wife and I kept on top of the refrigerator. Handing her a Manhattan, it was hard not to ask if she'd heard from Big Jim, or if she was going to write the foreword to whatever biography he might be working on.

Ava discovered or invented another dozen primitive artists. One woman in particular brought in the money that Big Jim had once provided. This woman built beds of nails out of old car cigarette lighters. Me, I invented a board game called "Vietnam," but it never made it to market.

JESUS, BEANS, AND BUTTER RUM LIFESAVERS

Monroe Thompson

Thirsty Martin had been following the man all the way from the blood bank. What caught his eye was the overcoat the guy was wearing. Now there was a real coat. A coat like that could get you through the Alaskan winter. That coat was made for weather like arctic storms and sixty below and hundred-mile-an-hour winds. A man could live in a coat like that. They must have had to shear a whole herd of sheep to make that coat, Thirsty thought.

Now the current temperature was probably between fifty and sixty. It might be a little cold for mid-September, but couldn't be below fifty. It just didn't get that cold in New Orleans. With a coat like that, the guy had to be a snowbird. With a coat like that, the guy was definitely from out of town. A man couldn't buy a coat like that in New Orleans.

At the blood bank Thirsty had caught a snippet of the guy's accent. Sounded kind of like up east, New York or Boston, or maybe Buffalo. The guy had a hoarse, bitter voice, like a baseball umpire. Yankee, for sure.

He hadn't seen the guy come in the blood bank, because he had been on the table, squeezing the little rubber pad, feeling the tendons and muscles press against the needle thrust into his vein, and watching the blood bag wiggle back and forth. When he had pumped his bag full, the nurse pulled the needle out and had him sit on the side of the cot with his arm up in the air. So he had been sitting there with the alcohol and liniment smells burning his nose, pressing a cotton ball against the little hole the needle made, and looking out the door at the receiving desk. And that was when he first saw the fellow.

When a donor goes in, the big nurse at the front desk stabs the guy's finger and squeezes a drop of blood into a beaker of blue stuff, and if the drop doesn't do right she won't buy it. She is an overbearing bitch anyway. After she gets through asking all these personal questions, she grabs the poor bastard's hand and shoves the little blade in like she was darning a sock. If he flinches, she says, "Now, now, Mr. So-and-So, that little prick didn't hurt you." After all that, it's an ego thing, and to get turned down is embarrassing even if it were not for the financial considerations.

She turned the guy in the coat down and wouldn't take his blood, and he had been really pissed.

"You ought to pay me something for trying," the guy said.

And the nurse told him, "You may have a doughnut and some orange juice, sir, and you really should see a doctor."

"Hey, you shove 'at doughnut up your ass," the man said. He lifted that huge coat with both hands and sort of walked into it, picked up his shopping bag, and shuffled out the door.

Thirsty wanted to follow him. He wanted to meet him and talk to him. He wanted to get a close look at that coat, and he hurried the nurse.

"It's okay," Thirsty told her, pointing to the little blood clot in the bend of his arm.

The nurse studied the puncture and covered it with a Band-Aid. " You be careful, Mr. Martin," she said.

Thirsty wolfed down his doughnut, tossed off the orange juice, which tasted like Listerine and aspirins, and hurried out the door with the seven dollars in his hand.

The man in the overcoat was about a block ahead of him. Snowbird. Yeah. They started drifting in this time of the year, early fall. Some of them stayed and some of them drifted on south and wintered in Miami or Orlando or Tampa. They were gray-faced men, smoked with diesel fumes and peppered with railroad dust, wearing shoes without laces and pants without belts and carrying crumpled paper bags, and they moved across the face of the earth in their seasonal migrations like gray herds of grazing animals, north in the spring, south in the fall. Thirsty wondered about men who couldn't stay put.

The man walked east along Prytania Street, turned left at Lee Circle, and continued along St. Charles. It was a dim September afternoon, with rain threatening, and there was the occasional rumble of distant thunder. A chill wind fluttered the pennants at the car lot on Julia

Street, and a wet, shiny streetcar rumbled down the tracks, carrying a Budweiser ad on its side. On the poster was a picture of a group of smiling young men and women gathered around a fireplace, holding up schooners of beer and looking like they were having the time of their lives. A beer would taste good, thought Thirsty Martin, and he watched the streetcar waddle away down the tracks, dragging its tail against the overhead wire, receding in the distance in the direction of the tall statue of Robert E. Lee, carrying with it the images of warmth and comfort and belonging.

When he looked back down St. Charles, the man was gone, and he felt a little bump in his heart. Shit. He wanted to talk to him, see what he was about, find out where he was from, take a close look at that god-damn coat. Well, what the hell, he thought, and he felt the little fold of bills from the blood bank. Seven dollars. He bought a fifth of Italian Swiss Colony white port at the liquor store on Magazine Street, and as soon as he was out of the door he unscrewed the cap and took a hefty drink, screwed the top back on, wadded the bag around the neck of the bottle, and walked across the street to Lafayette Park.

And there was the man from the blood bank, sitting on a bench in the middle of the park, all hunkered down in that monster wool over-coat, with his big Kmart shopping bag beside him. He was rolling a ciga-rette from a can of Prince Albert. There was a light mist falling now, and the canopy of old oak trees gathered it from the air, collected it, con-densed it, and sent it to the earth in huge, random whistling drops.

Thirsty stopped before the man, careful not to invade his space, standing a courteous five feet away. "Mind if I roll with you?" Thirsty asked.

The man cut his eyes up without moving his head. First he regarded the crumpled paper bag that Thirsty held loosely in his hand and which was molded to the shape of the wine bottle; and which Thirsty was jig-gling slightly, the way a keeper at the zoo might dangle a sardine before a trained seal. The man raised his head, peeping out like a hermit crab in an oversized shell, and held out the can of Prince Albert.

"Paper's in the can," he said.

Thirsty received the can with his left hand and held out the wine with his right. From high in the oaks, big drops of water were falling with loud singing smacks, and the wind was humming through the power line and shaking the limbs and leaves. Thirsty sat on the bench beside the man in the coat and worried with the Prince Albert can. He saw the man hold the wine bottle in both of his hands and look at it. The man peeled back the paper sack on the neck of the bottle, unscrewed the cap, wiped the mouth of the bottle with the heel of his hand, and turned it up. From Thirsty's angle the man's head was hidden in the flare of the turned-up collar, and it looked like some headless apparition was pouring wine down the open collar of a huge coat, and he could hear the air gurgling up in the neck of the bottle.

When the man took the bottle down he said, "Oh, Jesus!" and "Thanks, I needed that," and he set the bottle on the bench between them.

Thirsty finished making the crooked cigarette, licked the full length of the paper and held it up. "Look at that son of a bitch," he said. "A Camel would walk a mile to put his brand on that."

The streets were quiet, except for a few slow-moving cars with their lights turned on against the gathering gloom, and the regular rattle and hum of the St. Charles streetcar. The wind had died down and the drizzle had stopped. Now the smells of cooking were riding on the soft cool air, and the two men sat in the empty park and drank the wine.

Once, Thirsty said to the man in the overcoat, "You look like Hoagy Carmichael," and the fellow replied, "Who the hell is Hoagy Carmichael?" and Thirsty didn't feel like getting into it. They finished the bottle of wine, and then got up and turned over every rock in the park because Thirsty told the man that sometimes people hid money under the rocks. They walked over to the liquor store on Magazine and bought another fifth of wine, and walked back to the park and sat on the same bench and passed it between them.

Finally, Thirsty asked him, "Hey, where the hell did you get the coat?"

And the man said, "I found it in a bus station in Charlotte, North Carolina."

Thirsty nodded. That made sense. "It's a hell of a coat," he said.

The man agreed. "Just about perfect."

"A man would give a lot to own a coat like that."

"It ain't for sale."

"Bullshit. Everything is for sale."

"Everything but this coat."

The streetlights came on and the sky faded to a smoky black. They passed the bottle between them until it was empty, and then Thirsty laid it on its side under the bench. The wind was rising again, and the big oaks were still dropping unexpected splatters, winking against the hazy glow of the lights.

"You got a place to stay?" Thirsty asked.

"Yeah," the man replied.

"I mean indoors," Thirsty said.

"I don't need to sleep indoors," the man said.

Thirsty knew he was right. With a coat like that, he could sleep anywhere. Hell, he could float down the river in it and stay warm. But Thirsty was concerned for this fellow. He had seen him at the blood bank, and he had followed him, and they had drunk wine together and turned over rocks, and the guy looked like Hoagy Carmichael, and he probably needed something to eat. So Thirsty said, "Listen, I know you ain't asking for nothing, but I know if your capital, surplus, and undivided profits were giving you tax problems, you wouldn't be visiting no blood bank. So look, I got a place you can sleep warm, and if we hurry we can get some beans before we turn in."

"Where's that?" The voice came from deep inside the open collar of the coat.

"The Baptist Mission," Thirsty told him.

"No thanks," the man said, "I don't go for that Jesus shit."

"What are you, a goddamn atheist?"

"No, I'm a Lutheran, but I don't go for that emotional bullshit."

"Man, it ain't no emotional shit, you just sit there and listen to the guy preach about fifteen minutes, and then you eat your beans and they give you a cot. It ain't the Waldorf, but it's clean, and it don't cost nothing. What you pay is your time. You just sit there and listen."

The man heaved a sigh. He stood. "Okay," he said, "but you better watch those assholes trying to save my soul. I don't like it."

"Them assholes ain't gon' try to save your soul, man. They just gon' give you some beans." Thirsty said, and he realized there was a lot of wine swimming around in this old guy's brain. He would have to watch him. "By the way," Thirsty asked, "what's your name?"

"You writing a fucking book?" the man asked.

They walked over to Poydras, and down to Grady Street. There was a crowd of men at the front door of the mission, and a couple of them recognized Thirsty and spoke to him. The man in the coat was staggering and weaving, and Thirsty guided him inside and seated him on a bench near the door. Settling in next to him, Thirsty picked up a stray songbook and put it in the rack on the bench in front of them. The man said, "Hey, you want me to lead the goddamn singing?" and Thirsty was surprised at how clearly his voice carried in the big chapel. It was like he had a megaphone. Thirsty held his finger to his lips and the guy looked at him with disgust, turned his face to the front, and turtled down in his great coat.

The men from the sidewalk filed in, coming in twos and threes, filling the pews from the back to the front, climbing over one another, scooting along the pews to make room, and finally, when the doors were closed, the chapel was filled wall to wall with bleary-eyed gray-faced men, who sat suffering as quietly as they could, waiting for the final "amen" from the pulpit which signaled the opening of the kitchen, and the beans, and the warm cot where they would sleep out of the rain with their shoes under their pillows against the midnight thieves. It was quiet except for the shuffling of feet, a few shattered coughs, the squeaking of the pews, and the animal fizzle of growling stomachs.

The preacher marched deliberately across the platform and looked over the gathering with fire in his eyes. He was a new one on Thirsty, but the message was not new. Thirsty had heard it a thousand times, the old story about change and giving one's life to the Lord, and about losing a life to save it, and seeking God's will, and sin and repentance. Thirsty tuned the guy out and thought about happier days. He remembered

Marcel's Gym in the fifties, when he had been a middleweight contender, and the day he put Kid Gavilan on his ass in a sparring session. People appreciated him in New Orleans back then. He could have walked into any bar on Bourbon Street and his money would have been no good. Everybody bought him drinks. They loved him back then.

Thirsty noticed by the clock behind the pulpit that fifteen minutes had passed, then thirty minutes, and he could feel the turmoil seething in the breast of the man beside him. From time to time a low moan issued from inside the gaping turned-up collar.

Finally the man in the pulpit neared his climax. Thirsty could feel it coming. The preacher stepped away from the pulpit and thrust a thick, limp Bible over his head in one hand. With the other hand he aimed an accusing finger at the congregation. "What you men need," he cried in a loud voice, "is JESUS!"

It was too much for the man in the overcoat. He sprang to his feet, threw open his coat, and in a voice several decibels higher than the voice of the preacher, screamed in bellowed outrage, "WHAT I NEED IS THEM FUCKING BEANS!"

The effect was like pushing the button on a doomsday machine. All the bums and drunks came out of their seats screaming, and somebody started singing "The Battle Hymn of the Republic." The doorkeepers grabbed the man in the overcoat and rushed him out the door. Thirsty ran behind them yelling not to hurt him, and they asked if he was his friend. Thirsty told them he was, and they threw him out, too.

And when the door slammed behind them, there they were again, on the street, in the rain, sloshing along from streetlight to streetlight, stepping around the puddles illuminated in the cones of light, splashing through them in the dark.

The man in the overcoat was laughing, holding his belly and coughing between paroxysms, and Thirsty was laughing, too.

"Look, pal," Thirsty said, "I still got four bucks and change. What say we go get another bottle of wine?"

"Sounds like a winner to me," the man said, "and you can call me George, buddy, that's my name." George dug deep in the pocket of his coat. "Here," he said, and he held up a small roll. "Have a butter rum Lifesaver."

"Thanks," Thirsty said, and he popped one into his mouth. "Beats the hell out of beans, don't it?" And they turned up Magazine toward the liquor store. The Lifesaver tasted good.

"Where did you get them?" Thirsty asked.

George laughed. "They came with the coat," he said.

ARNOLD'S NUMBER

Sidney Thompson

On weekends, at the top of each hour from noon till five, a crowd entered the backside of the depot where the buses were parked and refueled. Those who did not pass through the front doors into the downtown streets of Memphis, but massed in the depot for an exchange, would refilter during the hour through the back doors, which the announcer over the loudspeaker called gates. These were the passengers Arnold knew. Today, Sunday, at twelve o'clock sharp, he ran across Union Avenue and pushed open one of the front doors and marveled at all the people he could choose from. They were poor, or close enough for Arnold to call them that. People who survived by being friendly, charmingly naive, and easily charmed. And regardless of the depot he visited, he always dressed down.

He was wearing the red, white, and blue plaid flannel shirt tucked into the black suit pants his wife, now ex-wife, had given him eleven years ago for Christmas with matching coat and vest. And he wore, of course, his navy blue windbreaker with the missing snap, which he had removed himself.

He smiled as if he'd seen someone he knew and walked in her direction. There was a vacant chair beside a lady holding in her lap a baby wrapped in a pink blanket. She rocked it with her legs.

"Isn't she cute?" said Arnold, sitting down and laying his duffel bag between his high-top sneakers.

"This 'she' you referring to's a boy," she said. "And, yes, he is cute." She looked at her baby. "He's my little wonder."

"Always happy, is he?"

She turned and glared at Arnold as though he had insulted her child for the second time and would take no more.

"He ain't never cried but once. Nobody believes me when I say that and you don't have to neither. But it's the honest-to-God truth. Cried at

303

birth and takes all else like a man."

Arnold looked her straight in the eyes. He said, "I believe." He tickled the boy's palm and watched him clutch his tiny pink hand around his fingertip.

Arnold laughed. "How old is he?"

"Seven months, two weeks," she said. "Name's Verdi." She raked his thin blond hair with her fingernails, and Verdi released Arnold's finger.

"That's a nice name," said Arnold.

"It's Daddy's name, his middle name. Grandmomma come across it while listening to the radio. Said it followed a beautiful song. And when I heard that touching story I swore I'd give it to my son, too. Ain't that right, little Verdi," she said, tickling the baby's nose, then looking up from the baby's smile to smile herself at Arnold.

Arnold smiled, crossed his legs, and folded his hands on his knees. That was, a year ago, one of the first things he had to learn in the depot: where to place his idle hands. They could look like dangerous implements if you weren't careful. If he was standing, they fell kindly in front, woven, and if sitting, they went on his knees. But you had to place them so that the person saw you place them, saw that gentle nature, or, he was convinced, you had to repeat the gesture until it was noticed.

"Verdi loves me to death," the woman said. "And he don't love just anybody. You know, when Lionel—that's his daddy—come home from work, Verdi won't even hug him. How about that?" She grinned, and Arnold could see cavities. "Ain't that something?"

"It's important for a boy to love his momma."

"Yes, very, very."

"My daddy ran out on Momma and me," said Arnold, and the lady shook her head in disgust. But he was lying—it was his mother who had left. "Daddy ran off with the next-door neighbor, a clerk at a convenience store, worked the graveyard shift. Yes, she was convenient, all right. So I know how this little guy feels. He knows nobody loves like a momma."

The mother patted Arnold's folded hands. "I wish Lionel could hear you say that. He gets jealous over the littlest thing."

"You and Verdi headed home?"

"No, well, yeah," she said. "Holly Springs, my first home. Visiting his grandparents. How about yourself?"

"Nashville," he said. But the only place he was going, between five-thirty and six, was back across Memphis beyond the city limits to his dusty, near-empty house in the suburbs.

The loudspeaker clicked on, and Arnold listened to it hum over the chatter and the noise of televisions at the front of the depot, and he breathed in deeply. "All boarding for Birmingham/Atlanta go to Gate Nine." Arnold didn't like the announcer's voice. It was gravelly, guttural, and the tone plainly indifferent, if not contemptuous altogether. But Arnold liked the sound of the loudspeaker: an ocean breeze rushing in with the tide. Though he enjoyed the travelers, he detested their tobacco and would meditate on the humming of fresh air, breathe it in deeply, rhythmically.

The lady brought baby Verdi to her chest and stood, lifting a large suitcase. "That's my bus," she said.

Arnold reached under his jacket and pulled out a stack of postcards from his breast shirt pocket. He flipped through them until he found one showing Elvis and Priscilla Presley embracing their newborn Lisa Marie and each other.

"Here, a little reminder of your brief stay in Memphis." Arnold slipped the postcard between her fingers that were under Verdi's head.

"Thank you," she said, "and you have a safe trip to Nashville."

He watched Verdi and his mother make their way through the crowd to Gate Nine. Arnold devoted each weekend to one of five depots. He had initiated this rite in Memphis for no other purpose than to pass the time until he could own again the blissfulness of schedule. Then, afraid of being discovered a loiterer, he began to rotate from Memphis to those bus stations in the four nearest cities—Nashville, St. Louis, Little Rock, Jackson. Still, despite the routine, it was always a disappointment to see his friends walk away.

He turned to see who remained in the room. When he saw an elderly woman sitting by herself, he hurried to a stall in the restroom and opened his duffel bag to the paper sack of campaign buttons for Bush-Quayle, Clinton-Gore, Ross Perot (Arnold never did make up his mind whom to vote for), and buttons promoting Pro-Life, the NRA, and the Sex Pistols; his solid black mourner's tie that wrapped around a pair of sunglasses; and beneath these items lay the manila envelope with the horsehair mustache and the glue. What he wanted this time was the arm sling and the elastic bandage, which he always wore for meeting elderly women.

"Someone sitting here, ma'am?" he asked, pointing to an adjoining chair.

The woman looked up, cut her eyes back down and shook her head, so Arnold sat, waited a moment, then let out a slight moan. He waited, then moaned again, slightly louder.

She turned to him. "You okay, son?"

"I hope so, ma'am. My arm's paining me some. You see, my wife and I had a little dispute."

"Oh," she said, her pupils dilating. She slid away into the empty chair beside her.

"No, we didn't exchange blows, ma'am."

"Whew, that's good," she said, returning, with her ear even closer. "Well, tell me what happened."

"She said she didn't want children and I said I did. I said it was selfish of her not to want to bring any into the world."

"You're absolutely right," she said. "Barney and I—rest his soul—brought in six, and if we hadn't, well, who would've? Answer me that. Who would've, if we hadn't?"

"Nobody," said Arnold.

"So what happened to your arm? Shame it's your right one."

"Wouldn't you know?" he said. "That's the kind of luck I have. Well, just to be blunt about it, she left me. She packed up right in front of me, hopped in our only car, and drove off with me standing right there pleading for her to come back."

"My, my," she said.

"I was so mad, and I turned around and saw the plural on the mailbox. Saw it said The Hamptons. It was such a bald-faced lie I knocked the box off its post. That's when I fractured my arm."

The lady shook her head. She patted his good arm. "You poor thing," she said. Then her mouth dropped open, she looked intently into his eyes. "You aren't going after her now, are you?"

He shook his head. But a year ago, when she left, he had gone after her. From the hospital, with a splint on his arm, he took a taxi to the depot, and after a three-hour bus ride to her parents' house, he'd begged for thirty minutes through the screen door for her to come back. He even promised he'd never pester her any more about children. Then her father said, "Okay, Arnold, you've had your say," and slammed the door.

"No, I'm taking a trip to be with my folks," he said.

"That's a good idea. Especially if you live here. Do you live here in Memphis?"

"Practically. I live in the county."

"You need to be careful then," she said. "Memphis's going to fall one of these days. Fall hard and sink fast."

"Armageddon, you mean?"

"Heck, no, son," she said. "The quake. There's a quake coming. And they're predicting a big one. That's why I'm taking a bus out of here. Going to Florida, where the weather's safe. No sir, I won't be around to see the New Madrid Fault suck this city into the river. It's called Continental Drift, son. So I suggest you stay with your family as long as you can."

"You must have children in Florida."

"My youngest daughter," she said, "but I'm not moving in with her. I wouldn't put that burden on anybody unless they asked for it."

She began to talk about the retirement village awaiting her in St. Petersburg, then stopped, opened her purse, and brought out brochures to show him pictures of the view she'd have of Tampa Bay.

Arnold and his wife had vacationed in Florida one summer, had beach-hopped from Fort Walton to Destin to Panama City back to Destin and again to Fort Walton, she with the tanning oils, sun blocks, and sunscreens, and he with his metal detector.

The lady pointed at the palm trees in the pictures, at the pretty flowers she didn't yet know by name, at the whiteness of the sand, while Arnold studied the beachcombers wading in the surf, the gray-haired ladies strolling with linked hands by the flower blooms, the aged couple sitting in wrought-iron lawn chairs with tropical drinks, with umbrellas adorning their drinks as the palm trees towered and fanned above to adorn the couple in the depths of luxurious chit-chat. How lovely it must be to be given a life, Arnold thought, in which every day passes like Saturday or Sunday at the depot. He realized then that this lady couldn't be poor, even if her plain dress and scarred shoes suggested it. She was just frugal. She was probably richer than he was, but wasn't she friendly?

Just as she had put away the brochures and snapped her purse closed, the bus to Tampa was announced for boarding. Arnold rose to help her with her luggage, but she insisted she could manage alone. She shook his good hand, and he gave her a postcard bearing a photograph of Elvis hugging his mother, Gladys, whose forlorn eyes gazed at someone or thing outside the frame. She told Arnold she loved Elvis ("His gospel songs, that is"), warned him again of Memphis and the muddy Mississippi opening up to swallow, and walked to her gate.

Arnold thought it was funny that in their own private vernacular each had witnessed to the other. Like priest and rabbi.

After changing out of the sling and bandage, he sat back down and looked up at the clock on the wall—ten minutes till the next wave of passengers. He scanned the depot for the next friend he'd make, but there was no one to talk to, no one alone. And that was one of his rules: Always converse with singles. He had ten whole minutes.

He decided to browse the tiny gift shop, which stood near the front of the depot between the ticket counter and the announcer's glass cage. Arnold walked past the row of beige seats. Bolted on the armrest of each one was a coin-operated television. He refused to look in the direction of the cage. He'd caught a glimpse of the announcer many months ago, and that was enough. He was a stout, orange-haired man in a wheelchair, and he could go to hell, Arnold told himself months ago, if he thought Arnold would sympathize with his shade of pumpkin.

In the gift shop, Arnold noticed that the toy buses had gone up fifty-five cents. He scanned the rack of postcards that anybody in any depot would ever want to receive: the overweight Vegas Elvis; the G.I. in Germany Elvis; the black belt in karate Elvis; the badge-flashing, pearl-handled-pistol-packing deputized Elvis; the President Nixon hand-shaking Elvis, who was also the newly appointed special agent of the Bureau of Narcotics and Dangerous Drugs Elvis; and there were others, but none Arnold didn't already have. Gradually approaching the snack food display, he admired the models on the magazines, ignored the newspapers, and as he purchased his ritual bag of vanilla wafers, he ignored the clerk, who never spoke a word to anybody. Who do you think you are? Who are you trying to fool anyway? thought Arnold, looking at the fringe of gray neck-hair protruding from the clerk's black toupee. Arnold could teach him a thing or two.

Sometimes Arnold considered saving a few wafers to share with a passenger, and every time deciding that no one would accept food from a stranger, would suspect him of poison if he offered. So he ate them all and all the crumbs and afterward always drank from the water fountain between the restrooms.

He was again sitting when the next group of passengers entered the depot at the top of the hour. One was a young man in his twenties, clean-shaven, but wearing a tie, and Arnold never talked with anyone wearing a tie, unless it was black. Otherwise, the person reminded him too much of his other life, the one that was busy, thankfully, but that he neverthe-less preferred to forget. But behind the man with the tie walked a bearded man who wore a sweatshirt, jeans, and a Navy pea coat and carried a notebook and a backpack. Though interested in talking with him, Arnold declined, because as soon as the man sat down he began writing in his notebook. One of his most important rules in the depot was never to disturb someone who is reading or writing. He'd done it once. On a summer Sunday morning in St. Louis, he asked a young woman, high-school age, if she'd seen his mustache comb anywhere. He was wearing his fake mustache, as he did for young women. And she looked up from her paperback romance, politely closed it with her finger keeping the place, rather casually collected her belongings, said, "Excuse me," and moved to another row of seats. He was so humiliated he hurried out of the depot, out of the state. He drove straight home.

Ever since then, Arnold had always dismissed immediately his interest for the reader and the writer both. But this bearded man obviously was not writing a letter or making a grocery list, like all the other mere scribes who mocked Arnold by mirroring him, himself a technical writer. This one would cross something out and turn to the next page of his notebook. It seemed he was writing and revising something important. But then Arnold thought of the elderly woman. How could he be sure about anything anymore except the one thing he knew absolutely? Which every weekend of the past year had supported—that the stranger is kinder than the lover or friend and is unable to attack your blind spots that you yourself exposed in confidence.

Arnold grew fatigued. After twenty minutes of watching the writer, he needed somebody he could talk to. There was a college boy at the end of the row in front of him. He was wearing a Louisville letterman's jacket. Arnold liked college kids because they looked for reasons to brag on their fraternities or ball teams or whine about their grades or the cost of textbooks. And with the help of a letterman's jacket, the subject of discussion was a given.

Arnold began to limp very casually around the waiting room, until he arrived at the back of the Louisville letterman. He raised his hand to tap the boy's arm, eager to tell his knee injury anecdote from the sixth grade—of course, he'd place it at the University of Kentucky to add some spice—but then the loudspeaker started to hum, and Arnold stopped to listen. Arnold inhaled and he could smell, as he stood in the depot, the warm fresh salt air of the Gulf.

"Huh," he said to himself, remembering he'd forgotten to meditate the last time the loudspeaker had come on, which was surprising since he and that nice rich old lady moving to St. Petersburg were discussing Florida itself.

The Louisville/Lexington bus was called for boarding, and the college boy jumped up and scrambled away so fast that Arnold coughed.

Damn cigarette smoke, he told himself, rubbing his eyes. Damn rude announcer. Insensitive ingrate.

Arnold suppressed the urge to scramble, too. He strolled to the chair from which he had earlier watched the writer. But the chair had been taken over by a fat woman in plastic. She was wearing a polyurethane miniskirt and a red raincoat. Arnold wondered if she'd traveled all the way from Seattle, Washington. But there was no empty seat near her. None near anyone alone. He cursed under his breath and rushed to the bathroom.

He splashed water on his face and spat air into the streaming water. He dried his face and neck on paper towels, wiped his hands and sleeves and looked at the mirror, then at himself in it: emotionless, featureless. He smiled. He smiled with parted lips. He smiled with eyebrows raised. He frowned. He squeezed the paper towels into a ball and dunked them into the trash. He thought he smiled for real this time and looked. Nothing.

He stepped out of the bathroom and looked in the direction of the writer. But the writer was gone. Arnold turned his head to the left, and there he was, standing beside a waste can tearing pages from his notebook and tossing them into the can. His faded-green backpack sat on the gray tiled floor, and he was putting the notebook inside it. He tied up the pack and raised it to his shoulder, walking out the front doors.

Arnold hurried to the can, thrust an arm into the trash, and pulled out the papers. He sat down in a chair against the wall and read what appeared to be poetry. Many words were crossed out, and there was scribbling in the margins and arrows intersecting and pointing here and there. But each page was more comprehensible than the last. And there was one page, most probably the completed version of the poem, that had been edited very little except for the title, which had been changed several times.

The announcer interrupted Arnold's concentration on his first and second readings of the poem. Damn times two, thought Arnold. Every fifth weekend he came here hoping to hear a friendly voice over the loudspeaker—not that the announcers presiding over the other stations were motivated by any end higher than salary, but at least on occasion they would say, "Greetings" or "Pardon me."

Finally, on the fourth reading, he translated the near-hieroglyphic script:

> I have an eye
> Beautiful to look at,
> Clean,
> Kept beside my bed
> Inside a drawer
> In a condom box.
> The iris is
> Blue as my other eye
> (With its limited orbit),
> And the pupil painted black
> Cannot be caught in the unfolding
> Or enclosing of a living iris.
> I see half-worlds,
> Have stepparents and half sisters,
> But I know whole the trickeries of sight,
> Of love, the fool's perceptions.
> The danger of a tornado?
> The eye has connections.

Arnold decided he liked the poem—for its brevity, "the soul of wit." Though he would have liked it more if there was even more brevity. It was the first poem he'd read in years, since his wife's thirty-fifth birthday when he gave her a collection of Emily Dickinson, which his wife had wanted until she owned it.

He walked over to the trash can and threw away the other drafts, then folded and placed the final one in his shirt pocket along with his postcards. Arnold returned to his chair and leaned back. It felt good to shut his ears as well as his eyes and to relax within himself. He didn't even need vanilla wafers. He could spend a few minutes in peace like this. He decided it was possible.

He was jostled by movement in the chair next to him, and he opened his eyes to see a black woman sitting down, a young woman in her twenties, richly perfumed with the sweetness of roses. Leaning toward him from the side of her head was a small yellow hat, shaped like a dog bowl. He sat up, watching her dig in her tiny white purse, looking at her white dress with yellow and purple flowers, the fruit basket wrapped in cellophane in her lap, the two red suitcases sitting in front of her two yellow shoes.

"God," she sighed. She nudged him. "Have a light?"

"Sorry," he said and bit his lip. He didn't have his mustache on either. He hated it when he was caught off guard like this.

"Have a cigarette?" she asked.

"No. I wish I did though. I've been dying for one." Arnold stood up. "What do you smoke?"

"Camel."

"Be right back."

He hurried to the gift shop. The clerk tossed the pack of cigarettes on the counter, saying nothing as usual.

"I need a lighter, too," said Arnold, and the clerk pointed to a bucket. Arnold had to read the total on the register himself.

The clerk chuckled while handing him his change. Arnold looked up but saw no evidence of humor in the man's pale face.

"Lost your taste for your biscuits, have you?" The clerk spoke with a cockney accent, and as soon as the surprising voice quieted, his face resumed its fallen, tired rigidity.

Arnold wanted to tell this Brit he ought to mind his own damn business since he obviously didn't know the first thing about conversing with American strangers. He decided to give him back what the clerk had been shoveling out himself. Arnold turned, without saying a word. But it wasn't satisfying. It wasn't Arnold.

At the shop's entrance, he whipped around. "From now on," he declared, "I'll be bringing my own damn vanilla wafers. Did you hear that? *Wafers*, not biscuits!"

The clerk retained his frozen glaze, but the relinquishing of resentment satisfied Arnold. Hell, liberated him. It was something he couldn't do in the office at work, something he thought he wouldn't want to do here, or need to do.

The young fragrant woman with the yellow hat was radiant in this beige, gray, faded depot. He warmed as he approached.

"I don't know why I didn't go get them sooner," he said, sitting down. He opened the pack and knocked one out for her to take, lit it, then lit one for himself. He was aggravated he couldn't fold his hands on his knees. He had to hold his cigarette out to the side to keep the smoke from his face.

"Where are you headed?" he asked.

"Chicago."

"Nice place, Chicago."

"You like it there?"

"I liked it," Arnold said, thinking of the elevated trains. She raised her eyebrows as though she couldn't believe it. "But, of course, that was a long time ago," he said. "Things change."

"I'm going to see my momma. But when she dies, I'm done with Chicago." She took a long drag on the cigarette, then slowly whistled the smoke into a stream that warmed his face. Arnold held his breath until the air cleared.

"My daddy lives here," he said, but his father had been dead for six years. "That's why I'm here," he said. "No telling where my momma is. She ran off with the next-door neighbor." He puffed his cigarette but didn't inhale.

"Where you stay?" she asked.

"I live in Jackson, Mississippi."

"I like Missipi," the woman said. "I's born outside Tupelo. Lee County." She smiled. "Them was the good old days." She looked at Arnold. "What'd you do?"

"Excuse me."

"What'd you do? For a living?"

"Oh, I'm an auto body man," said Arnold. "But on the side, I'm a writer. A poet."

"You write love poems?" she asked.

"When I find the right person, I do."

"Well, tell me one." She held on to the fruit basket and turned her body toward him.

"I came up with one just a while ago. How about it?"

"I'm ready."

He dropped his cigarette on the floor and stomped it. He withdrew the poem from his pocket, cleared his throat, feeling slightly ashamed for wanting to pass it off as his. He'd always told, in his own way, his own story. He smiled at her, and she smiled, and his smile suddenly felt real. He hoped his was as pretty as hers, and he began to read.

"Wait," she interrupted. "I don't understand. What you talking about?"

"Let me read it all," he told her. "You have to get the big picture. You'll see." He started over. When he got to the end, he looked at the woman, at her wrinkled expression.

"You sure that's a poem? It don't rhyme."

"It's a poem, all right."

"Don't sound much like one." She bent closer to him. "Hey, you got brown eyes. You ain't got blue eyes."

"They used to be blue—when I was young," said Arnold. He folded the poem and put it back in his pocket.

"With your dark hair, I don't see how you could ever had blue eyes. You sure they was blue?"

"Okay," he said, shrugging his shoulders, "I exaggerated a little. Poetic license, you know? See, I wear contact lenses." He leaned toward her, stretching his lids open with his fingers. "I have a tinted pair at home. I'm just not wearing them today."

"Huh," she said, nodding. "I might get me some. How much they cost? They expensive?"

Arnold felt himself slipping. How could he be an auto body man and afford tinted contacts? Realizing his hands were empty and idle and she was looking at him and he was almost caught in a lie, he laced his hands on his knee. "I don't remember exactly," he said. "There was a going out of business sale, so they were cheap. Cheap cheap."

She raised her hand, and an inch from his face pointed accusingly her index and middle fingers, the cigarette between them forming a cross. Smoke streamed straight up as though confined by banks. "You such a lie," she said and tapped his nose with her long red nail, as if to punctuate. "Not that I mind," she said, waving her hand, then landing it on his arm, "but you so sorry at it."

Arnold gaped, knitting his brow and looking into the black hole of her left eye, then her right.

"You have me all wrong," he said.

"You college educated, ain't you?"

"I wish I was." He shook his head, gradually lowering his face. He thought if he looked at her, saw her smile a moment longer, he might smile back and blow his tenuous cover. "I wish I was," he repeated sadly, but what he wished, for a split second, was to be an auto body man.

"You never wrote that poem, did you?"

"Damn, you won't give up, will you?"

She slapped his thigh. "Got that right," she said. She laughed, and, looking up, he saw that her deeply brown eyes shone white from the glaring bulbs above.

"Okay, all right already, you win," he said. "I'm a lie. Just exercising my poetic license."

"Darling, I used to write love poetry, my own, understand? And they was pretty good, too. Rhymed like music." She flicked her ashes on the floor, rested her hand on his leg. She said, "Darling, want me to show you what love poetry is?"

Arnold nodded. "I'd love you to."

"Well, you in luck then. I got one handy."

She opened her tiny purse and pulled out a clinking mass of keys and key chains and charms. "This is Willie," she said, handing him the ring. He saw that at the end of a chain hung a pendant that contained a picture of a dark bare-chested man holding up a string of catfish. She tapped at the wooden disc beside the pendant, and Arnold turned to it, saw it was engraved with rows of words.

"I wrote it for Willie," she said, "and my brother Stanley burnt it on there for me to give him. Want to see if I can say it by heart?"

"Sure."

"It's called 'Fun.'" She said, while he read:

> *Late last night Willie, he come by on a tractor,*
> *And I was rip-ready and he was attractor.*
> *Well, he done drove us deep into corn,*
> *And our clothes we shucked and coulda made porn.*
> *Then he got sweet and on the lips he kissed me,*
> *And oh how I shivered and felt all set free,*
> *For the rest of the night 'til up peeked the sun.*
> *Damn, we sho had fun!*

"Yeah, you did it," said Arnold, handing her the key ring. "That's good. That's a good love poem."

The hum of the loudspeaker and the voice that followed interrupted their conversation. The announcer called for the boarding of three different gates. The buses were rolling in, and one was the bus to Chicago.

"What's your name?" she asked, dropping her cigarette butt on the floor without bothering to stamp it out.

"Barney," he said.

She brought out a pen and a slip of paper from her purse before dropping in the key ring. "Barney, I'm going to give you my name and number."

"What for?"

"You was trying to pick me up, wasn't you?" She wrote on the slip and handed it to him. "I want you to work on your poetry. And next time you in Memphis, give me a ring, okay?"

He stared at her curly handwriting.

"I hadn't had no fun in a while," she said.

He felt she was waiting for him to look up. He tapped the smoking butt with his sneaker and raised his head, scanning the garden of her dress, roses yellow and purple, to her dark, powdered face, to the red painted lips. She winked.

"Not since Willie," she said. "He died couple seasons ago. Head-on collision."

"I'm sorry to hear that."

She shrugged her shoulders. "Well, God's will. So, you going to give me a ring?"

"Of course," he said, "I'll call you, Rosetta."

"I mean it now. You lying to me?"

He raised his right hand, palm outward. "So help me God," he said, believing his own lie this time.

"Then I'll be looking for a love poem." Cradling the fruit basket between her forearm and chest, she stooped to gather her bags.

"Let me help you," he said.

Arnold walked slowly as though the heavy suitcases were heavier than they were.

"Did you and Willie have any kids, Rosetta?"

"Not that I know of," she said and nudged him with her elbow.

"But do you want any?" He pushed open one of the back doors and held it for her as she stepped outside. "I mean, does the pain scare you at all?"

"Shoot, any woman be scared of that."

Arnold watched diesel fumes swimming around Rosetta's bus.

"But nothing ever amounts to much, does it now, Barney, if there ain't no risk of it hurting you none, getting you killed or what-not. You know?"

He nodded. "Yeah, I know," he said.

When they reached the bus, he handed the suitcases to the driver, who loaded them swiftly into the luggage compartment. Arnold turned to face Rosetta, crossed his hands in front of him, wrung them.

"Call me Arnold. Barney's my middle name, but Arnold's my first."

"All right, Arnold Barney," she said with a grin. She leaned forward, pressing the fruit basket against his chest, and kissed his cheek. "Thanks for the help, and for the smoke. You didn't have to."

"My pleasure," he said. He took the Camels from his windbreaker.

"Here, take the rest. To tell you the truth, I usually smoke Marlboro."

"Thanks, sweet," she said.

"Hey," he said, remembering. He opened his windbreaker, pulled out his postcards and nervously flipped through them. "The King. A souvenir," he said. He fanned them out. "Which one would you like?"

"You got any Chuck Berry? Now there's you a man can sing *and* write his own songs."

He shook his head, put his cards away, and dumbfounded but not unhappy, not insulted or defeated and ashamed but neither glorious nor assertive, he pocketed his hands in his trousers.

She leaned forward once more, to kiss him on the lips but stopped short, eyeing him from an inch away. "You want me, don't you? You can't hide that. Tell me, Arnold, tell me you want me to wet your lips with a big old kiss."

He was breathing her breath. He swallowed.

"Why don't you just hop on this bus with me? What's stopping you right now from going all the way to Chicago?" She leaned a little closer and backed away without kissing him, then smiled. "I doubt your daddy'd mind," she said and turned to the bus.

He watched each bend of leg as she climbed the silver stairs. Soon there was no more leaning yellow hat, no more flowered hips, her yellow shoes vanished. He watched her ghost travel the aisle, then seat itself more clearly at the darkly tinted window. He waited for her to look at him. He was waving goodbye. A boy sitting behind her, wearing a cowboy hat, returned the wave, but she, Rosetta, stared directly ahead, at the back of an empty chair. Below her, the driver was closing up the luggage compartment.

Arnold trudged back inside the depot. He wondered if his desire to call her in days to come was rash, too risky. He passed a trash can, then stopped and backtracked, plucked the eye poem from his breast pocket and returned it to where it should have stayed. The postcards followed. Then, protecting himself, he dropped in Rosetta's slip. And though he'd already memorized her phone number of threes and twos, he felt his tongue curl up in the dust of his mouth, his lungs shrink. Afraid he'd eventually forget the number, angry that he cared, he shoved his duffel bag into the can, thrust it down hard to the bottom. He had never been made such a fool of in a depot, and never with as much respect and promise. He didn't know what to do. He hoped he was doing right.

The loudspeaker clicked on, and he paused, taking in one last deep breath, feeling sentimental about the depot, about Rosetta, feeling resentful about the loss of her, and that damn announcer broke in.

Arnold stomped to the announcer's glass cage and peered in. The man held the microphone between his hands, like he was praying with the thing.

Arnold rapped on the glass, and the announcer turned and scratched his orange head.

"Hey," yelled Arnold, "don't you have any religion?"

Arnold watched him mouth obscenities, but it was over the loudspeaker he heard them.

He laughed. "Is that it? Is that the best you can do?" Arnold spun around, facing the gates and beyond: the bus to Chicago, idling at the exit. Then he watched it pull onto Union Avenue and disappear. A new crowd was pushing its way into the depot.

He started toward the trash can but veered, deciding to lead the onrush of passengers through the front doors. Arnold stopped and stood on the sidewalk, and while mumbling, he held open the door and nodded to each one who entered the city. And he mumbled all the way to his car, while also tapping his hands on his thighs. Perhaps someone who saw Arnold believed that the singing of his lips over the same faint refrain happened by rote or was ushered by the quaking of new love. But it was willed by fear. And the penning, the securing of that arrangement of numbers onto the back of his hand, once he'd seated himself behind the wheel, only elevated the fright. The music.

The Dead Girl

Brad Watson

Parnell Grimes, son of Mercury's most prominent local funeral director, possessed a general grief for such as those unclaimed and unmoored in the world. By the time he was fourteen he'd developed a working fascination with his father's profession, and had begun to sneak down into the preparation room to see the corpses that would be embalmed and presented the next day. And on some few occasions during that time, and always when the people had been mauled in accidents or contorted in some terrible death, he'd gone down in the wee hours to find them simply gone, disappeared, and had fled back to his room terrified that these walking dead would grasp him at every corner. The next day, their funerals would go on as planned, closed-casket. He'd been too terrified to say anything or ask, except once, and then never again. He'd pushed it deeply into a place where he would not have to think about them all the time. He was able to do that. Until the time he thought himself to blame.

The summer he was sixteen years old, he had been awake in his room one night and listening out the window to the occasional automobile rumbling past on the street. He'd seen the oscillating red of the silent ambulance light before he'd heard the car's engine, and knew then he'd heard the telephone ringing earlier, as he'd thought, though it had awakened him from a deep sleep and he hadn't been sure just then that it hadn't been a dream. But he heard it now pull up out back, the whining sound of its transmission as it backed up to the preparation room doors, heard the two doors of the ambulance open and shut, heard the longer creaking of the heavy rear door, and then the rolling of a cart being removed and the voice of his father greeting the men quietly, and the men greeting him in return. And then the closing of the doors, and the ambulance driving off, with no red light now flicking, and then quiet. He rose and slipped into his clothes and shoes and crept down the stairs, in case his mother hadn't awakened.

This was in the year before the strange and mysterious illness of first his father, who died a horrible suffocating death about which no one had an explanation, followed just a week later by his mother. He'd been horrified by the strange noises they made in the room outside of which he crouched fearfully, old Dr. Heath going in and out, weary, and washing his hands, it seemed the old man washed his hands so furiously in the pail in the hallway outside the room. And the doctor would not let him assist with their preparation, not that he'd wanted to but he'd thought it proper, almost an obligation. Dr. Heath laid a hand on his shoulder and said, "Son, it may be catching." And when first his father, and then his mother, lay in their caskets and he stood over them one after the other in the parlor, as he had over so many they'd prepared themselves, he felt a separation of himself from something he couldn't pin down, death reversed upon itself, become something less clinical and more strange, as if all the making way they'd done for other people to that point had been slowly absorbed by them until it became them, too. And so he felt it then, himself, that he'd already gathered some of his own dying, and it would be a lifelong process of accumulation.

There was no explanation of what had happened for some two years until Dr. Heath saw the article that led him to suspect the psittacosis, and then investigated to find out that the gypsy woman his father had embalmed just before he got sick had been a breeder of imported parrots. And had died in much the same way. And when word leaked out, a veritable posse of men from town, friends of his father's, went out to the camp with torches and drove the gypsies away on foot, warning gunshots popping the air, burned the gypsies' wagons, tents, and all their belongings in a conflagration of hatred, grief, and fear. Parnell had seen it from some distance away, having run to follow the men at a safe distance. What he remembered was the terrible sounds of the birds in their cages, trapped there and burning, their shrieking like women and babies, which settled into an awful silence replaced by the quiet crackling of the burning wagons—and the stench, faint but coming to him in little waves, of burning flesh and feathers. He could not stand a bird in a cage to this day.

But on the night he'd awakened to hear the ambulance bring its cargo he'd crept downstairs and quietly opened the door to the preparation room to see something that made him catch his breath. The figure on the table was a girl near his age that he knew from school, though he'd never spoken to her as she was a year older and a quiet girl, though he'd admired her. Her face seemed a sleeping face, not one with the contortions of pain or even the blankness of death, but with her mouth parted and her chin lifted just so, she seemed to be in an expectant sleep, as if she might wake any moment from the dream she kept alive by somnambulant will. His father turned and saw him, and pulled the sheet back over her face.

"I know her," Parnell said.

"You go on back to bed. You can't help with this one."

"What happened to her?"

His father looked down at the form beneath the sheet.

"Nothing," he said. "This one's a mystery. Her parents are beyond grief. She went to sleep and never woke up."

"How long has she been asleep?"

"She's dead, son."

"I mean, how long was she asleep?"

"A week or more," his father said. Then after a moment he said, "She's too close to your own age, Parnell. I don't want you helping me with the young ones. There's time later in your life for that sad business."

"Yes, sir. There won't be an autopsy, then?"

"The parents said they can't abide the idea. There's no evidence of foul play."

"Will you do the embalming tonight then?"

"No," his father said after a moment. "I've had my toddy tonight. I think I'd better wait till morning."

"Yes, sir."

"You go on back to bed. Here, I'll wash my hands and come up, too."

So he waited while his father washed in the sink, though Parnell's eyes never left the vague figure of the girl under the sheet. He looked at the shape of her feet beneath it and could tell she wore no shoes. He imagined she was in the nightgown she'd put on the night she lay down to sleep from which she would never awaken.

"Father," he said. "Was she even sick?"

"Ran a little fever, is all, nothing much." His father turned, drying his hands and looked at the girl. "I cannot imagine anything more awful. I hate to know it can happen. But I knew it before. I'll try to forget again, if I can. Though you should, more than me." He smiled at Parnell. "It's you with your child-rearing days ahead of you."

Not something Parnell could imagine, though. He walked with his father back up the stairs to the parlor level, then up the curved staircase in the foyer to their living quarters, and his father kissed him on the forehead before leaving him in his room and going back to bed with Parnell's mother. Parnell undressed, took off even his underwear and socks, and got into his bed. Some minutes later he heard his father's steady sonorous breathing, and some minutes after that, stepping into his slippers and pulling on his cotton bathrobe, he stole back down the two sets of stairs and into the preparation room. He felt his way in the dark around the wall to the sink, switched on the little lamp there above it, and turned around.

She was like a ghost there under the sheet. He could imagine, felt almost he had been there with her when she had drawn her last breath. The sweet expiration. This loss to him, to Parnell, of that which had never been his nor could be in life, and now here alone with him in death, she was. His heart ached with it.

He drew the sheet away from her face, his hands trembling, and the shock of her features, more alone with him than he'd ever imagined a girl could be, moved through him like a mild electric current.

He hadn't noticed her much, but a few times, passing her in the hallway at school he had noticed her shyness, how she walked with her chin tucked down in her neck, her dark brown eyes glancing up to make sure she didn't run into anyone or get run over in the between-class rush, hardly daring to make eye contact with anyone. Glance up with a smile that seemed almost apologetic, then look down again and make her tentative way along. She was beautiful, he could see now, but no one would have noticed this, she'd been so demure and invisible. Now so visible it seemed a crime that she had never been admired by anyone but her parents, or maybe some boy just as shy as she was, someone who'd never have had the nerve to talk to her or ask her to a game, or ask her to dance at one of the dances they sometimes held at evening in the gymnasium. Someone like Parnell. She was a little dark, and her dark eyebrows were narrow but thick and defined, with a little arch like a V pointing upward in the middle of each one. And her eyes, closed, were wide-set. But it was her mouth that transfixed Parnell. It was broad and full, her lips a little dry and cracked, and now parted in death he could only imagine how expressive it must have been when she was at home, with family, and uninhibited by her shyness, how much joy she must have given to her mother and father, how much they must have hoped for her.

It was the hint of exotic in her features that began to sink into him now. What exotic locale they suggested he could not imagine, but someplace different. It was not the look of a gypsy. Until the woman with parrot's fever, which ended it all, his father had often embalmed and buried gypsies. He had a friendship with the old gypsy queen's son. He'd buried the queen, in that grand ceremony they'd conducted down Eighth Street to the old cemetery west of town, Rose Hill. But she was not gypsy. Her name, now he remembered, was Littleton, that was fitting. Constance Littleton, they called her Connie. Little Connie Littleton, here alone with Parnell. He leaned down and kissed her lips. Dry as desiccated clay. No give there. No, there was the faintest. She was not entirely cold. Still fresh in death, still sweet in passing. Still between the living and the dead, her spirit not entirely removed. He gently pulled the sheet down across her body, and off her small toes, and let it drop to the floor.

She was all small. And if she'd worn her nightgown in death his father had removed it, to prepare for embalming. She barely had feminine breasts. Her arms and legs were thin, her wrists no bigger round than stalks of sugarcane. Her shins and ankles almost bird-narrow, ending in the slim flat feet. Her waist was like a boy's, not narrow and flaring into her hips. Her hands were turned up, as if she were consciously laid out in sacrifice, merely drugged by the high priests who'd laid her there.

He imagined that if he had known her, they would have walked to a little clearing in the, woods. She would be silent, as always, and hardly able to look at him in her shyness. And in his own, little else to say. They would have sat together in slanting afternoon sunlight and let the quiet sounds of the woods gather around them for their company. He took the robe off and stood there a long moment with his eyes closed.

"I love you," he said to her. "You have to know that."

He began to cry a little, his eyes welled up. He had loved her and he hadn't even known it. He began to be flooded by memories of her. He'd seen her eating by herself or with a couple of almost equally silent girl-friends in the school cafeteria. He'd seen her sitting on a bench beside the stadium reading a book and eating an apple one day. She wore a sweater and a tartan skirt and penny loafers. He imagined her helping him remove them, one by one, the light sweater, the skirt and shoes and socks off her feet, her underwear and a little brassiere there more for modesty than support.

The table hardly creaked when he climbed atop it and lay in the narrow space beside her. "I do love you," he whispered. He had hardly to push apart her thin legs, she was in the attitude to receive him already. At her neck, and behind her ears, in her hair, the musty sweet-and-sour smell of a week's neglect in her bed. He could hardly hear the sounds he made for the louder sound of the blood rushing behind his eyes.

As he laid his weight upon her, her lips parted and an almost imper-ceptible exhalation escaped them, the odor of something strange and familiar too, an animal's breath, and rotten flowers, the scum of an iron-rich creek near the swamps, the odor of richly decaying life, life in death, the dying always overtaking the living so the richness of the roots of life must push up unevolved from the earth and into an almost instant decomposition. She was thick and solid in her tissue, hard in parts of pro-truding bone like stones beneath a mat of firm moss, and cool but dry. Inside her was thick and cool and close but not entirely unyielding, his hard prick like a rigid fetus inside a cold womb. He moved himself deeper, slowly, with a wild restraint born of his barely contained respect and love for her, which fought within each second in his mind with a violent lust. He gripped the delicate knobs of her shoulders, which fit snugly into the palms of his own small, childlike palms. His mouth was at her ear, and into it he whispered desperate declarations of his passion, her beauty, oh how she was giving more of herself to him each moment. Some heated current ran its hot millipede fingers up his spine, shocked through his brain and out his scalp, his follicles pure heat valves, his jaw thrown open as if to eject his own heart, some shout must have rolled out of his diaphragm though he could no more distinguish sound from some other force than if it had occurred in a world yet to know any living, breathing thing, his drool on her neck making a wet spot he could see, when he could see again, spreading beside her lank dark hair on the white sheet beneath them.

He closed his eyes and lay there, his breath returning slowly to normal, his heart returning to a dreaded calm, when he heard the little noise that made him open his eyes again. It was a sound like the first little cheep you hear sometimes outside your window at dawn when a bird wakes up in its nest. And when he looked he saw first her mouth move, the lips press together, and then her narrow brow furrow over her thick dark eyebrows. His own breath caught in him like he'd been delivered a blow just as she caught her own, and her eyes opened like those of a child who's been sleeping long and hard and he was up and off her still thumping gently with the last of what he'd done, and standing there watching her.

She lay there blinking for a long moment, then sat up.

"Mama?"

Her voice small and crusty, weak. A thick gray cloud in her eyes, clearing.

"Where am I?"

Parnell had retreated farther away from her into a darker corner. Now she was blinking her eyes and looking at him.

"Where am I?"

He couldn't move. She stared at him a moment, then felt on her right shoulder where Parnell had drooled, looked at the faint glint of moisture on her hand. She looked down and tentatively touched her lower abdomen, her tummy, felt herself, made a quiet hnngh sound, an almost delicate expression of puzzlement. She saw the sheet still bunched at her feet and reached down to get it. She pulled it up over her waist, and then held it while she got down from the embalming table. Her bare toes flexing as they touched the cold concrete floor. She fixed the sheet around her shoulders like some kind of biblical robe and found the door with her eyes and started for it slowly, like a sleepwalker. She had forgotten him. She was not fully awake. He did not know what. He did not know what this was. Her hand found the doorknob and she opened the door and then stood there a minute in the doorway, looking out, looking up the stairs. And then she started up the stairs, going slowly, a little shaky, her hand on the railing. At the top of the stairs she opened the door to the main floor and stepped through.

Parnell snatched up his robe and put it on and followed her quietly in his slippers. When he got to the top of the steps she was almost to the front door at the end of the entrance hallway. She pulled on the door a second, and Parnell almost cried out, thinking she would not be able to open it and his parents would wake at her rattling the knob. Then he heard the lock tumbler click and the door creaked open, not too loudly, and she walked out into the streetlamp light on the front porch. He hurried forward to catch the door before it shut to and just did catch it and opened it to look out. The girl was out to the sidewalk now, still looking about her as if in a dream.

He was paralyzed with terror, but what could he do? In the mist of the bare light before dawn she became naught but a diminishing figure wrapped in a white sheet, her dark hair and bare white feet exposed, a slip of leg when she took her steps, wavering, like a child drunk or a poor corpse wandering toward its gloom as a ghost, until she disappeared in the faint light, a wisp becoming one with the misty fog, and he closed the door quietly, leaned against it trying to catch his breath, and then stole up the stairs and crawled back into his bed and lay there for what seemed hours until he heard his parents stirring.

He lay there curled in his bed unable to move, his mind a wild jumble of fear and horror. What had he done? What would become of him now? He was more alive and awake and full of terror and wonder than he had ever felt in his life. He waited for the news to spread to the proper authorities who would come to arrest him, and thought about what he would say.

It could have been a few minutes later, it could have been an hour, he couldn't tell, when he heard the telephone ring. And in a minute he heard the door to his parents' room open, and his father rushing down the stairs. And then his mother calling down to his father, and he heard her go by his room and down the stairs. And he waited longer, lying under the sheets and awaiting whatever would happen. And then he heard their car start and leave. And then nothing. And he stayed there until some long time later, it seemed, his mother opened the door to his room and stuck her head in, a queer look on her face.

"Parnell, hon, come on down to breakfast."

"What is it, Mama? I heard Papa leave."

She stood there a second, looking at him a little blankly.

"That Littleton girl," she finally said, and looked then as if her senses came back to her. "She just up and walked out of here sometime last night!"

"The dead girl, Mama?"

"Well," his mother said slowly then, "I suppose that's what she was. But now she's alive and down at Heath's."

"She's at the hospital?" He lay there breathing hard and looking at his mother, but she seemed distracted. "How can that be?" he said barely above a whisper.

"How can anything be, darling?" she said. "How can anything be? My good Lord, to think we came close to burying that child, and her alive the whole time."

Parnell could hardly find the words, but finally he said, "How did she come to wake up like that?"

His mother looked at him oddly then, and his heart seized up for what seemed the hundredth time that day.

"I don't know," she said slowly. "I guess she'd just slept long enough."

When his father came home and went downstairs, Parnell waited

until he was alone and went down there and went quietly into the preparation room, where his father sat on a stool looking over some papers
beneath the small lamp he had set up there.

"Papa?" he almost whispered.

His father looked around at him over his glasses, then turned back to
his work.

"Your mama tell you what happened?"

"Yes, sir."

"Very strange business."

"Papa," he said after a minute. "Is that what happened to those other
people?"

His father turned slowly to look at him, removed his glasses.

"What other people, Parnell?"

"The ones that would be gone."

His father said nothing, just stared at him. Then he saw him glance
at the dark corner over the by the sinks and he saw old black Clint, his
helper, standing there staring at him also, and a chill ran through him.

"The ones, I would come down and they would be gone?"

His father continued to stare at him. Then he spoke slowly.

"It's been a hard night for all of us, Parnell. I don't know what you're
talking about. You need some sleep, son."

"I'm sorry," Parnell said. "I wasn't spying on them."

"You should never come down here alone, Parnell," his father said.
"Not yet. There are things you don't understand." He paused. "Will I
have to put a lock on the door?"

"No, sir."

"Go on to bed, son," he said then.

His father watched him as he turned and walked out of the room and
closed the door behind him and stood there a moment, and heard mur-
muring conversation between his father and old Clint but couldn't make
out what they were saying. He went upstairs to his room and lay there all
day with no coherent thought in his head until sometime in late afternoon he dozed off, and would not come down to eat supper. His mother
brought him a sandwich up to his bed and sat on his bedside smoothing

back his hair as he ate, and whispering, "Poor boy, sometimes I wish we weren't in this business, it's no place for a little boy to grow up.".

"Yes, ma'am," he said, and forced some bites of the sandwich down, though his mind still raced wildly, and for the next several days, when he feigned sick to stay out of school, terrified to go there lest the other children see in his face what he'd done. Until finally he was forced to go back, and he crept the halls more fearfully than ever, more invisibly than ever, and spoke to no one, and became again simply the strange Parnell all the children had always known, who kept to himself and would be a mortician when he was older, and was therefore an oddity to be abided with some amusement and unarticulated dread. And after some time, late in the year, the dead girl returned to school, as well.

He would see her in the hallways, after that, but like Parnell she was more the way she had been than ever before. She clutched her books to her thin chest, she kept her eyes down at her feet, and moved quickly from class to class. But Parnell, when he saw her now, saw more than he could bear. Her life, her living, the vital self she carried through the drab hallways, seemed a continuous miracle and the source of a deepening shame, even as the horror at what he had done became for him in his private and unchallenged thoughts something commonplace. Replaced, as it was, by simple shame, a secret and unmentionable embarrassment. In what little niche of her memory was she aware of what had happened? In what dream that visited her in the hours she could not recall, long before she would awaken, this miracle of awakening every day? What part of Parnell existed in there, to be known by no one but Parnell and a part of Constance Littleton that might never resurface, and if it did could not be believed? Some students, some of the boys, called her the Dead Girl and would laugh. Other students said she had no memory of anything from when she went to sleep until she woke up in the hospital. Wandered from the funeral home like some risen mummy and went straight to the hospital. It was like an angel had guided her there, some of the pious girls said. But if it was an angel, Parnell said to himself, it was a fallen one, awakened now to see the darkness of the world all around him.

The Right Kind of Person

Steve Yarbrough

Ann had just bent over to put on her shoes when she began to feel as if her head was full of fog. For the longest time her mind stayed cloudy. When she finally had a thought, it was, *All my life thinking's been easy and now it's hard.* She bet she'd had a darned stroke.

"Momma?"

She stared at the mirror over her dresser. She didn't look the least bit different. Her hair was still more red than gray, her teeth were still white.

"Better hurry, Momma, or we'll both be late."

Her daughter Darlene stood at the door.

Maybe the stroke was just a little one—else she wouldn't have recognized her daughter, would she? When her sister Lena had the stroke two years ago, she didn't even know her own husband. Ann bent and put on her shoes easy as eating an egg.

She was waiting in the car when Darlene opened the door. "I hope it don't sleet," Darlene said. "The weatherman's saying sleet and snow and I don't know what all. Johnny says every time Billy sends him to Jackson the weather turns awful."

All the way downtown Darlene ran her mouth. Stroke or no stroke, Ann did what she always did. She tuned out to avoid thinking ill of her daughter. Darlene was like her daddy had been. She talked all the time because she was afraid that if she shut up, even for a minute, you might tell her something she didn't want to hear.

Darlene stopped the car in front of Kenwin's. Ann opened her door and climbed out.

"Bye, Momma."

Ann said, "Bye."

Or tried to: Nothing came out. Her bowels loosened a little when she realized she was standing in the middle of the street in downtown Indianola, with her mouth hanging open. She shut it quick, "Mmm," she

333

mumbled. She smiled at Darlene—to keep her from having a heart attack in the unlikely event that she'd noticed anything unusual—then she slammed the car door and went in to work.

All day long she refused to open her mouth. She just smiled when someone spoke to her. A couple of customers looked at her funny, but thank the Lord she had sense enough to show them whatever they wanted; she could still tell a skirt from a pair of panty hose. Thank the Lord too that this was Christmas rush. The place was so busy Velma Boyle couldn't come yapping.

When they closed at five, Velma said, "Ann, are you feeling normal? You've been awful quiet."

Ann grinned and waved good-bye.

Darlene talked all the way home, but this time Ann felt glad. She'd slipped into the bathroom around three-thirty and tried to say, "Good day." She had "Good day" in her mind, she knew how it ought to sound, but her mouth couldn't seem to form the words. She'd decided the stroke was probably worse than she'd first thought, but she still believed she could lick it if they'd just leave her be. She was happy Johnny Garber had gone to Jackson. If the weather got bad and iced the roads, she might have time to bring herself around before he returned. Her sister had died in a Rolling Fork rest home last summer. Ann didn't want to give her son-in-law the chance to pack her off to Care Inn.

At supper Darlene found her out. She asked her two or three questions about did she want this or would she like that, and Ann couldn't muster an answer. She might have solved that problem simply by filling her plate and then shoveling food into her mouth, but her right hand had gone numb and she knew she couldn't handle a fork. She sat still and quiet, the hand asleep in her lap.

"Momma." Darlene's eyes were getting bigger. "Momma, what's wrong?"

Her voice cracked on "wrong." Ann wanted to say, "Don't commence, Darlene."

Darlene shoved food at her, crying, "This! Can you say what this is? Or this?"

Johnny got home before too long, and Ann guessed it was a good thing. Darlene was about ready to roll on the floor. She'd done that the night her daddy died, though she was nearly fifty at the time.

Johnny Garber stood over Ann. She wished she could get up from the table, but her right leg felt funny. If only she hadn't sat down. She should have known better.

"Ann," Johnny said. "Are you sick?"

She looked up at him and shook her head no. Then she did something she'd almost never done. She smiled at her son-in-law.

"We better call the hospital," he said.

Darlene cried, "Oh, Jesus!"

Ann shook her head no, no, please no, but Johnny was already dialing.

* *

"Stay in the car," Johnny said. "I'll come around and help you out."

She waited until he slammed the door; then, using her left hand, she opened her own door. She heaved both her legs out of the car and somehow managed to stand. Back at the house, when she realized Johnny intended to tote her, she'd willed herself to walk. Now she aimed to do it again.

Cold rain pelted her face. "Goddamn it," Johnny said. He held his umbrella over her head and tried to steady her with his arm, but she shook him off like an unpleasant dream. She walked around the car and up the wheelchair ramp to the building. She tried her best to hurry because the highway was only a few feet away and she didn't want anybody to drive by and see her.

A nurse was waiting for them. "Come right in here, darling," she said. She led them into an examining room filled almost entirely by a leather-covered table with white paper rolled over it. "Let's have you lie down."

While the nurse strapped the blood-pressure contraption onto her arm, she asked Johnny how Ann had been behaving.

"She won't say anything."

"Is she normally very talkative?"

"She usually expresses her opinions."

The nurse took her blood pressure, wrote it on a clipboard, and said Dr. North would be there in a few minutes.

Johnny had left Darlene behind to collect insurance papers. She and North appeared at the same time. North looked at the nurse's clipboard, shined a light in Ann's eyes, listened to her chest, and told her she'd had a mild stroke.

Upon hearing the word "stroke," Darlene squealed and slid to the floor.

While her daughter occupied Johnny's and North's attention, Ann hopped off the table. But something went wrong, her legs had turned to cheese, and the next thing she knew, she was on the floor too, scant inches away from Darlene.

* *

Ann had moved in with her daughter and son-in-law three years ago when Early died. She'd moved because Johnny begged her. "You can't live out there in the country by yourself," he said. "What in the world would you do?"

"I'd do what I've always done."

"What if you get down sick?"

"If I get down sick, I'll get up well."

"Somebody might bust in on you."

"They do, I'll blow them halfway to Jackson. I got a shotgun for just such as that."

"Well, then," he said, "you ought to move in with us for Darlene's sake. She'll worry."

It hadn't occurred to her that this might happen. She'd always figured that if Early went before she did, she'd stay on her farm and work till she died. But now, she saw, Johnny was fixing to beg her to come live with him—else Darlene would keep him awake every night for the rest of his life—and while she didn't want to live with Johnny any more than he wanted her to, she truly loved this whole minute, and she wished she could preserve it, seal it in a jar.

"Ann," he had said, looking down at his toes, "please let me move you. Don't make me beg too long."

"There's certain conditions I'll want met."

His blue gaze grew wary. "What kind of conditions?"

"I'll apprise you of them," she said, "as they come to me."

The morning after he moved her, she rose early, lugged her orange trunk with the leather handle into the living room, and took out her pictures. The pictures of Grandpa Michalson in his coffin, she decided, would look nice hanging over the TV. She pawed through the trunk until she found her hammer and nails.

Johnny's walls were white Sheetrock, smooth and unmarked. She positioned a nail.

The loudness of the first blow thrilled her. She began to beat the hell out of the wall. A second nail was halfway in when she sensed an unhappy presence. She glanced over her shoulder. Sleepy-eyed Johnny wore a pair of blue shorts. "Morning," she said. "Remember them conditions I mentioned?" She hit the wall another blow. "I thought of what one of them is. I have to have my pictures. They'll make me feel at home. If she sees I feel at home, Darlene won't worry about me so much, and if Darlene don't worry—"

Johnny turned and trudged away.

Later that same morning, at breakfast, she forgot and read the paper aloud. She'd been doing that for years, because if she didn't Early would jabber on and on about his ingrown toenail or Hiram Knight's new John Deere, and she didn't want to hear that; because she didn't want to plant the notion she was senile.

She'd just gotten through the part about how the child-murderer down in Crystal Springs buried the body of his own three-year-old in a grave on the banks of the Pearl River, when Johnny threw down his fork, stood up, and stomped out of the room.

"He feels like life's full of bad news," Darlene told her the next day. She was explaining it in such an orderly fashion that Ann knew Johnny must have written it down for her. "You know, he's never been too happy with his job, and Billy didn't give him a raise for next year. Most everybody else at the plant got one. He says we'll make it, but just barely.

"He says with things being bad in general, it just upsets him to hear about disaster and killing when he's trying to eat."

"Things *are* bad in general," Ann said. "But if Johnny was the right kind of person, he'd fall down on his knees and thank God they're not worse."

That evening, as Johnny sat slumped on the couch, a six-pack at his side, Ann said, "Tomorrow I'm going out and hunt me a job." She'd planned on finding a job anyway, even though she knew Johnny wouldn't like it. Now he'd given her an excuse. "Between your little salary and Darlene's and mine, we'll make it just fine, don't you worry."

"Shit." He slammed his beer can down on the coffee table. "You're seventy-three years old. Job, my ass."

"I start work in the morning," she said at supper the next night.

Johnny's fork halted halfway to his mouth.

"The weatherman," Darlene babbled, "he says it might rain. Or it might not. There's only a fifty percent—"

"Shut up, Darlene," Ann and Johnny said together.

Darlene did. Blessed silence.

"I don't know who'd be fool enough to hire a woman your age," Johnny finally said, "but whoever it is, you can just call them up and tell them thanks but no thanks."

"When the Lord gets ready for a person to lay down and quit," Ann told him, "they'll know it. Quit'll be all they *can* do. Till then, everybody ought to strive. I'm gonna be a salesgirl at Kenwin's."

Johnny laid his fork down and stood up. "Ann," he said, "you're impossible. God help you."

"God won't help me," she said, "if I don't help myself. You've got to be willing to meet Him halfway.

Every time Johnny rose from his chair that first night, the cushion sighed. She'd hear his soles clop twice, then she'd feel him standing over her.

And she'd wonder what he saw when he saw her. She remembered the way her sister looked the last time she saw her at the rest home: a pale green bib tucked under her chin, applesauce oozing from the corner of her mouth as a teenaged nurse spoon-fed her. She'd be damned if she aimed to be spoon-fed.

The next morning North pried her eyes open and shined his infernal light in each one. He listened to her heart, he glanced at his clipboard, then he told her she was doing just fine.

"Would you be doing fine," she wished she could ask, "if you couldn't raise up and say, 'Scat'?"

"And," North went on, "your daughter's fine too. She'll be in to see you in a few minutes."

He left without saying a word about sending her home.

Johnny came to stand by the bed. She stole a peek at him to see if he looked like he pitied her. If he did, he was masking it well. He looked like regular Johnny. "You want to watch the television?" he asked her.

She shook her head no.

"How about the paper? Want to read the paper?"

She didn't care what was happening to anybody but her, and the paper couldn't tell her a thing about that. She shook her head again and closed her eyes.

Darlene flittered in. She poked her face right down in Ann's. "We took us a tumble last night! Wonder we didn't bust something!" she chirped. "I'm going to stay with you and let Johnny go home and take a bath."

As soon as Johnny had closed the door, the TV blared on. "Let's us watch *The Guiding Light*," Darlene said. "Won't that be a good way to spend the time?"

"Yes, Darlene," Ann longed to say, "that's every bit as good a way to spend the time as twiddling your thumbs or picking your nose."

She guessed having her daughter for a wife must be every bit as trying as having had Early for a husband. She wondered where she and Johnny Garber went wrong.

She had lived with her son-in-law before.

When Johnny left the Navy in the fall of '46, he came back to Mississippi and began dating Darlene. He was the first boy she'd ever gone with, so Ann was surprised that winter when Darlene said she wanted to get married.

Her inclination was to say no, because Darlene was just sixteen, but Johnny's daddy, Mr. Lee Roy Garber, came to her and said, "Ann, Darlene's the most harmless girl in the world, and I don't want you to worry about Johnny being good to her, because if he's not I'll kill him."

They got married in March. Mr. Garber fixed them up a house on his place, and he bought them an old school bus, which he and Johnny equipped with an ice-cream freezer and a soft-drink box and a couple of candy counters. For a good three years Johnny and Darlene supported themselves by driving the rolling store around the countryside and selling stuff to hoe hands and tractor drivers.

Then Mr. Garber passed away. By this time Ann had seen enough of Johnny to know why his daddy had made a merchant of him instead of a farmer. Johnny was lazy. For the past two or three months he'd operated the rolling store alone—Darlene was working in town at Morgan & Lindsey's—and a couple of times, as she hauled a load of cotton to the gin, Ann had come upon the school bus parked beneath a shade tree by the side of the road. Through the window she glimpsed Johnny on the candy counter napping.

When Mr. Garber died, his wife sold the farm and moved to Arizona to live with her sister. The man who bought the farm said Johnny and Darlene could keep living there, but of course they'd have to pay rent.

"Mark my words," Ann told Early. "They'll have to move out. Johnny's not making any money. If I was Darlene's daddy, I'd whip his tail. A man's supposed to provide for his wife."

Early said, "Time to slop the hogs," and went outside.

Darlene came to ask if she and Johnny could move in with her parents. Ann could tell she was embarrassed. She kept her big eyes trained on the floor. "It'll just be for a little while," she said. "Johnny says he's thinking about buying us a house in Belzoni."

"Why Belzoni?"

"He says Belzoni's a nicer town than Indianola."

"What makes it nicer?"

"Well . . . they've got the livestock auctions there."

"Does Johnny aim to ranch cattle?"

Darlene said she didn't think so.

"Then why would the auction being there make it nicer?"

Darlene ran her tongue over her lower lip. Her face brightened. "The Yazoo River runs near there."

"Oh, honey," Ann said. "You've married a trifling man."

Darlene erupted. While she cried, Ann held her and smoothed her blowzy hair. "You know you can come here," she said. "What's mine's yours."

They moved in the next weekend. Ann gave them the big room at the back of the house. She'd always loved that room because when the wind blew, the branches of the big old cedar tree that stood nearby made music; and sometimes, when Indian Bayou flooded, you could hear water lapping tree bark. Of course, she guessed if it ever flooded bad enough, the water might get in the house. It amused her to imagine Johnny Garber trying to paddle out in a boat. *Between him and Early*, she thought, *we'd doubtless spill and drown.*

One afternoon, after he'd been living there a month or so, Johnny came home about three o' clock. Ann was sitting on the couch shelling peas. When Johnny walked in, she said, "Did you sell much?"

"Not too much."

She glanced up at him. He was a nice-looking young man, tall like all the men in his family, slim-hipped, jut-jawed, and he had a pair of powder-blue eyes.

"If you didn't sell much," she said, "maybe you ought to get back out and beat the bushes."

He stood before the mantelpiece, studying the pictures on it. "Ann," he said, "what is it about dead people that appeals to you?"

"What?"

"You've got nine pictures up here," he said, "and four of them are shots of people in their coffins. You've even got two pictures of the same corpse taken from different angles."

"That's my grandpa. Grandpa Michalson."

"That *was* your grandpa. In these pictures he's something else altogether."

"I don't have no pictures of him living," she said. "You're coldhearted, Johnny, if you can't love your dead."

"When somebody's dead there's nothing to love. I respect a corpse enough not to hop around popping pictures of it."

"If you don't like my pictures," she said, "you can always move into the bus. You already spend a lot of time sleeping in it."

He faced her. "Did you know I sleep there most nights?" he said. "There's just one bed in your room. My presence might make your daughter uncomfortable." He walked out before she could reply, which was probably a good thing, because she didn't know what to say.

The next day, he didn't speak to her or Early. She did her best to act nice. At mealtime she asked him did he want some blackeyes or some turnips, but he just sat there, not making a sound. He parked his chair at an angle to the table, so that Ann saw only his back. And the day after that, while she was chopping cotton in the field across the road from the house, she saw a pickup truck turn into her yard and let a man out. The pickup pulled away, and the man stood in the yard conversing with Johnny. Soon, Johnny and the man shook hands. The man climbed into the bus, cranked it, and drove off.

She dug her hoe into the soft dirt on top of her row and left it standing there to mark her spot. When she got to the house, Johnny was lying on the couch reading. She pulled the book out of his hand.

She looked at the cover. "*The Sea-Wolf*," she said. "Twenty-four years old and laying up reading animal stories." She handed the book back. "Who was that in the bus?"

"Raymond Ferris."

"From the tractor company?"

"Yeah."

"What's he doing with the bus?"

"He bought it."

"Bought it?"

"Yeah. Or anyway he's buying it. He don't have the money yet."

"How do you plan to make a living from now on?"

"Darlene's working."

Ann's heart began to pound. "I know she's working," she said. "She's working. Early's working, I'm working—and you're too lazy to drive that damn bus down the road and sell Popsicles to niggers. How much energy can it take to sell a nigger a Popsicle?"

"More than I've got," Johnny said and reopened his book.

She was amazed. "So you don't aim to do any work for the rest of your life?"

"What reason have I got to work?"

"Reason?" she said.

"When you work you're supposed to be working toward something. I don't see no end in sight."

"I work," Ann said, "because a person's supposed to earn their living by sweat of their brow."

Johnny swung his legs off the couch. "I'll tell you why you work from daylight till dark," he said. "You do it to forget you're married to a man who don't have stomach enough to shoot a stray dog. You do it because it keeps you too busy to wonder how you'll make it through the day when you can't do it no more."

She waited until she was sure her voice would sound calm. "Johnny," she said, "I want you out of my house by tomorrow night. With no roof over your head and no grub in your gut, you'll have ample reason to toil."

* *

Christmas passed. She stayed in the hospital day after day, feeling worse and worse. For one thing, she still couldn't talk; yet once a day a nurse brought by a poster board on which had been glued drawings of a piece of pie, an apple, a glass of milk, all sorts of foods and drinks. "Can you remember the word for this?" the nurse would ask, pointing at a greenish-looking hamburger. When she didn't answer, the nurse would withdraw the poster, promising, "You'll tell us tomorrow."

She couldn't walk anymore either. Every time she tried, her right leg gave way. Once, when Johnny was helping her to the bathroom, her left leg went rubbery, too. When she fell, Johnny caught her. She heard a raspy "goddamn," and for an instant felt almost gleeful—she'd said something—but then she realized it was Johnny's "goddamn" and not hers. She would've said it if she could.

She quit eating because nothing tasted right and also because she couldn't control the muscles in her mouth. Food oozed down her chin, and Darlene wiped it off, cooing, "It's just a little mess is all." When she refused to eat, they stuck a needle in her arm and fed her through a tube. They catheterized her and laid a plastic bag on the bed.

She no longer felt responsible for keeping herself alive. It was someone else's doing.

Looking at Johnny Garber, tired and graying in his chair, she thought . . . *This is where you was when you was laying on my couch. I made you get up and turn a hand.*

* *

"Here we go, Mrs. King," the nurse said.

Ann barely knew who she was. She let Johnny and the nurse lift her into the wheelchair. The day before, she'd heard North tell Johnny that as soon as she got stronger, she'd have to go to the rehabilitation center in Jackson. He said they might be able to help her regain the use of her arm and leg; they might even teach her to talk. Her sister had gone to the rehab center after her stroke. Then it was on to the rest home in Rolling Fork.

They rolled her out to the parking lot, talking to her all the way, but she paid them no mind. She closed her eyes.

Johnny got out of the car, then opened Ann's door. She let him lift her in his arms.

She saw the strain on his face as he toted her across the yard. *You're not a young man anymore, Johnny Garber,* she thought. *And me, I'm an old, feeble woman.*

He carried her not to her bedroom but to the living-room couch.

"You need to make a daily habit of sitting up," he said, "even if it's just for a few minutes."

Ann felt weaker than most folks' faith, and she knew she'd hoed her last row. But she sat there half an hour, looking out the window, and watched some neighbor boys shoot baskets in the yard across the street.

MARLIN BARTON lives in Montgomery, Alabama. His first collection of short stories, *The Dry Well*, was published in 2001. His stories have appeared in *The Southern Review*, *Shenandoah*, *The Sewanee Review*, and the *O. Henry* collection.

RICK BRAGG writes for *The New York Times*, and won the Pulitzer Prize for journalism in 1996. He is the author of *All Over but the Shoutin'* and *Ava's Man*. The University of Alabama Press published a collection of his feature columns, *Somebody Told Me*.

SONNY BREWER owns Over the Transom (www.overthetransom.com) Bookstore in Fairhope, Alabama. He has been editor of the city magazine in Mobile, Alabama; associate editor of an Alabama weekly newspaper; feature columnist; freelancer and ghostwriter; magazine publisher of the now-defunct *Eastern Shore Quarterly*; author of a parable on aging cleverly disguised as a children's book, *Rembrandt the Rocker*; and a book of dime-store philosophy called *A Yin for Change*.

JILL CONNER BROWNE is THE Sweet Potato Queen and best-selling author of *The Sweet Potato Queens' Book of Love* and *God Save the Sweet Potato Queens*. She lives with her mother and daughter in Jackson, Mississippi.

C. TERRY CLINE, JR., began writing short fiction and articles when he was seventeen. He has since published nine novels of suspense, including *Damon*, *Missing Persons*, and *The Attorney Conspiracy*. He lives in Fairhope, Alabama, with his wife, novelist Judith Richards.

PAT CONROY's novels include *The Prince of Tides*, *The Great Santini*, *The Lords of Discipline*, and *Beach Music*. He lives on Fripp Island, South Carolina. This essay is from his forthcoming book, *My Losing Season*.

TOM CORCORAN has been a Navy officer and photographer. St. Martin's Press publishes his Key West–based mysteries: *The Mango Opera* in 1998, *Gumbo Limbo* in 1999, and *Bone Island Mambo* in 2001. *The Octopus Alibi* is set for January 2003 release.

BETH ANN FENNELLY is the recipient of numerous awards and prizes for her poems, including the Pushcart Prize. Her book *Open House* won the *Kenyon Review* Prize for Poetry and was published by Zoo Press in March 2002. Beth Ann is married to fiction writer Tom Franklin; they have a daughter, Claire.

PATRICIA FOSTER is the author of *All the Lost Girls: Confessions of a Southern Daughter* (winner of the PEN/Jerard Fund Award) and editor of *Minding the Body, Mending the Mind* and *The Healing Circle*. She is an associate professor in the MFA Program in Nonfiction at the University of Iowa and also teaches in Italy and France.

TOM FRANKLIN is the John and Renee Grisham Writer-in-Residence at the University of Mississippi and a 2001 Guggenheim Fellow. The title novella of his collection *Poachers* (William Morrow) appeared in *New Stories from the South, 1999* and in *Best American Mystery Stories of the Century*.

WILLIAM GAY is the author of the novels *The Long Home* and *Provinces of Night*, and his third and fourth novels are almost complete. His short stories have been published widely and consistently anthologized.

JIM GILBERT is the author of rambling sketches disguised as book reviews for the *Mobile* (Alabama) *Register*. He is a founding board member of the Fairhope Center for the Writing Arts.

W.E.B. GRIFFIN has published more than 170 books, all but three or four of them written in Fairhope. His most recent efforts have produced four series of books, all published by G. P. Putnam's Sons, New York, many of which—including the last thirty-nine—have been on the *New York Times* Bestseller list.

WINSTON GROOM is the author of twelve books, including *Forrest Gump, Better Times Than These, As Summers Die,* and the prizewinning Civil War history *Shrouds of Glory.* His nonfiction book *Conversations with the Enemy* was nominated for a Pulitzer Prize. His latest nonfiction is *A Storm in Flanders.* He lives in Cashiers, North Carolina, and Fairhope, Alabama.

MELINDA HAYNES's works of fiction include *Mother of Pearl,* an Oprah pick for the summer of 1999; *Chalktown;* and *Willem's Field,* due out in the spring of 2003. A painter for most of her life, she now lives in Mobile, Alabama, and writes full-time.

FRANK TURNER HOLLON lives and works in Baldwin County, Alabama. His first novel, *The Pains of April,* was published in 1999 by Over the Transom Publishing. Frank's second novel, *The God File,* was published by MacAdam/Cage in March 2002 and was selected by Barnes and Noble as a national "Discover" pick for Spring 2002.

SILAS HOUSE is the author of *Clay's Quilt* and *The Parchment of Leaves.* Chosen as one of the ten best emerging writers by the Millennial Gathering of Writers in 2000, he is a frequent contributor to National Public Radio's "All Things Considered." He lives in eastern Kentucky with his wife and two daughters.

As a graduate student, SUZANNE HUDSON won a Hackney Literary Award and a $5,500 National Endowment for Arts and Humanities prize, then withdrew from the publishing world for twenty-five years until last year's publication of *Opposable Thumbs,* a collection of stories. A novel is in the wings.

A native of Fort Smith, Arkansas, DOUGLAS KELLEY now makes his home with his wife and two children just across the Oklahoma state line. His travels as a corporate pilot facilitated his research for his book of the sea. *The Captain's Wife* is his first novel.

Tom Kelly is a frequent contributor to national sporting magazines and has published six books, among them *Better on a Rising Tide* and *The Boat*. He has been in the timber business for more than fifty years.

Michael Knight is the author of *Divining Rod* and *Dog Fight and Other Stories* (Dutton). A Mobile, Alabama, native, he has had short stories published in *The New Yorker* and *Playboy*. Michael and his wife, Jill, live in Knoxville, Tennessee. His new book is *Blackout and Other Stories* from Grove/Atlantic.

Bev Marshall, a native of McComb, Mississippi, spent her adolescent years in Gulfport. She holds degrees from the University of Mississippi and Southeastern Louisiana University, where she taught in the Department of English. Her short stories have appeared in *Maryland Review*, *Potpourri*, *Xavier Review*, and elsewhere. Her novel *Walking Through Shadows* was published by MacAdam/Cage in 2002.

Barbara Robinette Moss, a visual artist whose work is in galleries around the country, won first place for personal essay in the William Faulkner Creative Writing Competition for her essay "Near the Center of the Earth," which became the novel *Change Me into Zeus's Daughter*, published by Scribner's. Her new book *Sing to the Wild Cat* is due out in Spring 2003 from Scribner's. A native of Alabama, she lives in Iowa with her husband, Duane.

Jennifer Paddock received her M.A. in creative writing from New York University. Her fiction is forthcoming in *Louisiana Literature* and *The North American Review*. She lives in Fairhope, Alabama, with her husband, Sidney Thompson.

Judith Richards has written five novels. *Summer Lightning*, which is about her husband, author C. Terry Cline, Jr., has been published in seventeen languages and is under option for a film. She and Terry live in Fairhope, Alabama.

RICHARD SHACKELFORD died of cancer in Pensacola, Florida, in 1997, leaving three unpublished novels and a screenplay. He was a poet and a newspaperman, a ghostwriter, and the author of two published books of nonfiction.

GEORGE SINGLETON's first collection, *These People Are Us*, was published by River City Press in 2001. It will be available from Harcourt's Harvest line in Fall 2002. A second collection, *The Half-Mammals of Dixie*, will be published by Algonquin in September 2002.

MONROE THOMPSON is the author of two published novels, *The Blue Room* and *A Long Time Dead*. When he died in Fairhope in 1998, he left behind a collection of short stories and two unpublished novels.

SIDNEY THOMPSON received his MFA in creative writing from the University of Arkansas. His fiction has been published in *The Carolina Quarterly* and *The Southern Review*. He lives in Fairhope, Alabama, with his wife, Jennifer Paddock, and teaches at UMS-Wright Preparatory School in Mobile.

BRAD WATSON's *Last Days of the Dog-Men* (Norton, 1996) received the Sue Kaufman Prize for First Fiction from the American Academy of Arts and Letters. "The Dead Girl" is from his novel *The Heaven of Mercury* (Norton, 2002). Watson has taught at the University of Alabama and now teaches at Harvard University.

STEVE YARBROUGH, a native of the Mississippi Delta, lives in Fresno, California. He is the author of five books, including *The Oxygen Man* and *Visible Spirits*.